P9-CRZ-863

Call Me Wild

ROBIN KAYE

PLAINFIELD PUBLIC LIBRARY
15025 S. Illinois Street
Plainfield, IL 60544

sourcebooks
casablanca

Copyright © 2012 by Robin Kaye
Cover and internal design © 2012 by Sourcebooks, Inc.
Cover design by Dawn Adams
Cover image © Fancy/Alamy

Sourcebooks and the colophon are registered trademarks of Sourcebooks, Inc.

All rights reserved. No part of this book may be reproduced in any form or by any electronic or mechanical means including information storage and retrieval systems—except in the case of brief quotations embodied in critical articles or reviews—without permission in writing from its publisher, Sourcebooks, Inc.

The characters and events portrayed in this book are fictitious or are used fictitiously. Any similarity to real persons, living or dead, is purely coincidental and not intended by the author.

All brand names and product names used in this book are trademarks, registered trademarks, or trade names of their respective holders. Sourcebooks, Inc., is not associated with any product or vendor in this book.

Published by Sourcebooks Casablanca, an imprint of Sourcebooks, Inc.
P.O. Box 4410, Naperville, Illinois 60567-4410
(630) 961-3900
FAX: (630) 961-2168
www.sourcebooks.com

Printed and bound in the United States of America
VP 10 9 8 7 6 5 4 3 2 1

3 1907 00291 4520

To Laura Becraft and Deborah Villegas

You are the best critique partners I can imagine,
the best friends I could ever want, but most of all,
I'm blessed to have you both as the sisters of my heart.

Chapter 1

JESSIE'S EYES DARTED FROM ONE NAKED MAN TO THE next. As a sports reporter, she'd done her share of major league locker room interviews over the years, but today it was as if every player knew something she didn't. She couldn't remember when she'd seen more balls—and not the kind you hit with bats, unless you were a jealous husband or wife.

Jessie squared her shoulders and pressed the record button on her iPhone—just for audio—she certainly wasn't going to film this nightmare.

Tonight the men on the team showed as much skin as possible. She hadn't had that problem since she was a cub reporter they thought they could shock easily. Every now and then, she had to teach a rookie a painful lesson, but for the most part, the guys were polite and kept their towels in place. Until today.

Wiping her suddenly clammy hand on her Ally McBeal skirt, at almost six feet tall, Jessie had no problem looking most men in the eye. She zeroed in on the shortstop. "Carter, is that you?" She'd never liked the obnoxious man and figured he was as good a victim as any. Jessie dropped her gaze to his package for a few beats and pointed to his junk hanging unencumbered and proud—well, it had been until a second ago. Now it looked even smaller, having evidently wilted under her scrutiny.

An uncomfortable silence filled the room—at least it was uncomfortable for Carter. His face turned a putrid shade of red, a few shades deeper than his carrot-colored hair, and then his smile crumbled like a winning streak after a team photo on the cover of *Sports Illustrated*.

Jessie kept her focus on Carter. "For a moment there I thought I'd walked in on a peewee baseball team. My mistake."

The team laughed, and when her gaze slid over each player, she found they'd rediscovered their manners and their towels, or at the very least, their jockeys.

Nakedness didn't bother Jessie; lack of respect did. After quieting the team's laughter, she got down to business. She did her interviews and left, wading through the throngs of fans on the way to her Eighth Avenue office.

In the elevator, Jessie wondered what caused the scene in the team's locker room. Maybe it was a full moon? A nudist baseball player's convention? She wasn't sure, but she knew something was wrong. It was as if they were humoring her. The reporter in her sensed a juicy story. She'd do some snooping around after she filed her column.

The newsroom always felt different this time of night. Most of the staff was long gone, and a quiet settled over the usually insane place. There were no clacking keyboards, no raucous conversation, no slamming of the editor's door. Jessie dumped her messenger bag on her desk, tossed an old Starbucks cup into the trash, and tried to ignore the itchy feeling crawling up the back of her neck. Something was off.

Looking through her game notes, she checked her stats. Her memory had never failed her before, but she wasn't about to chance screwing up. The readers of her column and blog knew the stats almost as well as she did, which was saying something. She played the interviews she'd recorded, still trying to ignore that niggling feeling, and wrote her story, leaving out the part where the team lost their shorts, jockstraps, and manners, and filed it well before her deadline.

Spinning her chair toward the window, she stared out over Eighth Avenue. She supposed she could go home, but thanks to the coffee and the win, she was too hyped to sleep. She picked up her phone and called her best friend Andrew in LA.

"Hey, sugar," his deep voice came through the phone. "What's up?"

Jessie leaned back in her chair. "Good, you're alone."

"How do you know?"

"You never call me sugar when you have a girlfriend around."

"You caught me. Nothin' personal, but most women don't believe my best friend is female and that at least one of us is not secretly in love with the other. I've found it easier not to mention you arc."

"Not mention I'm what?"

"A woman."

"You're kidding." Jessie twisted in her chair until her back cracked. For once she was glad she didn't have a social life. No dating, no explanations. Then again, no dating, no boyfriend. No boyfriend, no sex. Yeah, that last one was a real bitch. Jessie didn't miss having boyfriends, she did, however, miss sex. A lot.

Andrew continued. "They assume you're a guy, so if I were to call you sugar, they'd wonder if I was bi."

"I'll bet. I guess that's one of the downsides of dating."

"Sugar, all you see are the downsides." Andrew cleared his throat. "What are you doing? I thought you'd be writing your column. I caught the end of the game."

Thank God he changed the subject. Smart man. Jessie twirled around in her chair. "It's filed."

"Okay, so cross off writer's block. What's the problem?"

"What do you mean?"

"Don't give me that. Something's wrong. What is it?"

Jessie shook her head. "Probably nothing. I'm just overreacting." She should be used to Andrew's hypersensitive, highly accurate, best friend ESP.

Andrew remained quiet, which made her nervous.

"Fine, I went into the locker room for interviews, and every last player lost his shorts. They were playing a trick or a game, and I was the only one not in on it."

"And what'd you do?"

"I told Carter that I thought I'd walked into a peewee team's locker room. It'll take him a few weeks to heal from the wound to his manhood. For such a big prick, who knew his would be so little?"

"You're skating on thin ice, Jess."

"Enough about me. What's up with you? How's work?"

"It's a soap opera, but it pays the bills."

Jessie spun her chair around and clicked on her email, sifting through the trash while she and Andrew spoke. She still couldn't believe her best friend since freshman year at Columbia was writing for a soap opera, even if the money was damn good. Whatever happened to his dreams of writing for film? "Have you been working on your screenplay?"

"Have you been working on your novel? See Jess, two can play that game."

"Hey, I'm living the dream. I'm a sports reporter for the *Times*—I've already achieved my goal. You gave up on yours."

"I didn't give up. I have a day job so I don't have to live in my car while writing my screenplay. I'm an artist, just not a starving one."

Andrew talked about how hard it was to get into the film business. She knew from experience it would take awhile for him to go through his litany of excuses. Instead of wasting her time, she did what every woman was capable of; she multitasked and went through her hundred or so emails. At least by doing that she had a prayer of finding something original and or new, maybe even exciting.

She scrolled through the usual junk—drugs to enhance the size of her nonexistent penis, an ad for dates with naked women. She wondered if it was her androgynous name that brought all this crap to her email box or if everyone got it. She deleted it all without reading, while saying her "uh-huhs."

Jessie flagged the emails from fans of her column and blog, moving them to her file to be answered—an early morning task she did over coffee. She opened an email from her boss, and for the second time that day, wondered if she'd entered an alternate reality.

She pushed suddenly sweaty bangs off her face with a shaking hand and looked around the deserted office. Had she been *Punk'd*? "Oh God."

Andrew stopped kvetching mid-word. "Are you even listening to me?"

She blinked at her computer, and it was still there—an electronic pink slip.

She swallowed hard. "I think I just got downsized."

This couldn't be happening to her. She worked all her life for this position—her dream job. She loved it, she was great at it, and now, they were taking it all away.

"What do you mean?"

"Look for yourself." She hit send. "I'm forwarding you an email from my boss." It should have been high-lighted in pink. She hadn't heard about any more layoffs. There was no warning. No sign anything was up. Was she the last one to know about her pink slip?

Jessie checked the time stamp. Noon. Her editor must have assigned another reporter to cover the game. No wonder the guys in the locker room had been naked. They obviously hadn't expected her.

She rubbed her stomach. If she'd had some warning, she would never have eaten that second hotdog at the stadium. Gray spots danced on a transparent veil hanging over her computer screen, and she swallowed back the saliva gathering in her mouth—the usual preamble to violent illness. She pulled her trash can out from under her desk just to be safe.

"Oh shit, sugar. I'm so sorry."

"I just signed a two-year lease on my apartment last week." She pressed the heels of her palms against her eyes to keep from crying. "I can't afford my apartment without a paycheck."

"Don't worry. We'll work this out."

Who'd have thought? A pink slip didn't need to be pink to pull the Astroturf right out from under her feet.

———～～～———

Fisher Kincaid gazed across Starbucks, over the top of his *Idaho Statesman* newspaper, at the woman sitting behind her MacBook Air, staring at a blank Word document, and chewing on the cardboard lip of her venti cup. This was the second time he'd seen her today. Since it was barely 7:00 a.m., he hadn't slept with her, and she wasn't a patient, that was notable—even for a city as small as Boise.

"Checkin' out the new customer, Fisher?" Laura, a barista with the voice of an angel and the body of a porn star, handed him his daily refill, which meant it was almost time to leave to make rounds at the hospital.

"I took a run earlier and followed her for five miles." He didn't mention that he'd barely kept up with her.

Laura raised her perfectly plucked eyebrow.

"What was I supposed to do?" Fisher's hands went up—coffee cup and all. "She was in front of me and turned at my usual place by the park."

"Five miles, huh? So that's how you keep in shape." Laura ran a hand down the button band of his shirt, stopping just above his belt buckle, and making her way slowly back up his chest.

Ah, to be twenty again. Those days were long gone, and so were nights with anyone like Laura. She turned her back on him and was already belting out a Lady Gaga tune and hamming it up for the regulars. She spun around, grabbed his free hand, and lifted it high before dancing under it. He set down his coffee and dipped her until her ponytail touched the floor, receiving a round of applause from the crowd.

Fisher pulled Laura up and released her. He nodded toward the woman with the amazing ass and even more impressive stamina he'd followed just that morning. "What's the deal with her?"

"Not sure." Laura wiped the counter, looking at Mac-chick chewing on her cup.

The woman was nervous—the kind of nerves that couldn't be blamed on coffee, even if she'd downed a few venti quads. Her eyes darted around the small store in a sweep of the area, not meeting anyone's gaze, but missing nothing.

Pacific Northwesterners never had a problem looking strangers in the eye. Obviously, the woman wasn't from around here. With her self-imposed isolation and the way she frowned at the copy of the *Times* she'd bought off the rack, Fisher pegged her for a tourist from the east coast.

He hadn't seen her type a word on that computer since he walked in and recognized her, taking in her blank face and her blank screen. He'd said hello to the morning regulars, talked golf with his buddy Dana, and fishing with Alan, as they joked with the baristas and each other. All the while he'd had the distinct feeling he was being watched.

"What's her name?" Fisher asked Laura. If anyone there knew, it would be Laura. She had a great memory for names and drinks.

"Jessica. The two of you have a drink in common, but she likes her venti Americano with sugar-free vanilla instead of a half cup of sugar, and she doesn't bring in her cup for the discount."

"I don't do it for the discount; I just hate cold coffee." He threw his arm around her shoulder. "And I love the way you always heat up my cup—it keeps my coffee hot longer."

Laura tilted her head toward him. "Too bad the only

person getting hotter than your coffee is me. Yeah, hot, bothered, just sayin'."

Fisher stepped away as he watched Jessica open the *Times* to the sports page and scowl. Not many women he knew went right to the sports without first checking out the front page and the lifestyle section. Hell, most women he knew never made it to the sports page at all. That's why he hadn't had to buy a paper in ages. He usually found it littering a table just waiting for the next guy to read.

Steph, the manager, sauntered out from the back of the store. "Hey, Fisher. What are you still doing here? You're running late today."

He checked his watch. Damn, she was right. Heading toward the door, he waved good-bye to the baristas, gave Steph a wink, and walked straight into Jessica. His arms went around her as her body slammed into his. He instinctively tightened his hold, drawing her close, doing his best to keep them from falling, as he struggled to catch his balance without spilling his coffee all over her.

Her solid muscles vibrated with what seemed like barely contained indignation. She was tall, just a few inches shorter than him, and at six feet three inches, it was unusual for him to be eye-to-eye with a beautiful woman. She was lean with sharp angles, sinewy muscles, and what looked like keen intelligence, once you got past the pissed-off, icy glare. Even her expressions were hard. The only things soft about her were the breasts pillowed against his chest.

Her deep brown eyes were shot with specks of gold and blasted insults loud enough to be heard without speaking.

"I'm sorry." Fisher did his best to steady her, moving his hand to her small waist. No hint of softness there either.

She jerked away as if he'd zapped her with a defibrillator.

"Easy, I was just trying to make sure you were steady on your feet."

She grabbed a handful of her long chestnut hair and tossed it over her shoulder. It was not the usual look-at-me hair flip. No, hers was pure exasperation, not a come-on, which was a damn shame even *with* her prickly attitude. "I thought this was a coffee shop, not a dance club."

Fisher did his best to squelch his urge to smile. "Coffee's a requirement, dancing is optional." He took a deep breath and caught her scent. It was somehow familiar, but unknown, arousing without being overbearing, light and a little dark at the same time. Captivating.

"Obviously not for me." Jessie had spent the last half hour watching this guy and wondering what the odds were of running into the man again after he'd followed her on her morning run. It had damned near killed her to outpace him.

His untamed white-blond hair curled over his collar and looked as if it had been gelled and slicked back in a vain attempt to rein in the wild curls—at least temporarily. His bright green eyes were clear and crisp as the high mountain lake she and Andrew used to hike to. He was at least six three, and ripped in all the right places. He looked like a surfer doing a really bad job of impersonating a professor.

In the half hour she'd been at Starbucks, she'd watched him schmooze every female barista and customer, and most of the males too. Oh yeah, she knew his type. He was the guy who spends half his time working on his tan and the other bleaching his teeth, all the while living in his mother's basement.

Jessie gave him the Bronx stare, the one that deflated a professional athlete's ego faster than you could say Goodyear Blimp, only to be met by a grin—a dimple bracketing one side of his mouth and a Tic Tac commercial smile. Crap, the guy must be thick too.

"If you're uncomfortable dancing here we can go to Humpin' Hannah's or Shorty's."

Jessie struggled to keep from rolling her eyes. "Not interested, but thanks anyway." She was surprised to see his smile widen.

"Okay, then. I guess I'll see you around."

"Not if I see you first."

He shot her a wink before he turned toward the door. His smile hadn't dimmed one little bit. Yeah, he was definitely not a member of Mensa. Maybe he had processing problems. He'd figure out that he'd been turned down sometime in the middle of next week.

Jessie took her place in line and waited. Once the couple in front of her placed their half-hour-long, amazingly complicated order, and paid—having to not only dig for their gold card, but also refill it—she told herself to calm the hell down. After all, she wasn't in New York, she wasn't on deadline, and it wasn't as if she even had a job to go to.

For the first time in her life she had more free time than she knew what to do with. No wonder her mother had always warned her to be careful what she wished for. Jessie had always wanted to have the time to write a novel—she just didn't want to lose her job and sublet her beloved apartment to get it.

She let out a sigh, pasted on what she hoped was a friendly smile, and stepped toward the counter.

Starbucks's answer to Lady Gaga with a go-go dancer twist leaned toward Jessie, wide eyed. "Fisher asked you out, and you blew him off? What's wrong with you? Are you married?"

"No."

"Gay?"

"No." Jessie had worked with people for six years who hadn't asked her such personal questions. The woman had only served her a cup of coffee, and she wanted her life story?

Andrew had warned her that people were a whole lot friendlier in Boise. He didn't say friendly was synonymous with nosy.

"Why the third degree? So, a guy asked me out, and I said no. What's the big deal?"

"Hmm. Maybe you have a vision problem. Did you look at the man?"

Jessie did roll her eyes then. "Just because he looks great doesn't mean there's anything there, if you know what I mean."

The barista appraised Jessie's outfit, a Mets T-shirt, holey, ragged-out jeans, and black Converse high-tops. "I guess there's no accounting for taste."

Jessie wasn't sure if Lady Gaga referred to her taste in men or clothes. She decided it didn't matter. "May I have an employment application, please?"

"Applications are all online. Just go to Starbucks dot com, slash careers, and you can fill it out there. Lucky you, we're hiring. I'm sure Steph, our manager, will give you a call."

"Great, thank you." Jessie ordered a lemonade iced tea, and after a barista with a pixie face and curly brown hair slid it across the counter with a smile, Jessie went back to the document on her computer that contained nothing but a blinking cursor. At least she had a plan for her forced sabbatical. Write a book and work part-time at Starbucks for the health insurance. It wasn't much, but it was her plan.

—⁓—

Fisher rubbed his stiff neck as he got out of his ancient Toyota Land Cruiser in front of the local Albertsons grocery store. He lifted the door a little to make sure it closed properly. His brothers always teased him about driving a beater, but he didn't mind. He loved his old truck. He'd bought it used and put another quarter of a million miles on the darn thing, and except for having to replace the engine a hundred thousand miles ago, just as the odometer passed four hundred K, he hadn't had one problem with it. The same couldn't be said for his BMW Roadster, or his BMW sport-touring motorcycle, even though he loved both with the unbridled passion of a sixteen-year-old.

Fisher grabbed a cart from the parking lot and made his way into the grocery store—the same store he'd shopped in since he was in diapers.

There was something to be said about shopping at the original Albertsons. He remembered when Old Joe Albertson, who had been one of Grampa Joe's best friends, used to give him and his brothers penny candy right out of the bins.

Fisher knew his way around the store with his eyes

closed and even knew every cashier who worked there. At least there were some places where nothing much changed. He wished he could say the same about his life. He'd been in a bit of a funk lately.

For a moment that morning when he'd asked Jessica out, he'd wondered if the root cause was lack of sex. It had been awhile since he had a date. Now that he thought about it, he wasn't sure why. She was the first woman he'd asked out in months, which was strange. Still, even though he crashed and burned in front of an audience of alert coffee drinkers no less, he couldn't say he was in any more of a funk than he had been before.

Fisher made his way to the produce aisle and grabbed the makings for a nice, healthy salad. Good food, strong body, strong mind, and all that. After tossing most of the produce aisle into his cart, he ran through the rest of the store looking for inspiration. Nothing looked good, but after the kind of day he'd had, it wasn't surprising.

He'd done back-to-back knee replacements on patients so obese, their joints deteriorated under their weight. After seeing what those poor people went through, he bypassed the frozen food aisle, looking at the shoppers who lived on chemically engineered, processed foodstuffs, and then did a double take when he recognized Jessica.

Okay, it wasn't her he recognized, but the shapely ass he'd followed that morning. The memory of it was branded on his psyche. Yeah, and he hadn't exaggerated its perfection either. Jessica had her ass sticking out and her head buried in the frozen food case, while she tossed Lean Cuisine meals into her cart at an alarming rate.

Fisher's cart glided down the aisle as if it were

self-propelled, while he checked out the rest of her cart. Two cases of diet cola sat on the bottom rack—hadn't anyone ever told her the hazards of drinking that? The day he'd seen cola take the finish off an antique wood table was the last day he drank it. In the empty child seat beside her purse sat a loaf of processed white sandwich bread. He did his best not to gag. He almost failed when he saw the cereal beside it. She *wasn't* buying cereal with colored marshmallows in it and a prize in the bottom of the box, was she? Maybe she had small children, but who would feed small children that? God, her cart looked like something that should be featured on a television show titled *What Not to Eat*. How could a woman in great shape survive on what she'd dumped in her cart? He didn't see one fresh fruit or vegetable and nothing whatsoever from the dairy aisle. Of course, depending on the direction she was shopping, maybe she hadn't hit it yet. One could only hope. "Hi."

Jessica jumped at his greeting. "What? Oh, it's you."

Fisher leaned on his cart and checked her out—still amazed that her beautiful body could run on such low-quality fuel. "We meet again."

Jessica dumped a stack of chicken meals in her cart and looked him up and down. "Yeah, looks that way. I didn't see you first."

She couldn't fool him. Her words might say she was unhappy to see him, but her body language said different. Hell, from the fit of her T-shirt, she looked downright thrilled to see him, though that could just be from spending five minutes with her head and chest stuffed in a freezer case. Still, he wasn't about to complain. "Do you actually eat all that?"

She looked from her cart and back to him. "Yes. That's why I'm buying it."

Fisher shook his head, tossed aside a few of the frozen meals, and picked up a jar of marshmallow spread that rested next to the peanut butter. "What are you, like six years old? This stuff will kill you."

Jessica took the jar of Fluff out of his hands and returned it to her cart. "It's comfort food, and right now, I'm not about to question it."

"I was just heading over to the butcher block, hoping for inspiration, when I saw you and thought I'd be neighborly and say hello."

"We're neighbors?"

"We must be if you shop here. I live in the North End, and I assume you do too." He moved his cart closer, blocking her in. "I was thinking a nice piece of sea bass, maybe some tuna, rainbow trout, or salmon. How's that sound to you?"

She shrugged.

Fisher chose to ignore her lack of an answer. "Yeah, barbecued fish, a side of yellow rice with roasted vegetables, and a big Caesar salad sounds good. There's plenty for two if you want to come over and keep me company."

Jessica leaned against her cart and stared dumbfounded—that was the only way he could describe the look on her face. "Do you do this often? Pick up total strangers at the grocery store and invite them to dinner?"

"You're not a stranger. I've seen more of you today than I do most people in a week. I know that your name is Jessica, you have a thing for venti Americanos with sugar-free vanilla syrup, and you're new around here." He leaned a little closer to her. "FYI, for the most part

Boiseans are friendly people. This"—he motioned from him to her and back again—"is nothing unusual."

"Seriously?" She stepped back as if he had bad breath. "You do this often? How many women have you picked up while grocery shopping?"

"I'm not picking you up. I'm inviting you to dinner. As for how many women I've invited to dinner while at this store, I'm not sure. I've never thought about it. But really, Jessica, from what I see in your cart, you could use a good, healthy meal. I'm offering one, and I'm a great cook."

"And modest too." She took what looked like a mental inventory of each cart before giving him a seemingly self-conscious shrug. "Thanks for the invite, but I have a lot of work to do tonight."

"Shot down twice in one day. I don't know if my bruised ego will ever recover."

She looked as if she was searching for a way to escape. "I can't imagine it being a problem. I'll see you around."

Fisher nodded and rolled his cart out of her way. "Only if you don't see me first. Right?"

"Right." The side of her lips quirked as if she wanted to smile and wouldn't allow it.

Oh yeah, right then and there, Fisher decided he was going to see that smile. If he had to chase her for twenty-five miles uphill in a head wind—hopefully with good visibility—he'd see her smile.

Chapter 2

THERE ARE TIMES IN LIFE WHEN YOU JUST HAVE TO man up and tally your losses—Fisher just never thought he'd lose this big. "Knitting classes?"

He'd known he was too old to bet on getting laid. Okay, not too old, since Fisher had, after a few shots and some brotherly arm-twisting, reluctantly agreed to the bet. Unfortunately, he'd picked a fine time to grow a conscience, or whatever it was that had kept him from taking home the first gorgeous, willing woman he'd encountered… or the second, or the third. Hell, he'd lost count. He hadn't known what, but something was missing—something important. He just hadn't been sure if it was something missing in him, or them. Shit, maybe he was going through a midlife crisis, although thirty-two was way too young to be having one.

Fisher sat at the bar at Humpin' Hannah's and ignored his twin brother's smile—one exactly like his own. He concentrated instead on the wagon wheel mounted from the ceiling and the florescent orange bra, a recent addition to the collection of shoes and undergarments decorating the wheel like Christmas tree ornaments.

Hunter was a brown-haired version of Fisher, with a little more brawn and a lot less brain—okay, maybe not a lot less, but right now, Fisher wasn't feeling charitable. Unfortunately, Hunter didn't let the lack of eye contact stop him. "The payback is ingenious, isn't it? I wish I could take the credit, but it was Trapper's idea, and you did lose the bet."

Any reaction Fisher had to his fate would only add to his brothers' enjoyment, so he kept his face expressionless. Trapper and Hunter were having a good enough time at his expense without him adding to their fun. No, he'd take it like a man and make the best of it, even if it killed him. And really, after being blown off by the same woman twice in one day, how much lower could he sink?

Trapper, their older brother, had a rebel without a cause attitude and long, curly, dirty blond hair, the same build as Fisher, and got paid to work in his robe. Sure, the getup came with a bench, a gavel, and the last Fisher knew, a pretty hot bailiff named Traci who called Trapper "Sir" and "Your Honor." No matter how often Trapper pulled the judge card, Hunter and Fisher never fell for it. Well, not unless court was in session, and then, only because they were certain Trapper wouldn't hesitate to have their asses thrown in jail on contempt of court charges.

Trapper set down his beer and slid a paper across the bar. "Here's a gift certificate for the beginner's knitting class at Knittin' Chicks—"

Obviously his brothers discovered an all new low. He cursed his fate, while Trapper droned on, as judges are wont to do.

"Class begins at six o'clock Thursday evening. That's tomorrow." If Trapper was trying to keep a straight face, he was failing spectacularly.

"I know what day of the week it is."

Trapper took a break long enough to finish his beer

and slid the empty mug to their sister and bartender, Karma, for a refill. "Dalia will fix you up with supplies. Now the deal is you have to make one project in class—"

"And one project outside of class." Hunter held up his beer to clear the bar.

Fisher followed suit when he caught Karma holding a full mug and eyeing the bar like a pro bowler with a seven-ten split.

The Kincaid genes ran strong. Karma was a female version of Fisher with Trapper's hair. She wore hers only a few inches longer then Trapper's shoulder-length locks and was tall and lean like the rest of them—Karma was a beauty. Behind the sweet, girl-next-door-with-a-killer-body look came a sharp mind and a wicked temper. She loved her family, but turned being a pesky little sister into an art form.

Hunter's gaze followed Trapper's frosted mug as it zipped by unobstructed, before setting down his beer. "I know you're not above talking some pretty young thing into knitting for you, even though you struck out at taking one to bed. We need proof that you can knit something on your own."

Fisher raised an eyebrow and held back a groan. Of course Hunter would have all the bases covered, he was always the sneakiest of the three. Still, he couldn't hold a candle to Karma. "Fine. I can't believe my own brothers would torture me like this."

Trapper laughed. "Oh, come on. It's only three classes, and you'll be surrounded by women. The way I see it, we're doing you a favor and helping you get over that little problem of yours."

"I don't have a little problem."

Hunter punched his shoulder, hard. "You're right, little brother, you haven't gotten laid in over two months. You have a big, big problem."

"First of all, I'm bigger than you, and being born five minutes after you hardly makes me your little brother, so cut the shit, Hunter. Secondly, how long did you go without before you met Toni?"

Hunter shrugged. "Hell, I spent months in the mountains alone."

"Bullshit, you had Bianca Ferrari all over you. I should know. She mistook me for you, remember?"

Hunter scrubbed his face and looked around— probably for his wife. That was still a touchy subject for Toni. "Bianca wasn't my type."

Trapper scowled. Hmm. Maybe it was a touchy subject for Trapper too. Interesting.

Fisher hid his smile behind his mug. "Yeah, well, none of the women at last week's Ladies' Night were my type either."

Trapper set down his beer and pushed his cowboy hat off his forehead. "Then I guess you shouldn't have made the bet. The first rule of gambling is don't play if you can't pay."

"You know, Trap, I haven't seen you out with any women lately. Not since I heard a rumor about you and a hot blonde getting busy in Toni's room at the hotel right after the wedding. Of course, you were gone for several days after the wedding too. But ever since then, you and I have been holding up the same bar. Sounds to me like you need the class worse than I do. After all, you're older."

"Wild Thing" played in the background, and Fisher

caught Hunter looking for his wife, Toni. He caught her eye like he had her heart. She left her conversation with Karma, slid under her husband's arm, and leaned into his side. "Fisher? You're taking a class?"

"Looks like I am."

"I just love continuing education. Hunter, why don't you sign up too? It will give the three you some real male bonding time before we're stuck on the mountain all winter."

When Hunter paled, Toni slid her hand up his chest and rubbed her nose against his throat. Hunter's Adam's apple bobbed.

"Step out of your comfort zone." Toni whispered in that deep sexy voice of hers. "Isn't that what you're always telling me, you wild thing, you?"

Hunter just about choked on his beer. God, Fisher loved his sister-in-law. Toni was perfect for Hunter from the top of her Goth head to the bottom of her combat boots. He looked down to find she wasn't wearing boots. Her shoes looked girly, and well, except for the plat-form sole, almost normal. Come to think of it, in the weeks since she and Hunter had come home from their wedding, she'd really toned down the shock factor of her clothes. She was still Goth, but definitely not over-the-top anymore. Fisher kind of missed seeing his rather straitlaced brother's reaction to his wife's originality.

"Okay." Hunter stood and grabbed his wife, holding her in front of him—probably a necessity. The man had it so bad, Fisher almost felt sorry for him. Almost. "Now that we've got you all set, little brother, Toni and I are going home." Hunter didn't waste time on good-byes as he steered Toni out the door, leaving Fisher with the tab.

Fisher rested his elbows on the bar and contemplated the bottle of Macallan 18 Karma kept for him. "God those two are disgusting. Hunter was here less than an hour, and one word out of Toni's mouth and he's running for the bedroom."

Trapper shook his head. "Yeah, they need to take a real honeymoon and get it out of their systems. Then everything should get back to normal."

"Look at Ben and Gina. They've been married over a year, and they're still acting like horny teenagers." Fisher didn't know whether to be jealous or appalled— they both felt wrong. Almost as wrong as the thought of taking a knitting class.

———

"It's all Andrew's fault that I'm in Boise in the first place." Jessie looked up from her beer to the bartender at Humpin' Hannah's. "What did you say your name was again?"

"Karma," she said as she built a Guinness for a man six stools down named Dick.

He must have been a loyal customer if his Humpin' Hannah's golf shirt and the time Karma took building his Guinness was anything to go by. When she finally finished the pour, she slid the full mug down the bar.

Jessie watched the beer slow and stop right before hitting Dick's open hand without even sloshing over the side. "Impressive. How long did it take you to perfect that?"

"A few years." Karma gave a nonchalant shrug before folding her arms, resting them on the bar, and leaning in. "So, about your best friend, Andrew. What kind of friend is he?"

"What do you mean?" Jessie stared into Karma's

deep green eyes. They were somehow familiar, but she
didn't know why. She'd never seen Karma before this
afternoon when she ducked into the bar after exploring
downtown Boise.

"Is he just a friend, friend? A bed buddy? A frenemy?
An ex? Girl, there are all kinds of"—she held up two
fingers of each hand to form quotation marks—"'friends,'
if you know what I'm sayin'."

"Oh, no. Andrew's more like a brother from a different mother. But then I really wouldn't know since I'm
an only child."

"Must be nice."

Jessie shrugged, wondering if Karma was serious or
not. "Andrew and I met at college orientation. We were
both English majors, so we had all the same classes. One
night, after way too many of these"—Jessie held up her
beer and took another sip—"we talked about dating, but
we were such good friends, we decided not to take the
chance of ruining a perfect relationship."

Karma gave her the all-knowing-bartender with a
twist of Jujitsu-grand-master nod. "Ah, so there's no
sexual chemistry, huh?"

Confused, Jessie could do nothing other than shrug.
Karma's eyes penetrated hers as if she could see far
more than she let on. "I don't know. Like I said, we
never tested the waters." When Karma threw her blonde
head back and guffawed, Jessie's face heated. Every
customer stopped what they were doing and stared.

"Jessie, there's a whole lot you don't know about
chemistry. If it's there, nothing in the world would have
made you think about not testin' those waters. Strong
chemistry gives you no choice in the matter. One minute

you're talkin', and the next you're exploring the other person's tonsils and rubbin' up against the bulge in his Wranglers. Thinking is not required."

"Right, like I believe that."

"Honey, if you don't, you're a fool. But that's neither here nor there. So you were on the phone with your friend. Andrew, is it? Is he good-looking?"

"I don't know. I never thought about it. He's about six one, dark brown hair—almost black. Brown eyes. He's smart and funny."

Karma licked her lips and looked as if she were imagining the "Can't Say No" sundae at Serendipity 3—Jessie's favorite place to binge in New York. Karma must have had a very good imagination. "Good body?"

Jessie pictured Andrew in her mind's eye. His face was clear, but his body was a bit fuzzy. "I guess. I never really paid much attention."

"Yep, like I said—no sexual chemistry." Karma walked her fingers across the bar and took the beer Jessie had all but finished without noticing. Karma grabbed a chilled mug out of the cooler. Without even looking, she hit the right tap and waited, her eyes never leaving Jessie's. "Moving on."

Talking to Karma was like trying to watch a TV show while someone flipped channels. "While I was on the phone with Andrew, I dug through my work email and opened up a pink slip—"

"You got fired? From where?"

"I wasn't fired. I was laid off."

"Sorry." Karma looked anything but.

Jessie told herself that the newspaper business was shrinking, and she was the lowest female on an all-male totem pole. Getting laid off shouldn't have been a shock. "I was a sports reporter for the *Times*. Andrew talked me out of jumping out the window—which, when you consider my fear of heights and the fact that none of the windows were even operable, greatly diminishes any heroism on his part. He urged me to sublet my apartment and move into his house here in Boise. I can stay as long as I want, rent-free, on one condition—"

Karma slid the beer to her. "What's that? Does it have anything to do with testing those waters we talked about?"

"No." God, what was it with people in Boise? They serve you a drink and expect information about your sex life? Or in her case, the lack there of. It had been so long since she'd had sex, she wouldn't be surprised if her hymen had regenerated.

"Touchy subject, huh?" Karma wiped down the spotless bar. "Interesting."

"Not touchy, really. I'm just not used to talking about who I sleep with."

"No gal pals then?" Karma leaned forward and smirked. "I guess I'd better tell you, just in case you don't know. Testing the waters rarely involves sleep—unless you test them and it's so good you decide to wake up together and try it again to make sure it isn't a fluke."

Silence descended, well, as much silence as you could get at a bar as big as Hannah's on a Thursday afternoon. Jessie figured it was time for a change of subject. She cleared her throat. "Um… about the whole gal pal thing. You see, all my friends are guys I play basketball or softball with, or professional athletes. You're different from any woman I've ever met, Karma. Talking to you is like talking to a nosy guy with boobs."

Karma spun around, taking the order off a waitress's tray and pouring drinks. "I'll take that as a compliment." She shook a martini, strained it into a glass as she twitched her nose, and then smiled. "It's probably because I have three brothers and a cousin who thinks he's my big brother—well, until he asked me to marry him that one time. Thank God he found someone else to drag down the aisle." She feigned a shiver. "But that's a whole other story—you see, historically, the women in my family have been grossly outnumbered by men. But don't worry, I'm working on correcting that."

Jessie took a much-needed sip of her beer, trying to figure out how Karma could almost marry a cousin. Wasn't that illegal? Then again, maybe they were second cousins, or maybe she misheard. Since Karma was now the only friend Jessie had in Boise, she really didn't want to know if Karma was weird. Right now, she needed a friend. "Where was I?"

"The condition."

"Oh, yeah. Andrew dared me to write the book I've talked about since we were students at Columbia." She should have known Andrew wouldn't just be a nice guy and give her time to lick her wounds in private. "It's so unfair because he knows I can't resist a dare. So here I am. I just applied for a job at Starbucks, and I'm going to write a novel."

"What kind of novel?"

Jessie looked to make sure no one was within earshot. "You promise not to tell anyone?"

"What's it matter? I'm the only person in Boise you know."

"That's not true. There's my stalker."

Karma's eyes went wide. "Man, you work fast. You've been here less than a week, and you already have a stalker?"

"I don't know. I've been wondering about it for the past few days. Every morning the same guy runs with me—uninvited, he shows up at Starbucks without fail, and twice now, I've run into him at the grocery store. The last time, I spotted him first and ducked down the feminine hygiene aisle just to avoid him. He turns up everywhere I go. It's weird."

Karma bent over the sink and washed out the beer mugs and glasses. "What's he look like? Is he a creeper?"

"No. He's actually gorgeous. It's as if the sun is always shining on him, you know? Everyone I meet thinks he's God's gift to the female population. When he asked me out and I turned him down, one of the baristas at Starbucks questioned both my sexuality and my vision. It's as if wherever he goes he has a fan club. I know Boise's a lot smaller than New York, but running into him three times a day is ridiculous." She sipped her beer and tossed a pretzel into her mouth. "If he's not a stalker, the man missed his calling."

Karma shrugged and wiped down the first in a long line of liquor bottles. "I don't know how it is in New York, but we don't get many stalkers who are highly thought of here in Boise. Maybe the two of you just have a lot in common. You could share a circadian rhythm or something. Stranger things have happened." She plucked up another bottle and continued wiping. "Still, three times in one day is a bit of a stretch even for Boise. But hey, look at the bright side. A hot stalker is better than an ugly one. And if you're not interested in him, you know you can introduce him to your BFF."

"Why would I introduce him to Andrew? Andrew's not gay, and I can assure you this guy Fisher isn't either. The man's got more testosterone than the entire Giants' defensive line put together. He could bottle it and have enough to supply the eastern seaboard."

Karma stopped wiping down the bottle of Macallan 18 and stared at Jessie. "Your stalker's name is Fisher?"

"That's right." She tipped her beer mug up, foam clinging to her upper lip. "Fisher. My hot stalker."

"You're kidding." Karma slipped on her poker face—it almost killed her, but she didn't want Jessie to know that her stalker could very well be Karma's big brother—not that Fisher was a stalker or anything. He just had very precise habits, and so, it seemed, did Jessie. This was just too funny, not to mention perfect. "What's he look like?"

Was it horrible that Karma wanted to make her big brother squirm a little? Uh-huh, probably. What could she say? She was way more naughty than nice, and so far, it had worked for her. She wasn't about to change her tactics now, especially since she was having so much fun. How else could a girl with three older brothers survive if not by blackmail?

Jessie leaned forward. "He has the most amazing curly, white-blond hair, and the prettiest green eyes I've ever seen on a man."

Bingo. Karma's mind spun with all the ways she could use this information to her advantage—the possibilities were endless. Outside she played the perfect bartender, while inside she was doing the Snoopy "Happy Dance." Her brother was the only blond man named Fisher Karma knew in Boise, and her position at Hannah's insured she knew almost every single man over the age of twenty-one in Ada County. She was positive Jessie's stalker was none other than her big brother, Dr. Fisher Kincaid. And, from the dreamy look on Jessie's face, Karma could almost guarantee that Jessie and Fisher had enough chemistry to fuel the Idaho National Lab's Advanced Test Reactor. The girl couldn't describe her best friend, but she was having absolutely no problem describing Fisher, who she'd only seen a few times.

Jessie stared into Karma's eyes, and for a second Karma wondered if Jessie, smart girl that she was, had put two and two together. Looks-wise, Karma was the female version of Fisher, well, except her blonde was more dishwater than platinum. Leave it to the man to get the killer platinum blond hair. Sometimes life was just too unfair, although with this information, Karma could definitely tip the scales in her favor.

Jessie shook her head as if she was silently talking herself out of something. "Fisher's eyes are almost the same color as yours, but his have a circle of blue around the pupil. He's a few inches taller than me, I'd say about six two or six three, dresses like a preppy surfer, and is built like David Beckham. He has washboard abs and a lean, flat, well-muscled chest, and an ass worthy of a limerick."

Karma certainly didn't want to talk about Fisher's ass. She also saw no resemblance between Beckham and Fisher. Not that she compared their bodies or anything— that would have an exceptionally high *ick* factor. She made it a point never to check out her brothers or cousin. Yuck. Beckham was a god among men. Even though Fisher never had a shortage of women falling all over him, she couldn't believe he and Beckham were even in the same league. It was clear that Jessie had either fallen under Fisher's spell, or she was certifiable. "I love Beckham. That man can park his cleats under my bed any day."

"Tell me about it." Jessie fanned her face. "Beckham's even hotter in person than in the pictures."

Karma jumped up to sit on the cooler. "You know him?"

Jessie shook her head. "I don't know him, know him, but I've interviewed him a few times. One time he was in the locker room and only wore a towel. That man's abs are a thing of beauty."

"Talk about a job with perks. You get to interview half-naked professional athletes." She poured Jessie another beer and slid it over. "I'll clear your tab if you can produce pictures of Beckham in a towel or less."

"No problem." Jessie tugged an iPhone out of her pocket and scrolled through pictures. "Here's one with me and Beckham without his shirt on. His ink is amazing."

Karma ripped the phone from Jessie's grasp. "The hell with his ink, look at that body. Holy moly, batgirl! Wow, you got to touch my dream man. Who wouldn't want to be you? So this Fisher dude has as a body like Beckham, and you shot him down? What's wrong with you?"

"Nothing. I'm not here to date; I'm here to write. Besides, that guy Fisher flirted with anyone missing a Y chromosome. Plus, he didn't strike me as the strongest brew in the coffeehouse, if you know what I mean. When I wouldn't go out with him, he just smiled. He's either thick or mentally challenged."

Karma had just taken a sip of club soda—thank God she swallowed, or it would have shot straight up her nose. She should be writing this stuff down. After all, her job as a younger sister was to stick pins in Fisher's overinflated ego, not to pump it up. "A mentally challenged stalker. How… interesting. Now back to your story. If you're here to write a book, why is it such a big secret?"

"It's not a secret. It's just embarrassing. I'm a trained journalist with a degree from the best journalism school in the country. Now, if I'm lucky enough to get the job I just applied for, I'll be pouring coffee and writing a trashy romance."

"You're a romance writer? I love romance, and I've been reading it for years. Hell, I even hooked my cousin Ben's wife, Gina, and Toni, my new sister-in-law, on romance after swearing them to secrecy." She leaned closer. "If one word of my addiction got to my brothers or cousin, my hard-won position as an almost equal in their eyes would disappear faster than a vegetarian at the Rocky Mountain Oyster Feed."

Jessie took a swig of her beer. "I'd always planned to write literary fiction, but after looking at my severance package and my bank balance, if I have any hope of surviving, I'm going to have to get published pretty darn quick. I can't afford to spend a year writing a masterpiece. I'll spend six weeks writing a romance and turn around and sell it before my bank account hits the danger zone."

"You think you can write a book in six weeks and sell it? Who do you think you are? Nora Roberts?"

Jessie waved Karma's objections away. "Everyone knows that the easiest way for a debut author to break into publishing is to write a trashy romance. I'm a successful journalist. I should be able to do it with one hand tied behind my back."

"Jessie, when was the last time you read a romance?"

"Me?" She looked as if Karma just asked her what her favorite sexual position was. "Never."

"Have you done any research? I don't think publishing a book, even a romance, is that easy. There's a romance writer in Boise who comes in here every now and again. She once told me it takes the average romance writer seven books and ten years before getting published. And that's the average. For a lot of writers, it takes even longer."

Jessie drank the rest of her beer, reached into the bag she carried, and slid a romance face down across the bar, doing her best to hide the cover. "I'm doing research. I bought a dozen best-selling romances, and I'm going to read them even if it kills me. Honestly Karma, there's nothing like flashing a book with a bare-chested man on the cover to make a woman's perceived IQ drop a dozen points."

Karma just smiled.

Jessie tossed down a handful of bills. "I guess I'll go home and work on research. Say, do you know of any tennis courts with walls for practice?"

Karma took the bills and stuffed them back in Jessie's hand. "You showed me a picture of Beckham without a shirt, so we're square. I play tennis at Ann Morrison Park. How 'bout we meet to hit some balls tomorrow morning. Say about ten? That way we can discuss your research, and you can tell me what you think of this book." Karma flipped over the book and sighed when she caught a glimpse of the cover model. "It's on my TBR pile."

"What the heck is a TBR pile?"

Karma shook her head. "To Be Read pile. You might want to pick up a copy of *RT Book Reviews* too. It will give you a good picture of the romance core demographic as well as all the different subgenres."

"Tennis tomorrow for sure." Jessie pulled a card out of her wallet. "Here's my number if you need to cancel."

Karma wrote her cell number on a bar napkin. "Here's mine. I'll see you at ten."

Jessie shouldered her bag. "I'm hoping that all the exercise will counteract the depressing state of my life."

Oh yeah, Jessie was in for a shock. Reading a good romance will take her down a few pegs, not that Karma could really hold her attitude against her. Ten years ago Karma wouldn't have been caught dead reading a romance in public, and now the only thing keeping her from coming out of the romance closet was the fear of her brothers' and cousin's retribution. She couldn't afford to be thought of as a girl—not when she'd almost reached equality. "I'm looking forward to hearing all about it tomorrow."

"Right. The last thing I want to do is beef up on how to write a trashy, formulaic romance. Crap. I'm a journalist, not a writer of sex-infused purple prose."

Chapter 3

JESSIE CRAWLED OUT OF BED, TORE THROUGH A PowerBar, and chugged a glass of juice before going on her morning run. She considered skipping it. She was meeting Karma later for tennis, but since she didn't know if Karma was any good, she decided to get her run in anyway. She got cranky if she didn't get enough exercise. Besides, if she skipped it, she might not see Fisher, who had turned up in her dream last night.

It wasn't as if she'd meant to dream about him, but there was no mistaking the eyes she stared into while he did amazing things to her body. Too bad she woke up before the grand finale. Between reading that hot romance last night and dreaming about Fisher that morning, she'd woken up feeling… edgy. Edgy was not good.

Maybe it was time to start dating after all. Not that she'd date a guy like Fisher, but heck, there must be a nice, single guy in Boise.

She grabbed her iPod, shoved it into her armband before stuffing her key into the pocket of her running shorts, and slammed out of the house. After a few warm-up stretches, she was off. She took it slow for the first few blocks and then quickened her pace as she hit Camel's Back Park. It was nothing like Central Park with lush trees, lawns, and blacktop running paths. Camel's Back Park looked like the inside of a salad bowl. The bottom was green grass, and the sides looked as if they'd strip-mined a foothill at a forty-five-degree angle. It was a striking contrast to what she was used to. At first, the barrenness shocked her, but now, she noticed all the subtle colors—a palette dotted with earth tones from dark ocher, to sepia, to taupe, softened by sagebrush and punctuated by the backdrop of a cerulean sky. It amazed her that at seven in the morning the moon hung like an orb over the foothills that rose above her in the bright morning light. It was almost surreal.

She passed the tennis courts and took the path toward Hull's Pond. She hadn't gone a hundred yards before she heard the thud, thud, thud of running shoes against the hard-packed earthen trail beside her. She checked her watch. Fisher was punctual, if nothing else. Okay, punctual and hot. Today, instead of following her, he was running with her. Pacing her.

<center>~~~</center>

Fisher had been running late and hadn't had time for a real warm-up before Jessica ran by at full throttle. He poured on the speed, wishing he'd grabbed a water before leaving the house. "What'cha listening to?"

"The Exit, 'Don't Push.'"

He hoped that was the name of a band and a song— not that he knew which was which. He'd never heard of either. Fisher matched her pace, but couldn't say anything intelligent about the music. That was what happened when you'd had your head buried in academia for ten years. College, med school, residency, and then his fellowship took over his life. When he finally got home, he was all about studying for his boards and buying into a partnership. There was no time for a relationship more demanding than a roll in the hay. Even then, sometimes that was too much, which might explain why none of his relationships got past the hot sex stage. If it hadn't been for Hunter and the rest of his family, Fisher would have had no contact with anyone outside the medical community.

"This is my hard-run playlist. It keeps me moving."

"I gathered that." Fisher's calves burned as he ran beside her into the foothills below the Boise Front, the chain of mountains just north of Boise. "You do realize we're gaining elevation, don't you?" Unfortunately, the steepness of the trail hadn't slowed her down any.

"Yeah. That's apparent. They don't call it Camel's Back Park for nothing. You just gotta get over the humps."

They passed Hull's Pond, which shone green in the morning light. It looked as if God had taken a huge spoonful of earth out of the foothill, leaving the clear pond in its place. Jessica didn't bother slowing down to admire the view. She just turned off the trail and kept climbing onto Owl's Roost.

Fisher ran beside her as the North End took shape below them. Boise spread out, the greenbelt became clear—a lush green stripe of grass and deciduous trees running on both sides of the Boise River against a brown background. The Capital Dome and the few skyscrapers that made up the downtown shone in sharp relief in the September sunlight, against the endless blue sky cut only by a few jet trails.

"I run hard for four songs, I take it down a step for another four, then I'm back to running hard before I slow it down, and then I stretch. It's a great workout."

He didn't bother asking which songs, since his entire repertoire of music predated 1995.

They crossed Mile High Road and continued to climb past a few incredible McMansions with amazing views of the city. "What were you listening to the first time I followed you?"

"Probably my girl power playlist. You know, Gwen Stefani, Meredith Brooks, Pink, Sheryl Crow, Nelly Furtado, and your girlfriend's favorite, Lady Gaga."

Yes, it was time to update the music collection. Fisher had a hard time keeping up with her and talking, yet he couldn't help but laugh. "Laura's not my girlfriend. I only go out with adults. I'm flattered, thanks."

"Don't mention it."

"Is that why you won't go out with me?"

Jessica checked her watch. "No. I told you. I'm not interested. It's nothing personal."

"Sure. Like I believe that." Fisher didn't know why it mattered so much, but he was happy to see he might be wearing her down. Her mention of Laura meant she was at least curious, didn't it? Maybe he was suffering delusions due to lack of oxygen to the brain. He took a deep breath and did his best not to huff. "How can disinterest be impersonal?"

She actually turned her head and looked him in the eye. "I'm here to work."

Fisher wished she'd slow down so they could talk. "I'm not keeping you from working. What do you do, anyway?"

"I'm a writer." She turned up the volume on her iPod, tapped her watch, and then poured on the speed.

Shit. That was a great conversation killer. He figured four more kick-ass songs added up to at least twelve minutes of sprinting. Thank God they were running on a slightly downhill slope. Still, the woman was a machine. Either that or she really didn't want to talk. She didn't have to worry about it now, or in the near future. He couldn't have talked if his life depended on it. Dry air burned his lungs. His arms felt like lead, and his leg muscles were screaming. If she ran this way every day, it was no wonder she had a world-class ass. He just prayed he'd survive the playlist. If it didn't kill him, the endorphins alone should get him out of his funk. He swallowed back a groan and did his best to keep up with her.

After running for what seemed like miles, he followed Jessica past more houses that were way above his pay grade, but not for long though. He banked a lot of his salary, even after paying his partnership buy-in. The mortgage for his North End cottage was ridiculously low, and he always bought his toys used, so they were paid off. Everything he'd worked his whole life for was coming together. He was financially stable, he loved his work, he had a great family, but something nagged at him like an annoying gnat. No matter how many times he swatted, it wouldn't go away.

They turned onto another trail. He hadn't been out this far since he wrecked his dirt bike—the memory was still painful. There was nothing like digging rocks out of your ass for a week, but even worse was the ribbing he'd taken from his brothers. It had been a favorite topic for at least six months. Hell, they'd even given him a set of training wheels for Christmas, complete with a deck of cards for the spokes. At least they hadn't given him a meep, meep horn or a bell—an oversight on their part.

Karma had made up for it though when she put a set of pink and purple handlebar streamers in his stocking. He'd never live it down.

East Ridgeline Drive sprang up out of nowhere— like the beginning of a Hot Wheels track missing the next piece. He was thankful for the drop in elevation as they headed toward the valley. Jessica hadn't slowed her pace, but at least they weren't climbing. Maybe he would finish the run without collapsing at her feet and blowing chunks after all.

It seemed an eternity before she backed off on the speed. He'd be lucky if he could walk in an hour. It was going to be a long and painful day. Good thing he didn't see patients until one o'clock. It would take a few hours in his hot tub to get his muscles to function.

Jessica passed the pond and headed toward the park, stopping at the top of Camel's Back Hill. It was steep as hell—at least a forty-five-degree drop. He should know. He'd been sledding on it every time they got more than a few inches of snow since he was old enough to climb the damn thing with a saucer in hand. For a second, he thought she was going to run down it. Not a bright move. He took her arm. "You don't want to run down there." He could barely get the words out, because he was huffing like a four-pack-a-day smoker. "Come down this way."

Fisher led her down the switch back, which took them to the North End on Bella Street. Back on level ground, she ran the rest of the way at a slow jog, cooling off, and then stopped at a house with a picket fence. She opened the gate and waited. It wasn't quite the invitation he'd hoped for, but she didn't close the gate on him, so he followed her into the well-kept yard.

She pulled out her earbuds, and he heard Usher's voice singing "Nice and Slow." The song made him think of sweaty sex and satin sheets. Damn the woman was intriguing. Unfortunately, the only muscle in his body showing interest in a workout wasn't going to see any action.

"Do you want a water?"

Fisher wiped the sweat from his face onto the hem of his T-shirt. "Right now, I'd drink sand."

She dug into a hidden pocket in her shorts, pulled out a key, and motioned for him to follow. "I'll get a few waters, but then I need to stretch. You can come in if you like, but I stretch on the porch."

"I'll wait here since you're coming back out." He wanted to collapse on the porch swing hanging from the rafters—just not in front of her.

"Okay, I'll only be a minute."

"Take your time." He'd need more than a minute just to keep from embarrassing himself.

———⁓———

Jessie let the screen door slam behind her. It was such a nice day; she had all the windows open. Indian Summer had hit Boise with a vengeance, and she was going to enjoy the heck out of it. As she passed the open window, she heard Fisher groan as if in pain. She looked out to find him bending over with his hands braced above his knees, looking as if he was about to puke.

She was surprised he'd been able to keep up with her, and frankly, she was surprised she'd been able to run like she had today. She was way too competitive for her own good, pushing herself harder than she had even at the Marine-inspired boot camp she'd gone to for an article she'd written.

Jessie grabbed a few ice-cold waters and headed back to the porch. By the time she'd gotten out there, she was happy to see that Fisher had straightened up and was stretching his calf muscles on the bottom step.

She jumped off the porch to hand him his water. Fire shot from her knee to her hip. "Fuckity, fuck, fuck, fuck," she belted out the all-time worst of her curses. Her left hamstring seized—not cramped. She'd had cramps before. The damn thing seized.

"Jessica, you okay?"

"Fuckity, fuckity, fuck." She saw spots for the second time in her life. She was seeing spots, and surfer dude had to be the only living witness. She hopped on her right foot as pain shot from her ass all the way down to her foot.

Fisher dropped his water and grabbed her instead.

This was just great—not to mention incredibly embarrassing.

"Lie down."

"What?"

"It's your hamstring, right?"

"Well, duh."

"Lie down. You need to stretch it out." The man tackled her, and the next thing she knew, she was flat on her back in the grass with her leg up, and her ankle resting in his right hand as he bent over her, his bright green eyes staring into hers.

Talk about déjà vu. It was a freakin' replay of her dream. She was still writhing beneath him, only the take-me-now tingles had been replaced with searing pain.

"Breathe." Strong hands massaged her calf, moving

higher—all the way to her ass and back again. She would have kicked him if she was able to move her leg and wasn't about to scream in agony. He stretched it a little farther with each pass of his hands from calf to ass, and it was all she could do to keep from crying. "Better?"

"I'm fine."

"No, you're not."

Of course, he was right, but she'd die before she admitted it. If anyone should be on the ground writhing in pain, it should be him. Okay, so she was pouting, it wasn't her finest hour. "What are you, an expert or something?"

"On women's legs?" He shot her a breathtaking smile that was a mixture of smug and sexy, making her wonder if he was enjoying her embarrassment or picturing her naked, maybe both. "You bet."

"Why am I not surprised?" Yeah, Fisher's smile was definitely *smexy*. She'd just coined a new word—one of her favorite things, but even that didn't make her feel any better—a true testament to her pain level.

"What you need is a banana, Gatorade, and a hot tub—not necessarily in that order. Do you have any of the above?"

"What do you think?" She sucked in a breath when his fingers brushed against her inner thigh way too close to home plate, not that it seemed to register on his face—she was sure hers was changing colors, first to pale and then to bright red. "You're the one who took an inventory of my shopping cart a few days ago."

"Where are your car keys?"

"In my purse, why?"

"Because we're going to my house. I live a few blocks away, and I don't feel like carrying you."

"I'm fine. I don't need to go to your house for a banana, a hot tub, or anything else."

Fisher leaned over her, his face just above hers, and his hands still kneading her left ass cheek. God, he had amazing fingers. Too bad she couldn't enjoy them. "If we don't treat this cramp, you'll damage the muscle, and then where will you be?"

He sure sounded as if he knew what he was talking about. Maybe it was personal experience. In any case, the way he spoke with such supreme confidence was unnerving, yet effective. "Okay, my keys are in my purse on the hall table."

Fisher smiled and handed her water. "Drink half of this. Slowly. It will hold you until we can get some electrolytes into you. It'll help deal with the lactic acid buildup."

"Yes, doctor." Okay, so she was being a smart-ass, but she couldn't help it. Pain made her cranky—although what Andrew called it was not so generous. She didn't know what the hell Fisher did with his time, but if he ever wanted to get a real job, he'd make a great masseur.

Fisher gave her ass a pat and smirked. He had the kind of smirk that pissed her off and turned her on at the same time. The pissed-off part she attributed to her crankiness. The turned-on part she'd much rather forget—along with the early morning sex dream, and the déjà vu thing, and Fisher's brush over home plate. God, it was a sexually frustrating hat trick. When he turned away, she found herself ogling his ass again. She'd be better off just pouring the whole water bottle over her head.

He returned a minute later with her purse thrown over his shoulder, bent down beside her, and before she could figure out what he was up to, picked her up.

Jessie let out a yelp and ended up spilling the rest of her water all over them. Her T-shirt clung to her sports bra, and the girls stood at attention. "What do you think you're doing?" She pulled her wet shirt off her skin and tried to think straight. Not an easy thing to do when his hand rested just below her very wet, very cold breast, while she clung to him, her arm wrapped around his neck.

"I'm putting you in the car."

"I'm not a piece of luggage. I can walk."

"No, you can hop. I imagine it would be fun to watch, but this"—he gave her a squeeze—"satisfies my latent caveman tendencies. It's a win-win."

"I'm driving."

"It's a stick, right?"

"Yeah, so?"

"So… your left hamstring is not going to appreciate having to be on and off the clutch. I'll drive."

The man had skills. He could carry her after a hard run, open the door to her Mini Cooper, and set her in the seat without decapitating her. Fisher dropped her purse in her lap and closed the door, while she dug out her keys. He also drove like a race car driver. In less than a minute, they were pulling into the driveway of a clinker-brick craftsman cottage. "It's beautiful." There were flowers everywhere. "Are you a gardener?" That would explain his tan and his muscles.

"Nah, my mom did all this. She enjoys it."

When he carried her through the front door, any hope she had that he didn't live with his mother was dashed. Too bad, she was beginning to question her initial impression of him. The place had all the touches of a woman's home. A mirror by the front door, a table below it to put a purse on, a soft throw over the back of the couch to curl up in, and a cozy armchair beneath a reading lamp close to the fireplace. This place was definitely not a bachelor pad.

"Do you want to put on a bathing suit or just soak in your running shorts? I know there are a few suits fresh out of the wash."

"I'm not going to wear one of your girlfriends' bathing suits."

He stopped in the middle of the hall. "I thought we cleared that up. I don't have a girlfriend. The suits are my little sister's. She comes by and uses the hot tub whenever she wants."

Okay, sure. She believed him. After all, it must be awkward having women over when you live with your mother.

He carried her into the kitchen, set her down on the counter, and grabbed a banana off the bunch hanging on a strange looking rack. He tossed it to her before opening the refrigerator. "Orange or lemon lime? I think I might have a blue one in here too." He leaned into the refrigerator, and Jessie avoided staring at his ass again.

"Orange, please." The blue was her favorite, but for some reason she didn't want to have a blue tongue and lips around him. She peeled the banana, which didn't help her stop thinking about sex, and took a bite. She was determined to look at anything that wasn't part of Fisher. The kitchen was immaculate. Hers was clean, probably because she never did anything but reheat in it, but this kitchen literally sparkled. The sink shined like a car on the showroom floor for crying out loud. It wasn't as if the kitchen didn't look used—it did. It just looked used by a neat freak. There were no piles of junk mail, no odds and ends lying around the countertops. Heck, there weren't even any grocery bags stuffed between the wicked cool fridge and the cabinets beside it. It was like a freakin' *Martha Stewart Living* kitchen.

Spices lined one wall on a stainless steel rack Jessie could swear she'd seen the last time she grabbed a quick bite at Dean and DeLuca in the city. Fisher's mom must be one hell of a cook if she used even a quarter of the spices on the rack. Jessie hadn't heard of half of them.

Fisher cracked the top of the Gatorade, traded it for the banana peel, and threw it in a porcelain crock by the sink.

"What's that? The world's smallest garbage can?"

"It's for the compost pile. My mom's garden loves it. Come on." He helped her off the counter.

Surprisingly, her leg felt a lot better. She didn't know if it was the banana, the Gatorade, or the massage that did the trick. She really didn't care, but the next time she hit the Albertsons, she was definitely going to stock up on the two she could buy there.

"A nice soak and a couple of Motrin, and you should be back to normal in a few days." Fisher kicked off his running shoes and carried them back toward the front of the house.

"You mean a few hours." Jessie spoke to his retreating back. "I have a tennis date at ten."

Fisher dropped his shoes by the door. "At ten this morning? No way. It's almost eight-thirty now."

"I don't want to miss it." She took a step and then toed off her shoes. "I'll be fine after a soak in your hot tub. I'm feeling better already."

Fisher grumbled something—she didn't know what.

The scary expression on his face and the tension she saw in his shoulders as she followed him down the hall, toward the back of the house, was enough to tell her he was not happy with her declaration.

Too bad. She'd never missed a game before. Besides, she wasn't stupid—well okay, so she occasionally did not-so-smart things like pushing herself and him to see who would fail first. Still, she'd learned her lesson. She was not the bionic woman, and she was really not into pain. She'd take it easy and be careful.

He grabbed a few towels out of a wonderfully organized linen closet—yeah, definitely an OCD woman lived here—before stomping into a man cave. It had a huge flat-screen TV that took up an entire wall. Damn, she'd give her eyeteeth to watch a game on that behemoth. A computer, Xbox, and a Wii, rounded out the toys. Movies, games, and music all in alphabetical order, took up most of another wall. A deep brown leather couch, love seat, and chair provided seating with mission-style tables that you could set a drink or your feet on. The ceiling was dotted with recessed lighting, and Frank Lloyd Wright–inspired table lamps finished the room off, adding a golden glow.

A beautiful Navajo rug hung over the stone fireplace, and a larger version of the same rug covered the uneven, walnut hardwood floor. The walls were painted a rich maroon, and the windows were covered with blackout shades. Since the room faced due west, she figured they were a necessity if you wanted to watch TV in the late afternoon.

Fisher opened the French doors and stepped onto a deck sprinkled with clay pots overflowing with flowers and surrounded by gardens. He pulled off the cover of a large Jacuzzi hot tub that had to seat five or six adults. While he was busy, Jessie pulled off her T-shirt and running shorts. Heck, she had a sports bra and running underwear that covered her better than her racing bikini. She thought about soaking in her T-shirt and shorts, but she wasn't about to sit on her leather car seats in chlorine-soaked clothes.

—◦◦◦—

Fisher turned around to say something—what he couldn't remember—when he saw Jessica wearing what looked like the world's hottest bikini. Not that the suit was anything extraordinary, but the body it barely covered, well, that was an entirely different story. Jessica had a flat, firm, muscular torso and what looked like a very nice set of C-cup breasts. Her long, lean muscles were defined without being bulky. She looked one hundred percent female. She lifted her arms and showed off a set of guns Jillian Michaels would be jealous of. Raking her hands through her hair, she tied her ponytail into a knot at the top of her head, so that the ends fanned out and stuck straight up. She should look ridiculous, but it only made her look hotter. All his blood flowed south, and his mouth watered.

Jessica shrugged her shoulders. "I didn't want to get my shorts and T-shirt wet. It's not as if I'm naked."

Fisher saw naked women, or at least partially naked women, on a daily basis. Sure they were patients, but no one he'd ever seen, girlfriends, supermodels, or *Playboy* centerfolds when he was twelve, had the ability to throw him off his game before. Maybe it was because he hadn't expected her to strip down like that. Or maybe it had been way too long since a woman undressed in front of him. Whatever the reason, it rendered him incapable of speech.

He pulled his shirt over his head, stalling for time and hoping to get the problem in his shorts under control. At least he was behind the hot tub. Of course he'd have to get into the damn tub too. He leaned over to adjust the jets and climbed in trying to ignore her, or at the very least, think of her like a patient. He'd never had this problem with a patient. Unfortunately, his dick knew Jessica wasn't a patient, and if it had its way, she never would be.

He watched as she carefully climbed into the Jacuzzi. He could study the ripple of muscle over bone for an eternity, the way her ribs were defined when she bent over. The delineation of her spine as she stretched her back before sliding into the hot water made him want to run his hands over every bump and curve on her body. She moaned as she slid beneath the surface—the sound only added to his discomfort.

Jessica stayed on the opposite side of the tub, which was just fine with him. His mind was getting him into enough trouble without her being close enough to touch.

"God this feels like heaven."

Inappropriate thoughts flew through his mind with the speed and clarity of fireworks, one more spectacular than the next, and he did his best to shut them down, or at the very least, ignore them.

Jessica laid back, closed her eyes, and soaked in the sun and the warm water. She hadn't said anything, but then she was a woman of few words. He'd figured that out on their run. The silence wasn't uncomfortable, and

it was nice just soaking without having to listen to someone run off at the mouth. Yeah, Jessica was not your
typical female.

He checked his watch and was surprised to find
they'd been soaking for about twenty minutes. "How's
the leg?"

"Good. Do you want to feel it?"

Did she just say what he thought she said? "Feel it?"

"It wouldn't be the first time. It isn't as if you didn't
have your hands over every inch of my leg from ass to
ankle less than an hour ago. What's the big deal?"

She stood, the water cascading off her body, drib-
bling between her breasts and over her rectus abdominis, sliding down her transverse abdominis and external
obliques. Unfortunately, thinking in Latin just made his
problem worse. Did she really expect him to answer
when all he wanted to do was catch the droplets of water
running down her torso with his tongue?

She rested her foot between his legs. Thank God he'd
turned up the jets. There was no way she could see how
hard all the talk of feeling her up had made him. As if
they had a mind of their own, Fisher's hands wrapped
around her slim ankle and slid to her calf, supple skin
over tight, smooth muscle. No spasms there. His hands
crept higher. There was no sign of swelling or bruising to indicate rupture, no apparent myofascial pain, or
even tenderness. He ran his hand up the back of her right
hamstring to compare the two and check for swelling.
He found none. The only change he could detect was in
her respiration. "Am I hurting you?"

"Um… no. You're fine. I mean… I'm fine. I mean…
no, it doesn't hurt."

He did his best not to smile, but damn if he didn't feel a tic in his cheek.

Jessica backed away so quickly she slipped on the edge of a built-in lounge and landed in the seat with a splash. Her face flamed.

Something about her just tugged at him, making him leave his gentlemanly tendencies at the door. "There's nothing to be embarrassed about. It's human physiology. It's sexual chemistry—you're just experiencing a normal reaction to physical stimuli. Don't worry, it works both ways."

"B... both ways?"

"I'm just as affected as you are." He stood and almost laughed as her eyes just about bulged out of her head. There was no use trying to hide it, not that he could if he'd wanted to. "If you don't want to miss your ten o'clock date," he said as he handed her a towel, "you'd better dry off while we talk about what we're going to do about it."

She stood and wrapped the towel around her like a shield. If he didn't pay close attention to the straps running up behind her neck, he could almost pretend she was naked. He never thought he'd admit it even to himself, but maybe his brothers were right. It had been way too long since he'd dated a woman. And the thought of this woman going on a date—even just for a game of tennis—didn't set well with him.

Fisher was getting used to Jessica's lack of conversation skills. Still, it didn't keep him from wanting to give her a push. "So, what do you think we should do?"

"Nothing." She wrapped her arms around herself. "I'm going home, and you're going to do whatever it is that you do."

Fisher stepped closer, and her eyes widened. Still, she didn't step back. He liked that about her. She was cautious, but not afraid. "Ignoring it isn't going to make it disappear."

"No, it won't make it disappear, but ignoring you might do the trick." Jessica smiled, but not the kind of smile he'd hoped to see—he wished he could trade the determined grin for a compliant one. Somehow he figured the word "compliant" was never used to describe Jessica. Willful, headstrong, and truculent, certainly—compliant, never.

She shook out her T-shirt and pulled it over her head before sliding the towel down and looking him in the eye. "It's nothing personal, Fisher. You seem like a really nice guy, but I'm just not interested in dating, no matter how much chemistry there is between us. Just because you can raise my blood pressure, and I can raise your—" She motioned to his quickly deflating hard-on. "It's nothing more than lust. Unlike you, I've got a lot of work to get done in a short time. The last thing I need is another distraction. So even though you're the best-looking distraction I've ever imagined, I'm going to say thanks, but no."

He inched closer. "So you've imagined me and you—" Oh yeah, she didn't even need to answer, the way her eyes darkened and her breath caught gave her away. He was glad to know he wasn't alone.

"Thanks for all your help today—the banana, the Gatorade, and you know"—she motioned to her leg—"whatever." She tugged her shorts up under the towel and then pulled it off, folding it over the rail around the deck. "I'm sorry if I did anything to lead you on. That wasn't my intention at all. As a matter of fact, I was trying to avoid you."

He stepped to the left to block her escape, but she pivoted right. "You were? When?"

"When I saw you at Albertsons last night. I slipped down another aisle. Look, let's just pretend this never happened. I'll get my shoes, and I'll be out of your hair."

"Jessica, wait."

She shook her head and walked through the French doors. He couldn't say a damn thing to stop her. She'd made up her mind, and all he could do was hope she figured out that ignoring him wasn't going to make the chemistry they shared go away.

Chapter 4

"SORRY I'M LATE." JESSIE HURRIED THROUGH THE GATE of the tennis court Karma occupied, tossed her bag in the corner by the fence, and grabbed a can of balls and her racket. "I had another run-in with my stalker, and things got a little out of hand."

"How out of hand did it get?"

Jessie shrugged and opened the fresh can. The scent of brand new tennis balls assaulted her. It was like a drug. God, she loved it. New-tennis-ball scent was as powerful and fleeting as new-car smell. By tomorrow, the balls would lose their new-ball smell and just a smidgen of their bounce. It was sad. But today, she put a ball to her nose and inhaled, they were perfect.

"I had a nasty hamstring cramp this morning, so I need to take it easy today. I'm sorry." She tapped one over the net to Karma, who caught it and stuck it in her pocket. Jessie followed suit and then bounced the other around on the top of her racket, checking her strings. "Would you mind if we just volley instead of playing a game?"

"We don't have to play at all if you're hurt." Karma adjusted her visor. "We can just go to Starbucks and talk. There's one a few blocks away."

"No, it's fine." The last place she wanted to go was the Starbucks that she and Fisher shared. She didn't want to run into him again so soon, if ever. But then the thought of never seeing Fisher didn't sound too good either—even after his threat of a come-to-Jesus meeting about the whole wild, rampant, scary, sexual chemistry thing. "I was just trying to run my hot stalker into the ground this morning, and well, by the end of the run, I was the one on the ground." Jessie hit a ball to Karma. "Of course, in order to get me there, he had to tackle me."

Karma let the ball fly past her and walked toward the net. "Your stalker tackled you?"

"Yeah, but he was only trying to help, I think. Though with him, there's always that lingering doubt." Jessie shrugged. "He's a guy, and he gave me a hell of a leg massage. Between the massage and the soak in a hot tub, I'm almost as good as new."

"A massage, then a soak in a hot tub? Sounds like foreplay to me."

Jessie would be the last person on earth to admit it, but it felt a lot like foreplay too. She just hadn't realized it until way too late. She plucked at the strings of her racket as Karma approached her.

"You have a hot tub?" Karma didn't give Jessie even a second to answer. "Isn't that convenient?"

"No, I don't have a hot tub, and no, it's not convenient at all." Jessie backed up and took the spare ball from her pocket, bouncing it against the court with her racket to avoid making eye contact. "Fisher took me to his house, fed me a banana and Gatorade, and let me go for a swim in his Jacuzzi. It was medicinal, not foreplay." She didn't mention the end part where she practically ran away from a fully aroused, not to mention well endowed, incredibly hot man. Or the part about being as aroused as he was. Her only saving grace was that he lived with his mother. She'd made that mistake once before, and she was never doing that again. No momma's boys for her.

"You went home with your stalker?"

Jessie let the ball bounce once more before hitting it over the net. "Uh-huh."

Karma returned the volley right to her, and Jessie backhanded it, making Karma run.

Karma smashed the ball. "So it sounds like he's becoming less of a stalker and more of a boyfriend."

The ball flew back toward Jessie, but not right to her. She hopped sideways. "Not a boyfriend. I made that clear." Jessie sliced it back over the net, so Karma had to run for it. "I refuse to date a grown man who lives with his mother."

Karma returned a half volley that would make Roger Federer proud. Karma obviously knew her tennis. "Did you say he lives with his mother?"

"Yes." Jessie hit a crosscourt shot, making Karma run for a ground stroke, and bounced back to the middle, favoring her hamstring. "I mean, I think he does. His house has to be run by a woman with a major case of OCD. The kitchen sink shined, the house was immaculate, the gardens were spectacular, and his videos and music were in alphabetical order. Fisher's mother must be like Martha Stewart on steroids. Even the linen closet was so tidy it looked staged."

Karma lobbed the ball to her. "You didn't ask him if he lives with his mom?"

Jessie skipped back into no man's land and returned the ball with an overhand smash down the line. "Hell no. I don't want him to think I'm interested because I'm definitely not. No matter how hot he is. Fisher and his mom even have a compost pile. It's… unnatural."

Karma returned with a drop shot and let out a laugh. "Composting is unnatural? God, you make it sound almost incestuous. A lot of people compost here. There's nothing kinky about it, believe me."

"Maybe not." Jessie ran to the net to scoop up the ball and missed. Maybe tennis wasn't such a good idea. She turned and hopped back toward her tennis bag. She motioned for Karma to follow.

"Now spill. Did hot stalker guy ask you out again?"

Jessie looped her bag over her shoulder and rummaged through it, finding nothing. "I didn't give him the opportunity. I left." She gave up and collapsed, resting the bag on her lap. Her hamstring cramped again, making her almost as uncomfortable as Karma's questioning.

"You ran?"

Jessie shaded her eyes and looked at Karma with the sun at her back, her blonde hair tied in a ponytail and a visor shading her face. "I didn't run, I left." Jessie needed to drink the Gatorade she'd picked up on her way, and take some Motrin before her hamstring seized up on her again. Dammit, she hated that Fisher was right. She could just picture the smug look he'd have on his face if he found out about this.

Karma slid down beside her. "Looks like the game between you and your stalker is at forty-love and you, my dear, are on the losing end."

Jessie searched the pocket of her bag for a pill bottle. "I don't believe in love, not off the court at least. There, I found it." She took a look at the expiration date. "Shit. They expired two months ago."

"They're fine. They don't go bad when they expire, they just lose some of their effectiveness."

Jessie shot her a questioning look.

"My brother's a doctor." Karma shrugged. "He's forever going through my medicine cabinet and tossing stuff, but even he wouldn't complain over a few months."

Jessie reached into her bag and pulled out the couple of drinks. "You want one?" She cracked open a Cool Blue Gatorade, not caring if her lips turned blue. She handed one to Karma before tossing four pills into her mouth and chasing them down.

Karma leaned her racket against the chain-link fence and brushed off her hands. "What do you mean, you don't believe in love?"

Jessie should have known Karma wouldn't let that go. She might have only met Karma twice, but she could tell she was one of those people who wouldn't let anything slide. "I think people love their families. You know—parents, siblings, friends, and pets. But I don't believe in romantic love. It's not love at all. It's lust, plain and simple. It's not pretty, so people try to dress it up with hearts and flowers and cute, chubby babies armed with arrows. The whole concept of romantic love is nothing but spin and a boon for the entire greeting card industry."

"You've got to be kidding." Karma took a swig of her drink and wiped her mouth with the back of her hand.

"Nope. I'm serious." Jessie pulled up her left leg and tried to massage her hamstring—Fisher was way better at it. The man had magic hands. Not that she was thinking about him or his hands or anything else. What was she talking about? Oh yeah. "You see, Karma, before the year 2000 and the dawning of true gender equality, women were dependent on men."

"Not my mom. That woman wouldn't be dependent on a man."

"Okay, fine. Not every woman. I grant you that women have been increasingly less dependent on men in the years approaching the turn of the century. Still, even thirty or forty years ago, the majority of women were dependent on men for everything—food, shelter, money, you name it. Men married women, and after the lust died, women had no choice but to stay with their husbands because of that dependency, not to mention the social stigma carried by divorce. Not divorced men, mind you, just women. In the last thirty years that's all changed. Women are no longer dependent on men, and divorce is no longer the proverbial scarlet letter. There's no reason for a woman to stay unhappily married. We can take care of ourselves."

Karma laughed. "We women might be able to 'take care of ourselves,' but a vibrator doesn't keep you warm at night or bring you coffee in bed in the morning. This I know."

"I don't mean take care of ourselves sexually. Hell, there's never a shortage of men to sleep with, if that's what you're looking for—I'm talking about financial and social independence. When the lust peters out, which studies show happens between a year and a half and two years after the first roll in the hay, women of the past would lie to themselves about how much they adored their husbands. They did the whole wifely duty thing because there was no escape. Now we're finding that the relationship is left to wither and die, eventually ending in divorce or an ugly breakup."

Karma took another drink and stuck out her hand to stop the conversation. "Let me get this straight. You don't believe in love, and you're writing a romance novel? How can that be?"

"Romance is fiction. Do authors of novels about serial killers have to kill people to write them?" Jessie stretched out her leg in front of her. "Romances are nothing but formulaic stories with three point five sex scenes. Boy meets girl, boy and girl have sex, fall in lust, boy, girl, or both do something stupid, girl breaks up with boy or vice versa, and then they somehow overcome their flimsy external and internal conflicts, or the horrible misunderstanding, only to realize they can't live without the other. They kiss, make up, have one more hot sex scene, and live happily ever after. The end."

Karma had a funny look on her face, but Jessie wasn't sure she wanted to know what Karma was thinking. She finished off her bottle of Blue Ice. "I wonder if Fisher would let me use his hot tub again."

"You've never been in love." Karma said it with such certainty it was eerie.

Jessie didn't lie. Well, not usually at least. "Okay, fine. I've never been in love. Not even close. I've been in lust and in like, but never love, because romantic love doesn't exist."

Karma picked up her empty bottle and Jessie's too. "I'll recycle these."

Was Karma just going to leave it like that? She wasn't going to argue?

Karma offered her a hand up, and Jessie took it, grateful for the lift. Good thing Karma was strong. Jessie was able to get up without putting any weight on her left leg.

How she was going to drive was a mystery. Maybe the Motrin would kick in before she got to her car.

"Well," Karma said as she bent to get both her bag and Jessie's. "I believe in love. Hell, I've seen it. My brother married the love of his life and so did my cousin. They're disgustingly happy. There's no sign of the lust petering out with either."

Jessie found herself hobbling beside Karma in the general direction of the parking lot. "They're still in the lust stage. Just wait a few years, you'll see. The average first marriage lasts about six and a half years. Of course, not all marriages end in divorce. I guess it depends on what the couple has in common outside the bedroom."

"My grandparents were married for over forty years before my grandmother died. I'm not buying it. A woman as intelligent as you can't actually believe that love doesn't exist." Karma tossed her bag on a nearby picnic table in the shade and threw her leg over the bench.

Jessie shook her head. "Your grandparents lived before the new age of gender equality. They don't count."

"Of course they do. Gramps is so rich, if his wife had wanted out of the marriage, she'd have had no problem living off the money from a settlement and would have gotten in a divorce. She loved him, plain and simple, and he loved her until the day she died. There's never been anyone else for Gramps, which is kind of sad, really."

Jessie stretched her sore leg as Karma patted the table. "We might as well make ourselves comfortable. I don't think you're going to be able to drive like this."

Karma was probably right. Dammit. Jessie leaned against the table. "My parents are still married, but my mother's always been a stay-at-home wife and mother. My mom met my dad in college, married, and she's never worked a day outside the home. She's the last of the dependent generation."

"Maybe she's happy with her life." Karma kicked the dirt and watched the plume of dust rise and fall in the stillness. "Have you ever asked her?"

"No." Jessie stared at the ground and flexed her leg. "What's she going to say? I'm her daughter. You don't tell your daughter the sex is boring, and you'd rather be anywhere but staring across the dinner table at your husband."

Karma laughed. "Believe me, my mother lets everyone know when she's not happy. Maybe your mother is content. There are worse things to be. Life isn't all sunshine and happiness, no matter how great a marriage is."

"I don't know. They're always there, but separate, like a pair of bookends. You wonder what they have to talk about after all these years."

Karma took her visor off and pulled out her ponytail. "I think a solid, contented relationship would be wonderful."

"Is wonderful synonymous with boring?"

"No. You don't understand." She tossed her visor in her bag. "It's like baking. You can sprinkle in happiness like cinnamon sugar on a coffee cake—too much is overwhelming, and too little is bland. But when you get the right mixture, it's comforting and enjoyable. I think that's what a good marriage is like after the hot sex cools a little. That's what I remember when I think back to Gramps and Gran. Even after my cousin's parents died. They were sad, but close—inseparable, holding each other up through a really tough time. One always had the other's back. They were one hell of a team."

Karma leaned against the table and looked out toward the river. "I wish I had my fly rod in the trunk. There's nothing like tiptoeing to the edge of the river and casting to work out the kinks and relax. Do you fly-fish?"

"No, I've never tried it. It looks like fun though."

"If you want, I can ask my brother if we can use his cabin. It's right outside of Stanley, and it's gorgeous. It's only about three hours away in the mountains, right by the Salmon River. I'm taking the whole weekend off, so I don't have to be back in town until Wednesday when Hannah's opens again."

"Sounds like a great little vacation."

"I'd better take the time off when I can get it. My bartender's wife is prego and due in a few weeks. He's going to stay home with her and the baby for a month, so my hours are going to be insane after the kid's born. This is probably my last chance to get out of the valley before Hunter closes up the cabin for the winter."

Jessie stood, put her foot on the edge of the table, and stretched.

"Feeling better?"

"Yeah, a little. I guess Fisher was right about tennis not being a great idea." She stretched a little farther. "I don't think I damaged it though."

"That's good. On the bright side, the cabin has a whirlpool Jacuzzi tub in the master bedroom and a natural hot spring in the river. What do you think? Are you interested in a girl's weekend away? I was going to head up alone, but this will be much more fun."

Jessie put her leg down on the ground and took a

tentative step. "I'm definitely interested. But I don't have any fishing gear, and until I see how my finances shake out, I can't really invest in any."

Karma patted her arm. "Yeah, you have nothing to worry about there. May I remind you that I have three brothers and a cousin? Those guys collect gear like Imelda Marcos collected shoes. I'm not worried about finding you a fly rod. I even have an extra pair of waders if you want to use them. Let me ask Hunter if the cabin's free, and I'll call you. When can you leave on Friday?"

"Anytime, really. I don't start training at Starbucks for a few weeks. I guess I'm replacing some guy who's moving to San Diego. Right now, the only plan I have is to avoid my hot stalker. I'd love to see Stanley, and I can always bring my laptop with me and work if I get the itch."

Karma stood and brushed off her butt. "Great. Hunter's always got the cabin stocked full of food, so I'll just bring some milk, eggs, cheese, and whatever else I find in my fridge, so we'll be set."

Jessie stepped closer. "I'll bring wine and beer."

Karma walked with her toward the parking lot. "Sounds like a plan. I'll give you a call tomorrow with the specifics. You're going to love it up there."

"Great. Thanks for the invite. It sounds like fun."

Jessie smiled and waved as she climbed into her Mini Cooper, thinking a weekend at a secluded cabin was just what the doctor ordered.

Karma felt a smile tugging at her lips as Toni and Hunter walked through the doors of Hannah's arm in arm. She didn't see how anyone could look at them and not believe in romantic love. With those two, you'd need a hazmat suit to avoid exposure. Hell, after seeing Toni and Hunter so ecstatically happy, not to mention Ben and Gina flying in and out of town in wedded bliss, even Karma, the woman voted most likely to become a cougar, was softening when it came to the idea of a long-term relationship. Marriage, not so much, but then, she was smart enough to never say never. Toni had sworn up and down she'd never marry, and now she had to live with all the I-told-you-sos. Karma knew what info could be used against her by her family and learned never to volunteer it.

She poured a beer for her brother and a dirty martini for her sister-in-law and set them on the bar. "Thanks for coming by, guys. Tonight's tab is on me, if you'll lend me the cabin this weekend." She tried for her innocent smile. Toni looked as if she bought it. Hunter, unfortunately, knew better.

He took a sip of his beer as he studied her over the rim of his mug. "Who are you going with?"

Damn, she couldn't get away with anything. Good thing not getting away with it was her plan all along. Her brothers were so predictable. "What makes you think I'm going with anyone? Maybe I just want a weekend alone."

"Karma." Hunter turned on his no-bullshit voice and raised an eyebrow.

"Fine. I'm going with my new friend, Jessie James. Jessie's just moved here from New York." God, this was like taking candy from a sleeping baby. You'd think a guy like Hunter would make it a little challenging at least.

Toni smiled, and the gleam in her eye matched

Gina's when she was in deep matchmaking mode. Sheesh, the two of them were horrible. They were the last ones to want marriage and a relationship. They'd been so thick, they hadn't known they'd fallen headfirst into the love machine reactor until someone like her hit them over the head with a two-by-four. Now they'd turned into modern-day yentas, trying to fix her up with every Tom, Dick, and in this case, Jessie in Boise. Thank God Jessie had an androgynous name. "What does Jessie do for a living?"

"Sports reporter for a big paper in New York or something. Now Jessie's taking some time off to write a book."

Hunter scowled, but being the strong, silent type, he didn't say anything. Toni, on the other hand, was a babbler.

Toni sat up a little straighter, obviously warming to the subject. "You're going out with someone who doesn't even have a job?"

"I'm not going out with Jessie. I'm just going to fly-fish. Jessie's interested in learning a new sport. So are you going to lend me the cabin or not?"

Toni slid her arm through Hunter's. "Of course we are. Besides, it's not as if we're going to be up there for the next few weeks anyway. You'll be doing us a favor."

Hunter all but sneered at his wife. "I don't like the idea of Karma going up to the cabin with someone I've never met."

God, he was going to pay for that later. Good thing, he seemed to like it when Toni was pissed at him. Strange man.

Toni rolled her eyes. "Someone you've never threat-ened, you mean. Give it a break, Hunter. Karma doesn't need you putting the fear of God into her boyfriends. She's more than capable of taking care of herself."

"Yeah, right." Karma stared him down for a few beats and tried not to laugh at how well Toni had him trained. God, who'd have thought her lone wolf brother would turn into such a lapdog. Toni led him around by the nose. He knew it and didn't seem to mind. Amazing. "Don't worry, Hunter; Jessie is harmless. We're just going to soak in the hot spring and catch some fish. Heck, Jessie's even planning to bring a laptop and work at night in front of the fire while I read. It'll be… cozy."

Hunter muttered something, gave his wife a kiss, and headed upstairs to the pool tables with his beer.

Karma checked her watch and followed Hunter's progress up the circular stairway, before turning her attention to her sister-in-law. "How much you want to bet that Trapper and Fisher will be here in under a half hour?"

"You don't think he's going to call them about your weekend away, do you?"

"I don't think, I know. I'll bet you a Jackson that Trapper and Fisher will be waltzing through those doors before you know it."

"You're on." Toni shook Karma's hand across the bar. "It will serve Hunter right if I lose. Men, especially the *über*macho ones like Hunter, think we need them to run our lives."

Karma mixed a batch of margaritas for a waitress. "Yeah, you think Hunter's bad with you. I've had to deal with him all my life—times four. Fisher, Trapper, and Ben aren't any better."

Toni sighed. "I don't know how you keep from hurting them. Honestly."

Karma turned on the blender and couldn't help but smile. She salted the glasses and whispered. "You want to know my secret?"

Toni leaned in. "Of course."

"You'll have to swear you won't say anything to anyone, especially not Hunter. Ever." She poured the drinks and set them on the tray. "It's a girl thing, and guys—even married guys—can't be trusted with it."

"I pinky swear." Toni held out her little finger.

Karma hooked hers around Toni's. It was great having sisters. "Here's the thing. Ever since you and Hunter got married, well, Fisher's been a little depressed."

"Fisher's depressed because of me?"

"No, no, no. Toni, Fisher loves you."

Toni's face paled, and her mouth fell open.

Oops, Toni definitely got the wrong idea. "Not loves you, loves you. He loves you like a brother. Calm down, it's not the end of the world."

Toni nodded, but didn't look convinced. Maybe this was all a big mistake. Karma felt like giving herself a head slap. She should know better than to open her big mouth. "Fisher's really happy for you and Hunter. Hell, I doubt he even knows what the heck is wrong with him. Men can be so obtuse."

Toni frowned and toyed with her olives. "I didn't know Fisher very well before Hunter and I got married. I guess I still don't. I didn't have a clue he was unhappy."

"Calm down. It's not that bad. Hell, Fisher probably doesn't even realize it. But I've been watching my brothers all my life; I know what's going on with them even before they do. Take Hunter for instance. I knew he was over the moon in love with you the minute he called asking me to buy him that dating book. Where do you think he got that industrial-size box of condoms?"

"You?" Now Toni was turning bright red.

Better embarrassed than ready to pass out. "Yeah, you're welcome. I knew his were probably expired, and as much as I'd love to have a little niece, I didn't want an accidental one."

Toni's eyes bugged out. The poor girl might need something stronger, but Karma didn't know what was stronger than a Grey Goose dirty martini—well, not that Toni would drink anyway. Besides Karma didn't have time for this. If she was right, Trapper and Fisher would be there in less than fifteen minutes, and she was usually right. She poured Toni another. "Here, drink this."

Toni did as she was told, and after she finished the first and downed a few gulps of the second, her color evened out.

"Good. Now the way I see it, Fisher just needs someone to fill that empty space, kind of like you did for Hunter."

"You're going to set him up with someone?"

Karma couldn't help but smile and give herself an imaginary pat on the back. It was an ingenious plan, if she did say so herself. "Yes, and I have the perfect victim… I mean, woman. Don't worry. Fisher's already interested in her. He's been stalking her for a week now."

"What?"

It was going to take Toni a little time to adjust to the craziness of the Kincaid men, obviously. "He's not stalking her really, but she's been wondering. It seems they're on the same schedule. They go running at the same time, show up at Starbucks at the same time, shop at the same time. He's also asked her out more than once and even got her into his hot tub." She waggled her eyebrows and caught some guy looking at her. Men— they all think the world revolves around them. She shot him a not-in-this-lifetime look and returned her attention to Toni. She waved away the question she found there. "Look, I don't have time to explain everything right now. I'll tell you later, because I laughed so hard I nearly peed my pants when I heard the whole story. Sometimes being a little sister has its perks after all. So here's my plan…"

Chapter 5

FISHER PRACTICALLY RIPPED THE HINGES OFF HUMPIN' Hannah's door. He hadn't slept in two days, was still recovering from his last run with Jessica, not to mention the hot tub incident, and barely survived his first knitting class with his masculinity intact—although he had been given the phone numbers of the daughters and grand-daughters of six of his classmates. After hearing what the ladies had to say about their beautiful and talented offspring, he had less than no interest in ever dating any of them. God, women could be scary. Was nothing sacred? After packing up his knitting and walking to the back of Knittin' Chicks where he'd hidden his truck, he was called to the hospital for an emergency and had been there ever since. He needed a shower, a shave, a meal, and about twelve hours of uninterrupted sleep.

Karma slid a cold one across the bar, which he caught just before it hit the edge. The girl could sure hump the beer. "Thanks, Karma."

"Hunter's upstairs." She smiled that wicked smile of hers, which always made the hair on the back of his neck stand straight up.

Shit. That wasn't a good sign. He figured that since he'd been out of the loop for a few days, whatever her dastardly plan was, it most likely didn't involve him. It was a good thing too. He wasn't up to going toe-to-toe with Karma, literally or figuratively. She might be a girl, but he knew from personal experience how dirty she fought and the damage she was capable of exacting, both to his body and his reputation. He didn't even want to go there. "I'll head on up then and let you and Toni continue conspiring." Fisher kissed Toni on the cheek as she counted out twenty dollars and handed it to Karma. God only knew what that was all about. He didn't have the energy to ask. When it came to his crazy family, including the new additions to it, he had a firm don't-ask-don't-tell policy.

Fisher dragged himself up the stairs and found Hunter brooding in the corner. "What the hell is so all fired important that I had to come here instead of going home and sleeping for the first time in over forty-eight hours?"

Hunter looked up, and Fisher cringed when he saw the worry written all over his twin's face. So much for only staying for a quick beer. He pulled out a stool and sat opposite him at the high-top table. "Sorry, I'm just beat."

"You look like shit. I would think you'd be used to the lack of sleep by now."

"Yeah, yeah. Are we just gonna chitchat like a bunch of women, or are you going to tell me what the hell the problem is?"

"Trapper's on his way. I'd rather only have to say it once, so keep your shirt on."

"Trouble in paradise?"

"No, it's our pesky little sister."

"Damn, I knew she was up to something."

"Something or someone."

Fisher had never wanted to get involved in Karma's personal life. He'd just assumed she didn't have one. Especially when it came to guys. The last thing he wanted to think about was a guy doing anything with his little sister.

"She's taking some dude—a sports reporter from New York named Jesse James, of all things—to the cabin this weekend."

Fisher got cuffed on the back of the head. He didn't need to look to see it was Trapper—no one other than his brothers or his cousin Ben would have the balls to try it.

"What ran over you? You look like shit."

"So I've heard." Fisher elbowed Trapper right after he set the pitcher of beer on the table. No use spilling perfectly good beer. Fisher did his best not to smile when he heard Trapper's rapid exhalation. He may be tired, but he could still get one over on his big brother. At least that hadn't changed.

Trapper pulled over a bar stool and picked up his mug as he eyed Hunter. "Let me guess. Toni finally figured out what a loser she married and asked for a divorce?"

"Very funny." But Hunter wasn't laughing. "My wife is still blissfully unaware of the fact I'm a mere human, thank God. And the last thing I need is the two of you filling her in. The problem I'm having is the same damn problem I've had for the last twenty-five years."

Trapper set his beer on the table and smiled. "Karma."

Hunter nodded and stared into his beer. "She talked Toni into letting her use the cabin for a long weekend starting Friday."

Trapper looked between him and Hunter. "So, what's the problem?"

Fisher rested his boot on the rung of his stool and winced when his quads screamed. "The problem is she's going up there alone with some sports reporter—"

"Jesse James." Hunter added as he filled his mug and looked at Trapper. "Have you met him?"

"No."

"Yeah, I didn't think so." Hunter rested his elbows on the table and sipped his beer. "Karma said the guy's new in town. He's here from New York, and he's writing a book or something. I don't like it."

"If you didn't like it, then why did you lend her the cabin?" Trapper pushed his cowboy hat back and stretched his shoulders. "I swear, after you said 'I do' you seemed to have lost the ability to say no."

"I have not. Toni said yes before I could get the word out. Besides, this is easy to fix."

Fisher tried not to fidget when both sets of eyes turned to him. "Don't look at me. Hunter, you created the problem, you fix it."

Trapper took his hat off and ran his hand through his long hair. "I'm out. I've got a thing this weekend, and I can't get out of it."

Fisher wasn't going to let him off that easily. "A thing? What the hell is that? At least be honest about it. You've got one of your famous seventy-two-hour flings."

"Hey, at least I'm not living like a freakin' priest. It's been so long since your dick has seen anything but your own hand, it's a wonder it hasn't shriveled up and fallen off. Which is why you should be the one to go crash Karma's little party. You have nothing better to do anyway."

Fisher wished he could call bullshit, but Trapper was right. The only plans he had for the weekend were getting some much-needed sleep; although, since he and Jessica got into the hot tub together, things were definitely looking up. He had proof that his dick hadn't shriveled up and died—something he had begun to wonder about, not that he'd ever admit it to his brothers. And no matter how much Jessica denied it, she was interested in him.

Hunter set his empty beer mug down a little harder than necessary. Sometimes it sucked that his twin could all but read his mind and knew when it was going off on a tangent. At least it worked both ways, though since Hunter married, Fisher wished he could filter the info he'd picked up.

Fisher wasn't able to avoid Hunter's stare.

"Good. At least we've got that settled. Fisher's going up to babysit our little pest and her new boyfriend. You might want to shave and get some coffee first. You're supposed to look tough enough to scare him, remember."

This sucked in too many ways to even count. "Hunter, what's wrong with you? Why do I always get stuck doing your dirty work?"

"Nothing's wrong with me. I have a new ski lift being installed, and I have two crews working all weekend. I have to be on the mountain. If I didn't, believe me, I'd have Toni up at the cabin, and Karma would not be invited."

Fisher stood, stuck his hand in his back pocket to grab his wallet to pay for the beers, and then changed his mind. He was going to let them take care of the tab. That was the least they could do. "I always have to do the dirty work for you two while you're out having fun. What the hell am I supposed to say to Karma when I get there?"

Trapper patted him on the back. "You'd think a guy with your education would be able to figure that out on his own. But I'll give you some advice. You might want to duck when you walk in. She's gonna be as pissed as a mountain lion with PMS when she sees you."

"Thanks for the advice. Now tell me something I don't know."

"It sounds like our baby sister has plans for a romantic weekend." Trapper leaned in and lowered his voice, prompting Hunter to follow his lead. "And your mission, Fisher, should you accept, is to make sure you screw them up."

Hunter smiled for the first time all night and let out a low chuckle. "Yeah, she said she's going to teach this dude to fly-fish. Like I believe that. Guys named Jesse James don't drive three hours to a secluded mountain cabin just to catch fish. That's for damn sure."

Fisher had to agree with them. Shit. Sometimes he wished he were an only child. "Fine. I'll head up in the morning. Maybe then I'll finally be able to get some sleep. After being on call for three days and nights, I don't have to see patients until Tuesday." He finished his beer. "Call me if anything changes. I'm going home to pack and catch a few hours sleep before I head back to the hospital. My patient stabilized, but I want to leave orders for my partners if I'm going to be out of town all weekend."

Trapper checked his watch. "I'm headed to the airport. I have a plane waiting. Have fun dealing with the hellcat, Fisher. And Hunter, you'd better go collect that wife of yours before Karma starts rubbing off on her or filling her in on all your earlier escapades."

Hunter stood. "Good point. Karma might look harmless, but we all know she's anything but."

As they collected their mugs and the pitcher and headed down to the bar, Fisher wondered how he ended up with the short straw again. Now all he had to look forward to was a weekend of Karma's wrath.

———⁓———

Jessie tossed her duffel and messenger bag into the back of her Mini, set her iPod to her New York playlist, and pulled out the directions Karma had emailed her. She backed up, half expecting to see Fisher jogging by, but he wasn't there. Hell, he hadn't been there or anywhere else she went for three days. She wondered what had happened. Maybe when she ran out of his house he'd given up, which was just fine with her. After all, she really didn't need the distraction, and Fisher was definitely that. She'd gotten through almost half the romance novels she'd purchased and had to admit all those love scenes left her hanging. When she packed her apartment in New York, she'd only taken what she could fit in her car—her clothes and her computer—and put everything else in storage. Bringing the contents of her bedside table had never occurred to her.

Billy Joel's voice singing "New York State of Mind" filled the car, and she wondered if moving here was a mistake. She missed her apartment, she missed the noise of the city, and she really missed the deli down the street. If there was anything missing in Boise, it was a good Jewish deli. What she would give for a good knish. She adjusted her Bluetooth and speed-dialed before turning up Warm Springs Avenue toward Lucky Peak Reservoir. Her mom answered.

"Ma, hi. It's me."

"Jessie, how are you?"

"I'm good. How are you and Dad doing?"

"We're fine. Is everything okay?"

"Yeah, it's great actually." She pictured her mother fixing lunch. Ever since Dad retired, it seemed her mother's entire life revolved around their next meal. "I'm driving up to Stanley to spend the weekend fly-fishing with a friend. Karma said she'd teach me, and I've never fished anywhere but off the back of Dad's boat. This should be fun. It'll be nice to get up into the mountains. I look at them every day, but I haven't been up there since I arrived."

"Have fun dear, but be careful. There was a man killed by a bear just the other day at Yellowstone. The woods there aren't the same as they are on Long Island, you know. There are wild animals there."

"Yes mother, I know. I've been out here before with Andrew, remember?"

"Of course, but you're not with Andrew now, are you? It's just going to be you and your girlfriend. It would be nice if you had a man there to protect you."

She shook her head. God, you'd think it was the fifties the way her mother spoke, but then her mother was born in 1943 and was a definite product of the fifties. "I'm capable of protecting myself. I don't need a man to do it for me."

"You know, Jessica, you can spout off all you want. It doesn't change the fact that sometimes men are nice to have around. I'm not saying you need them, but there's something to be said for having a partner to hold through the good and the bad."

"In this case the bad would be scaring off man-eating

bears? Didn't you say that the bear attacked a *man*? Times change mom."

"Times might change, but you're still human. A woman has needs, and don't go spouting off about being financially independent either. You know what I'm talking about."

"Excuse me. Who are you, and where is my mother?" Her mother never talked about sex unless she absolutely had to, and she certainly never brought it up.

"Very funny. Just because your father and I keep it inside the bedroom doesn't mean that all we do in that bedroom is sleep. Did you think you were an immaculate conception?"

"No, I thought I was an accident."

She heard a sharp intake of breath. "Oh honey, no. Never an accident. We'd tried for years to conceive, and we'd given up. We were looking into adopting when I found out I was pregnant with you. I thought you knew that."

"Ma, how could I know that? It's not as if you and dad ever talked about it."

"We never in a million years wanted you to think that you were anything but wanted and cherished."

"I did. I just thought I was a surprise, that's all. I knew you loved me. Speaking of which, I was wondering if you could do me a favor."

"Of course. What is it?"

"Could you send me bagels and lox, potato knishes, and black and white cookies? You know, send them in dry ice. I'm going through withdrawal."

"So you *are* homesick." She heard the smile in her mother's voice and felt herself smiling back.

She *had* been listening to her New York playlist more often than ever, and although she loved Boise, she did miss certain aspects of living in the city—like twenty-four-hour takeout. "Yeah, I guess I am."

"You're still coming home for Thanksgiving, aren't you?"

"I don't know, Ma. I just got a part-time job at Starbucks. I'll see if I can get Thanksgiving weekend off. Since I'm not starting for a few more weeks, I wouldn't count on it. Maybe you and Dad can come out here. I have plenty of room, and I think you'd really like Boise. It's so different from Long Island, and it's beautiful."

"I'll see what your father says, but if you're going to be working, what would be the point of us coming all the way out there?"

"Mom, I'm only working part-time. When I'm at work, you and Dad can do whatever it is you do. My Starbucks is close enough to walk to, so you can have my car." The connection started breaking up. "Look Mom, I'm heading into the mountains, so I better get off. I'll call you soon. I might not be home until Wednesday. If you send food, make sure it will arrive after that, okay?"

"Okay, have fun and be careful, honey. I love you."

"Love you too, Mom."

The scenery changed as she gained elevation. It went from high mountain desert—where if you don't water it, it won't grow—to thick pine. She wasn't sure what time Karma planned to arrive at the cabin, so she was in no rush. Karma had told her where a spare key was hidden, but Jessie didn't feel comfortable walking into a stranger's house. So when she saw the sign for Idaho

City a half hour into the trip, she pulled off the highway to do some exploring.

She'd learned that Idaho City had once been a huge mining camp when gold was discovered on Grimes Creek during the early years of the gold rush. It looked as if it had been stuck in a time warp. It was so authentic that they could have filmed a spaghetti Western there.

Jessie toured the old jail, had lunch at Trudy's Kitchen, and even poked around the old Boot Hill Cemetery. By the time she got back in the car it was well after noon. She checked the directions again and headed farther up Highway 21 for another couple of hours through some of the most beautiful mountainous country she'd ever seen. Following the directions, she turned onto Highway 75 and drove until she saw the nondescript, signless, gravel road with the split rail fence described in the directions Karma had given her.

The gravel quickly turned to a washboard nightmare. Her little car bumped along on a road that seemed, in some places, barely wide enough for her car alone. It snaked back and forth, climbing in elevation, and turning into a ribbon of parallel ruts. She'd thought Idaho City was high at almost four thousand feet, and she'd been climbing steadily the entire trip.

Things were going well until her car hit a big rock that had fallen in the road. She grabbed her cell to call Karma, but there was no signal. Fabulous. It didn't take a genius to realize she was seriously screwed. She just hoped that Karma came looking for her or was behind her. She started wondering if her mother hadn't been right after all. Damn, she'd feel a lot better if she had a man with her. Which was ridiculous, because really, if she had a man with her, he'd be just as helpless as she was. She got out of the car and looked underneath it. The puddle of oil quickly seeping into the dirt road wasn't a good sign.

Great! This was just what she didn't need—a huge repair bill, not to mention how much it would cost to have her car towed. Maybe if she found a clearing she could get a cell phone signal and call for help. She got out of the car and walked a little way up the road. There was nothing but dense forest and not a car in sight. Worse, it was getting cold.

Fisher took a swig of his cold Americano and tried to keep his eyes open as he drove the last leg of the trip to Hunter's cabin, cursing his brothers the whole way. He couldn't believe he got suckered into babysitting Karma, while both his brothers were most likely having sex and a lot of it. He couldn't remember the last time he even came close. Oh, yeah, there was that time with Bianca Ferrari, but he was unconscious through most of it. She'd been after Hunter and jumped in bed with the wrong twin. God, even when he was in med school or working the insane hours of a resident, he had a better sex life than he did now.

The road made a sharp turn to the west, and Fisher had to slam on the brakes to avoid hitting a bright red Mini Cooper that some asshole had left in the middle of the road. He put his flashers on and climbed out, glad that he remembered to toss his toolbox in the back. When he saw the New York plates, he did a double take. That couldn't be Jessica's car, could it?

Fuck, Jessica... Jesse. Karma was coming to stay with her friend the sports reporter, Jesse James. Jessica said she was a writer... and Jesse was supposed to be writing a novel. He'd come here to watch his sister and her girlfriend—the one woman who didn't want a damn thing to do with him. He had half a mind to just turn around and head home. He looked inside the car and saw Jessica's keys hanging out of the ignition. When he'd driven her car last week, he'd been surprised by her huge keychain. It had every New York sports team's logo hanging off it and a miniature statue of liberty. It probably weighed half a pound and made a racket whenever the car hit a bump. God, was he thick or what? A New York sports reporter named Jessie—he was either stupid or a complete chauvinist. But then he hadn't slept in what felt like an entire week, so his brain was not firing on all cylinders. He knew there were female sports reporters.

What the hell was his New York reporter thinking driving a city car like that into the mountains? And where the hell was she? She should know better than to walk away from a vehicle. God, what if she hadn't walked away? A thousand nightmare scenarios ran through his mind. What if someone had picked her up? He put his hand on the hood; it was still warm but not hot. She couldn't have been gone for more than twenty minutes at most. Still, it didn't help him figure out where the hell she'd gone.

Maybe Karma drove by and picked her up, but Karma would know to push the damn car onto the side of the road. Shit. He had a bad feeling about this. He grabbed his satellite phone off his belt and speed-dialed his sister.

Chapter 6

KARMA GRABBED HER CLIPBOARD AND COUNTED THE bottles in the storeroom. She hated doing inventory almost as much as she hated doing payroll. Still, both had to be done. She hummed along to the tune on the radio, snuck a peek at her watch, and told herself that everything would work out just fine. It wasn't as if Fisher and Jessie weren't attracted to each other. They just needed a little push to get things moving.

"You're doing inventory?"

Karma jumped and put her hand to her heart. "Kevin, damn you. I told you not to sneak up on me like that. I'm gonna put taps on your shoes."

"Or spurs."

"Hell, no, you'll ruin my floors." Kevin, her bartender and best buddy, smiled. "You only do inventory when you're worried. Sharon's fine."

"I'm not worried about Sharon. And speaking of Sharon, why aren't you at the hospital? Weren't they supposed to induce this morning?"

A broad grin spread over Kevin's face. "No need. Sharon had Violetta at 1:10 this morning. They're both doing fine, and they were sound asleep ten minutes ago when I left the hospital."

"Oh my God! Why didn't you call me?" She dropped her clipboard and gave Kevin a big hug. "So, tell me all about her."

"Violetta Rae weighed in at seven pounds, nine ounces, and twenty-two inches long. She's tall and skinny just like her mama with a full head of black hair. She's beautiful, perfect in every way. Hell, you can go see her now if you want. I'll take over the inventory until you get back."

"Yeah, about that." Karma pushed her hair behind her ear. "What are you doing here? You're on leave, remember? Don't you want to go home and get some sleep?"

Kevin rubbed his unshaved chin. "Na, I can't sleep without Sharon anyway."

Karma shook her head. What was it about her and happily married couples? She'd fixed up Sharon, one of her suitemates from college, with Kevin two years ago, and they were married less than nine months later. She had the golden touch when it came to everyone else's relationships but hers. "No, I'll stop by the hospital when Roy comes in. I'll give him a call and ask him to come an hour early. You need to go home to shower and change. I'm sure if you go back to the hospital the nurses will take pity on you and give you a Barcalounger to sleep on."

"You okay?"

"Me? Sure, why?"

Kevin didn't say anything. He didn't need to. Karma remembered what Jessie had said about Andrew, how he had some strange kind of best friend ESP. When Jessie mentioned it, Karma knew exactly what she was talking about. Kevin had it too. Damn him. He just stood there with his arms crossed, waiting.

"Fine, okay. I'm just a little worried about Fisher."

Karma killed the urge to squirm under Kevin's scrutiny. When his laser gaze locked on hers, it was more effective than truth serum.

"What about him?"

"I kinda sorta fixed him up, but he likes her already." Kevin didn't look like he was buying it.

"If he likes her, why did you have to fix them up?"

"Well…" Karma put her clipboard down and walked around him into the bar. "Jessie—that's her name—just doesn't know she likes Fisher yet."

"Karma," he said, in his deep I-mean-business voice. "I thought you learned your lesson when you tried pulling this kind of crap with me and Sharon. I can't believe you're setting up your own brother."

"Hey. Look at you, Mr. Happily Married, new daddy. It all worked out in the end."

Kevin let out a bark of laughter. "Yeah. No thanks to you."

"Bullshit." Karma slid under the pass-through of the bar and grabbed a bottle of champagne she kept in the back of the cooler just for days like these—to celebrate Violetta's birth and tamp down her nerves. She cut the foil off the bottle's caged cork. "You're happily married because of me. If I hadn't thrown you and Sharon together, you'd still be single." She popped the cork and ignored his muttered curse.

Kevin came around the bar and reached for the champagne glasses, checking to make sure they were dust- and spot-free. He took the bottle and poured. "Look, do your brother a favor, and stay the hell out of his love life from now on."

"I'd gladly stay out of Fisher's love life if he had

one. He hasn't been on a date that I know of since Hunter got married."

"Is Fisher in the habit of telling you, his little sister, about his dates? I doubt it."

Karma laughed at that. "You know as well as I do, not one of my brothers or my cousin, for that matter, have a prayer of keeping anything away from my prying eyes and ears. I have a whole network of contacts feeding me information on a twenty-four-hour basis. It's taken me a lifetime to establish, and it works like a charm." She picked up her champagne glass and held it high. "Here's to Sharon and Violetta. May they both have a healthy, happy, quiet, and sleep-filled future."

Kevin touched his glass to hers. "To Sharon and Violetta, the two females who rule my heart."

Karma took a gulp of her champagne and jumped when the *Roadrunner* theme song blared from her phone—Fisher's ringtone. She forced a smile. She wasn't sure if she was nervous or relieved, but at least the dreaded waiting was over. Too bad Kevin was there to witness the conversation. Of course, he wasn't gentlemanly enough to give her some privacy. He knew Fisher's ringtone as well as she did. Shit.

"Hey, Fisher."

"Where is she?"

Karma kept her face neutral, even though the tone of Fisher's voice made all the hair on her arms stand up. "Where is who?"

"Don't play games with me, Karma. Jessica. Is she there with you?"

"No."

"Fuck!"

Karma couldn't believe her ears. Fisher almost never cursed and certainly not in front of her. This was the first time in her life he let the F-bomb fly in her presence. "Calm down, Fisher. What's the matter?" She turned so she wouldn't have to see Kevin's accusatory stare. Too bad there was a mirror behind the bar. She squeezed her eyes shut.

"What's the matter? Her car is sitting in the middle of the fucking road on the way to Hunter's cabin—"

"So?" Beads of perspiration gathered at her hairline.

"And she's not in it."

"Where is she?" She almost whispered.

"How the hell do I know?" Fisher was yelling. He never yelled. "I thought she was supposed to be with you. You know, Jesse James, the big-time New York sports reporter you said you were spending the weekend with? You played us all like freakin' windup jack-in-the-boxes, making Trapper, Hunter, and me think you were going off to play house in the mountains with some strange dude. What's the deal?"

Karma put her hand to her breast, trying to calm her racing heart, and went with her first instinct—plead the fifth or confusion, maybe both. "I have no idea what you're talking about."

"Right. Sure. Look, I don't have time to play your games. All of Jessica's stuff is in her car. Her keys are in the ignition. And Jessica, the girl you invited up to Hunter's cabin, is nowhere in sight."

"You know Jessie?"

"You know damn well I know Jessica. Now Karma, stick to the topic here, or when I get my hands on you…"

"Fisher Kincaid, your threats don't work with me, so stop busting my chops."

"Just tell me, Karma. Where in the hell is she?"

"I don't know. Really, I don't. I gave her directions to the cabin. Maybe she's there. Have you checked?"

"No. I went around a switchback and almost plowed into the back of her car—the one she left in the middle of the fucking road. The one she had no business driving off the main highway. Have you seen it? It's no bigger than an M&M on wheels. You know better, Karma. She could be hurt or worse. You'd better get your sorry ass down here and help me look for her."

"Up."

"Up what?"

"Get my sorry ass *up* there. I'm doing inventory at Hannah's at the moment. You see, Kevin's wife had the baby this morning, and I just found out about it. I'm not going to be able to make it to the cabin after all."

"Oh really? And just how were you planning to let Jessica know? Oh, that's right. You tricked me into going up to the cabin. The one you conveniently can't get to."

"I did no such thing. I didn't have a clue you were going up there. What am I, a freakin' mind reader?"

"No, you're a pain in my ass, and you and your little stunts are going to get you, or some poor, unsuspecting woman hurt."

"Hunter lent me the cabin, not you. And for your information Dr. Smartypants, I was planning to call John Rotchford. You know, that hot new ranger at the Stanley ranger station, and ask him to go over and tell Jessie I wouldn't be able to make it. I just didn't have a chance to call him yet, because I'm too busy being abused by you. But don't worry. I'm sure John would be happy to look after Jessie for me."

Both Kevin and Fisher let out inventive strings of curses. She covered where she thought the mouthpiece of her cell phone was—not that she really knew—so Fisher wouldn't hear Kevin. "Why don't you just turn around and go home? I'm sure you have better things to do than look for Jessie, a woman you don't even know. Hey, how did you know that was Jessie's car, anyway?"

Fisher growled. "Karma, cut the crap. I'm worried about her. She left her car. She didn't even pull it over to the side—"

"It's a jeep trail, Fisher. There isn't a freakin' side."

"She left the keys in the ignition."

"Well, who's going to steal it? It's in the middle of freakin' nowhere. No one but us goes up past the Jones's place."

"Karma, what if she's hurt?"

"I'm sure she's fine." She had to be fine. Jessie was an athlete, definitely not a shrinking violet. She was the toughest woman Karma had ever seen. Hell, Karma would give Jessie even odds against any of her brothers. "Have you called out for her?"

"No."

She heard embarrassment in Fisher's voice and resisted the urge to say "well, duh," just as Fisher screamed Jessie's name in her ear and nearly blew out her eardrum. "Do you mind not screaming in my ear? Damn, Fisher."

"Shh… I'm listening for her."

"While you're listening, why don't you head toward

the cabin? I'm sure she's hiking the rest of the way. Call me when you find her. In the meantime, I'll call the ranger station and put them on standby."

The line went dead. Fisher hadn't even said good-bye. Karma looked at her phone. He'd never hung up on her before. That nagging you've-gone-too-far-this-time-and-the-shit's-hit-the-fan feeling settled in the pit of her stomach.

Karma jumped when Kevin touched her shoulder. She'd forgotten he was there. "Oh God, what if Jessie's hurt, or worse?"

Kevin pulled her into a tight hug. "I'm sure she's fine, just like you said. Now take a deep breath and call the station just in case. Let them know they might need to put together a search party if Fisher doesn't find her in the next hour or so."

"Right." Karma's hand shook as she pulled up her contact list and found the station. Kevin, as usual, was the perfect best friend, quietly supportive. She was glad he hadn't said "I told you so." She knew as well as he where that line between calmness and tears was. Right now, she was dangerously close to crossing it, and nei-ther wanted that.

———∿∿∿———

Fisher gathered his backpack with his emergency medi-cal kit and tossed in two bottles of water. So much for his plan to spend the weekend fly-fishing and trying to screw his own head on straight. Sure, he knew he'd have to put a crimp in Karma's romance plans, but the rest of the time he could have done some serious fish-ing therapy. Once he had a fly rod in his hands, life suddenly made more sense. Now he was stuck finding and babysitting Jessica.

He took in his surroundings. He was only a few miles from Hunter's cabin, but there were plenty of dense woods between here and there. Too bad Jessica had no way of knowing that.

What kind of idiot took a car like Jessica's up a mountain trail? God only knew what kind of trouble a city girl like her could get into while in the wilderness.

He called her name until he was hoarse, hearing nothing in return. He stopped, listened, and looked for any sign of her. The trail was hard-packed dirt, no dust to show footprints, no sign of her or anyone else for that matter. It was as if she'd disappeared.

"Jessica—" He pushed back the fear and tried to put himself in her shoes. What would she be looking for? A Starbucks? The cabin? A cell phone signal? There was no hope for a cup of coffee or cell coverage past Idaho City, but Jessica wouldn't know that. He walked faster.

Most people had the mistaken belief that if they climbed, they'd get a signal—it was a myth. He poured on the speed, fueled by pure adrenaline. He hadn't had a bite to eat since the cold pizza he'd gnawed on prior to falling into bed the night before.

He climbed another hundred yards when he noticed a flattened sapling on the edge of the track that looked as if someone had stepped on it. He stopped. Sure enough, it was fresh, and so were the indentations in the pine needles littering the ground where the track cut through forest. He picked up the pace and followed her trail through the woods, stopping as he crested a ridge.

Shit. There in the distance, Jessica scaled the side of a steep hill that anywhere east of the Rockies would be considered a mountain.

He worked his way closer silently, afraid to startle her. He had to admit she was one hell of a climber— never looking down, always keeping her eye on the next hand- or foothold. She was strong, and he admired her agility and grace, even though climbing alone was one hell of a stupid stunt.

He drew a relieved breath as she crawled onto a ledge a good thirty feet above him.

She held her cell phone over her head, shielding her eyes from the sun, and turning in a slow circle.

She was definitely going to be disappointed. "If you're looking for a signal, you won't find one above Idaho City, and even there, it's iffy."

Jessica jumped, and Fisher swore his heart skipped a beat until he was sure she wasn't going to tumble down on top of him.

She pressed her back against the sheer wall behind her. "What in the hell are you doing here? Are you following me again? What are you—some kind of weird stalker?"

Was she serious? "Don't flatter yourself. I came up to babysit my little sister when I almost rear-ended your car. Have you ever heard of pulling off the road?"

"I would have if I'd been on a road in the first place. Besides, I hit a rock and broke something in the under-carriage. I couldn't turn the wheel. It wasn't moving no matter what I wanted it to do. Believe me. Stopping be-fore I reached my destination was not on my 'to do' list."

"Look, why don't you come down from there before you break your neck? What were you thinking climbing alone?"

"I was thinking I could call for help. It didn't look so high from down there." Her voice shook, and she hesitated before taking a tentative step toward the edge. She took what looked like a deep breath, got on her hands and knees, and dropped her feet over the edge, feeling around with her sneakered foot for a hold, clinging to the edge with her arms.

Fisher ran directly beneath her, ignoring the stones raining down on him. He shielded his eyes. "To the left, dammit!" God, his voice was shaking too. He probably strained his vocal cords yelling her name for the last half hour. "Jessica, open your eyes for God's sake. Look where you're going."

She shook her head as her foot inched to the left. "I can't look down. I'm afraid of heights."

"Of all the—" He cut himself off. Calling her names, even if she did deserve them, was not going to get her down safely. "Okay, just a little bit more. There. You got it. Now wait for me. I'm coming up."

"Why?"

"So I can talk you down."

"I'll be fine."

"Yeah, I can see that."

She grabbed a new handhold and slid her right foot farther down, hitting a solid foothold without his help.

Fine, he'd stay put. "There's a better handhold to your right, down a little farther. There."

He directed her, staying directly below in case she fell. He wondered how bad it would hurt to break her fall. Hell, he still hadn't recovered from their last run. The woman was going to be the death of him.

When she jumped the last four feet, he was forced to

step out of her path and didn't know if he wanted to hug her or strangle her.

———————

Jessie wiped her raw hands on her jeans to keep from throwing her arms around Fisher and making a complete fool of herself. That was way higher than it had looked from the ground. She'd be damned if she ever did anything like that again.

Fisher clenched his jaw, and a vein popped out on his forehead. She thought he looked hot when he smiled, but oh mama, when he had a full head of steam, he was downright incendiary.

She swallowed hard, resisting the urge to fan her face, and reminded herself that she was supposed to be indifferent, not turned on. She put her hands on her hips and looked him up and down. "What is your problem?"

Fisher brushed dust, dirt, and a few rocks out of his hair and off his shoulders. "You are, apparently."

"I never asked you to follow me."

"I was minding my own business, until I almost hit that windup toy you call a car that you abandoned in the middle of the road." He clenched his fists in time with the throbbing of that vein. "I was not following you. I was rescuing you."

"In your dreams maybe."

"Nightmares more like. Believe me, the dreams I have about you do not involve scaling rocky cliffs." Fisher turned and stomped away.

She stood there watching him. He dreamed about her? That was kind of sexy in an awkward-take-me-now kind of way. Still, she'd be damned if she was going anywhere. Not with him.

He looked back over his shoulder. "Are you coming?"

"Where?"

"I thought you were heading to the cabin. You'll probably have an easier time finding it if you drive with me. It's about a three-mile hike, and I'm too tired to follow your ass any farther."

"What cabin?"

"My brother's cabin. The one Karma invited you to. Oh, and by the way, she asked me to tell you she's not able to make it. There's a new addition to the Humpin' Hannah's family, so she's covering for her bartender, who is doing whatever it is that new fathers do."

"She's not coming?"

"The last time I spoke to Karma, she was working. But here." He held out a cell phone. "Call her if you want. My sister's number is on speed dial—she's number four."

"Karma's your sister?" Oh God. This can't be happening.

"Unfortunately." His grin widened. If he was doing his Joker impression, he was right on target. "Even though the resemblance can't be denied, my brothers and I still checked her birth certificate just to make sure. And yeah, it's legit."

She'd thought Karma's eyes looked somehow familiar, but she hadn't put it together. Of course, she'd never seen Karma and Fisher side by side. Jessie shut her mouth, which she realized had been hanging open, and remembered all the things she'd told Karma about Fisher. Her face flamed, but there was nothing she could do to hide it, so she didn't bother trying. She closed her eyes and shook her head.

"Don't be too hard on yourself. You're not the only

one who fell for her stunt, and while I can't prove it, I have a feeling she set us both up. Karma's a master manipulator. To her credit, she usually means well. Of course, that doesn't keep me and my brothers from wanting to kill her on a regular basis."

Jessie shoved past him toward her car. "I can't believe she'd do this to me. I thought we were friends."

"Oh you are." Fisher fell into step beside her. "You should take it as a compliment. Karma only manipulates the people she loves. The fact that she manipulated you after knowing you such a short time—" He took hold of her arm, stopping her, and shot her a don't-bullshit-me look. "She *has* only known you a short time right? You didn't know her in college or something?"

Jessie pulled free of his grasp and rolled her eyes. "Oh yeah, Karma and I are old friends. I'm the one who talked her into tricking you, so that I could get you alone. All those times you asked me out, I was just playing hard to get, so I'd have a chance to trap you in a secluded mountain cabin and take advantage of you."

"Well, a guy can hope, can't he?"

"You know, maybe my first impression of you was right after all."

"Yeah, what was that?"

She stepped over a fallen tree and scanned the surrounding area. "And to think my mother was worried about bears. She never warned me about the locals."

"If you don't tell me, I'll just get it out of Karma eventually." That Joker smile peeked out again, a little bit evil and a little bit hot.

It stopped her dead in her tracks.

"Believe me, it won't be difficult. She'll be crowing

about how the four of us fell for it. It must have been a doozy to spur Karma to go to the trouble of pulling off a complex con like this—it takes planning."

"She wouldn't dare tell you." Without even looking where she was going, she stomped into the woods.

"Oh wouldn't she?"

She sliced a path with her arms. "You really want to know my first impression of you? I thought you were a little slow on the uptake. Are you happy now?"

"I guess we're even then." He trudged after her. "I thought the same thing about you when I almost rammed into the back of your Barbie-mobile."

If he was trying to piss her off, he was doing a fine job. "I told you, I couldn't move my car if I wanted to." Why she was explaining herself to him was a mystery. "It just went kathunk and stopped."

"Kathunk? Is that a technical term?"

She fought the smile tugging at the corners of her mouth. How did he do that? He was the only person alive who could piss her off and make her laugh at the same time. He was impossible.

"Jessica?"

Damn the man. Even his voice could get her heart pounding. He was the reason she was up here in the first place. She'd thought it would be safer to be far away from him, and now he was within touching distance. Not that touching him ever entered her mind.

"I really am sorry you got caught up in one of Karma's schemes."

And now he was being nice? "Me too. But believe me, it won't happen again."

"Uh-huh. Where have I heard that before? Oh right.

From my brothers." He took a bottle of water from his pack and held it out to her. "It's amazing. The three of us know Karma and the damage she's capable of, and still, we never see it coming."

"Thanks." She took the bottle. Holding the cuff of her sweatshirt, she unscrewed the cap and took a long drink. God she was thirsty.

"Did you even think to bring water with you?"

"No, just beer and wine."

"I meant as part of an emergency kit, not a damn hostess gift."

"What would I need that for? This isn't the Antarctic. And I'd appreciate it if you would stop yelling at me."

Fisher yanked off his baseball cap and raked his hand through his hair, dislodging more dust. "I'm not yelling. I'm just saying you need to carry survival gear in what you insist on referring to as a 'car' in case you get stuck in the wilderness like you are now. You shouldn't leave the Treasure Valley without it."

"Overreact much?"

"No, I don't." He took her arm again, effectively stopping her. "I don't think you understand." He spoke slowly, in a controlled voice. It would have been believable if she hadn't seen the heat of anger in his eyes. "This isn't New York, Jessica. Almost two-thirds of Idaho is public land—wilderness, desert, mountains. The City of New York has over eight million people in three hundred square miles. Idaho has one and a half million people in eighty-three thousand square miles. Forty percent of them are in the Treasure Valley. You do the math. If I hadn't come along when I did, God only knows the next time someone would. Probably not for weeks. If you'd fallen and broken your neck up there, who knows if someone would have ever found you."

"You did."

"I was looking for you, dammit. I had fresh tracks to follow. And I was damn lucky to see a snapped branch. If you had stayed with the vehicle like you're supposed to, at least you would have been easy to spot by plane."

"Karma knew where I was going. If I went missing, she would have called someone."

"Shit." He tossed his empty water bottle in his pack and reached for his phone. "I forgot to call her."

"Call her how? There's no cell coverage, Einstein, remember?"

"That's why I carry a satellite phone." He hit a few buttons and held it to his ear, his not-so-evil grin exposing itself again. "Ingenious, isn't it?" It was there for a second and gone just as quickly as it appeared. "I found her no thanks to you. Call the ranger station and tell them we don't need search and rescue."

"Search and rescue? Seriously?" Was he nuts?

His hand rested on her shoulder, and then he shook his head. "Yeah, well, I'm not sure she wants to talk to you." His eyebrows rose in question.

"I'll call her later."

"You heard Jessica. She said she'd call you later. And no, I'm not going to cut you a break. I'm tempted to wring your little neck, but I won't because then Mom would kill me." He did a teenaged eye roll that would make any mother want to smack him. "She could have been hurt, Karma. You should know better than to send a lowlander into the mountains in a two-wheel drive car with six-inch clearance and no emergency kit." He released her shoulder and turned his back as if she wouldn't be able to hear every word out of his mouth. "I don't care if she is in good shape. People need water—she brought beer and wine like she was going to a damn party."

"Hello. Remember me? I'm standing right here, and for your information, I was going to a damn party."

"Call your boyfriend at the ranger station and tell him I've got her." He kept right on ignoring Jessie and yelling at Karma. "I wonder what he'll think when he finds out all the trouble you caused. And no, this is far from over. You and I are going to have a nice long talk when I get back." He pressed the end button and cursed under his breath. "Brat."

Fisher turned, and Jessie caught sight of his face just as his scowl disappeared. He didn't look happy. No, he looked exhausted. Maybe he'd spent too many late nights with the ladies. He certainly hadn't been on any early morning runs with her—not that she'd missed him or anything.

Waiting for him to pop up suddenly had been like walking through a haunted house expecting a ghost to jump out of the darkness and yell boo. The tension had taken its toll—she'd been edgy, irritated, and a little bit bitchy, or so Andrew had said. But the thing she'd resented the most was the way Fisher had invaded her thoughts, dreams, and life without her permission.

"Come on." He took her arm. "I'll take a look at your car and see if I can fix it."

"No, but thanks anyway. I'll call a tow truck when we get back to town." She wished Fisher would stop touching her. His touch created all sorts of tingles when she wanted none. Well, none from him at least.

"I'm almost as good at working on cars as I am at working on legs." His gaze dropped from her face and did a slow perusal of her body. The corner of his mouth tipped up as if he was fighting a cocky grin. "How's the hamstring?"

"It's fine, thanks." All her blood rushed to her face. God, what was it with this guy? His voice got deep and gravely, and her body reacted like an ice carving under a heat lamp. Oh yeah, she definitely needed to find a date. Maybe she'd go to Humpin' Hannah's for Ladies' Night *after* she forgave Karma. She wasn't sure how long that would take, but Karma was the only female friend Jessie had ever had. Maybe this was what girl-friends did to each other—trick them and fix them up with their brothers.

Jessie hadn't seen it coming—she hadn't even had an inkling Karma had been up to something, and she'd always been able to read people really well. There hadn't been one slip on Karma's part to even hint at her being related to Fisher.

Jessie made a mental note never to play poker with Karma Kincaid, but she wouldn't mind learning a few of her secrets. She was especially curious as to why Karma would fix her up with Fisher after everything Jessie had said him. She'd called Fisher a dim-witted stalker with processing problems. But then she'd also said he was gorgeous and told her about the leg and ass massage. Just thinking about it had her melting again.

Jessie needed to get her mind off the fact that the guy was beautiful, built, and although she wouldn't go as far as to call him bright, he maybe not as dim as she'd first suspected. She'd never had problems dealing with

good-looking men before. She would treat Fisher just
like she did every pro sports player she'd ever worked
with. She just wished her body would cooperate.

When they finally made it back to her car, she opened
the door to sit. He walked right on past, and she couldn't
help but notice the way he filled out his jeans and T-
shirt. Oh yeah, if she had to design a dream body, it
would be Fisher's, although it would have a different
head attached. It wasn't as if his face wasn't perfect,
it was. Jessie just wanted her dream man to have a different mind-set. He'd be a man on a mission—and not
for the perfect tan. No, her man would have direction
and goals. If she were ever to get into a relationship,
even for a short time, she'd want a man who was maybe
not wealthy, since she wasn't interested in anyone
else's money, but he'd have a career he loved and the
ability to support himself without having to live with
his mother. He'd be comfortable with himself, which,
despite Fisher's circumstances, he was, and then some.
Fisher looked as if he was on top of the world, which
just told her he was delusional.

Fisher stepped behind an old Toyota Land Cruiser
that looked as if it was held together with duct tape and
rubber bands, and opened the back with an earsplitting
creak that bounced off every hard surface. He hauled
over a beat-up toolbox that was in the same shape as his
Toyota and disappeared behind her car. "Looks like you
took out the power steering pump and the oil pan."

"That's not good." She walked to the passenger side
and squatted beside him to look underneath. His body
was so big he barely had room to reach under the car.

"I'm not going to be able to fix it without a lift. We'll

have it towed to my garage—I have a lift there. I'll order the parts, and then rig it with a skid plate to protect your power steering pump and oil pan. Damn, it looks as if the pump has a fan too." He slid his shoulder out and sat up like he was doing a crunch.

Crouched down, she was eye to eye with him. "You don't have to do that. I'll just have it towed to the dealership."

He shook his head.

What? Was she speaking in tongues or something? He looked as if he hadn't even heard her.

He stood and slapped the dust from the butt of his jeans. "I'll just push it off the trail, so no one else will hit it. Get your things and put them in my Cruiser."

There was no point in arguing; he wouldn't hear her anyway. Jessie grabbed her purse, duffel, and messenger bag.

Fisher took them off her hands—obviously not a man who had a problem carrying a girl's purse. "Pop the trunk, so I can get the beer and wine. No use letting it go to waste."

"I can get it."

"Suit yourself." He set her things on the bench seat of his Toyota as she waited with the liquor box containing a few six-packs and two bottles of her favorite Shiraz. When he reached for it, his hand met hers, and his brows rose until she let go. She stepped back and hugged her sweatshirt to her. "Go ahead and get in if you're cold." He handed her the keys. "I'll just push your car out of the way."

"Don't you need help?" At least she'd found her voice.

Fisher looked over his shoulder. "You're kidding, right?"

Guess not. Men. She could really do without the

whole I-am-man macho thing. She'd seen enough of that in her years as a sports reporter to last a lifetime.

He pushed her seat all the way back, put her car in neutral, and with the driver's side door open, gave it a push. You'd think the car weighed no more than a grocery cart the way he steered it off the path and over the ruts. He pushed it well off the trail before he put the car in gear and set the brake. He tossed her keys to her and jumped into the Toyota. "Next time, you might not want to abandon your car with the keys in it."

"I'll make a note of that. Thanks."

He started up the Cruiser and looked over. "Buckle up. It's going to be a bumpy ride."

"Right." Jessie did as he asked, and then turned toward the window. This car was five times the size of hers, but as soon as Fisher got in, it seemed to shrink. Maybe it had to do with the size of his overinflated ego.

They drove in silence. Fisher turned off the jeep track onto what looked like a path that animals used. The Cruiser bumped along the uneven trail. When they crested a ridge, it was as if the cabin jumped out in front of them.

Oh my Lord, she'd thought Karma had meant a cabin in the woods, like a bungalow. This place was massive and looked more like an expensive ski chalet than a cabin. It was made of huge split logs with enormous windows, and a gleaming, high-pitched, green metal roof. It was all sharp angles and majesty. She sat there, taking it all in. "It's beautiful."

Fisher shrugged and grabbed the box of beer and wine.

"What are you doing?"

"Taking your things inside."

She scrambled out to stop him. "Why?"

He set the box on the hood of his truck, his fingers denting the cardboard. "Do you have a problem with me giving you a hand? Is that it? If you want to do it yourself, have at it." He left the box sitting on the hood and opened the tailgate.

"No, I mean why take it in? We're just going to turn around and go back to Boise."

"Sorry to disappoint you, but I'm not getting back into my truck until after I have at least eight hours of uninterrupted sleep." He walked past her with a duffel bag slung over his shoulder.

"You're staying here? With me?"

Fisher stopped and turned, exhaustion oozing from his every pore. "Don't get your panties in a knot. There are six bedrooms. We won't be sharing if that's what you're afraid of. You can take one on the other side of the cabin for all I care." He rubbed his stubbled chin. She hadn't really noticed it before because he was so blond, but the way the sun hit his face made the stubble on it shine and the dark smudges beneath his eyes more pronounced.

"I'll drive."

"Do you honestly think I'm gonna let you drive my baby after what you did to your car? Not in this lifetime. Now, do you want me to help you inside with your stuff or not?"

"No. I want to go home."

"Call Karma then." He tossed her his phone. "I'm going in, making something to eat, and then going to bed. Alone."

Chapter 7

FISHER DRAGGED ASS TO THE FRONT DOOR. WERE ALL women as exasperating as Jessica and Karma? With his luck the answer would be yes.

He unlocked the place, tossed his bag on the bed in the bedroom he always used, and listened for Jessica. She was probably still standing outside fuming. Damn her. Hadn't she caused enough trouble for one day? She'd already scared the life out of him with that stunt she pulled climbing a fuckin' mountain when she was afraid of heights. Who the hell did that? And now, she expected him to turn around and take her home?

He went back through the cabin, wishing he could just fall into bed, but he needed to keep an eye on her. He didn't trust her not to go off half-cocked and pull another stupid stunt. Fisher stopped at the door and found Jessica standing right where he'd left her. "If you're waiting for me to change my mind about leaving, it's not going to happen. Not today. Possibly not even tomorrow. I need to sleep." And from the looks of it, so did she, but he was smart enough to keep that observation to himself. "Did you call Karma?"

"No."

"Then what are you doing?"

She shook her head. Some of the thick hair she'd gathered into a ponytail loosened and curled around her chin. She was really beautiful in a Lara Croft, Tomb

Raider kind of way. "Fine. I'll come in. I don't have much of a choice."

"True." He didn't wait for her before raiding the kitchen to see what he could make for dinner. He was starving. With his head in the freezer, he called out, "You don't have anything against red meat, do you?"

"No."

"Good. Then we're having steak for dinner." He took two steaks out and wondered if he should grab a third. He figured if there was a question, he might as well. They could always have steak and eggs for breakfast in the morning. It wouldn't go to waste with him there. He heard Jessica plop the box of beer and wine on the counter and then head back out to the truck. Stubborn woman. He'd have carried all her things in for her if she'd stop treating him like a leper.

He pulled a few potatoes out of the bin and scrubbed them within an inch of their lives. Hell, he took off most of the skin. He was so damn pissed his hands shook. He grabbed a cold beer and everything he needed for a salad. It was a good thing Hunter and Toni left the place stocked just a few days ago. There was plenty of fresh food to hold them for as long as they wanted to stay. If he had his way, it would be awhile. A long weekend in the mountains was just what the doctor ordered.

He twisted off the cap of the beer and took a big swig just as Jessica dragged the rest of her things through the door. "Take your pick of bedrooms. I tossed my stuff on the bed of the room that I use. You can use Karma's room at the end of the hall if you want. She won't mind, but you might. She's kind of a pig."

"I'm sure it'll be fine."

She obviously didn't know Karma well, but that wasn't his problem. He'd be sure to tell her about how when they were kids, Karma's room looked more like a nasty science experiment than a bedroom. Hell, her apartment still did, unless she expected company. It seemed that the clean gene skipped her entirely—another reason he and his brothers questioned if she had been switched at birth. He shook his head and wondered when Karma would stop giving the family grief.

Fisher oiled and rubbed Kosher salt on what was left of the skins on the potatoes, poked them a few times with a fork, and stuck them in the oven to bake. He tossed the steaks in the microwave to defrost and finished off his beer while he made a salad.

By the time Jessica reappeared, the steaks were almost defrosted. She came out of Karma's room carrying a laptop, set it on the bar next to the kitchen, and booted it up.

"There's a desk in the study if you want to work there. I can clean it off for you."

She peered at him over the screen as if she questioned his motives. Women.

He shrugged. "I just thought you might be more comfortable there. But work wherever you like."

"Thanks. I'm fine here. I'm good at tuning things out when I work."

She'd already tuned him out, which was just as well. He was in no mood to deal with her, not when the fear he'd felt when she'd been missing was still so fresh in his mind. He'd done search and rescue in these parts, and he'd never felt the way he had today. Heck, he hadn't even known if she was in trouble. It didn't stop the nightmare scenarios from racing through his mind at the speed of light. He didn't want to think about what that meant. Maybe the lack of sleep was catching up to him.

After checking the freezer for vanilla ice cream, he grabbed a jar of his mother's peaches and threw together a quick cobbler. He hadn't had a decent dessert in ages. Since he had to be awake, he might as well keep cooking.

When he had the salad made and everything cooking, he headed to his room, pulling off his shirt on the way. He debated whether or not to just trash it, but tossed it into the hamper in his bedroom. He'd grab a quick shower, so after the dinner dishes were done he could crash.

———————

Jessie did her best to ignore the way Fisher moved around the kitchen as if he had been born in one. He seemed to know where everything was, and more importantly, what to do with it. She'd learned more trying to ignore him than she had from all the cooking shows she'd ever watched put together. Granted, there hadn't been a lot of those, but still, everything Fisher did, whether he was massaging her leg, crawling under her car, or putting together a meal, was impressive.

The man had taken a weird-shaped jar of what looked like peaches, poured them into a pan, juice and all, and then without measuring a darn thing, dumped a bunch of ingredients into a bowl, stirred it together with a fork, sprinkled it on top of the peaches, and popped it into the oven like a pro.

Whatever he'd concocted smelled heavenly. He hadn't even set the oven timer. How would he know when everything was done?

The sound of a distant shower running filled the silence. And it was silent here; she didn't think she'd ever been anywhere so quiet. She and Andrew had taken a few camping trips, but there were always other people around. The silence told her that she and Fisher were really alone. And like Fisher had said, there might not be another person for miles.

She listened to the clock tick in the next room, the refrigerator hum, and the sound of her own breathing before opening iTunes and playing something, anything to keep her from thinking about Fisher naked with water running down his body.

Yeah, that picture wasn't helping her write her romance. She wasn't sure what would, since reading them wasn't helping either. She'd read a half dozen and invariably ended up losing herself in the story every time. She'd forgotten the reason she was reading them in the first place was to dissect them, see how they were written, and figure out the damn formula. She had to admit, the formula had taken a backseat to the stories. They were good, and hot, and sexually frustrating. They did nothing but leave her edgy and hanging and looking at Fisher through rose-colored glasses.

She opened her new writing program and pulled up the character sketch loaded on it. Name... hmm... Frederick. No, Frederick wasn't a sexy name. Fisher was, but that would be too weird. God forbid he bought it and found his name in the damn book. He'd think she'd written about him. Like that was going to happen. He so wasn't hero material. Frank? No, not sexy. And what was it with the letter *F*? Shaun? Seth. Oh yeah, Seth was a sexy name. Seth Kirkland. That would work.

Role in Story: Hero.

Occupation: Not a bum.

Physical Description: There's something wild about him, maybe it's his curly platinum blond hair, which has a mind of its own, but no matter what, makes a girl's fingers itch to run through it. It could be the blond stubble that accentuates his square jaw when the light hits it just right, or the forest green eyes with blue around the irises—the man might as well have a sign across his forehead that says Call Me Wild.

Hmm… that wouldn't be a bad title for the book. *Call Me Wild.* She filled in the title and went back to the description. Fisher—no, dammit—delete, delete, delete, delete, delete, delete. Seth is tall and muscular, but not muscle-bound, with long lashes and dark eyebrows that make you think the hair is either out of the bottle or sun-bleached.

Fisher didn't seem the type to dye his hair, so she figured his was sun-bleached. Yeah. Okay, so her hero looked a little like Fisher, but people always say to write what you know. In the last few weeks she'd spent an inordinate amount of time thinking about and watching Fisher Kincaid. It was her job as a journalist to people watch, and since Fisher and Karma were the only people she knew in Boise, it made perfect sense to study them. That wasn't so odd when you thought about it in a realistic light, and if she could be called anything, it was a realist.

"Working hard?"

She jumped and almost fell off the bar stool. "Don't sneak up on me like that. You scared me."

"Sorry." He smiled, but he didn't look the least bit contrite. He'd shaved. The scent of shaving cream and

Ivory soap assaulted her. He'd changed into a clean pair of jeans and a white T-shirt. His wet hair hit the collar, leaving damp spots around the neck and shoulders. He ran his hand through it, and the curls took shape. It looked darker when it was wet, almost golden.

"I was going to start the steaks. They'll take about fifteen minutes, depending how you like yours. Is that all right?"

"Is what all right?"

"Do you want to eat in about twenty minutes? Are you at a good stopping point, or do you want me to wait awhile?"

"I thought you were starving."

He opened the oven just enough to peek in, and then closed it before turning back to her. "I'm hungry, but I can throw together a snack if you need more time."

"No, but thanks. Twenty minutes will be fine. I don't want to keep you waiting on me."

He leaned against the counter and crossed his bare feet in front of him. "It's not a big deal."

Maybe it wasn't a big deal to him, but it was to her. She'd never had a guy cook for her, and certainly not one who offered to serve her when she was at a convenient stopping point. "I'm a little hungry too." And she was. The smell of that peach thing he was baking made her mouth water.

"I'd offer to help, but I'm useless in the kitchen. I do excel at setting a table though." She slid off the bar stool and headed into the kitchen. "I'll set the table, if you just show me where the plates are—"

He took her by the shoulders and nudged her back to her computer. "No, you came up here to work, so work. I can take care of the table while the steaks are cooking. I don't want to disturb you. Can I get you a beer, some wine?"

"A beer would be great." She looked at the next line of her character sketch.

Personality: Hmm… he's considerate and sensitive to the heroine's needs. Like offering to wait on dinner until the heroine is at a good stopping point in her work. He's sincere, polite, smart, and funny, of course.

He pulled a beer out of the refrigerator and poured it into an iced mug. "Here you go." He slid it across the bar.

"Thanks." She sipped the beer and sneaked peeks at him as he seasoned the steaks. He washed his hands and then rubbed the seasoning into the meat. She'd never been jealous of a slab of beef before. She sure was now.

After washing his hands again, he put the meat on the grill. The scent and sound of sizzling meat stopped any progress she'd been making.

Habits/Mannerisms: Seth is a darn good cook and is a real health food nut. He's in great shape and runs every day. Drinks a lot of coffee, but not the designer girly drinks. He flirts with everyone female, but then doesn't seem to take anything too seriously—well, except for having survival gear in your car and poor parking habits.

Even though Fisher had turned on the fan, the scent of grilling meat made it impossible to think of anything other than food. Okay, food and the way he looked with a man's grilling apron tied around his waist. Any other guy would look like the Galloping Gourmet, but not Fisher—it only framed his perfect butt in faded denim. The jeans were tight. They fit like a well-worn glove, lovingly hugging his tush.

He reached for a bowl in an upper cabinet, his arm muscles rippling and stretching the sleeves of his T-shirt. God, she had to stop this—it was maddening.

"What are you making now?"

He looked over his shoulder and seemed surprised to find her staring at him. "Salad dressing."

"What? You've never heard of store-bought?"

Fisher looked as if he were trying not to laugh as he gathered spices. "Why would I buy dressing when it's so easy to make, and it tastes ten times better? Do you want Italian, Greek, Ranch, Thousand Island, or French?"

"Really?"

"Yeah, I'm not in the mood to make Caesar. I'd have to coddle an egg and peel a bunch of garlic. Plus, I don't have fresh lemons, and I'd have to open a whole can of anchovies—"

"Gag."

"Not a fan of anchovies, huh?"

"That's putting it mildly. I am a huge fan of ranch dressing though."

"Good. That's easy."

He pulled plain yogurt and mayonnaise out of the refrigerator, and then vinegar, and even more spices out of another cabinet. She'd never seen so many spices used in one dish. He scooped out yogurt and mayo without measuring again, poured in the vinegar and spices, and whisked it together in less than a minute. He dipped the tip of a spoon into the bowl and held it across the counter for her. "Taste and tell me that doesn't beat any ranch dressing you've ever had." He cupped his hand below the spoon so it wouldn't drip on her laptop.

She bent forward as he slipped the spoon into her

mouth. Their eyes met, and she was certain hers almost rolled to the back of her head. God, it was tangy and tart and creamy and smooth. It was heavenly, and he was right. She'd never had anything even remotely as good as Fisher's homemade dressing. "Oh God, how'd you learn how to make that?"

He shrugged. "I don't know. I just experimented. It's not a big deal."

"Not a big deal? It is for me. You didn't even measure anything. I can't cook at all, and you just pour stuff into a bowl and turn it into ambrosia."

He turned and gathered the plates. "I could tell by your shopping cart—no ingredients." He walked past her into the dining room and set the table. "My mother always told us that if you can read, you can cook. All it takes is the ability to follow directions."

"Says the man with natural talent." She sat back at her computer and looked over her work.

Background: It sounds as if he has a close-knit family. More info on that later.

Internal Conflicts: Peter Pan syndrome?

External Conflicts: Hmm… no idea.

Fisher flipped the steaks, opened the oven door, and poked at the potatoes. "Perfect. How do you like your meat?"

"Medium rare."

"Good. The steaks will be ready in a few minutes. Can I get you a glass of wine, or do you want to stick with beer?"

"Either is fine with me."

"Wine it is." He pulled a bottle of red out of the wine rack and went about opening it without the usual fuss she'd seen guys use. "I was up in Washington State last year, and I got this incredible merlot, Velvet Devil. I liked it so much, I bought a whole case."

She stuck "independently wealthy" under background. It was fiction, right? She couldn't very well have a hero who was broke. She saved her work and smiled at what she'd accomplished. "Can I help at all?"

"Sure." He took the butter and sour cream out of the refrigerator and set them on the counter. "You can put these on the table. I think the salt and pepper are already out there. Oh—and the salad."

She ferried them all to the table, folded the napkins she found in a bowl on the sideboard, and placed them under the forks. At least that was one thing she knew how to do. By the time she returned to the kitchen, Fisher had the steaks and potatoes on serving platters, and the peach thing sitting on top of the stove.

He picked up both platters. "All we need now is the wine and glasses. They're hanging over there." He nodded in the direction of a glass-front cabinet. Sure enough, wine glasses hung just below it.

Jessie grabbed the bottle and two glasses. When she reached the table, he took the wine, set the glasses by their plates, pulled out a chair, and waited.

She wasn't sure what the heck he was standing there for until he took her hand and seated her. "Yeah, sorry. I missed that one completely." She shut her eyes and did her best not to blush, not that she could control it, but if there was a way, she really wished she'd figure it out. That knowledge would be good right about now.

"It's not a big deal."

Again, it was to her. But then she wasn't used to men

treating her like a girl. She wasn't used to men treating her like anything but one of the guys.

Fisher stabbed a steak. "Medium rare for you." He placed it on her plate and passed her the potatoes. "So, what kind of book are you writing?"

"Genre fiction."

Fisher cut his steak. Jessica did a great job of avoiding his gaze. The red tinge to her cheeks confirmed his feeling that it was probably covering up something pretty juicy if it would cause her to blush. Erotica? God, wouldn't that be cool? He could help her come up with some interesting scenarios and positions. Since he'd met her, he couldn't look at her without thinking about hot sex. Shit, the thought of her just writing hot sex was enough to tent his pants.

"Which genre?"

She looked away as if she was deciding which lie to tell him.

"What are you hiding?"

"I'm not hiding anything."

"Okay, sure." He finished chewing his meat and picked up his wine, swirled it around the sides and watched its legs as it flowed back into the bowl.

"I'm writing a romance."

"What kind of romance?"

"Contemporary."

He nodded. "That's a smart move. I read an article recently that said romance readers read on average ten books a month. Did you know it's the only genre that's actually increased sales during the recession? That's amazing. They said a woman would put down a steak in the grocery store and opt instead to buy a pound of ground beef and a romance."

"You read that?"

Fisher cut his potato and loaded it with butter and sour cream. "Yeah, I read all kinds of things. Do you belong to RWA?" Jessica's blank stare told him no. "Romance Writers of America. It's a national group that has local chapters all over the country." One of his patients belonged to it and was a *New York Times* best-selling author, not that he could mention it. Sometimes HIPPA really sucked. "There's a chapter in Boise."

Jessica took a sip of wine and watched him over the rim. "No snarky comments?"

"Why? I always thought they were darn good books. I've even read a couple. Of course, I didn't really know they were romances before I picked them up. I'm told what I read were cross-genre. Once I got hooked on a particular author though, I read her other stuff too. It wasn't until someone asked if I was buying them for a girlfriend that I put two and two together. I don't know what the big deal is. Most books have a romance subplot at least. Look at *The Bourne Identity*."

"True. I never thought about it. I'd never read a romance until a few weeks ago."

"Really? Why not?"

She held up her finger. "One: the covers were enough to put me off food for a month. Come on, I wouldn't have been caught dead carrying around a book with Fabio on the cover."

"Yeah, but that's all changed now. Have you looked at the romance covers lately?"

She speared a piece of potato and chewed. "I suppose. Still, they all have headless, shirtless, waxed-within-an-inch-of-their-lives guys on them."

"At least they're not the bodice rippers of old. And face it, sex sells. Since the target demographic is women, it only makes sense to put a hot guy on the cover. No one complains about a beautiful woman on the cover of *Playboy*."

"Are you equating romance to *Playboy*?"

"No, the women's version of *Playboy* is *Playgirl*. I'm just saying if you want to attract women, putting a hot guy on the cover will do the trick."

"Point two: I can't stand purple prose. I'm a reporter, and we're trained to write succinctly—we get to the point and avoid overly long, flowery descriptions. And three: I don't believe in it."

He froze with a piece of meat speared on the tines of his fork hovering near his mouth. She wasn't joking. At least she didn't look like she was. Maybe he misunderstood. "You don't believe in what?" He pulled the meat from his fork and waited for her to come up with an answer.

"Happily ever afters, romantic love. It's all a hoax. But I guess that's why romance is fiction."

He chewed his meat, taking care not to choke on it. Wow, that explained so much. He waited until he'd swallowed and washed the bad taste in his mouth away with a big gulp of wine. Had someone hurt her so badly that she'd given up on love? Maybe that's why she was so damn skittish around him. Always looking for an angle, as if he was trying to pull one over on her. Sometimes it sucked being a nice guy. He wondered if he'd spend his life repairing the hearts and bodies of women who were abused in one way or another by asshole men. "Bad experience?"

"With what?" She didn't seem upset. She ate her food as if she hadn't a care in the world and a decent meal in a millennium—which was a possibility.

"Men, love… Has someone hurt you?"

"Me?" She shot him an incredulous look. "No. Why do you ask?"

Something flickered in those dark eyes of hers, but the emotion was gone before he could even name it. "I've just never met a woman who wasn't a dyed-in-the-wool romantic. Even my sister-in-law, Toni—her mom's the female version of Hugh Hefner without the ascot. I think Clarissa's on husband number five or six. Toni may have sworn off love, but she always believed in it."

Jessica held up her fork. "Lust is constantly mistaken for love." She cut her steak and speared it along with a piece of potato. "Love doesn't exist. It's just a prettied-up version of lust that keeps the greeting card companies and divorce lawyers in business." She popped the food into her pretty mouth as if she were adding a punctuation mark.

"So every guy who wined and dined you struck out in the love department?"

"I don't date much."

"Then you've never fallen in love." He sat back and rolled the wine in the bottom of his glass.

"No. I've never fallen in love because love doesn't exist. I've fallen in like and in lust, sure, but that doesn't last long."

He found himself leaning forward, looking for any sign of fallacy. The woman was a knockout. Why didn't she have men falling all over her? Maybe it was because they couldn't keep up with her? "When you say you don't date much, what do you do?"

"What do you mean?"

"I'm assuming you're not a virgin."

"Hardly."

"So, who are these guys you sleep with? How do you get from 'Hi, my name is Jessica' to rolling around in bed without dating?"

"They're guys I know." She picked up her wine and took a sip. "Friends, teammates, guys I work out with. It just happens sometimes."

"And do you tell these guys your theory on love?"

"Yeah, I guess. It's not a secret. It's a fact." She stared into his eyes as if willing him to contradict her.

He held her gaze. "And when do you tell them this?"

She finally broke eye contact, sat back, and thought about it. "I'm not sure. Different times."

Fisher placed his napkin beside his plate. He'd lost his appetite. Leaning back, he steepled his fingers. "Let me guess. You and a guy have a good thing going, you get together once or twice a week, you grab a beer after work or after a workout. He starts feeling you out about relationships, and you tell him your theory."

"Okay, yeah." She shrugged and pulled her leg up, hugging it to her chest. "That sounds about right."

"Then within a couple weeks the lust has cooled down, and the guy or you back off, thus proving your theory."

"Uh-huh."

"Well, all that proves is that you're wrong."

"I'm wrong?"

"Hell yes." He pushed his plate away. "What guy in his right mind is going to get closer to a woman who doesn't want or even feel the slightest hint of love for him? It's not *all* about the sex, you know—even for guys. Why would a man waste time with a woman who doesn't care for him?"

"I care for them… as friends…"

He stood and gathered their plates. "And that's the kiss of death. Telling a guy you love him like a friend is like a guy telling his best buddy the girl he fixed him up with has a great personality. He might as well label her a dog."

"You're wrong." She sounded sure of herself, but she definitely didn't look it.

"I'm not going to argue the point since there's only one way to prove it. So tell me, if you haven't been romanced, how are you going to write about it? I assume your hero and heroine will eventually fall in love, something you have no experience with and believe is an urban myth. How are you going to pull it off?"

"Research."

He stopped what he was doing and stared at her. "You're going to date poor, unsuspecting men for research?"

"I hadn't considered that, but I suppose it is a possibility."

"Okay."

She stood too, and tossed her napkin on the table. "Okay what? What is okay?"

"Okay, I'll date you. Now you finally have a reason to go out with me. Call it research." He didn't wait for her reaction. He picked up the plates and took them to the kitchen. She deflated and sat down hard, staring into her wine as if it were a looking glass depicting the future.

Poor girl, she didn't know what she was up against.

Fisher might not have done it for a while. Hell, he'd be the first to admit he was a little rusty when it came to romance—he couldn't remember a time when he actually had to work to get a woman in his bed. Probably not since he was a horny teenager, but he figured it was like riding a bike.

He looked over at Jessica again, while he rinsed the plates and loaded them into the dishwasher. She was like no other bike he'd ridden before. Those training wheels and handlebar streamers might just come in handy after all.

Chapter 8

JESSIE DIDN'T KNOW HOW ON EARTH SHE'D GOTTEN herself into this mess. Fisher did the dishes, whistling a tune, like the earth hadn't just tilted off its axis.

She couldn't date him. Could she? Sure, she could sleep with him. Lord knew there was no lack of attraction between them, but then what? What would happen when they worked off that whole sexual need thing? What would happen then?

He tossed a towel over his shoulder and leaned on the counter. "Do you like ice cream?"

"For what?"

"To eat. What were you thinking about?" He laughed this low, gravely laugh that set her hair on end and had the girls standing at attention. Fuckity, fuck, fuck, fuck—that was such a bad sign.

"I was just going to put it on the cobbler, but if you have any other interesting ideas, I'm completely open. So do you want it with ice cream, or without?"

"With." She poured the rest of the wine into her glass and drank it in one gulp.

"Dutch courage? Come on, Jessica. I'm not that scary."

He had no idea. She gathered their glasses and carried them to the kitchen, where he was dishing up cobbler. God, it smelled great.

"Coffee?"

"Okay."

"Regular or decaf?" He spun the stand holding a plethora of K-Cup coffee options.

She couldn't care less about coffee. She felt as if she'd just jumped off a proverbial cliff. She held her breath, waiting for him to catch her, and he was talking about coffee. "Whatever. Caffeine doesn't bother me, but neither does decaf, if that's what you want."

He slid his arm around her. "Darlin', I'm so tired tonight, nothing but you could keep me awake. You've caused me more sleepless nights than anyone I can re-member." His hand rested on her hip as he pulled her tight against him. "So, it's your call. Am I going to sleep, or am I going to bed?"

"Nice layup there." She relaxed against him. Her hand rested over his racing heart, while hers sped to catch up. She took two Wolfgang Puck Jamaica Me Crazy K-Cups, put one in the machine, and pressed the button. "You're going to need all the caffeine you can handle."

He toyed with the waistband of her loose-fitting jeans, slid his hand under the hem of her T-shirt, and then stroked the heated skin of her stomach. "I do so love a decisive woman."

She sucked in a breath. "It's lust, not love." He needed to know that almost as badly as she needed to say it. She couldn't afford to become another victim of her mother's fairy tales. She wasn't immune—she was human after all. Great sex was supposedly like having a runner's high—or so she'd been told. The body craved the en-dorphins that orgasms created. Fisher, if he were as good as she suspected he was, would be more addictive than chocolate-covered crack. Their gazes locked as she de-bated whether to run away or take the chance. For once, she wished she were a sissy. There was a dare in his eyes, and since she never could resist a dare, she closed the distance between their lips of her own volition.

His kiss was slow and gentle and unbelievably soft. She hadn't known what to expect, but tentative tenderness was not it. His jaw was smooth to her touch; there was no scraping, no bruising. Fisher didn't plunder, he tempted. He traced the seam of her lips with the tip of his tongue, his hard body pressed against hers, and his hands roamed beneath her oversized T-shirt. His heart raced beneath her palm in stark contrast to the slow gentleness of his kiss and touch.

She went up on her toes, increasing the pressure in direct proportion to the need rocketing through her. In the background the coffee machine burbled, spurting the last drop into the cup.

Fisher ended the kiss and stared with eyes dark and mysterious, as if he were trying to make up his mind about something. "Coffee's ready." He reached around her, tossed the empty K-Cup on the counter, replaced it and the mug, and pressed the button for another cup.

She didn't move, didn't want to. His body surrounded hers, and he seemed happy to have her smashed against him. Her hormones weren't complaining either. She leaned in for another kiss and nibbled his full bottom lip, tasting the wine they drank with dinner, and toyed with the tight rein he seemed to have on his control. She wanted to shatter it.

His arms tightened and he changed the angle and tenor of the kiss, vying for dominance. Now that was more like it. Their tongues danced, swirling in her mouth, hers chasing his in a hot, wet tango.

When the coffee machine sputtered the final drop, the last thing she wanted was for this to end. She plunged her hands beneath the waistband of his jeans, and that wicked grin reappeared. This time, she figured it matched hers. He'd gone commando, and she couldn't think of a nicer surprise. She raked her nails over the ass she'd been admiring for far too long, and he groaned into her mouth, his erection pressing into her abdomen.

Fisher ripped his mouth from hers and dragged in a breath. "Jessica, if you want to drink the coffee we just made before it gets cold, you'd better get your hands out of my pants."

She raked her fingers toward the waistband, only enough to slide them around to the front and flick open the button on his worn Wranglers.

"Like I said, I do love a decisive woman." Before she knew what he was up to, he tossed her over his shoulder like a sack of potatoes, knocking the wind out of her. She gave a kick, but his arm was a steel band around her thighs. The kitchen flew out of view as he clipped down the darkened hallway. He stepped into a room and set her on her feet with a gentleness that threw her again.

Fisher removed the elastic from her hair and ran his fingers through it, tipping her chin so that her eyes met his. "Are you sure this is what you want?"

No question there. "Yes." She reached for his shirt and pulled it over his head. God he was gorgeous. Blond hair shone in the moonlight, highlighting the hills and valleys of his chest and torso. She traced her finger over the length of a scar that followed the angle of his oblique muscle between the hip and his abdomen and stopped somewhere below the waistband of his low-slung jeans. "What's this from?"

"Appendix, when I was eleven."

"Must have hurt." She bent to kiss it, tracing it from the top to the denim with her tongue.

"I had drugs. Too bad Hunter didn't."

"Your brother? What was wrong with him?" She slowly slid the teeth of the zipper down.

"If one of us gets hurt, the other feels it too. It's a twin thing."

He sucked in a breath as she kneeled in front of him. "You feel each other's pain?" Jessie kissed the skin she bared as she eased his jeans over his hips. She sat back on her heels and looked her fill. "What about pleasure?"

"Beats the hell out of me. With you looking at me like that, I'm not thinking about anyone's pleasure but ours."

She slid her hand up the inside of his leg, and his dick jumped and seemed to get even larger.

"Jessica. You're playing with fire, darlin'." He tugged her to her feet and kissed her hard as he unhooked her bra with one hand. His other pulled her shirt up and off. He stared at her, his eyes bright and dark and just a little too intense. She checked the urge to cover her breasts.

Her bra straps fell off her shoulders and hung in the curve of her elbows as he slid her jeans and panties down over her hips and took her hand as she stepped out of them. He didn't even blink. He just continued to stare, and the longer he did, the more she felt like a fool. She knew what she looked like—her stomach was way too muscular, and her thighs were too big—all muscle, but still, they weren't the kind of legs most guys drooled over. In her experience men only wanted women who had big boobs, a small waist with a sexy belly—women with soft, womanly curves and no definition. She didn't do curves or softness. Hell, she didn't do much when it came to the whole woman thing.

She'd never been modest before. After all, she'd trained hard to achieve the fitness level she had, but she couldn't remember the last time a man looked at her like he wanted to eat her up instead of just picking her for his team. It was disconcerting—almost as disturbing as the way her body reacted to his gaze as if he'd touched her. They'd only kissed a few times, and she was primed, ready, and way past needy. She'd never done needy until she'd met Fisher. She didn't see it as a plus.

"God, you take my breath away."

The way he said it, it didn't come out sounding like a compliment. It sounded more like a curse, but then she wasn't even sure of that. If she hadn't seen his lips move, she'd swear she imagined it. The only time she'd ever taken anyone's breath away was when she tackled him in football. "It's a body, Fisher. Mine is nothing special."

"If you believe that, you're a fool. You're every man's wet dream. I should know."

She opened her mouth for a smart retort, but Fisher was faster out of the blocks. He came at her, all two hundred pounds of hot man—mouth-to-mouth, chest-to-chest, thigh-to-thigh. Flames licked her skin followed by the edge of the bed. She went into a free fall, landing and sinking into the down cover with Fisher on top.

He ate her mouth with commanding diligence. Gone was the gentleness, displaced by a controlled burn. The heat of his body melted hers. His hands roamed, shooting sparks of pleasure and need wherever he touched.

He trailed kisses down her neck, licking and sucking as his hands explored her arms, sides, and back, before pulling her thigh over his hip. She heard herself moan as his erection pulsed against her core when he sucked her breast into his mouth.

Jessica was on sensory overload. Her back arched as her hand cupped his head, trying to make sure he didn't escape. Her womb tightened with every pull at her breast.

She couldn't seem to get enough air. He switched breasts, and his erection brushed over home plate and had her writhing and moaning beneath him like a cat in heat. She couldn't take much more. She wrapped her legs around his waist and raised her pelvis, reaching for completion, anything to uncoil the knot of need.

Fisher groaned and slid to her side. "Slow down, darlin', we have all night. Hell, I don't have to be back until Tuesday." His kiss was soft and teasing, but she wasn't in the mood for that. No, she wanted mindless heat.

She flipped them over and straddled him. She meant business. She sucked his tongue into her mouth, swirling around his, before she released it and nipped his lips. His fingers speared through her hair, massaging her scalp as she dragged her teeth down his neck to his collarbone, exploring his chest—nipping, licking. Muscles danced beneath her lips as she licked a trail over his abs, traced the ridges and valleys, and dipped into his navel before heading south.

Encircling his erection, she ran her lips over the length of it, feeling the heat, the hardness, the life pulsing through him. God he was beautiful. Swirling her tongue around the head, she tasted him, catching the drop of wetness. Oh yeah, she had him exactly where she wanted him. She opened her mouth to take him in, just as iron vices closed over her arms, dragging her against him, flipping them over. His mouth came down on hers, and all the air left her lungs. The sound of something crashing registered as she squirmed beneath him.

Fisher knocked the damn lamp off the bedside table in his haste to get a condom. He ripped his mouth away from Jessica's, and still holding her down, felt around the bottom of the drawer. His finger brushed the crinkled edge of a foil packet, and he almost cried with relief. At the rate he was going, he'd be lucky to last another five minutes. He'd never been with a woman who turned making love into a full contact sport. She definitely wasn't the type to lie there and make him do all the work, and Lord, when she tried to take charge, he'd been tempted to just let her go for it. If he didn't have such a hair trigger right now, he would gladly have let her take full advantage.

"Let me help." She reached for his dick and the condom.

He whipped the condom out of reach. "Darlin', if you do any more to help me, it's going to be over before it's begun. As it is, I'm just going to give you a blanket apology and swear I'll make it up to you next time, and the time after that, and the time after that."

He sucked air through his teeth as he rolled on the condom. His hands shook, and he wished he knew what the hell was going through her mind. She was unreadable. Sure he knew she was turned on, but when it came to anything other than the physical, he hadn't a clue. And he wanted to know what was going on behind those chocolate brown eyes.

Shit. He was supposed to be romancing her. God, he

was such an ass. He'd forgotten all about that the minute she shoved her hands in his pants. Now what was he supposed to do?

"Something wrong?" She sat up, and for the first time he saw some real emotion. He would have preferred it not be insecurity, but at least that was a starting point, a connection.

"I just remembered I'm supposed to be romancing you, and I'm doing a terrible job of it." He leaned over and kissed her. "I'm sorry."

She let out a brittle laugh; the insecurity was still there. She pulled away and scooted toward the other side of the bed.

"Whoa, where do you think you're going?" He wrapped an arm around her.

"Out of here." She tried to push out of his hold. "Look, it's fine. I'll just go sleep in Karma's room. No apology necessary. I know I'm not your type, and well, it was just research…"

"You think I'm rejecting you? Hell, I was apologizing for my lack of finesse. Any thought of romance flew out the window the second you grabbed my ass. I wanted you so bad I acted like a Neanderthal. That's what I was apologizing for. Jessica, you deserve better."

She stared at him with wide eyes. "You were worried about finesse?"

"Yeah. It's right up there with performance anxiety—for which, I should remind you, I've already offered a blanket apology."

Her lips twitched, and that golden spark in her eyes reappeared. Thank God. "I have no problem with your performance so far." The tension left her body, and she allowed him to pull her against him as she nuzzled his neck. "I'll let you know how I feel about it once I have a full understanding of your methods and practices."

"Methods and practices, huh? No pressure there." He pulled the covers down and laid her back against the pillows before kissing her, long and slow. He leaned back and looked into her eyes. "You don't think you're my type? What would my type be if not you?" He kissed her chin and moved on to her neck.

"I don't know—someone girly. You know, big breasts, stick legs, not a lot of muscle."

The pulse point on the side of her neck thrummed beneath his lips as his hand slid over her breast, her nipple pebbling beneath his palm. "Your breasts are perfect, and you're sexy as hell—beautiful and strong. I wouldn't change a thing about you. Your body is spectacular. It would be great if you'd let me keep my dignity once in a while when we're running, but that's just my male ego talking."

His mouth captured her breast, making it impossible for him to talk. He sure as hell hoped she was better at reading body language, because that was all she was going to get for a good long while. He wasn't coming up for air again, until he did every one of the things he'd dreamt about, even if it killed him. And it just might.

Oh God, Jessie had thought she was in trouble when it looked like he was rejecting her. But then, she was more mad than hurt, though hurt would have come later. What he did now was worse than she'd ever imagined. It made his possible rejection look like child's play.

Fisher worshiped her body—something that never had happened to her before. What was she supposed to do? He held her like she was a precious artifact, stroking and kissing and teasing. Drawing her up so tight, she'd swear she was going to implode, and then soothing her with his lips and tongue as if they had all night to touch and explore.

Every time she made a move to return the favor, he gently, but firmly, put her in her place, which was flat on her back. Finally, he held her hands above her head and stared into her eyes. His were dilated, dark, and so intense. "Just hold onto the headboard until I say so. Okay, darlin'?"

She was too dumbfounded to even answer, plus he picked just that moment to slip a finger inside her. Her body shook, and she keened like a wild animal, bucking against him. He pressed his thumb against her, and it was as good as flipping a switch. Her orgasm crashed through her, rolling like an earthquake, shocking her with its intensity and strength. She threw her arm over her eyes. God, it had been a year since she'd had sex… maybe longer. She didn't exactly write it on her calendar. It hadn't been that memorable.

His touch soothed, as she rearranged the shattered sections of her brain, tried to control her breathing, and released the death grip she'd had on his hand. She was just about to roll onto her side to either thank him or apologize—she hadn't decided which should come first—when he slipped between her legs. She opened her eyes and expected to see him hovering over her. Wrong. He wasn't above her at all.

He was down there, and… "Oh God, yes." What he was doing with his tongue, teeth, and hands was probably illegal in several states. He drove her back up so fast, she was glad she had the headboard to hold on to. "Fisher?"

He mumbled something, and the vibrations from his mouth, his voice—whatever it was—sent her flying.

She called out his name as he entered her in one swift thrust, filling her completely and triggering her orgasm, which rolled into another and shot her onto a plane she'd never visited, no less knew existed. Nothing in her experience had ever come close to this. She wrapped her shaking legs around his hips and dragged him closer as wave after wave rolled through her... through him.

"Jessica, you feel amazing." He kissed her softly as her body relaxed. She seemed to have lost the ability to move. Her arms slid from around him, and if her ankles weren't hooked around him, they'd be history too. She felt like a lump of clay—heavy and inanimate.

Fisher stared into her eyes as he rocked within her, slowly, gently, and with such tenderness, she had to look away.

Her mind raced trying to figure out how to please him when she was incapable of movement. But Fisher seemed to have the magic touch, and before she knew it, her fingers were sinking into his back, her heels digging into his butt.

No matter how much she demanded, he teased her with his slow, steady pace, just fast enough to have her on edge, but not hard or quick enough to throw her over.

He had her riding the sharp edge of madness, her heart pounding so hard she'd swear she was bruising something. When she couldn't take it anymore, she tilted her pelvis, clenched every muscle, and pulled him deep.

Fisher groaned, his face contorted with pleasure or

pain, she wasn't sure, and then he went wild, pistoning his hips, pounding her, hard, deep, and so damn good, she swore she saw stars. His whole body tensed, and he let out a pretty inventive string of curses before thrusting three more times and collapsing on top of her.

Jessie was in serious trouble. She covered her eyes again and did her best not to cry. She was scared, confused, and she couldn't think of a nice way to distance herself from Fisher long enough to pull herself together. He was lying on top of her, with his face in the crook of her neck.

She took a deep breath and tried to calm down, even though she was sure she'd lost her mind. She hadn't cried in years, and she had absolutely nothing to cry about. She told herself to suck it up, but every time she did, even more tears welled in her eyes, and blinking them away wasn't cutting it.

Fisher kissed her lips, and she let out a shuddered breath. Pinpricks of guilt shot down his spine. "Jessica? Sweetheart, are you okay?"

She nodded, but then with her arm thrown over her eyes, even with the moonlight shining on the bed, he couldn't tell for sure. He gathered all the strength he possessed and rose onto his forearms, which pressed him deeper within her. He did his best to ignore the way it felt and his body's instant reaction.

"Jessica, honey, please look at me."

She shook her head no, and bit her lip. He wanted to turn on the light, but he'd trashed the lamp earlier. Well, damn. Prying her arm away from her face was like Indian arm wrestling, but he won. Shit. He'd known something was wrong, but he hadn't expected this. Not for a million years. "Why are you crying, darlin'?"

She snuffled, and the tears continued. "I'm not crying. I don't cry."

Fisher kissed the side of her face and caught the tracks of her tears. "Tastes like tears."

She let out another shuddered breath, and it was as if another hole in the dike appeared. For a woman who wasn't crying, the tears were sure flowing.

She slammed her fist down on the bed. If he hadn't had her pinned, inside and out, he was sure she'd be stomping off somewhere. Damn she was fascinating— beautiful, intelligent, and at times, amazingly clueless. "Sometimes a physical release spurs on an emotional one. Maybe you just need a good cry."

Crying didn't bother him. His brothers and cousin would rather have their left nut removed than deal with a woman's tears, but he'd spent the last six years in hospitals where tears of grief, happiness, pain, and exasperation flowed around the clock. A mother's grief was the worst. Nothing in his experience could compare to that.

"I'm not crying. My eyes are leaking. There's a big difference."

"Okay, sure." He slid his arm around her and rolled them onto their sides. He might as well get comfortable. In his experience, when women who weren't normally criers started crying, they made up for lost time. Yeah, he had a strong feeling she'd be at it awhile. "Since your eyes are leaking, you might as well just let it go." He rubbed her back and kissed her forehead. "It's okay, sweetheart. I'm right here."

"Yeah, that's what sucks about this. You're right here, and my eyes are leaking. God, this is embarrassing. You probably think I'm a nutcase."

"Because you cry after amazing sex? I think you're a nutcase because you tried to drive a car with a five-inch clearance up a jeep trail, and I'm not even going to mention your diet."

She finally looked at him. "There's nothing wrong with my diet. I can outrun you any day of the week."

"Yeah, but then your hamstring cramps because you don't get enough potassium. Face it, Jessica, if you ate better you'd perform better—it's basic."

She ran a hand down his chest. "I didn't hear you complaining about my performance." She wiggled, and his dick reacted as if she'd just given it CPR. Her eyes widened, and for a second there, he wondered if she was fishing for compliments. Hell, she was definitely worthy of them, but he'd always been a big believer of actions speaking louder than words.

Her kiss was slightly salty—warm and open and deep. She nudged them both over, straddled him, and sat drying her eyes with the backs of her hands, showing off her inner six-year-old. God, she was a wild combination of hard and soft, cynic and innocent, all wrapped up in a perfect package of a lean, mean, sex machine. "Um… sweetheart, if you're going where I hope you are, we need to grab another condom."

"Um sure, but before that, I'm hungry. That peach thing you made smells amazing. Would you mind—"

"Feeding you? No, just as long as you tell me what you were thinking of doing with that ice cream earlier."

She bent over and kissed him, tears and embarrass-ment apparently forgotten. "How 'bout we go and get some, and I demonstrate?"

Chapter 9

JESSIE OPTED TO GRAB THE FIRST T-SHIRT SHE COULD get her hands on, threw it on, and escaped into the kitchen, since crawling under the bed like a wounded cat to die of embarrassment wasn't an option—not with Fisher watching her every move. She reheated their coffee and took the ice cream out of the freezer in an effort to hide her mortification.

Fisher strolled out wearing nothing but his Wranglers, zipped but not buttoned, and looking sexier than any man had a right to, even with the dark rings under his eyes. Rings that were probably put there from spending sleepless nights like this with other women. Not that she expected him to sleep with just her. Okay, well, yeah, she did. Maybe they should have gone over the rules before she agreed to play the game. And dating was a whole new game for her.

"What's wrong?"

She tugged the cover off the ice cream. "Nothing. I'm just hungry."

"And you're a rotten liar. Whenever something's wrong, you get this crease between your brows." He smoothed it with his finger. "So you might as well spill it."

"I'm just wondering about the rules."

He crossed his arms and leaned against the counter. "What exactly are we talking about?"

She pulled open the first drawer, searching for spoons. "I told you I don't date."

"Here." He grabbed spoons out of the drawer right beside him and started dishing out the ice cream. "So now that we're dating, you want to know the ground rules?"

"Yeah, pretty much."

"Dating rules? Sex rules? Relationship rules?"

"Sex rules, mostly." But now that he mentioned it, dating rules and relationship rules kind of wigged her out too. "You know, maybe this whole research thing was a big mistake."

"The only rules of sex are that while we're together, we have it. Often."

"And when we're not together?"

"Oh, so that's what this is all about. Are you doing *research* with anyone else?"

"No."

He handed her the cobbler and stuck a spoonful in her mouth. "I'd prefer it if you kept it that way."

She yanked the spoon out and pointed it at him. "I'm not the one with women falling all over me."

A dark brow rose, and the left side of his mouth tilted up, showing off a perfect dimple. "You have nothing to worry about. I don't have the time, energy, or interest to juggle women. Besides, you're the only one I want to make love to."

"It's research, Fisher. And dating, I guess. Not love."

"It's romance. Just in case you're not sure of what that involves, I'll spell it out for you. Romance involves getting naked, making love, playing, and eating. It means talking on the phone and checking in with each other and holding hands under the table. It's spending time together, and laughing, and crying. It's fighting about what movie to see, and what games to play. It's putting up with bad habits and each other's families. It's what couples do."

"But that's just it. We're not a couple. We're... research partners."

"Darlin', while you and I are together, we're a couple. Research partners don't sleep together, and they don't do half the things with ice cream that I'm contemplating right about now. So it looks like you have a decision to make." He sipped his coffee and stared at her over the rim.

"I have things to do. I really don't have time to date."

"Do the things you have to do preclude you from being with me?"

"Well, no. Not all the time."

"Okay, so you work. What's the big deal? Most couples work. I don't expect you to drop everything to cavort with me. Besides, my schedule's flexible. I don't think it'll be a problem. So, is it a deal?" He scooped up the last of his cobbler and stuck the spoon in his mouth as he turned to rinse the bowl.

"I guess."

"You better be careful, Jessica. If you keep up this level of excitement, it's going to go to my head."

"What do you want me to say?" She stabbed her spoon back into the cobbler. "This whole arrangement makes me uncomfortable, which is probably why I've never really done the whole dating thing before."

He dried his hands and stepped toward her, all barechested, barefooted, and barely dressed. "Change is scary, and you've scared the hell out of me since I met you. I think I'm a glutton for punishment." He motioned to her half-eaten cobbler.

It had tasted great, until they started with the rules discussion.

"Are you going to finish that?"

She shook her head and handed it over. "Go ahead. I can't finish it. It's great, but I'm stuffed." She shimmied up to sit on the granite counter. Shoot, she forgot she wasn't wearing underwear.

"Thanks." He stepped between her legs and shot her a sexy smile and scooped up a big spoonful. "This is just one more perk of coupledom," he said around a mouthful of cobbler. "I get to eat whatever you can't. Hunter has gained at least ten pounds since he married Toni— and believe me, it's not because she's a good cook."

"Hunter is your twin, right?"

"Yeah. Trapper is the oldest, and Karma's the baby."

She laughed. She couldn't help it. "Hunter, Trapper, Fisher, and Karma. There's a story there somewhere."

"My mom said Dad was trapping when Trapper was born, hunting and fishing when we were born, and going through a divorce when Karma was born. Needless to say, Mom named us."

He finished her cobbler and slid his arm around her. She jumped off the counter and instinctively reached for him, her arms wrapped around his waist, and the momentum brought them together. He fit her so well that it stole her breath. He looked down at her and had a little ice cream on his mouth. Jessie stood on her toes and ran the tip of her tongue over his upper lip. The flavor of vanilla and peaches vied for dominance, but the taste of Fisher, subtle and hot, overwhelmed them the same way he overwhelmed her senses. One kiss had her heart warring with her breastbone and the bulge in his pants pressing against her stomach.

Fisher ended the kiss and pressed his forehead against hers. "Let's go to bed. I'll take care of the dishes in the morning." He took her hand and led her out of the kitchen, turning off lights and locking doors on their way, and then as soon as they hit the bedroom, he pulled her shirt right over her head. "I think you wore me out today."

"You can't blame your exhaustion on me. You've been complaining about being tired since I found you."

"You didn't find me. I rescued you, remember?" She was still sputtering with indignation when he righted the lamp he'd knocked over earlier.

He switched on the light. It was a good thing the lamp proved to be indestructible. Fisher straightened the shade, tossed a few condoms on the table beside it, and tugged off his jeans. "Which side do you want?"

"You did not rescue me."

"You can have the one closest to the bathroom. I brought your bags in from Karma's room." He pointed out her duffel sitting neatly on the chair. Everything was neat. He'd even straightened the bed. "I'm going to brush my teeth. You can join me if you want."

"No, that's okay. I'll just wait until you're done." She'd never shared a bathroom in her life. Not even in college. She'd gotten her own apartment because she couldn't imagine living with a bunch of girls. The prospect of sharing a bathroom with Fisher wasn't much better.

"Okay." He kissed her before turning and walking out of the room.

Why'd he do that? Maybe he just liked messing with her head. If that was his intention, he was doing a great job.

She grabbed her ditty bag and was more than half tempted to drag her stuff back into Karma's room. She'd never slept with the guys she had sex with— not even the guys she thought of as friends, and she definitely didn't think of Fisher as a friend. He was too good-looking, too good at everything. The worst part about it was the way he looked at her—like she was a woman he wanted.

When it came to being just a woman, she didn't know how. Since she was old enough to ride a bike, throw a baseball, and sink a free throw with nothing but net, she'd always been in competition with guys. She'd fought to get to the top of her class, to be the best batter on the team, any team—it didn't matter if it was the boy's baseball team or the office softball team, she was the best. She didn't know how to live any other way.

She was competitive to a fault. People like her weren't good at sitting on the sidelines, and from what she saw of relationships, that's exactly what Fisher would expect her to do even though their relationship wasn't real, and definitely not long-term. Hell, when it came right down to it, the whole research thing was a convenient excuse to scratch one heck of an itch and maybe get a few ideas for her book. Still, by agreeing to date anyone, even temporarily, she put herself in a very untenable position. She'd have to turn into the one thing she never wanted to be—the supportive little woman.

"Bathroom's yours."

She'd been so lost in thought he startled her. She looked like an idiot standing naked, hugging her toiletries to her chest. She should have bolted when she'd had the chance. "Thanks." She hoped it didn't sound as sarcastic as it felt. "I… um… I'll just be a minute."

"I'll wait here." He slid under the covers and rolled onto his side to watch her.

Jessie closed the door with a click and leaned back against it, trying to quiet her racing heart. She'd had quite a workout for one day. Between her car breaking down, and then discovering Fisher, finding out she'd been tricked, and then falling into bed with him, she figured it would take hours to settle down. She caught her reflection in the mirror and gasped. God, she looked like a stranger. Her hair was a tousled mess, which meant it was going to take her an hour to comb it out in the morning, her lips were red and swollen, and her skin actually glowed. She couldn't believe her eyes. For the first time in her life, she had that just-got-fucked look.

She wasn't sure if that was good or bad. All her previous dalliances were so… civilized that afterward, most times she didn't even have to tighten her ponytail. They were perfunctory at best, but not with Fisher. No, she wasn't sure which one brought the wild out in the other, but damn, she wondered if she'd ever be able to settle for perfunctory sex again.

She brushed her teeth, washed her face, and tried getting a comb through her hair, but it was useless. The way Fisher ran his hands through it and tugged on it, forcing her to expose her neck to his assault, made the thought of detangling it before jumping back in bed with him seem pointless. Just the thought he might want a replay made it impossible to regret the rat's nest it had turned into. Hell, he could muss up her hair anytime.

She turned off the light and headed back to bed. Fisher lifted the covers for her as she slid in. He covered her up, threw his arm around her waist, and pulled her from the edge of the bed into the middle and right up against him. "There, that's better."

He spooned her and rested his hand on her stomach. She wasn't into cuddling, but unfortunately, it seemed Fisher was. He was also the world's fastest sleeper. She doubted it had been more than thirty seconds between the time he pulled her against him, and his light snore and steady breathing told her he was sound asleep. How did he do that?

She should have known it was too good to be true. All that talk about him making love to her again and again and again when he'd given her that adorable blanket apology had her looking forward to going to bed and not getting much sleep. Unfortunately, he was not going to deliver, at least not tonight. She might as well have brushed out her hair.

She glanced at him over her shoulder; he really did look as if he needed sleep. Lord only knew what he had done that had exhausted him so. She wasn't sure she even wanted to know. They had a deal, and the deal was, for as long as they were together, they'd only have sex with each other. As far as she was concerned, that was all that mattered.

Okay, so that was all that *should* matter. So, she'd have to work on it. She was only human, and Fisher was by far, the best lover she'd ever had. She just didn't know what would happen after the relationship thing was over. The thought of going back to her perfunctory sex life was not of interest.

—⁓—

Jessie fell asleep in Fisher's arms, his soft snore in her ear, his legs tangled with hers, and his hand holding her breast. She awoke to the scent of coffee—always a good thing.

She pried her eyes open to find Fisher sitting against the headboard, sipping a cup, and watching her. Scraping the hair away from her eyes, she did a double take. "God, it wasn't just another hot dream, was it?"

The corner of his lip curled, and his eyes sparkled. "You've had hot dreams about me?"

"No talking until after I've had coffee. I can't be held responsible for anything I say or do pre-caffeine."

That was all it took before he slid down in bed, reached across her, touching her in all the right places, and handed her a cup that had been sitting on the bedside table. He nuzzled her neck. "We don't have to talk at all. There are more interesting forms of communication."

He leaned over her, resting on one arm. She had to admit he looked as good in the morning as he did any other time of the day or night. She, on the other hand, did not. "You're going to have to move since I can't drink lying down."

"Spoil sport." He sat beside her, watching her every move, even though all she'd done since she awoke was breathe.

"Thanks." She pulled the sheet up to cover her chest, tucked it under her arms, and scooted up in bed as she took her first sip. Perfect. The coffee was still hot, but cool enough to gulp. Just how she liked it, strong and sweet— like her men. God, where had that thought come from?

Fisher slid his arm around her and pulled her to his

side before he nuzzled her ear again. "You're welcome, beautiful."

She rolled her eyes. "I've heard of night blindness, but never morning blindness. You might want to have your vision checked when we get back to town."

"Nope, it's twenty-twenty. So, what do you want to do today? I can teach you how to fly-fish, or we can pack a picnic, take a boat across Red Fish Lake, and go for a hike. Or we can stay here so you can write. Maybe we should do all of the above."

Jessie sipped her coffee and tried to get her brain working. "We don't have to stay. Don't you want to go back to town?"

"I'd rather be here with you." He kissed her shoulder and nuzzled her ear. "I don't have to be back in Boise until Tuesday morning. I thought you'd planned to hang here with Karma for the weekend."

"I did, but Karma's not here."

She felt him smile against her neck. "And for that I'll be forever grateful."

He took the empty coffee cup from her hand, set it on the table, and with absolutely no warning ravished her mouth. She didn't even want to think about what she tasted like, but he tasted of coffee and toothpaste, not a combination she'd ever found appealing before, but with Fisher, it was incredible.

Before her foggy mind cleared, she was straining against him, gasping for breath, and thinking he was a whole lot more potent than caffeine.

"I like having you all to myself."

Jessica had that wild-eyed look he'd come to recognize, the same one he'd seen right before she ran out of his house after the hot tub incident. Not exactly the reaction he'd been hoping for after last night. He'd been looking forward to a repeat performance, and she was right there with him until he opened his mouth. "When I said I wanted to keep you all to myself, I didn't mean that to sound creepy."

She pulled away and laughed it off. "It didn't. I'm just not much of a morning person. I can't do anything before I've had a quart of caffeine and a shower."

He'd never seen a woman so tense. He was relieved she was only escaping to the bathroom. "Okay." He stood and pulled on his jeans. "I'll bring you a refill and then get started on breakfast while you shower."

She stood, pulling the sheet off the bed and wrapping it around her like a very modest toga. "Fisher, you don't have to serve me. I'm more than capable of fixing coffee. Not much else, but coffee, especially with those K-Cups, is pretty much a no-brainer. As for breakfast, don't feel like you have to go to any trouble. A PowerBar is fine, and I brought some with me."

He'd really like to rip the damn sheet from her body. It wasn't as if he hadn't memorized every inch he'd touched last night, just like he'd memorized her taste and her scent. "I'm going to make myself breakfast, and it's just as easy to cook for two. But if you'd rather have a PowerBar than steak and eggs with hash browns, that's up to you."

"No, I didn't mean... well, steak and eggs sound good if you're cooking anyway."

"Okay then. I'll just go refill your coffee and bring

it in to you. And before you argue, it's not a big deal." He kissed her cheek and gave her a shove toward the shower. "Go ahead, before I decide to join you." That got her moving, which was a damn shame.

Jessie wasted no time running into the bathroom. She caught her reflection in the mirror, cringed, and ran her hand through her hair in a vain attempt to tame it. It was worse than a rat's nest. God, between the hair, the pillow marks on her cheek, and the white sheet, she looked like Medusa. White was so not her color. "But look on the bright side, Jess, it would be a great Halloween costume if you were out to scare men and young children."

A knock on the door made her jump. Okay, so she was a little bit freaked out and talking to herself. God, she hoped he hadn't been eavesdropping.

"Is it safe to come in?"

Shit, she didn't even have the shower running yet. She couldn't very well hide, and it wasn't as if he hadn't already seen her at her worst, several times in fact. She took a deep breath and opened the door.

Fisher's hair was wild, but not like hers. His was more windblown than bed-head. The sun streaming through the skylight caught the blond hair on his chest and accentuated his pecs and abs. Sometimes life was so unfair. He looked perfect in a dreamy, storybook way. She needed to stop staring.

Fisher smiled slowly, as if he could read her mind. With every quirk of his perfect lips, she felt herself shifting farther and farther away from her safety net. It was as if she were fighting a battle against an invisible, unknown enemy and losing spectacularly. She had that whole fight or flight thing going, but she didn't know why. She was so confused, she wasn't sure she knew what she was fleeing. She needed to get a grip.

"You okay?"

Hell, no. But she couldn't tell him that. There was only one person in the world she could tell, and her damn phone didn't work. "I'm fine. I just need to call my best friend to check in, and I can't get a signal on my phone. Is there a place nearby I can get cell coverage?"

"No need. Just use my phone." He set the coffee on the counter, grabbed his phone off the nightstand, and handed it to her. "Plug it back in when you're done, okay?"

"Sure." She took the phone from him and caught the sheet that was slipping off her breasts, watching him leave. "Fisher."

He looked over his shoulder.

"Thanks for the coffee and everything."

"I'll wait for you to finish before I start breakfast, so take your time. Talk as long as you want."

She nodded as Fisher closed the bedroom door behind him. Of course, he was really nice and generous, and well, wonderful. Almost perfect, except for the whole dating thing, and couple thing, and always showing up wherever she was thing—although that had come in handy yesterday. Last night had been perfect too—at least the sex part had. In fact, she awoke wondering if it was just another one of her romance novel–induced, multi-orgasmic dreams. Although in the past dreams, she'd always woken up hot and bothered, well before the big pay off, which made her realize that sex with Fisher had been no dream. Well, that and the slight twinge of sore muscles that hadn't been used in way too long. Last night was certainly one for the record books. She could claim most orgasms with one person, most orgasms in one day, and most orgasms in one year. Yeah, Andrew was right. She definitely needed to get out more.

Jessie took a deep breath and dialed.

"Andrew Monahan."

"Are you alone?" She turned on the water in the party-sized tub to drown out the conversation and be able to soak at the same time.

"Hello to you too. What's the matter? Why are you in Chicago? And why is water running?"

"I'm not in Chicago, and I'm filling the bathtub." She sat on the edge of the tub.

"It's a Chicago area code."

"I borrowed a friend's satellite phone. We're outside of Stanley, and I can't get cell coverage anywhere. Not even on the top of a mountain, I might add."

"You have a friend?"

"You're surprised I have a friend, but you're not surprised that I climbed to the top of a mountain to get cell coverage? What's wrong with this picture?" Jessie stepped into the tub, easing into the hot water while it continued to fill. "And need I remind you that you're my best friend in the world?"

"Sugar, I love you. You know that, but I'm your only friend, and that makes me your best friend. What can I say? The rest of the world is shortsighted."

"I have friends."

"You have acquaintances. Friends are people who will drop everything on a moment's notice and take the red-eye to see you throw out the first pitch in a minor league season opener."

"I totally smoked it."

"You did, but how many of your other so-called friends even crossed the Hudson to see it?"

"Yeah, you do have a point there. None, but I have two now." She leaned back, stretched out her legs, and rested her neck on the edge of the tub.

"Well, good for you. Didn't I tell you that people in Boise are friendlier?"

"Yeah, see that's the thing. I kinda need your help. You know the guy I met?"

"The stalker?"

Jessie rubbed her eyes and wondered why she told Andrew everything when he used it against her later, just like he was doing now. "His name is Fisher Kincaid, and I was wrong. He's not a stalker. We just have the same circadian rhythm, and he likes me."

"He likes you? Sugar, wake up and smell the Old Spice. He wants to get into your pants."

"How do you know? What am I? Unlikable or something?"

"Look at yourself." God she hated it when Andrew used his I'll-speak-slowly-because-you're-too-stupid-to-live voice. He picked it up when he minored in pop psychology, and she'd been waiting for him to lose it ever since. "You're gorgeous. What's not to like? You're sexy as hell in an I-don't-give-a-fuck way that dares a man to step up to the plate. But you've built so many walls. You're more impenetrable than a super-max prison."

"I don't have walls."

"Sugar, your walls have been firmly in place since your junior year in high school."

"You swore you'd never repeat what I told you."

"No, I swore I'd never repeat it to anyone else.

Repeating it to you is fair game. What that jock did to you was unforgivable, sugar. Taking your virginity on a dare was horrible, but it's time to get over it all ready." She had broken his nose when she found out and years later turned him down when he hadn't recognized her and tried to pick her up at her class reunion. She thought she had persuaded Andrew that she had moved on.

Jessie tried to erase the picture of the asshole-of-the-moment in her mind. "I'm so over Jamie Babcock. I was over him the second I broke his nose. I moved on years ago."

"Jessie, you like men. You may even have sex with them on occasion, but you only see them as the competition. You might be over Jamie Babcock, but you've never recovered. You've never trusted another man."

"I trust you. The last I checked, you're a man."

"You trust me and only me because I'm nothing like every other man in your world. I'm a writer, not a jock. I could give two shits about sports. Hell, in your eyes, I'm a girlfriend with a Y chromosome. In all the time I've known you, I've yet to see a man willing to fight the good fight and win. Sugar, I've seen you scare off more men than Mike Tyson with an iron deficiency."

Jessie chose to ignore the Mike Tyson crack, and the fact he dragged up an experience she'd rather not think about because she needed Andrew's help, and fighting with him wouldn't get her an answer any sooner. "Win what?"

"Your heart."

"I have a heart. I just don't believe in the happily-ever-after, fairy tale society has brainwashed women with since the beginning of time."

"That's old news and your convenient excuse to avoid getting hurt by men like Jamie Babcock. So, sugar, what's the problem?"

"It's Fisher. We're dating... sort of, and well, he's different."

"What does 'dating... sort of' mean exactly?"

"Since I rarely date—"

"Rarely?"

"You know, Andrew, this would go a whole lot faster if I didn't have to deal with comments from the peanut gallery. Do you want to help me or not?"

"Okay, calm down. I'm ready and willing to help you if I can."

"Good. Fisher knows about me writing a romance and my dating history."

"You told him about Jamie Babcock?"

"Hell no. Jamie is not the issue, never was, never will be. I told Fisher I don't date much, so he's offered to show me how a man romances a woman for research purposes."

"Well, that's one I've not heard before. Do you think he'd mind if I used that line?"

"Probably not. And guess what? It works."

"Really? Go on."

"Last night I was working on the book, while he made dinner. Before he put the steaks on, he asked if I was at a good stopping point, or if he should wait. And that was before we made our romance, dating deal."

"What did you do, shake on it?"

"In a manner of speaking." God, she felt herself blush. Talking about sex, even over the phone with her best friend, had her face heating.

"You had sex with him?"

She reached over and turned off the water, wishing she could dunk her head. "Well, yeah. You would have too if you were me, and he was cooking for you. He's amazing. He even made peach cobbler from scratch and homemade ranch dressing."

"I'm not seeing the problem here. Does he suck in bed?"

"Um… no. Just the opposite, he's perfect. Well, except he insists he rescued me when he didn't."

"And what would make him think he rescued you?"

She tapped her fingers on the surface of the water, watching the ripples. "Because my car broke down, and he found me climbing a mountain to see if I could get a signal to call for help."

"Sounds like a rescue to me."

"Of course you'd take his side, you're a man." She scooted down into the water to stay warm.

"Guilty. But back to the reason you're calling me at an ungodly early hour on a Saturday morning when you obviously like this man who cooks, is good in bed, and isn't a stalker or a rescuer. What's the problem?"

"I don't know. One minute I want to rip his clothes off, and the next I want to run as far and as fast as I can and hide. Maybe I'm PMSing. I'm not acting like myself. My eyes leaked."

"Your eyes did what?"

"Andrew, I swear, if you repeat one word I'm about to tell you, I'll write a tell-all book about you and send it to your aunt, the nun."

"Sister John Paul? You'd do that to her?"

"In a heartbeat."

"Fine, I swear. Now tell me what's wrong, so I can fix it and then get some sleep."

"After, well, you know."

"No, sugar, I don't know."

"What we did."

"Cook, eat, have sex?"

"Yeah, that last one."

"Okay, I'm following you. What happened after you had sex with Fisher, the rescuer?"

"Oh God, please don't make fun of me." She sat, pulling her legs to her chest and wrapping her arm around them, before resting her face on her knees. "I really don't think I could handle it, and honestly Andrew, you're all I have."

"Okay, I'll stop teasing, and I promise not to make fun of you. Now tell me what happened."

"Afterward, I started crying for no reason. I just bawled like a total whack job. And it wasn't as if I had anything to cry about. But I couldn't stop." She didn't hear anything, not even his breathing. She pulled the phone away from her ear to make sure the call hadn't failed. "Andrew, say something."

"I'm speechless."

"That's a first."

"Yeah, just like you crying. Maybe you're right, maybe it is just PMS. You know, you *are* a woman; you have hormones, maybe they just took over."

"They never have before."

"Unless you can't get your hands on chocolate, but then, if I remember correctly, you're more violent than weepy."

"I'm never weepy. I haven't cried in years, not even when I lost my job. Do you really think it was a hormonal malfunction and had nothing to do with Fisher?"

"I didn't say that."

"Andrew, your job is to make me feel better. You're dropping the ball in the best friend department."

"Sorry sugar, but I can't make a definitive diagnosis. Maybe it's PMS, maybe it's great sex, coupled with PMS, or maybe you're falling for this guy."

"That's ridiculous."

"Is it? Fine, but even you have to admit you have emotions. You feel love, hate, anger, jealousy, do you not?"

"I'm feeling angry right now."

"See, I'm right. You might not believe in romantic love, but you love me, you love your parents and mine. So, let's just take all emotion out of the equation. What's left?"

"Hormones."

"So, if it's true what you say, and you have absolutely no feelings for this guy you did the nasty with, then by process of elimination, your crying jag must have been due to a hormonal imbalance unlike any you've ever known. What else could it be?"

"Good. I feel much better now. I knew you would help me put things in perspective."

"Yeah, it figures you would. I think you're wrong, and I'm just telling you now for two reasons. First, you're too far away to slug me, and second, if I'm proven right, I can spend the rest of our lives saying, 'I told you so.'"

"You're right about the first and way off base on the second."

"Actually, if I were there, I'd be in the bathroom with you, and I have a feeling you'd have to stand in line behind Fisher when it came to a slugfest. Still, you're a hell of a lot closer than you were in New York. Maybe I'll fly out for a visit, so I can check out the guy you're dating for research purposes."

"Anytime. Just let me know when you're coming, and I'll introduce you to my new friend Karma. You'd like her."

"Are you okay now? Can I go back to sleep?"

"Yeah, I'll be fine." I hope. "Thanks. And you know… I really do love you."

"I know, sugar. I love you too. You have fun with Fisher, and call me when you get back to civilization."

Jessie severed the connection and set the phone on the vanity before soaking her head. She lay in the tub with her head tipped back, eyes closed, mouth and nose out of the water just enough to breathe, while she ran her hands through her thick hair, wetting it so it wafted around her head like jellyfish tentacles undulating with the movement of the water. She floated for a few minutes, letting the warmth soothe sore muscles, frayed nerves, and drown out all noise inside and outside of her head.

With her eyes closed against the bright sunlight shining through the big skylight above the tub, she lay still, calm, boneless, wishing she could stay there avoiding all the uncomfortable things in life—her job loss, her current occupation… Fisher. She didn't know how to handle him at all. Still, it didn't change the fact that he was waiting for her. She came out of the water, reached blindly for the shampoo, and hit human flesh that wasn't her own. Jessie wiped the water out of her eyes and crossed her arms over her breasts.

"I knocked." Fisher kneeled beside the tub, wearing nothing but a smile and his unbuttoned Wranglers. She could tell by the lack of elastic that he wasn't wearing a damn thing beneath them. "You didn't answer."

"I didn't hear you. Obviously." Fisher's eyes raked over her, and she was surprised the water around her wasn't boiling with the heat of his gaze. If her own hands weren't full, she'd be fanning her scorched face.

"Isn't it a little late for modesty?" His voice deepened and kicked her inner thermostat into high gear. He rested his arms against the tub and leaned toward her. His hair was wet from a recent shower and was just beginning to curl as it dried. "I kissed and licked almost every square inch of you last night and wouldn't mind doing it again. Did you and your girlfriend have a good talk?"

"Who?" Her brain was stuck on the kissing and licking part. It kept repeating like a scratched record on her parents' antique Victrola. Only this wasn't annoying, it was a turn on.

"Your best friend? The one you called."

"Oh right. Yeah. It was fine." God, she felt like a fool sitting in the bathtub holding her boobs and crossing her legs. She had no idea how to get out of the situation without either coming off like a bitch or a sex-starved maniac. "Did you need something?"

"I brought you towels and was hoping I could talk you into letting me wash your hair, scrub your back, and help you with the other hard-to-reach places."

"You want to wash my hair?"

"Ever since that day in the hot tub." He grabbed the bottle of her shampoo and took a sniff. "So this is what makes your hair smell so great." He shot her a grin that had his dimple winking at her and motioned for her to stretch out. "You'd better wet your hair again."

It was easier to close her eyes against both the embarrassment and temptation—her constant companions when Fisher was anywhere near. She slid under the water, telling herself he was right. It was nothing he hadn't seen before. She dunked under, ran her hands through her hair, and then sat quickly, spinning around with her back to him.

Cool shampoo plopped on the top of her head, and she expected the worst. Most guys she knew wouldn't think of shampooing a woman's hair, but then, maybe there were other sides to them she never saw.

Fisher's fingers dug through her thick hair, and he worked up a lather, massaging her scalp before drawing the shampoo through its length. He piled most of it on top of her head and then massaged her neck, moving to the base of her skull and up the back of her head. In less than a minute, he had her moaning.

His soapy hands moved to her shoulders and down her back. "Are you always this tight?"

She was unable to speak. A sigh escaped her lips.

He gently pushed her head toward her chest and ran his thumbs from the nape of her neck down either side of her spine.

"God, you're good at that."

He chuckled as he pressed her shoulders forward and massaged under the edge of her shoulder blades. "Glad you approve."

It was as if he knew every muscle, every pressure point, every sensitive spot on her head and back, and just how to touch it. One of Fisher's shampoos was better than every other massage she'd ever had, except maybe that one he did on her ass and leg. If she erased the memory of the pain she'd been in, she was pretty sure it would rank right up there next to his shampooing ability. She'd never noticed the tension in her neck and back until his magic fingers relieved it.

"I'll let you finish up while I start breakfast."

She looked over her shoulder. "You're leaving? Now?"

"Darlin', you're gonna get pruney if you stay in there much longer, and if I stay, we're never going to eat breakfast." He stood, the bulge in his jeans evident before he bent over, and gave her a peck on the lips. "You have ten minutes." He took another look at her, groaned, and left the bathroom.

Good thing the water was cooling. Still, she had a feeling she could be in a walk-in freezer with Fisher and still get hot.

Chapter 10

JESSIE DRESSED IN A PAIR OF SWEATPANTS, ROLLING THE waist to her hips, and a long-sleeved T-shirt, since she wasn't sure what they were going to do today. It would probably be smarter for her to talk Fisher into leaving, even though everything in her wanted to stay with him. She reminded herself that he wasn't her type—okay, physically he was, in bed he was, but the rest... She strode into the kitchen and found him in front of the stove.

"Great timing. The eggs are almost done."

He'd put on a shirt, and she tried to hide her disappointment. He piled steak, eggs, and hash browns on two plates and handed her a fresh cup of coffee.

"It looks wonderful. Thanks. This beats a PowerBar any day."

He followed her to the table and pulled out her chair. "Karma said you wanted to learn to fly-fish."

"I did, but I don't have to."

He leaned toward her. "It would be a real shame to come all this way and not get what you wanted."

Was it her imagination, or had his voice just dropped an octave? Visions of him above her, under her, and in the bathtub with her, flitted through her mind like fireflies on a hot, sultry summer night on Long Island.

"I'm the best around."

She ripped her eyes from his and stared at her plate. Yeah, she'd figured that out last night.

"I did it every summer from high school on. My brothers and I have a white-water rafting and fly-fishing guide company. Hunter's running it now."

She swallowed a mouthful of decadent hash browns and concentrated on not choking. He was talking fishing, and she was thinking about hot, sweaty sex. "A man of many talents, huh? A cook and a guide."

That dimple of his peeked out again. It was utterly charming. "Those are just two of my many talents."

Jessie cut into her steak and refused to take the bait. Still, it didn't stop her from thinking about the massages he gave, or the way he made love.

She caught him looking at her as if he could read her dirty little mind as well as he read her body. He made her uncharacteristically self-conscious. She pushed back her wet hair and wished she'd done something with it, or put on some makeup at least. Never one to put on makeup unless she was working or dressing up, all she'd done was put on face cream with sunblock and call it good. She was nothing like the women she'd seen throw themselves at Fisher. Just like she was nothing like the girls Jamie Babcock had dated before he took the dare. Still, she was all grown up and not looking for anything more than she and Fisher had. Sex was enough. Hell, it was all she wanted from Fisher or any man.

He took a sip of his coffee as she tucked into her meal. "Is it okay?"

"What?"

"The food."

"It's wonderful." She looked down at her plate. "It's also half gone. I'm not shy about eating… or much else, to tell you the truth."

."I like that about you. I can't stand when women pretend they don't eat anything. It definitely takes the fun out of cooking."

"I can imagine."

When he shot her a get-real smirk, she put her knife down and rolled her eyes. "Okay, I can't imagine cooking, which is probably why I don't. But it's got to suck if you go to all the trouble to cook for someone, only to have her put on an act, and pretend she's not enjoying it—especially if she's obviously holding out on you for nefarious reasons."

"That's an interesting word choice." He cradled his cup in his hands and sat back.

She shrugged. "That's what it is. Me—I'm a what-you-see-is-what-you-get kind of person. I'm not a good liar, and I don't care enough about what most other people think to bother lying about who I am. If they don't like me, that's their problem."

He raised an eyebrow and took a bite of meat.

"It pretty much made me an outcast during high school." It didn't help her that the entire school found out about the dare before she did.

"Were they blind?"

"I wore T-shirts and jeans when everyone else shopped at Bloomingdale's. I was a tomboy and better at sports than most of the boys, and they didn't like being bested by a girl. I stopped trying to fit in a long time ago."

"I'm sorry."

She shrugged. "I'm not. When I got to college I dated a few guys. It was fine."

"Still, that must have been rough."

"I went back for my ten-year reunion and wore a

dress, heels, makeup—the works. No one recognized me. When the bane of my existence asked me out, I told him who I was and left."

"It must have felt good to get even with him."

Not as good as breaking Jamie's nose had. She pushed her plate away. "Not really. I just felt stupid for showing up at all. I didn't think I wanted to impress them, just show them I'd moved on. But I only ended up feeling sorry for them. Maybe they'll change, but it seemed as if high school was the high point of their lives. Sure, a lot of them have married, a few more than once, but no one seemed to be soaring to the stars, you know? I couldn't find anyone who had achieved anything beyond the ordinary—at least no one who'd showed up. I had nothing in common with any of them."

"Have you soared?"

"I thought so. I had my dream job that I loved. I had exactly what I'd always wanted. Then a few weeks ago, I got laid off. For a while there I felt like my whole world crashed down around me. Now I wonder if soaring is all it's cracked up to be. The higher you fly, the farther you fall."

"So that's why you came out here? To get away?"

"That and I can't afford my apartment without a paycheck. I had to sublet it."

"And the book?"

"Fast cash. I'm staying in my best friend's house rent-free, but I still have bills. I can manage them working at Starbucks part-time, and that will keep me in health insurance too."

"Sounds like a good plan if you can sell your book."

"It's a romance. How hard can it be?"

He didn't say anything, but then he really didn't have to. He wore the same expression Karma had when Jessie posed the same question. She just hoped they were wrong. Fisher picked up his plate and reached for hers.

"Oh no, you don't." Jessie rose and took both plates. "I'm doing the dishes. It's the least I can do after you cooked, so don't even argue with me."

"Okay, if you insist." He followed closely behind her and leaned against the counter. "I thought I'd give you a fly-fishing lesson." He put away the butter and reached above her for a container before scooping up the leftover potatoes. God, the man smelled good. Even over the scent of the food he cooked, he smelled like pine, laundry detergent, Ivory soap, and something that was just him.

Fisher tossed the container in the refrigerator as she rinsed the plates and stacked them in the dishwasher. "With any luck, we'll catch our lunch and maybe even dinner. There's nothing better in the world than fresh rainbow or cutthroat trout. I swear I could live on it. Heck, I did every summer while I worked out here."

Jessie grabbed the cast iron pan and brought it to the sink. "Okay, but just because Karma tricked you, doesn't mean you have to teach me." She reached for the dish soap and he took it out of her hands.

"Darlin', you never wash cast iron with soap. You'll ruin it."

"What do you wash it with?"

"Hot water."

"But then it's not clean."

"Sure it is. If you use soap, you'll wash away all the seasoning, and then the iron will rust. Never, ever, wash cast iron with soap. And if it looks dry, just give it a nice coat of oil, and set it in a warm oven. It's better than Teflon if you take care of it. My grandfather has a fifteen-inch pan his ancestors brought over the Oregon Trail."

He took over rinsing the pan, scrubbing the bits of stuck on potato, and then dried it with paper towel. "As for staying, I'm not doing anything I don't want to do. Believe me, spending the weekend making love and fishing, and getting to know a beautiful woman, is no hardship."

She chose to ignore the whole beautiful comment. "Fine. I just didn't want you to feel as if you need to babysit me."

"Do you have a fishing license?"

"Of course." She put soap in the dishwasher and started it. "I bought one in Boise before I drove up."

"Good. Let me get a few things together, and we'll go."

Fisher led Jessica to the meadow. The river below filled the air with sound, cut only by the wind sliding through the pine trees on the opposite side of the clearing, and the birds calling out. The sun shone down on them. There wasn't a cloud in the sky, but the coolness of the morning lingered.

"Okay." Fisher laid the fly rod on the grass as he sat on the blanket he'd tossed down to shield them from the tall grass. He dug through the backpack he'd filled with bottled water, his ever-present first aid kit, and the practice leader he'd brought for Jessica's fly-fishing lesson. He tied one end of the leader to a piece of yarn cut from his project for his blasted knitting class, and the other to the fly line. He really didn't mind the knitting. Actually, he found it relaxing. He just wasn't sure how he'd get his homework done with Jessica around.

Jessica lay beside him, staring at the sky, focused on a hawk catching a thermal on the other side of the river.

"I have a practice leader on here. It's the florescent orange part, so it's easier for you to see." Grabbing the rod and stepping well away from the temptation lying on the blanket, he stripped some line from the reel and gave it a few false casts. "Are you ready for your first lesson?"

"Sure. Let's go down to the river." She got up and grabbed his backpack.

"Your first lesson is here." He slid the backpack off her shoulder and tossed it back onto the blanket.

Jessica picked up her baseball cap and stuck it on her head, pulling her ponytail through the back. She rolled her eyes before slipping on her sunglasses. "And just how am I supposed to learn to fish if there's no water?"

"You can't fish if you can't cast. Lesson number one is casting. The water and the fish would only get in the way."

"I thought the fish getting in the way of the hook was the general idea."

"Stand over here in front of me." He held the rod in one hand and her left hip in the other. "Feet shoulder-width apart, right foot slightly behind your left."

She adjusted her stance, and he stepped closer, holding the rod in front of her. "Your thumb sits on top of the cork handle. Now grip the rod like you would a golf club." The memory of last night and the way she'd gripped his rod, rose out of nowhere, and his body responded. Damn. He had to stop thinking about sex.

He wrapped his hand around hers, immediately feeling the tension. "It's a rod, not a bat. Relax your grip."

"Okay, it just feels weird."

It felt anything but weird to him. It felt amazing with her body tucked against his, his arm around her rib cage, her breasts resting against it. *Fishing, think fishing.* "First things first. You need to strip some line."

She turned her head, and her breath fanned his face. "I thought we were going to fish, not strip." She wiggled her ass against the growing problem in his pants. He held back a groan and taught her to cast.

By the time Fisher took her through the basics, coaching her on timing, rhythm, and motion, he was so sexually frustrated he couldn't see straight. He reeled in the line, his arms still around her, and then released her, stepping back, missing the press of her body immediately.

The sun caught the strands of gold and red running through her chestnut hair. God, she was stunning, and she focused fully on the rod in her hand. She hadn't even noticed he wasn't there behind her, guiding her, holding her.

Jessica stripped the line like a pro, cast, and gained distance—just like he'd showed her. Graceful, focused, beautiful, and if the grin on her face was anything to go by, she loved it. He couldn't wait to get her into the water. He adjusted himself and admitted he couldn't wait to get her back into bed again either. Hell, it didn't matter where they were. All he knew was he wanted to be inside her. Too bad she was more focused on the damn fly rod than on him. "Start reeling it in. I think you've got it down. I'll teach you the finer points in the river." He considered taking a swim. The ice cold water might help keep his mind on fishing.

Jessica spun around, and Fisher held up his hands to protect his face from being hit by a newbie angler with a nine-foot rod.

"Oh. Um… Fisher? What are the rules?"

God only knew what she was talking about now. "You lost me, darlin'."

She looked around and then at him. "Can I just put the rod down on the ground?"

"Yeah, or I can hold it for you."

"No." She gently laid the rod down and turned, looking up at him. "Thanks for teaching me. I think I'm really going to like it if I ever get the chance to actually fish."

Fisher stepped a little closer and pulled her shades off, so he could look into her eyes. "We can go now if you want, or we can eat. It's up to you."

"When's the best time to fish?"

"Early morning or at dusk."

She reached up and kissed him. It looked as if she were going for a simple kiss, but that wasn't at all what he wanted. He caught her about the waist, pulled her to him, and took full advantage of her surprised gasp to stake his claim on her mouth. She tasted like coffee, sugar, and excitement. Her whole body vibrated with it. He wasn't sure if it was the kiss that caused it or learning to cast. Either way, he wasn't going to question the outcome. He speared his tongue into her mouth and his thigh between her legs, tugging her closer. The scent of her, the meadow, and forest mingled, making an intoxicating combination.

She pulled her mouth away from his. "I've never had sex in a meadow before."

Finesse. He had none where she was concerned, and

he was supposed to be romancing her. What a joke! "We'll have to remedy that. Maybe tonight under the moon and stars, but for now, I didn't bring condoms. I didn't think—"

She pulled a handful out of her pocket and slid beside him as gracefully as a cat. "I did. We have a blanket and a half-dozen condoms. So now… what were you saying about stripping?"

He had her shirt off within a millisecond. With a flick of his wrist her bra followed, and thanks to her loose sweatpants, one yank had them slipping to her knees. She toed off her sneakers as he unzipped his pants, cursing the fact he'd put on hiking boots. "Shit. Give me a minute to get these off."

"No." She tackled him to the blanket, just about knocking the air out of him, pushed his shirt up, and before he knew what happened she had his shirt off, his jeans pulled down as far as they could go, and her mouth on his. She straddled him. When he opened his eyes, her face shielded the sun, and the light caught the colors in her hair.

God, she felt amazing. He pulled the ponytail holder out, dragged his hands through her thick hair, and angled her head to deepen the kiss. Tasting her like he'd wanted to for what felt like hours. "Jessica, let me get my boots and pants off."

"Oh, no." She shimmied down, and his dick came in contact with moist heat.

He sucked in a breath and slid his hands to her waist.

"I've got you exactly where I want you. You're at my mercy." She held his wrists and brought them up over his head, her breasts close enough to lick. So he did, and pulled a taut nipple between his lips, sucking it in deeper. She moaned, but didn't move, her hands still pressing his into the blanket. "God, you're good. You almost made me forget my plan."

"Plan?" He switched breasts, but didn't move his hands. He didn't need them. He used his lips, his tongue, and when he abraded her nipple with his teeth, he knew she was close. She rocked against him. One quick thrust, and he'd be in heaven. Before he could reach for a condom, she was on the move again.

"You keep your hands right there until I tell you, okay?" She gave him a quick kiss and moved to his ear. "I've wanted to do this since last night." She sucked on his earlobe and then nipped it with her teeth, sending bolts of heat right down to his groin. "I'm not going to let you deter me."

"But I want—"

She cut him off with a kiss. "Fisher," she mumbled against his lips, her eyes dark against the bright blue of the sky. "If you don't get what you want, you'll have your turn later. I promise." She didn't wait for a reply before she slid farther down, kissing his neck.

He did his best to control the urge to grab her hips and sink into her as she toyed with him, nipping his chest, licking a path down over his abs, sinking her tongue into his navel as his dick slipped between her breasts. "God, I've died and gone to heaven." The vision had his dick twitching and his hips rocking, thrusting, driving himself mad.

Her head lowered as he thrust, and his dick slid into the recesses of her open mouth. All control fled, and he bucked against her and let out a groan. "Jessica, please. I want to touch you."

She released him with a pop of suction and raised her dark eyes to his. They held enough mischief to make Karma look innocent. "Nope. It's my turn." Her hands held his sex. He started to protest, but when her tongue peeked out and licked the length of him, he lost all ability to speak.

Hot, wet, heaven. She slid her mouth over him, taking him deep, and when she sucked, the rush of blood drowned out the sound of the river below. He saw stars and wondered if it was from staring directly into the sun or from Jessica. Her hand held him in a tight grip. Her mouth and tongue danced and played tag with it, and all the while he could barely breathe. When her fingernail trailed over his balls, he couldn't help himself. He grabbed her, pulled her up against him, and then, wishing for the thousandth time he hadn't worn boots, he rolled her beneath him.

Jessie knew that was coming. Men could be so pushy. Unfortunately for him, his legs were locked together, and hers weren't. His kiss was searing, but she didn't let it distract her. She planted her foot on the blanket, and using a few wrestling moves of her own, rolled them back over and reached for a condom. "No hands. Today the tables are turned."

"What tables?"

She wasn't sure she could handle sex with all parts of Fisher engaged. She hadn't been able to last night and ended up blubbering like a baby. Maybe this way she could stay in complete control. She ripped open the package and tossed the wrapper in her shoe. The wind picked up, and her hair flew in front of her face, shielding it from Fisher's view and those hot green eyes of his. Even better.

Every muscle in his body tensed beneath hers as she rolled the condom down the length of him, sorry he'd interrupted her oral exploration. Today, he'd be the one losing control—at least, she hoped he would. She didn't have much experience with these things, but she figured it couldn't turn out as badly as last night had. The multiple orgasm part had been awesome; it was the waterworks after the fireworks that were the problem.

She laid over him, her gaze meeting his just as he raised his head, stealing her breath with a kiss, and thrust inside her—his tongue invaded her mouth with the same urgency his body had. They both fit so well. She almost came right then.

Fisher ripped his mouth away from hers. "Jessica, don't move. Please. Just give me a minute."

"No time-outs." She untangled her hands from his hair and sat, walking her hands from his shoulders to his stomach. His face looked carved in stone—tense, hard, and wild. She clenched all her inner muscles and rose above him, only to slide down in a heartbeat. Taking him in, loving the feel of him inside her, grinding against him, and doing a little hip swivel when their bodies met.

She set the pace, and he followed, sending her higher than she'd expected, so high she shot the spectrum of sound, color, and light. Everything blended into a cataclysmic crescendo that sent her reeling. She stared into Fisher's eyes, and they carried her like an undertow, so strong, so consuming, it was futile to resist. She'd always heard that if you just went with it, the undertow would eventually spit you out on shore, beaten and bruised, yeah, but alive. Whether or not you'd want to be when it was all over was the million-dollar question. The last time she'd been caught in Jamie's undertow, she'd been tossed back, all right. Only that time she hadn't wanted to live, and she never wanted to feel that way again.

Jessie collapsed on Fisher. Her gasps turned to tears, and fuckity, fuck, fuck, fuck. Her eyes were leaking again.

"This is getting to be a habit." Fisher pressed a kiss against Jessica's forehead and held her as her tears rolled onto his chest. He'd had the best sex of his life, twice, and each time it ended up with him getting cried on. "You want to tell me about it?"

She shook her head, trying to stop crying. It wasn't working. He rubbed her back, which only seemed to make it worse, but he knew whatever it was that bothered her needed to come out. The only way that was going to happen was if she let it.

Every tear that fell stabbed him like a knife. Still, he wished he could take all Jessica's hurt on himself. Anything would be better than watching her battle with the pain of whatever it was that would make the strongest woman he knew cry.

The real kicker was the tears probably had nothing to do with him, which sucked worse on too many levels to count. Not that he ever wanted to make Jessica cry, but shit, when a man has the best sex of his life with a woman, he'd want that woman to be thinking of only him. And except for a few arguments about Jessica's food choices, rescuing her, and dating her, she hadn't let him in far enough to hurt her. She had so many emotional no-trespassing signs posted, he wasn't sure how to get around them.

"I'm sorry." She slipped out of his arms and reached for her shirt, pulling it on. "Maybe this is a mistake."

Fisher rolled to his side, forcing a grin. "I agree. Remind me to never wear hiking boots around you again. It's not a good choice."

That made her stop, which was good, because she had her pants halfway up her legs. "What?"

"Look at me." He sat, bending his knees to his chest, and held out his arms, his shorts and pants bunched around his ankles. "I look ridiculous."

She let out a surprisingly girlie giggle and then sniffled. The way she dried her eyes with the back of her hands did something to his gut and had him wishing he could pound whoever was responsible for her tears.

"I think we're about even when it comes to the embarrassment factor." He dealt with the condom, stood, and pulled his pants up. As soon as he buttoned and zipped, he wrapped his arms around her. She didn't melt against him, but she didn't pull away either. "Let's take a hike before lunch."

"I have work I should be doing."

"It's not far, and it's in the opposite direction of the cabin. You can work all afternoon. I promise."

She stabbed her feet into her laced sneakers. Of course, she had runner's elastic laces. They gave more then regular laces, but still, it wasn't enough.

The tongues curled into her shoes, and he squatted and pulled them up for her. "You're going to love it." He kept waiting for her to agree. He was steamrolling her and wished it wasn't necessary. "It's where I go when I need time alone to think. It's a special place... to me at least."

He folded the blanket and threw it over his shoulder with his pack, grabbed the rod, and took her hand, leading her toward the river. "Gramps owns a bunch of land up here, and we've come camping here as long as I can remember. I was maybe six or seven when I stumbled on it. I was bummed when Hunter uncovered it."

"Why? I thought from the way you've talked about him, you two are close."

"We are... Well, we were... Aw hell, I'm not sure what we are anymore." Everything changed. How many times had he picked up the phone to call Hunter and put it down, not wanting to disturb him and Toni? How many days went by, seeing neither hide nor hair of his twin? They used to talk almost every day, or when their spidey sense told them to call. He hadn't felt that connection in a while, and that scared him down to his boots. "I suppose I needed my own space, someplace I didn't have to share—even with Hunter."

"Then why are you sharing it with me?"

She seemed as confused by that as he was. "I don't know." And he really didn't. It was completely unlike him. "Look, I don't know why you're upset, and I don't want to pry, but I do want to help. Hell, if you're anything like me, you might not even know what's bothering you. I've been there too."

"You have?"

"Yeah." Especially lately. "All I know is that when life takes a dump on me, I go there and always feel better. It might just help you too. It can't hurt."

She nodded and squeezed his hand. He wasn't sure what that meant. "When I was a kid, I used to think the place was magic. Sometimes I still do."

Fisher led her down the path he knew as well as the inside of his own home. He could run it on a dark, moonless night, and had not long ago.

Jessica kept up with him, which probably shouldn't have surprised him, considering the way the woman ran. He'd never enjoyed hiking with women, except for Karma, but then she wasn't a typical woman. In his experience, women either slowed him down, complained, or both. Jessica did neither.

He turned toward the river and helped Jessica over the boulders he'd thought had kept the rest of the world away. The sound of rushing water filled his ears, and he felt himself relax immediately. "Do you feel the river taking away the tension?"

"I'm not tense."

He placed his hands on her rock-hard shoulders and squeezed. "You're lying. I gave you a back rub, remember?"

"I remember, and I'm not lying. This is just the way I am. It's not tension. It's just normal."

He pulled her in front of him and pointed over her shoulder. "You see the circle of rocks up there? That's it, or it was before Hunter turned it into a glorified hot tub. Come on." He led her down the path he'd worn.

"How do you make a hot tub out here?"

"The area is full of hot springs. The water comes up so hot it will burn. Hunter encircled the spring with rocks, allowing just the right amount of cold river water to enter. I think he's got it at about one hundred degrees. Before Hunter hijacked it, you could scald yourself if you didn't know where to sit."

She looked at him with those big, deep eyes of hers. "You liked it better before."

"Yeah, it tended to keep people away, which worked for me."

"It must have really upset you. It's like when a guarded secret comes out, your pain is revealed to the world, you feel as if your privacy and self-respect have been stolen."

It just about killed him, but he didn't ask her what her secret was. He wasn't digging, though if she shared with him, it would be a big relief. Maybe if he knew, he could fix it.

"I wasn't happy when Hunter found it, but I never told him he'd discovered my sanctuary. Bringing you here is different. I want to share it with you. You're here by invitation, not invasion."

Jessica shot him a rabbit-in-the-crosshairs look, and he wondered who this conversation scared more—her or him. As much as it surprised him to say it, he didn't regret it. Having her here with him, holding her hand, and sharing this magical place, just felt right. That was enough to scare the crap out of him. The terror in her eyes didn't help either. He wrapped his arm around her waist and pulled her back against his front. "We can sit or soak—your choice. I'm fine with either."

"I'm not wearing a suit."

"That didn't stop you before, and you shouldn't let it stop you now, if you want to soak. The river traffic goes way down in September. There's not a soul around, but you and me."

He sat on a boulder and pulled her up, making space for her between his legs, wrapping his arms around her, guiding her to lean against him. He closed his eyes and drank in her scent, rosemary, mint, a hint of sex, and something that was all her. She melted into him, and he didn't say a word, letting the place steal her tension, her troubles, her pain. If she wouldn't share them with him, maybe for a while at least, she'd let the river wrestle with them.

Jessie rested against Fisher and watched the dappled sunlight sift through the trees on the river's edge. The sound of water soothed her frayed nerves. Their breathing in sync, in that moment everything felt right. Fisher made no demands, no comments, no questions. He just held her and let her lean against him. It felt natural to be close, which was strange. She'd never been physically close with anyone.

A picture of her and her parents at the Fourth of July fireworks flashed. Every other family seemed to be piled on one another, kids sitting on their mother's laps, men with their arms around their wives. She and her parents sat on opposite sides of their beach blanket, like stones holding down the corners, so the wind rolling off the Long Island Sound wouldn't pick it up. They were three people alone, together.

A picture of Jamie, holding her on his lap at a party in front of all his friends—people who wouldn't stoop to make eye contact with her, if not for Jamie. She'd gone shopping alone that afternoon to buy makeup and a sexy outfit for the party, and pretty underwear for Jamie. It had been the night they'd made love—or she had. Jamie had just been fulfilling a dare.

The next day, the loss of her virginity, and contrary to many people's disbelief, the fact she was indeed a woman, had become the talk of the school. She'd never gotten that close to another man again.

Not after Jamie.

Not until Fisher.

Sure she had a few affairs, but she'd never spent much time with the men. She'd never seen the point. Spending time with Fisher didn't seem to need a point.

"What do you think?" Fisher's voice rumbled through her back.

"I think you feel good. I think it's beautiful. You were right; it's a magical spot. But I also think there might be something to Hunter's glorified hot tub."

Fisher pulled her closer, his cheek resting against hers.

Jessie felt his smile. "It looks inviting. Maybe we should check it out later."

"Maybe you're right." Fisher's hold tightened, and she felt something slip a little farther out of her grasp. "I never considered bringing anyone else here, but with you, I can definitely see the advantages."

The way he said it sent a shiver through her. Advantages indeed. She'd never considered herself very sexual. Sex was okay when she had it, but it wasn't something she craved… not until Fisher.

With Fisher, she had a bad case of sex on the brain. Maybe he had an unusually elevated pheromone count—superpheromones. She reminded herself to get back to the library to research the physiopsychology of love, not that this was love—just extreme lust, but then with Fisher, *extreme* seemed to be the norm.

Jessie had never felt so relaxed around anyone, except maybe Andrew. But with Andrew, there was never this underlying current of sexual tension that threatened to overtake her entire body like whenever Fisher touched her. And Fisher touched her almost constantly.

She looked up at him. His hair was tucked under a backward-facing baseball cap. He should look like an idiot, but he didn't. He looked like a man comfortable with himself and his world. But then, she didn't know what there was to be uncomfortable about. It was obvious he hadn't needed to work for much. He lived with his mother. He probably had a trust fund from his rich grandfather. He came and went as he pleased.

What must it be like to live entirely without stress? That was one thing she'd never known. Her parents were fine financially, but after high school—after Jamie— she'd never expected them to support her, financially or emotionally. She'd never even considered asking for help with anything.

She'd worked through college to pay for whatever her scholarships didn't cover. She paid off her student loans within a year of getting her first job. She was completely independent, and she liked it that way. Still, being with Fisher had her on unfamiliar ground. *Wondering what he thought when he looked at her with those deep green eyes. Caring what he thought.*

"You're awful quiet. I thought you were getting over that."

"I was just thinking about my work. If we're not going fishing right away, I guess I'll get some writing time in."

"You could."

"That's a loaded statement. Did you have something else in mind?"

A smile played around his mouth. "Plenty, but I don't want to be accused of keeping you from your work."

"Now you're worried?"

"Not worried. I'm patient. I can wait. I'm a big boy."

Chapter 11

"JESSICA, ARE YOU ALL READY TO GO?" FISHER LOOKED up from where he was shoving supplies into his backpack and couldn't help but smile. Jessica wore one of Karma's fishing vests over a T-shirt, but she filled it out better than Karma did. Not that he noticed his sister's breasts or anything. He did his best *not* to notice them and made damn sure no one else did either. But he definitely noticed the way the too-tight vest hugged Jessica's. Damn, he'd never gotten half hard when he looked at a woman wearing fishing gear—not even the models he'd guided a few months before.

"Right." He zipped up his pack, threw it over his shoulder, and kissed her, watching the look of surprise that stole her expression every time he did. He was tempted to peel off her clothes again and make love right there on the dining room table. But that wasn't what she wanted. Hell, it had only been a few hours since they'd made love in the meadow. He didn't want her to think he was just after the sex, even if it was amazing. He'd wait. It would be painful, but shit, he was an adult.

He went over the list of supplies in his head: running shoes—check, condoms—check. He picked up the rods and wrapped his arm around her shoulders. Their legs were exactly the same length, which made walking close together much easier than with any other woman he'd ever walked with. She skipped, matching his step. It was as if his left leg was tied to her right in a three-legged race as they left the cabin and walked toward the beach.

Jessica had worked on her book the entire afternoon. Her fingers flew over the keyboard, and her beautiful face held such concentration. Sometimes he'd see her smile or hear that girly giggle that never failed to amaze him when it escaped. But even then, she was totally immersed in whatever she was writing. He'd give his eyeteeth to read it.

"How's the book coming along?"

She looked up at him and smiled. "I'm really beginning to like my hero. He's a lot of fun to write."

"And your heroine?"

"She's more difficult. I guess I just have a harder time relating to women. I grew up hanging around with guys. Women have so many layers, they're so complex, and they'll say one thing and mean another. I have a hard time relating."

He slipped his hand down to her hip and pulled her closer. "Tell me about it."

She turned as if she was revving up to do just that and realized he was just being sarcastic. "I always say what I mean."

"I'll give you that, but you can't tell me you're less complex than any other woman, or that you don't have more layers than a Vidalia onion."

Her face shone with exasperation. "You're not comparing me to an onion."

He laughed. "Hey, at least it's a sweet onion." He kissed her temple as they walked the path that led down to the beach, thinking about how he'd like to peel away her layers... and her clothes, and see everything that made up Jessica James—body and mind.

He wanted to teach her how to fish and watch her face when she caught her first trout, just like he watched her ride the wave of orgasm. He realized whatever he did with Jessica, whether it was making love, eating a meal, even fighting, was exhilarating. He'd never been much of a sharer before—sure, he'd shared just about everything with Hunter... well, until Toni. But he was beginning to understand that there were things between couples you couldn't even share with your twin. There were things about Jessica he'd never share even with Hunter, things that were just between them. With all his other girlfriends—even his real ones, he'd never felt that way. Maybe it was because he'd never loved his other girlfriends.

The thought stole the air from his lungs, and if he weren't in a freaking high mountain desert, he'd probably be sweating noticeably. Thank God for 15 percent humidity. His dead stop threw Jessica off balance, and she stumbled. If she didn't have great balance, she would have fallen right on her face, but he was too shocked to even react.

"What's wrong? You look as if someone walked over your grave."

Oh no. He wasn't falling in love. Was he? Hell, how should he know? Was there some kind of test? He'd never been in love before. He'd never wanted to be. But then, he'd heard the love bug tended to bite you in the ass when you least expected it. He'd had his share of love bites, but nothing like this.

"Fisher? You're looking really pale? Are you okay?"

"What?" Jessica stared at him, her big brown eyes filled with concern. "Yeah, I'm fine."

"Could have fooled me. Do you want to tell me what just happened?"

Shit on a stick. He couldn't very well say he realized he might be in love with her. She didn't believe in it. And wasn't that just the berries?

A ringing from his satellite phone broke the silence. He dug it out of the front pocket of his backpack. "Fisher Kincaid."

"Hey, you okay?"

His gaze returned to Jessica. "It's Hunter." He turned toward the river, almost happy that Hunter's spidey sense was still working. "Yeah, I'm great. How are you and Toni doing?"

"Fine. Are you sure you're cool? I got this weird feeling—"

"Yeah, I know what you mean."

"Can't talk?"

"Not now." Maybe not ever. Not about this at least. "It's all good."

"Okay, so something is wrong, but you can't talk about it. Nothing life-threatening though, right?"

"Right." It could prove to be painful, but not life-threatening. "I'll call you when I get back to town."

"Make sure you do. And don't forget you have class Thursday night."

"Like I'd ever forget that." He ended the call and took a deep breath. He was so screwed. Leave it to him to fall for a woman who didn't believe in love. How the hell can you prove the existence of romantic love? And how the hell was he supposed to know when he'd never been in it before?

—⁓—

Jessie pulled on the hip boots Fisher packed for her. They were Karma's, so they fit okay, even though they had rubber boots attached. The fabric was a pretty brown, gray, and green camo-ish paisley pattern and came up to her upper thighs, a few inches lower than her crotch. Karma's feet were smaller than her size nines, so the boots were tight, but not horrible.

Fisher stayed clear on the other side of the beach doing his own thing and ignoring her existence. He'd been Mr. Attentive all day, but ever since he'd stopped short on the path—as if he'd hit some kind of invisible wall, almost knocking her over—it was as if she didn't exist.

From the corner of her eye she saw him tugging on his waders and cursing under his breath. Cursing was out of character for him. She might not know him well, but the only time she'd ever heard him curse, even under his breath, had been the first time they'd made love. But then it was more a curse of awe than frustration. Because really, what did he have to be frustrated about? They'd both been having the time of their lives, or so she'd thought. This string of muttered curses was wrought with frustration, whether it was about his waders or whatever happened earlier, she hadn't a clue.

No matter how much he denied it, something had happened. Maybe it was the call from his brother that upset him, but she didn't think so. He'd looked as if he'd had a mental train wreck well before his phone rang. His color still wasn't good. Maybe he poisoned himself, but she'd eaten the same thing he'd fixed for lunch, and she felt fine.

She grabbed her pole and stepped into the river. She didn't need Fisher to tell her what to do. He'd already put a fly on her rod, so the rest was up to her. She could ignore people with the best of them. It wasn't her first choice, but if he was going to ignore her, she wasn't the type to run around asking what the heck was wrong. She didn't need his attention. "And he thought women were hard to understand. At least we don't lock ourselves in our virtual man cave," she muttered as she stripped the line and cast.

When the fly flew downstream on the river, she pulled it off the surface of the water, determined to tune him out and just enjoy the late summer sun bouncing off the quick flowing river. It really was breathtaking out here. She whipped the line behind her and forward a few times, picking up momentum before letting out line and catching distance. It felt good to be fishing, even if she had to ignore the man stomping around onshore behind her.

She heard Fisher stripping line downstream. So, he was going to keep his distance. That was just fine with her. She didn't want to know what was going on in that mind of his anyway. It was none of her business. She didn't have relationships for just this reason. She had never been interested in dealing with messy emotional crap—especially not someone else's.

The only thing she was interested in getting from Fisher Kincaid was sex and only on a temporary basis. If it turned out to be way more temporary than she'd planned, she'd be fine. She'd never had a problem going without before. Although she had a funny feeling going without wouldn't be quite that easy now that she knew what she'd been missing. Okay, so she'd like a lot more time rolling around with Fisher, but that probably had more to do with her PMSing than with him.

She pulled her rod back to cast again, but her timing

was way off—story of her life. Not only that, but she bent her wrist—what Fisher called breaking it in fly-fishing terms—lost her distance, and the line splashed a few feet in front of her. She looked over her shoulder and found Fisher staring off into space. Good, at least he'd missed her less than stellar performance.

Jessie ventured farther upstream—if he wanted to sulk, or whatever he was doing, she wasn't going to stop him. Tossing a glance over her shoulder, she realized she'd walked well beyond the beach. She turned to walk deeper into the river to keep from snagging her line on the bushes growing close to the shore. Reeling in some line, she talked herself through the cast before trying again. She didn't want to be caught screwing up. Just to be safe, she took another few steps. The riverbed beneath her feet disappeared, and the next thing she knew she was in over her head. Her waders filled with ice water as she kicked to get to the surface. She tried to kick her waders off, but the boots were too tight, and she was moving downstream fast. She bumped into a rock—a boulder. Pain radiated through her shoulder, and she turned so she could at least see where she was going, while she tried desperately to keep afloat as her waders dragged her down.

Fisher screamed her name just before she went under.

——⁓——

Fisher did his best to wrap his head around the whole idea of falling in love with Jessica. Maybe it was just the great sex messing with his mind. But then, he pictured the way she looked the day he'd met her. He'd been immediately attracted to her in a big way. It wasn't as if he'd never been attracted to a woman. He had, but his attraction to

Jessica grabbed him by the balls and made him do crazy things like run with her—maybe it wasn't love at all. Maybe he just had a latent death wish. Whatever it was had him worrying about what she ate. It made him want to know who had hurt her so badly she believed love didn't exist, and how he could go about fixing it. Damn, he had it bad. No wonder love was a four-letter word.

He stared downriver, hoping some answers would somehow magically appear. He didn't so much as look Jessica's way, because if he did, he might just blurt out his feelings, and that was the last thing she wanted to hear. He needed time to come up with a plan and make damn sure what he was feeling was love. Shit. Pretty soon he'd not only be knitting, but he'd be reading *Cosmo* too.

He heard a splash and then Jessica's scream. He pulled off his waders as she floated by. "Feet first! Jessica, point your feet downstream. Stay on your back." Fisher jumped in after her. How could he have been so stupid? He'd been so caught up the whole love issue, he'd neglected to tell her about the shelf, and she must have walked right off it.

He swam for her, and her head went under. With the fading light, she blended into the river, and he lost her.

He spotted her again just as she hit a boulder. It looked like she tried to grab the next one, but the river was getting rougher and pulled her down. Just a few more yards, he skirted the boulder she'd clung to, reached for her, and missed. Fuck.

Things were going to get dicier if he didn't get to her soon. Thank God, they were almost to the eddy. If he could get her to the eddy, they'd be okay. If not… That wasn't worth thinking about.

He kicked hard, ignoring the cold, and grabbed her arm, pulling her to him, holding her head above the water long enough for her to catch her breath. "Come on, Jess... Swim right, hard. Kick."

The boulder in front of the eddy was coming at them fast. Fisher spun them around, holding her close, protecting her body, taking the hit. He thought his back would take the brunt of the impact, but his head snapped back, and pain shot through him. He saw stars. He let the water pull them around the boulder into the safety of the eddy, letting them float in the whirlpool the large boulder he hit had created. The last thing he saw was Jessica's terrified, fuzzy face, before his world went black.

—⁓—

Jessie held onto Fisher as he sank. He was out cold. She held his head above water, thanking God she had her lifeguard certification and floated in what seemed like a whirlpool. At least the river had stopped dragging her down. She needed to get him on that big rock and out of the cold. For all she knew, he could be in shock.

She held onto Fisher and slipped beneath the water, testing its depth. When she hit bottom, she sprang up, pushing Fisher onto the rock. Damn, he weighed a ton. He was still hanging half off, but for now, he was stable. He was also unconscious and bleeding from the back of the head.

Shaking from cold and fear, she climbed onto the boulder, which was as large as a king-sized bed, but not nearly as comfortable. She grabbed Fisher under his arms and dragged him further up, trying to get as much of his body out of the water as possible, and then rolled him over. He was breathing, thank God. For a minute there, she wondered if she'd killed him.

She had to get him to shore, to his car, and then to a hospital. She just wished she knew how to go about doing that—supergirl she was not. They were only about three or four yards from shore. If she could get him out of the whirlpool, she should be able to swim for it.

Jessie pulled off the water-filled waders—not an easy thing to do with an unconscious man bleeding beside her—rolled them up, and threw them to shore.

Blood pooled beneath Fisher's head. She knew head wounds bled a lot, and the water in his hair made it look worse than it was—at least that's what she told herself. She took off the vest and T-shirt, wrung the T-shirt out, and wrapped it around his head. He was going to need stitches. "Fisher? Come on. You gotta wake up. I don't think I can get you to shore on my own."

The water had felt like ice, and even now that she was out of it, with the warmth of the rock seeping through her wet sweats, she shook uncontrollably. "Fisher, please wake up. Please."

She didn't know what to do. Should she leave him and try to get help? God, he could die out here. She heard herself whimper, something she'd never heard before, and fuckity, fuck, fuck, fuck, her eyes were leaking again.

"Damn you, Fisher. If you die on me, I swear I'm gonna kill you!"

She covered her eyes and cried. God this sucked so bad.

"I'm not dead yet."

Chapter 12

"STAY AWAKE, FISHER." GOD, EVERY TIME HE CLOSED his eyes, Jessie wondered if he was dead. She gave him another nudge, but she was afraid to take her hands off the wheel for too long as the Land Cruiser bounced up and down the steep mountain road.

She glanced at the directions to the hospital she'd hastily scribbled on a scrap of paper. Karma said it was a forty-five-minute drive during the day—once you hit the main road. But with night falling and the fact that she was driving a strange car down dark and windy, sorry-excuse-for-a-mountain-road, who knew how long it would take. But then, Karma had also said Jessie should take Fisher to the hospital if she thought it was necessary—as if Karma didn't.

Fisher had passed out for cripes sake. Sure, it had been for less than a minute, but so what? And he was bleeding. Okay, so the bleeding had stopped, or it seemed to after Jessie had washed the area and wrapped some gauze around his head. Still, she wouldn't be able to rest until Fisher got a clean bill of health.

She reached over to nudge him again.

"I'm up. Will you stop hitting me?"

"Don't go to sleep. You have to stay awake." She wasn't sure why, but she got the impression it wasn't a good thing for a person with a head injury to sleep.

"How could I possibly sleep after you stole my keys and insisted on driving my baby?"

Getting the keys wasn't hard to do, which just made her even more nervous. It was very clear to her that Fisher had an unhealthy relationship with the piece of crap he called a car. Lord only knew why, the damn thing had more ailments than a hypochondriac with a new copy of the *Physician's Desk Reference*. "I'm a great driver."

"Yeah, tell that to someone who didn't have to push your car off the road it never should have been on in the first place."

"God, are you going to bring that up again?"

She shot him a dirty look. Leave it to Fisher to still look hot with a bandage wrapped around his noggin, when she looked like something the cat threw up.

"I'd probably have a lot more to say if I could remember what the hell happened."

"I told you. You hit your head on a rock in the river, and I somehow pulled you onto that huge boulder close to your special place."

"Yeah, that's the part I don't understand. I wasn't planning to take a dip, and if I had, I sure as hell would not have gone that far downstream. It gets really gnarly down there."

Tell me about it. She sneaked a glance at him. At least she had his attention now, not that she'd wanted it before—back on the beach, before she'd fallen in.

Okay, so she had wanted him to turn back into Mr. I-can't-stop-undressing-you-with-my-eyes. She wouldn't lie to herself—not for long anyway. And she wouldn't lie to him… Hell, if he got pissed at her for causing his brain injury, at the very least, the anger might keep him awake long enough for her to get him to a hospital.

"I guess I went out into the river too far. I took a step,

and it was as if the bottom dropped out. The next thing I knew, I was flying down the river, and you were screaming at me. You grabbed me, but then you hit your head, and we ended up in a weird whirlpool. You fainted—"

"I didn't faint. I was knocked out."

"What's the difference?"

"Women faint with shock, if they have low blood pressure, for all sorts of reasons. When a man takes a blow to the head, he gets knocked out. There's a huge difference. Fainting is… prissy. I'm not prissy." He brought his hand up to the softball-sized lump on the back of his head. "It figures. I was rescuing you again."

She rolled her eyes. He didn't see it, which was just as well. "First of all, you need to retract the word again. That implies you've rescued me before, which you haven't. Secondly, I dragged you out of the river after you fainted. I ended up being the one doing the rescuing."

"You're going to have to show me proof, since I don't remember."

"Yeah, isn't that convenient?" She was sure the bloodstain was still on top of the boulder, but just the thought of it had bile rising in her throat. "Do you remember walking back to the cabin?"

"No, I remember waking up on the couch, wondering why my clothes were wet, and I had a headache like you read about."

That was a relief. "Isn't it interesting that you'd forget that I dragged you out of the river and through the woods? God, it sounds like a bad Christmas song." And felt like a nightmare. "You walked, like a guy on a three-day drinking binge. You said you were dizzy." She'd been scared to death his brain would swell, and he'd drop dead just like the bad guy in the last romance she'd read. She may have rambled on a bit about how the bad guy hit his head, and then a few hours later, he stood and fell flat on his face—dead as a doornail.

No, it wouldn't hurt her feelings if Fisher never remembered that, or the way her eyes sprang a leak when she'd thought he could die. God, just thinking about it made her eyes threaten to leak again.

"Do you even know where we're going?"

"Yes, I called Karma as soon as I retrieved your backpack. She gave me directions to the hospital."

A half hour later, Jessie pulled up next to the emergency entrance of the hospital and roused Fisher, something she'd been doing through the entire drive. Her arms were stiff either from dragging him from the river or just gripping the wheel like a lifeline.

"You're not supposed to park here."

"What the hell are they going to do? Give me a ticket?"

He pointed to the other side of the porte cochere. "You can park over there."

"By the sign that says Physician Parking? But I'm not a physician."

"What are they going to do, give you a ticket?"

At least he had his smirk back—that one with the winking dimple. She put the truck in neutral and put on the brake. "Let me get you inside before I park it, okay?"

"I'm fine. It's not that far. I can walk."

"Anyone ever tell you you're hardheaded?"

"I guess that's a good thing, considering."

Jessie parked in the doctors' lot, risking a ticket, tossed his backpack and her purse over her shoulder, and hurried around to meet him as he stepped out of the truck.

Fisher smashed up against her. She wasn't sure if it was because he'd lost his balance, or because he wanted her smashed against him.

She hoped for the latter, but was prepared to hold him up if need be.

"Now you smell like clear, cool river water and woods." He pushed her hair behind her ear and kissed her—just a sweet kiss that gave her a funny feeling in the pit of her stomach. His lips were so warm and alive, so unlike the way he'd felt a few hours ago. What a relief. He looked right into her eyes. His pupils were still the same size, which was good. "Thanks for rescuing me."

"And I was just beginning to believe you'd be okay, and you go and say something like that. Now I'm really worried. Let's get you inside and have your head examined."

"I'm not hurt… well, not badly. And I don't need my head examined. Unlike some people, I don't have a problem being rescued every now and then. It's nice to know I have someone watching my back. So thank you." He kissed her again and winced when her arm came around his neck.

"Oh, sorry."

"I feel like I got run over by a truck."

She wrapped her arm around his waist and led him through the automatic doors.

A petite blonde nurse looked up when the doors swished open and barreled around the desk. "Doctor Kincaid, what happened to you?"

Jessie saw the woman's lips moving. She heard her, but what she said just didn't compute.

"Doctor Kincaid?"

Whoa, something was way off. Fisher didn't know what happened, but Jessica stiffened under his arm and shot him a look that had him wondering if he should protect his privates. Jealousy maybe? Sure, Nurse Shaw was a flirt. Hell, she'd made more passes than Tom Brady, Aaron Rodgers, and Peyton Manning put together. It didn't mean he caught any of them. "Darla, this is my girlfriend, Jessica James. Jess, this is one of the ER nurses I work with when I'm up here, Darla Shaw."

"Great." Jessica tried to pull away from him, but Fisher held on to her. "Now that we've all been introduced, and we *really* know who everyone is, why don't you go back there and have your head examined?"

Fisher ignored her mumbling about lying, cheating men. Right now, trying to deal with his headache and the constant ringing in his ears was about all he was good for. "Darla, I need a CT scan. Could you see if they can squeeze me in?"

Jessica tried to disengage herself again, but Fisher kept his arm firmly around her. The nurse looked at Jessica and then him. "We need to look at that head wound before we do anything else, Doctor. And we'll need a doctor's order for the CT scan. You know the rules."

"I am a doctor. Just write up the order, and I'll sign it."

"Dr. Kincaid, today you're not a practicing physician. You're a patient. Go into exam room six, and I'll be right with you."

Darla had that don't-give-me-any-shit look about her, so he nodded, and immediately regretted the action as a wave of nausea crashed over him. Damn his head hurt.

Keeping his arm firmly around Jessica, he walked her into the ER and headed straight for the bed. He pushed his sore body up, wishing he could just sleep, but knowing Jessica wouldn't let him. He pulled her up beside him and probed the back of his head, wincing when he encountered the huge goose egg. Damn. No wonder his ears were still ringing.

Jessica sat rigid and madder than a wet hen. He might as well get this over with. He just hoped it wouldn't be as painful as the rest of the day had been... or would be. "Okay, what did I do?"

She speared him with another one of her killer looks. "If you have to ask, maybe you got your brains scrambled worse than I thought."

"What's that supposed to mean? Look, I don't remember anything that happened between the time I dove in after you and when I woke up on the couch. So if I did or said anything to piss you off in between, I'm sorry, but I really have no idea what it could be." Unless he told her he was in love with her. God, wouldn't that be awkward? But if he had told her, why would she be mad? She didn't believe in love. She'd be more apt to laugh at him than be mad, wouldn't she?

"You and Karma must have had a really good laugh at my expense, Dr. Kincaid. But that's just fine. I'll get you out of here, take you home, and that will be the end of it."

"The end of what? What the hell are you talking about?"

"This—you and me and this whole research fiasco."

"Darlin', I know I'm not as sharp as I usually am, but I haven't a clue as to what you're talking about. If there's something going on with Karma, if she said something, you'd better tell me about it. I don't have anything to do with it. If Karma is laughing at anyone, it's me. I'm the one who was set up to come out here, remember? Not that I'm complaining. Actually, I owe her a big fat thank you. Now, why don't you just tell me what the heck is bothering you?"

"I don't appreciate being lied to."

"To the best of my knowledge, I've never lied to you about a blessed thing."

"Bullshit. All this time I thought you were a trust fund baby living off your rich grandfather."

"Why would you think that?" It made no sense. "Hold on. If you thought that, why did you call me 'doctor' when you pulled your hamstring?"

"I was being facetious!"

"How was I supposed to know that? And if you thought I was something I'm definitely not, why is that my fault? If you wanted to know what I did, why didn't you just ask?"

"Karma knew what I thought, and she never corrected me."

"And I'm sure she had a good laugh at both our expenses. It still doesn't make it my fault. I would think you'd be happy to find out I actually have a real job."

Jessie didn't like feeling like a fool, but she had to admit that maybe it wasn't Fisher's fault. Jessie jumped to a lot of conclusions and never did ask him what he did.

The nurse rolled a cart in and looked at the two of them. "One patient at a time, Dr. Kincaid."

Fisher didn't look too happy to be interrupted. "Fine."

Jessie, on the other hand, was relieved. The sooner they got out of here, the sooner she could take him home and leave him in the loving hands of his mother.

Fisher released Jessie, and she wasted no time sliding off the bed. He grabbed her hand before she could get away—it was as if he'd read her mind and knew that had been her plan. She needed to get away—even for a little while. "I'll go wait outside."

He held tight onto her hand. "Don't go."

The nurse didn't even try to hide her curiosity. Jessie was sure that Fisher and his new girlfriend would be the subject of the next week's hospital gossip.

Jessie gave up her plan for an escape and stood when the doctor came in.

"Fisher." A hand came through the curtain and pushed it aside. "I heard you were giving Nurse Shaw a hard time." The doctor stepped through with a smile on his weathered face. His hair was gray, and he had some age on him, but his body and bright blue eyes belonged on someone much younger. The man was in amazing shape.

"Dr. Roger Gilg, this is my girlfriend, Jessica James. Jess, Roger's a neurologist, and we ski together whenever we get the chance."

"Nice to meet you." Jessie shook his hand and tried to get away again, to no avail. The doctor asked questions about how long Fisher had been unconscious, how disoriented he'd been, and how his motor skills were affected afterward—things only Jessie could answer. He ordered a CT scan and had the nurse clean the wound, before he closed the small gash with a few stitches. All the while Fisher stared into Jessie's eyes. The only time he let her go was when they took him for a CT scan.

Relieved, Jessie went to the waiting room and took a seat. She stared into space and tried to see Fisher as a doctor. Hell, she didn't even know what kind of doctor he was—not that it mattered. Though it did answer a lot of questions, like how he seemed to know her body even better than she did.

She picked up the hospital's brochure and paged through it. There was list of doctors, and there on the second page was a picture of Fisher. Fisher Kincaid, Doctor of Orthopedics. She read that he did his residency and sports medicine fellowship at Rush in Chicago, which explained the Chicago number on his satellite phone. He was even board certified. Wow, had she ever been wrong about him being a bum. It didn't happen often, and she wondered why she'd been so quick to jump to negative conclusions about Fisher. What did that say about her?

"Ms. James?"

Jessie stood when she heard her name. Dr. Gilg walked toward her. "Fisher's fine." He said quickly, even before she could ask.

"Good."

"He's refusing to let us admit him. He said he's in good hands and just wants to go home."

"Is that a good idea, Doctor?"

"Roger, please." He smiled and sat, patting the chair beside him. Jessie joined him, and he looked her over. "How are you doing?"

"Me?" What was he getting at? "I'm fine. Fisher's the one who took a blow to the head."

"He has a third-degree concussion. He also told us that you somehow got him out of the river. He's a big man. That couldn't have been easy."

"That's an understatement, but except for a few sore muscles, I'm fine."

The doctor removed a bunch of papers from a file. "Here's how this is going to work. Fisher's been given acetaminophen for pain. I don't want to give him anything stronger."

"Okay."

"The directions are all on here." He handed her the release orders. "You'll need to wake him every hour for the first twenty-four hours and make sure his eyes are dilated equally. If he vomits, I want to know about it. It's not unusual, but we want to monitor him."

"Great."

"Problem?" Roger raised a bushy eyebrow and waited.

Jessie wrapped her arms around herself to quell a sudden chill. "No problem." She got Fisher into this mess, she figured she could babysit him for twenty-four hours.

"He'll need to stay in bed for the next three days. He'll have some dizziness, and he shouldn't do anything more strenuous than walking back and forth from the bed to the bathroom. And knowing Fisher the way I do, you'll have to make sure he takes it easy."

"Sure, I can do that." Or his mother can. When the doctor rose, she followed.

"He's waiting for you in cubicle six. Here's my card. Give me a call if you have any questions or concerns."

She took the card and stuck it in her jeans pocket. "Thanks. I appreciate your help."

He smiled, looking a whole lot younger. "No, thank you. Fisher's been a godsend to us here at the hospital. We're all very relieved to know he's in good hands, and we're grateful for your quick thinking. From what Fisher said, this could have turned out very differently if you hadn't been there to save him." He took her hand and gave it a squeeze. "Unfortunately, I think rescuing him will seem easy compared to keeping him quiet for the next three days. Good luck, Jessica."

"Thanks, Doc. I have a feeling I'll need it."

—∿∿—

Jessie called Karma to update her on Fisher's condition. It sounded as if Karma was hard at work with a full bar, so Jessie didn't say much more than he had a concussion and was expected to make a full recovery. It wasn't as if she would ask Karma for help.

On the way back to Hunter's cabin, she made a plan. She packed their things before locking the house behind her. If she had to wake Fisher every hour on the hour, she might as well drive back to Boise. At least there was takeout in Boise, so she'd have something to eat, and once she dropped Fisher off at his house, his mother would be able to take care of him and follow the doctor's orders—letting her off the hook.

She needed to get back to work and get her book written. The last thing she needed was to play nursemaid. She so wasn't the type.

She drove from the cabin to the highway, past her beloved Mini. She made a mental note to somehow get it towed to the dealership and raid her savings account to get the darn thing fixed. This whole trip had been one disaster after another.

By the time she pulled up in front of Fisher's house, it was three in the morning. She'd already woken him up three times and was too tired to even think straight. All the house lights were off. She took the keys out of the car, left Fisher sleeping, and went to unlock the front door, hoping to wake Fisher's mother and give her instructions, before she passed out herself.

She banged her way into the house, turned on the lights, and went in search of Fisher's mom. The downstairs bedroom was empty, so she ran upstairs and found the two other bedrooms empty too. Where in the hell was Fisher's mother?

Jessie went to the car, opened the passenger door, and smiled when she heard Fisher's snore. His head had rolled back, and he was drooling. It was nice to know that he wasn't totally perfect. "Fisher, wake up. You're home."

When he opened his eyes, he smiled the sweetest smile, and his hand came up and caressed her cheek. "You're so beautiful, Jessica James."

"Are you sure they didn't give you drugs at the hospital?"

"Positive." He wiped the drool off the corner of his mouth on his sleeve and fumbled for the seat belt. She reached over him and unbuckled it, and the next thing she knew, he was kissing her. He pulled away, looked into her eyes, and pressed his forehead to hers. "Are you still mad at me?"

"No. It wasn't your fault. I should have asked you what you did instead of making assumptions. Let's get you inside. It's late, and I'm beat."

He held onto the door and stepped out slowly. She wrapped her arm around his waist and let him set the pace. "Where's your mother?"

"Mom? She's probably home. Why?"

"Well, I looked in all three bedrooms, and she's not here."

"Why would she be?"

She held open the screen door. "Because she lives with you... or you live with her."

Fisher let out a laugh as he headed toward the back of the house. "God, don't tell me you thought I lived with my mother too? It's no wonder you didn't want to go out with me." He laughed so hard, he ended up having to lean against the wall. His hand went to his head, and he laughed and cringed at the same time.

Jessie crossed her arms and rolled her eyes. "Okay, okay, it's not that funny."

"Sure it is. What the heck did you do? Tell Karma you thought I was a bum who lived with his mother?"

"Well, yeah." And she was sure Karma was still laughing about it.

"What made you think that? I brought you here, and you practically skinny-dipped in my hot tub."

"Have you looked at your house lately?" She motioned to the kitchen and shook her head. "The place looks like an advertisement for Merry Maids, it's so spotless. Even your linen closet looks like Martha Stewart came over and folded everything in it. And you said your mom did the gardening. What was I supposed to think?"

"So, I like a clean house. I thought women liked that."

"We do. We just assume your mom comes in and takes care of it for you."

He slid farther down the hall along the wall and turned into his bedroom. "Well, darlin', you have a lot to learn about my mother. She's been making us clean since we were in diapers. No one got out of it. Even Karma had to clean—of course, she gave it up as soon as she moved out of the house, but she knows how to do it. Mom likes to garden, so she comes over and plants flowers, but everything else is up to me."

"That's just great. Since your mom doesn't live here, it looks as if you're stuck with me."

"I already told you. I like being stuck with you." He slipped off his shoes and dropped his pants. He tried kicking them up to catch them and missed. "Damn. I'm afraid to bend down to pick them up."

"I'll get them. I suppose you put your shoes away too."

"Yeah, in the closet on the shoe rack."

Jessie picked up his pants and his shoes. "Anyone ever tell you that you're OCD?"

"All of my roommates. But then, I always cleaned up after them, so they didn't complain too much."

"At least not to your face."

Fisher held onto the edge of the bed and then the wall as he walked into the bathroom.

"Do you need help? Are you dizzy?"

"No and yes. I'm fine." He shut the door, and she waited for him to come out, picturing him passing out the whole time he was in there. By the time he walked back, his face was pale.

She checked her watch. "It's time for more acetaminophen. Lie down, and I'll get our stuff out of the car and bring you some water or something."

By the time she got back inside, he was snoring again. She set her cell phone's alarm for an hour and stripped out of her clothes, too tired to even throw on a fresh T-shirt, and climbed in beside him.

Every hour on the hour she woke him up, turned on the lights, checked his pupils, and then tried to get back to sleep. When she woke him up at eight in the morning, she felt as if she hadn't slept for three days straight. She set the alarm, rolled over, and like every other time, Fisher pulled her against him, spooning her, one hand holding her breast, the other on her stomach.

———

Karma pulled her Jeep out of the driveway on her way to check on Fisher and Jessie when her mother's ringtone blared from her cell phone. Shit. It was twenty minutes after ten, she hadn't gotten out of the bar until after three, and now her mother was on the phone. "Hi, Mom."

She drove through the North End and listened to her mother's worries about Fisher. "Mom, I told you last night, Jessie's taking good care of him. The doctor just told her to wake him up and check his pupils every hour."

Shaking her head, she remembered that her mother couldn't see her—well, not that she knew of, at least. "Look, they didn't get in until late, and I'm sure they're both exhausted. The last thing they need right now is people coming over at weird o'clock in the morning to check on them. Let them get some rest."

Karma ran her hand through her hair, which smelled like smoke. She'd been too tired to shower before bed like she usually did.

"You told the boys? All of them?" She cringed. "What exactly did you tell them?"

She turned on to Fisher's street and cursed when she saw both Ben and Hunter's cars parked in front of Fisher's house. "Oh, no. God, Mom. Fisher's gonna kill me. I've gotta go."

Chapter 13

LIGHT POURED INTO FISHER'S BEDROOM, AND EVEN with his eyes closed, the brightness made his headache worse. He groaned and slid Jessica's body closer to his, pulling the sheet over their heads.

Fisher had been having weird dreams all night, but this one took the cake. Beyond the constant ringing in his ears, he thought he heard someone come into the house and walk down the hall.

"Maybe that conk on the head was worse than the doctor thought."

That sounded like his cousin Ben, but what would Ben be doing here?

"Mom said Jesse James spent the night with Fisher, waking him up every hour." Hunter's voice cut through Fisher's foggy mind. "And there's definitely more than one body in that bed. I never thought I'd see the day my brother would be spooning with a guy."

"It could be a woman," Ben argued. "Maybe we should let them be."

God, this was no dream. It was a fucking nightmare.

"And miss this? Hell no." Fisher swore if he weren't already dead, he'd kill Hunter. "Besides, I know for a fact this guy Jesse James is the sports reporter Karma's dating. Look at them. If that's a woman, she's an Amazon. She's as tall as Fisher."

Hunter and their cousin, Ben, were standing over his dead body talking about Jessica.

But he wasn't dead. He couldn't be. If he were dead, he wouldn't be in so much damn pain.

Startled, Jessica moved in his arms as if she'd heard the same thing he had. Shit. Maybe it wasn't a dream or a nightmare after all.

A flash of heat flew through Jessie's body as her stomach tied itself into a knot. Not only was Fisher's family staring at her body covered with only a flimsy sheet, but they thought she was a man.

God, it was just like high school all over again. They'd dared Jamie to find out if she was a hermaphrodite—and taking her virginity had earned him bonus points. The memory of the stares and incessant whispering behind her back had her shaking and feeling like she'd just taken another dunk in the river.

The more things changed, the more they stayed the same. The only difference now was that this was the first time it ever happened in front of her. Worse yet, she could tell by the way Fisher tightened his hold, that he'd heard every word.

The front door slammed open, and she jumped.

"Ben, Hunter! Get the hell out of there."

Karma's voice screamed down the hall, followed by running footsteps. "Fisher, Jessie, I'm so sorry. I had no idea."

"You knew Fisher was sleeping with your boyfriend?"

"Hunter, Jessie's not my boyfriend, you ass. She's Fisher's girlfriend."

Jessie heard a grunt that sounded as if one of the guys just had the wind knocked out of him.

"Dammit, Karma. You didn't have to slug me. How the hell was I supposed to know?"

Jessie'd had just about as much as she could take. She removed Fisher's hand from her breast and grabbed the sheet that had sometime during the last hour been pulled over her head and brought it down under her chin, so she could see the group standing in the doorway. "Hi." She sat, making sure the sheet covered her breasts. "I'm Jessie, and I assure you, I'm one hundred percent female. Sorry to burst your bubble."

Fisher sat and grabbed his head. "Now would you mind getting the hell out of the room so we can get dressed and I can figure out how to apologize to Jessica?" Fisher did his best to smile, but the green tinge to his skin and the tension in his face just made him look scary. "Jessica, this is my brother Dumb, and my cousin Dumber, a.k.a. Hunter and Ben. You already know Karma, since the two of you have reportedly been dating."

The brawny guy stood there with his mouth hanging open. "Damn, you look like shit."

Fisher's arm came around her. "Hunter, you'd better be talking about me and not Jessica, or I'll really have to kill you."

"Of course, I'm talking about you. And hey, you can't blame me. Karma had us all believing Jesse James was a man."

"Yeah, but I was smart enough to put two and two together once I saw her. Then again, I've always been the brains of the family. Now get your collective asses out of here."

Ben waved a hand as he backed into the hall. "I knew

Jessie was a woman all along. Sorry for barging in. Fisher, Jessie—we'll wait for you outside. Take your time."

Karma shoved the still shocked and sputtering Hunter out the door and followed the guys, closing the door behind her.

Jessie let out a breath and covered her face with her hands. She didn't know whether to laugh or cry.

Fisher kissed her temple. "I'm trying to come up with an appropriate apology, but I'm at a loss. I don't even know where to begin."

Jessie knew her face was still flaming. She probably looked like she had a third-degree burn, but she'd have to face Fisher sooner or later. She pulled her hands away and did her best to smile. She must have missed the mark, because his face went from mad to enraged. "It's fine. They were just concerned about you. Are you okay? You look a little green."

"I'm pissed as hell, and if I'm green, it's only because I sat up too fast and my headache is kicking my ass. I'm so damn sorry. Remind me to get my keys back from them before they leave."

"You know, now that your family is here…" She scooted away from him. All she could think about was getting dressed and getting the hell out of there— preferably through the back door.

"Oh no, you don't. You can't leave me with those imbeciles."

"It's fine, Fisher. No harm done. I've heard a lot worse."

"What could be worse than what just happened?"

"Believe me, you don't want to know. Just drop it."

"Haven't you figured out by now that I want to know everything there is to know about you?"

"Why?"

"Because I care about you."

He was serious. She looked into his eyes and saw no deception, no agenda, no doubt. His lips quirked into the smile she'd come to know so well, a little tender, a little naughty, and a lot sexy, just before he kissed her forehead, her closed eyes, and then her lips. So soft, so warm, so gentle. His hand cupped the back of her head and drew her close. She wanted to sink into him, she wanted to believe, and she wanted to ignore the voice in her head screaming at her to run.

Fisher ended the kiss and watched the emotions race across Jessica's face. At first he'd felt her sliding towards acceptance and then do a U-turn straight into panic. "Breathe." Damn, it was a good thing he hadn't told her he loved her. That would have really gone over well.

Her eyes turned glassy, and for a second, he thought she was about to cry. If he was capable, he'd go beat the crap out of Ben and Hunter for upsetting Jess, but then, in his condition, he wasn't sure he'd even make it down the hall. "Darlin', you're gonna start turning blue if you don't breathe."

"I'm breathing." She dragged in a deep breath and blew it out. "Are you happy now?"

"I'd be a lot happier if I didn't have my family sitting in my den waiting for us."

"Us?" She blanched, and he tightened his hold on her as she eyed the door to the patio, looking for an escape. He couldn't blame her, but he sure as hell could stop her.

"Yeah, *us*, as in you and me." He took her clammy hand in his. "Come on. We need to get dressed. If we don't see what they want, we'll never get rid of them."

He stood, and his head spun.

"Fisher, I can't go out there."

"Sure you can. They're the only ones who have anything to be embarrassed about. It should be fun to watch the three of them grovel. Ben and Hunter have had a lot of practice lately, but it'll be good to see how Karma does. It'll definitely be a first."

"You think this is fun? God, Fisher, they thought I was a man."

"You were covered from head to toe. They had no way of knowing what a beautiful woman you are."

She let out a brittle laugh that made his heart ache as well as his head. "Yeah, right." She dug through the bag she'd tossed on the chair, pulling out clothes, examining them, and then discarding most. When she saw his questioning gaze, she threw a T-shirt on the bed. "I hadn't planned to meet anyone when I packed for a weekend in a mountain cabin."

Fisher held onto the wall as he approached her. Jessica, who'd always been so strong, seemed to wilt in front of him. He stumbled over to her, wrapped his arm around her waist, drew her back against him, and kissed her shoulder. "What you wear doesn't matter. You'd look beautiful wearing a potato sack."

She shot him a withering glance over the same shoulder he'd just kissed, grabbed a thong, a pair of yoga pants, a bra, and the Nike T-shirt she'd chosen, and then shot into the bathroom. It took him awhile to get there, because he had to hold on to furniture or walls to make sure he didn't fall over. When he slid in behind her, she had already dressed and was brushing her hair as if she were attacking it.

"Jessica, calm down, darlin'. Just give them a chance to apologize, and I'll get rid of them."

She stared at his reflection in the mirror. "Why don't you just go along without me? There's really nothing to apologize for, considering my size. They just jumped to a natural conclusion."

Fisher winced. "That I'd sleep with a man. I don't think so." He grabbed her hand and pulled her out of the bathroom. The movement made him nauseous, but shit, he just wanted this nightmare to be over, and the longer they waited, the worse things seemed to get.

Trapper stepped into Fisher's house and found Ben and Hunter running down the hall toward him, with Karma hot on their heels, hitting them over the head and screaming.

"I can't believe you guys just barged in on them. What the hell were you thinking?"

Hunter stopped short, almost running into Trapper. "We were thinking Fisher was in bed with Jesse James. That's what we were thinking. And we weren't that far off."

"What?" Trapper asked. "Did you just say Fisher was in bed with another man? Damn, and I missed it? Did Fisher know he was sleeping with a guy?"

Karma put her hands on her hips, and Trapper was tempted to step back. She looked madder than a hornet on flypaper. "He wasn't sleeping with a man. He was sleeping with Jessie."

"You mean that sports reporter?"

"Yes, Jessica is a woman, not that these two Einsteins could figure it out."

Hunter shook his head. "As soon as Fisher's better, he's going to kill us."

"You deserve it after what you just said about Jessie." Karma smacked Hunter upside the head again.

Trapper looked at his brother and cousin and raised an eyebrow.

Hunter threw up his hands. "She's gotta be six feet tall. Hell, she was able to drag Fisher's ass from the river to the cabin. She's no lightweight."

"You make her sound like Magilla Gorilla."

"We assumed exactly what you wanted us to, Karma." Hunter turned his attention to Ben and Trapper. "She set us up. Correction—she set Fisher up. Trapper, Karma knew you were leaving town, and that I couldn't get away from Castle Rock. If Fisher should be pissed at anyone, it's her."

Ben cleared his throat. "Okay, okay, this is getting us nowhere. Obviously, it's all Fisher's fault."

"What?" Fisher's voice came from down the hall. "How is it my fault that you two assholes came into my bedroom uninvited and insulted my girlfriend? And what the hell are you doing here, Trapper? I thought you were on one of your seventy-two-hour flings."

"Mom called."

"You answer the phone when you're with a woman?"

"Only if the caller ID comes up 'Mom.' And let me tell you, it's a mood killer for sure, especially when she tells me my little brother almost drowned in the damn river."

"I was rescuing Jessica."

Trapper gave the woman in question a thorough

once-over and winked. "I'm sorry. We haven't been introduced. I'm Trapper Kincaid, obviously the smarter brother. I'd have never mistaken you for a man."

"God, Fisher." Karma's hand flew to her mouth, and she sucked in a shocked breath. "Are you okay?"

Trapper sized up Fisher and cringed. His little brother looked about ready to fall over. He gave the phrase "pasty complexion" a bad name and didn't even sound like himself. "You look like the walking dead."

"Yeah, and it's great to see you too, Trap."

Jessie slid under the arm Fisher wasn't using to hold himself up and took some of his weight. It was as if they had some kind of silent communication. Fisher held onto Jessie like a lifeline.

Trapper had never seen Fisher lean on anyone. Ever. He would have sooner expected Fisher to crawl up the hall before he'd ever asked for help. He was always the one to carry the extra load.

Hunter stepped forward and looked Jessie right in the eye. "Wow, you sure look different than I'd imagined under the sheet. Then again, I'd imagined a guy."

Trapper sized up the group. Only Ben seemed smart enough to stay out of Karma's reach, and she looked ready to tear into Hunter again. One word from Fisher, and if Toni ever wanted kids, she and Hunter would have to adopt. Jessie looked mortified.

Hunter's stupid, crooked smile seemed to crumble, along with whatever was left of Jessie's composure. "Sorry about that," Hunter continued. "All I saw was the outline of your body, and you're really tall for a woman." He licked his lips. "I mean, well, I mean in a good way. Fisher's always been drawn to sturdy women."

Jessie's cheeks sharpened with color.

"You know, Hunter," Trapper said, "as a judge, I can assure you that when Fisher kills you, it will be considered justifiable homicide."

Jessie wanted to disappear—all five foot eleven and three-quarters of her. She had everyone's attention. She wished she was a half foot shorter, about sixty pounds lighter, and well, girly.

Jessie held Fisher up and cursed under her breath when she saw how much worse he looked than just a few minutes ago. "You need to lie down, and it's time for your painkillers." She spoke only to him, doing her best to ignore his family. "You should eat something too. We missed dinner last night." She walked him to the couch and figured it would be easier to get him into a sitting position if she sat along with him, holding him on the way down. She was afraid he'd drop like a stone if she didn't.

Karma, Ben, Trapper, and Hunter all stared with matching expressions of disbelief. She'd always used her height to her advantage; it had always been the great equalizer in men's locker rooms. But now, in front of Fisher and his family, it was turned against her. It wasn't as if she didn't know Fisher was way out of her league, even looking half-dead. She needed to get her game face back on. "I'll just run and get you some water for your pills."

"Hang on a second." Fisher kept his arm around her shoulder and held her firmly in her seat. For a guy who looked about ready to pass out, he was surprisingly strong. "All of you, apologize to Jessica, and then get the hell out of here. Oh, and give me your keys before you go."

The four of them spoke at once, either apologizing or

blaming the others, fingers were pointed, and the volume in the room rose.

When the front door opened, all chaos stopped, and Fisher groaned. "Oh God, it's Mom." He kissed Jessie's temple. "I'm so sorry about this."

Jessie tried to get up, but Fisher was holding her down.

Karma closed in on Jessie's other side. "And Grampa Joe's here too."

A woman in her early fifties walked through the door, hands on hips, looking fit to be tied. "Ben and Hunter, go out to the car and bring in the food I brought. Karma, you best put coffee on if you know what's good for you, and for God's sake, get Fisher some water and whatever painkillers he needs." Fisher's mom speared Karma with a do-it-or-die glare. Her green eyes looked so much like Fisher's, it was scary. "Trapper dear, how was your flight?"

Trapper took off his cowboy hat and kissed his mother's cheek. "Just fine, Mom. Thanks for asking. I came as soon as you called."

The one-woman tornado stopped directly in front of Jessie. "You must be Jessie. I'm Kate Kincaid, and I'm so sorry for whatever it is the three stooges did."

Jessie pushed Fisher's arm from around her and stood as an old man using a cane barreled in beside Kate. He tapped his cane on the hardwood floor. It looked as if he used it more as a prop than a necessity. "I'm Joe Walsh. You must be the little filly who saved my grandson's life. I'm grateful. I always knew Fisher needed a strong woman who could keep up with him. It looks like with you, Fisher's met his match. You can call me Grampa Joe. I'm looking forward to some fine, strappin' great-grand babies."

All Jessie wanted to do was strap on her running

shoes and bolt. Too bad the men were guarding the door. She knew she should say something, but words escaped her, and she sat down, deflated.

Fisher took her hand and leaned in. "Breathe."

Kate shook her head. "Don't pay any attention to that old goat."

Hunter carried in a box of what looked like food. "I've got to get back up the mountain. I left Toni waiting for the guys putting in the new quad-lift." He looked at his watch. "They should be there by now."

Ben followed him in. "Oh yeah, go hide behind your wife's miniskirt."

Hunter elbowed Ben in the gut. "Hey, I learned from the best. Like you don't have the plane waiting on the tarmac, so you can run back to Gina."

Karma jumped up to do Kate's bidding, and Gramps took her place on the couch next to Jessie. A bottle of water and an assortment of over-the-counter pain meds were procured.

Jessie shook her head. "Wait. Hold on a minute. Fisher can't be left alone for the next few days."

Kate smiled. "I talked to Karma, and it'll be fine. We know you don't cook, Jessie, so we'll be sure to bring over food until Fisher can get around on his own." She looked around. "Okay, everyone, let's leave these two to get some rest. Jessie, dear, you give us a call if you need anything. Anything at all."

"Wait, I can't... I mean... I've got to... don't you think Fisher would be better off with one of you? I'm not equipped. I have a hard enough time taking care of myself."

Grampa Joe patted Jessie's knee. "Aw, we'll be fine. We can take care of Fisher."

Kate's eyes flashed before she dragged Grampa Joe off the couch. "Oh no, you don't. Come on, old man. It's time for your Metamucil."

"You'd think with all the tree bark you feed me, I'd be as regular as a Rolex."

Kate spread her arms like a mother hen gathering her chicks and shuffled them out the door.

The snick of the lock sealed Jessie's fate. She was trapped.

Fisher wrapped his arm around her and tucked her under his shoulder. "Well, that was fun. Not."

She tilted her face towards his, so they were nose to nose. "What just happened here?"

He cracked a smile. That damn dimple was lethal. "Do you want the short version or the long?"

"Keep it pithy."

"The good news is the family likes you."

"And the bad news?"

"The family likes you. They'll be back."

"Fuckity, fuck, fuck, fuck."

Fisher pulled her with him as he lay back on the couch. "Okay, but this time you're gonna have to be on top."

"Sex is out of the question, no matter who's on top." Jessie ignored his mumbling, pulled away from Fisher, and rolled to her feet.

"Well, that's a damn shame, since it seems like my dick is the only part of my body functioning right now."

"You need to eat. Call it an early lunch. Then it's back into bed for you. Alone."

Jessie checked out the food situation. She wondered

when Kate had the time to prepare all the meals neatly stacked and labeled in the refrigerator. There was a big Tupperware bowl of homemade chicken noodle soup, that, amazingly enough, was still warm.

She reheated the soup in the microwave, brought it into the living room, and set it on a TV tray she'd found in the closet.

Fisher eyed the soup. "I'm not really hungry."

"Too bad, you need to eat. Doctor's orders." When he didn't make a move, she took a spoonful and held it up. "Either you eat, or I feed you."

He ate because she forced him. She ate because she was starving, and it was the best soup she'd ever consumed. She'd never seen homemade noodles before. Heck, she'd only eaten canned soup or wonton from the Chinese place down the street from her building.

After Fisher finished eating, Jessie helped him back to the bathroom. He tried to send her on her way, but she waited outside. He wasn't happy about it, but she didn't see why she should be the only one mortified that morning. It was a good thing she waited too. By the time he'd gotten the door open, he looked even greener than he had before, and she practically carried him back to bed.

She lowered the blinds, and then helped him adjust his pillows, before pulling the sheet over him. "Get some sleep. I'll wake you in an hour. Call me if you need anything."

"You're not coming to bed?" He grabbed her hand and tugged her to him. "You must be exhausted too. You've had less sleep than I have."

Jessie headed toward the door. "I'm fine. I've got to make a few phone calls and get to work. The book isn't going to write itself."

He looked like he wanted to argue, but he didn't. What could he say? She grabbed her computer and her phone and turned toward the living room.

"Jessica?"

She stopped and held onto the door frame, tempted to jump back in bed, curl into him, and forget everything that happened. "Yeah?"

"Thanks for staying."

"It's not a big deal."

He rolled over onto his side. "It is to me."

She shook her head and headed back to the living room. She turned on her phone, since she finally had cell coverage, and booted up her computer. When she looked at her voice mail messages, she didn't even bother listening to them. She just hit call and waited for Andrew to answer.

"You're back!"

Jessie laid on the couch, pulled the afghan over her, and put a pillow beneath her head. "Well, don't you sound chipper? Why all the phone calls, especially when you knew I'd be out of touch?"

"You didn't listen to your messages?"

"I knew I'd be calling you anyway, so why waste time?"

"Skype me. I want to see the look on your face when I tell you."

"I don't think you do."

"What's that supposed to mean?"

"It means I look like shit. I hope you have a strong stomach." She turned on Skype and clicked onto Andrew's account. His face popped up on the screen.

"Wow, you do look like shit."

"Told ya. Now what's got you so excited? A new woman in your life?"

Jessie sat back and smiled. She looked at Andrew through different eyes. She'd never noticed how handsome he turned out to be. When they'd started college, he was skinny and lanky, and well, geeky. In the last ten years, he'd filled out, worked out, and had gotten contacts. His bright blue eyes sparkled on the screen, a hint of a beard darkened his square jaw, and his smile showed off his parents' investment in orthodontia. How could she have not noticed how attractive he was before? "You know, Andrew, you're a really good-looking guy."

He squinted at her. "Are you feeling okay?"

"You really don't want to know."

"Of course, I do."

"Well, yesterday while I was fly-fishing for the first time, I fell into a raging river and almost drowned. Fisher jumped in after me and tried to save me, but ended up hitting his head on a boulder and passing out. I was the one who had to do the rescuing. He's got a third-degree concussion, and I'm sore in places that I never knew existed." She didn't mention that some of the soreness came from amazing sex, but there were some things Andrew really didn't need to know.

"Sounds like a good time. Where are you now?"

"Back in Boise, at Fisher's house. He can't be left alone, and his family has chosen me to play nursemaid."

"They obviously don't know you well. Either that, or they don't care much about your boyfriend."

"I tried to tell them, but they wouldn't listen." She didn't want to talk about Fisher's family. She still hadn't gotten over the sting of that morning's fiasco enough to laugh about it. She doubted she ever would. "So, what did you have to tell me face-to-face?"

"I was talking to a friend of mine over at ESPN, and he mentioned that they had an opening for a sports reporter. I sent him your stuff, and some of the online video interviews you did for your blog—part of the job is on camera, but the camera loves you almost as much as I do. You're a shoo-in."

"Oh, my God. Andrew, I love you!"

"I know." He looked way too pleased with himself.

"Mitch Seibert will be in LA the week after next. Just call his assistant, send her your resume, and set up a meeting. She'll make your travel arrangements. You can crash with me while you're in town. That will give you ample opportunity to thank me then in the usual manner." He waggled his eyebrows. "I hope you're up for an all-nighter." Andrew cracked a smile, and she wondered how much the tab would be in one of the swanky LA bars Andrew frequented.

"I'm up for anything. Paying up will be my pleasure."

"You know it, sugar. I can't wait to see you. It's been way too long."

"Yeah, it has. But don't forget, you're the one who left me in New York."

"You could have come with me."

"Yeah, right. What would all your women think?"

"No woman is as special as you. You know that."

"Aw, you sweet-talker. Look, I've gotta get some work done before I have to wake Fisher to make sure I haven't killed him yet."

"I wish him luck. He's gonna need it."

Chapter 14

FISHER SLID BACK DOWN THE WALL TO THE BEDROOM, praying his legs wouldn't give out and that he didn't throw up. He still couldn't believe what he'd heard. Jessica told the good-looking guy on her computer that she loved him—even after he'd left her. Was this Andrew the reason she'd given up on love? Fuck, he'd like to get his hands on that asshole and pound him into dust. And now, she was going to LA for an interview and planned to stay with him. And the worst part about it was that Fisher couldn't do a damn thing to prevent it.

Jessica had said she'd never been in love, that she didn't believe in it. Why would she lie?

Questions went round and round in his head as he lay in his empty bed, trying to figure out what to do.

A half hour later when Jessica came to wake him, he had more questions than answers.

"Fisher, wake up, big guy." He ignored her, until he felt the mattress dip next to him. She shook his shoulder, and he wrapped his arm around her, pulling her down for a kiss. He'd never felt possessive before, but by God, he did now. She was his. She might not know it yet, but he sure as hell did.

Jessica ended the kiss and put her shaking fingers to her lips. Damn, he'd never kissed a woman like that before—it was all he could do to rein in his feelings. As foreign as they might be, they definitely were there.

He didn't like it. Possessiveness, jealousy, and passion warred with his very real need to love her.

His hands slid beneath her T-shirt and snapped her bra open.

"What's gotten into you?"

"You have," he said and pulled her shirt over her breasts and took one into his mouth. He laved at her breast as he slid his hands into the waistband of her pants, pushing them down, feeling her wetness.

He rolled them down her long legs as he pulled her on top of him and slid into her moist heat.

Her eyes shot open and stared into his. Hot, wet, intense. He was gonna be faster than an owl licking a Tootsie Pop. One... two... three. Holy shit. No condom, but it was too late. She was coming, and so was he.

Jessica collapsed on top of him. He was breathing like a freight train, his head throbbed with the beating of his heart, and reality crashed down on him like a ten-foot wave of ice-cold water.

He closed his eyes and swallowed. Damn, he'd taken her like an animal. "Jessica."

"Hmm?" She nuzzled his neck before kissing his lips. "Are you okay?"

Well, at least this time she wasn't crying—yet. "I'll be fine, but we need to talk."

"Yeah, what about? Your performance? Considering all you've been through in the last day, I'm not complaining." She let out a girly giggle and then stopped when she looked at him. "Did I hurt you?"

"No, I'm fine. It's just that, damn, I wasn't thinking, Jess. I didn't use protection. I don't suppose that you're on any kind of birth control."

"No. I'm not."

"I didn't think so. I'm sorry. I've never lost my head like that before."

"Yeah, well, I wasn't thinking either. At least you have an excuse."

"No, I don't. So, I guess this is the time to ask how you feel about kids?"

"Fisher." She scooted off him. "It was just one time. I'm sure it will be fine."

He sat up and brushed her hair away from her face, so he could look her in the eye. "Darlin', one time is all it takes. Just ask my mother. Lord knows she told us all about it, over and over again, *ad nauseam*—not that it seemed to do any good, at least not where you're concerned."

"So now it's my fault?"

"No, it's definitely mine. I lose all control whenever you're near me. Jess, I love you."

Jessica blinked twice, and a flash of panic flew across her face before she schooled it. She took a deep breath. "No, you don't." She scooted away from him. "You took a blow to the head, and you're not thinking straight."

"Jess, I'm concussed, not crazy. Besides, I knew I loved you before we went for a dip in the river. That's why you were out in the river on your own in the first place. I was so busy trying to figure out what to do about it that I wasn't paying attention. I didn't warn you about the shelf."

"God, Fisher, what the hell do you expect me to say? You've known me, what? A week and a half? We've had great sex, three times. And now we're in forced confinement. You're confused. It's lust, not love."

"Sorry to burst your bubble, darlin', but I've been

in lust before, and this ain't it. This is about a billion times stronger."

"Well, stop it."

"I can't, and I don't want to. I love you, Jessica, so you better just get used to it. It's not going to change."

———

Jessie paced the living room. She'd been talking to herself for the last twenty minutes, and nothing she said made her feel any better. She hoped Andrew would be more help. "Andrew, he says he loves me."

"Was it in the throes of passion?"

"No. Just after that."

"Wow, I'm impressed. The guy's got a third-degree concussion, and he can still get it up?"

"Yeah, apparently that's the only part of his body that's functioning. He's definitely not thinking straight. Andrew, what the hell am I going to do?"

"Why do you need to do anything?"

She couldn't very well say, because they had unprotected sex, and she could be pregnant. God, she had terrible timing. She sank down on the sofa. "This dating thing is temporary." But a baby wouldn't be.

"Uh-huh."

"What's that supposed to mean? You're supposed to be supportive here. Tell me I'm right, and that he's nuts. He's known me a week and a half, Andrew. And I don't believe in love."

"Sugar, just because you don't believe in it, doesn't mean it doesn't exist. Hell, if our forefathers behaved like you, we'd still think the world was flat."

"Don't be ridiculous."

"You're the one having sex with him. You must care for Fisher, at least a little bit. After all, you're not acting like yourself. You saved his life, you're playing nurse-maid, and you're not running for the hills at the first sign of attachment. Don't knock love until you try it. It's not so bad, especially if the other person loves you back."

"Are you speaking from experience?"

"As a matter of fact, I am."

She heard something in his voice, a sadness that went straight to her heart. "What happened?"

Andrew cleared his throat. "Nothing. She never felt the same. It happens to the best of us."

"Who is she?"

"That's not important."

Jessie was stunned. She'd always thought that she and Andrew shared everything. Apparently not. "I'm sorry."

"Yeah, me too. Love isn't something you can control. Believe me, I've tried."

"Are you sure it wasn't just great sex?"

"Positive. I never made love to her, but I feel as if I've loved her forever."

"Well, if you're right, and love really does exist, she must be crazy not to love you. You're a lovable guy."

"Yeah, spoken like a woman who loves me like a friend. Enough about me. This is about you. What are you going to do?"

"Hell if I know."

"Do you like him?"

"Yeah, he's great. Well, except he's scaring the hell out of me. I'm still not convinced that blow to the head didn't knock a few screws loose. You'd think a doctor would have more brains than to fall in love with me."

"He's a doctor? I thought he was a bum."

"That's what I thought too until we walked into the hospital, and the nurse said, 'Doctor Kincaid, what happened to you?' Talk about a shock."

"How could you think he was a bum?"

"The same way I was convinced he lived with his mother."

"He's a doctor, and he lives with his mother?"

"No, turns out I was wrong about that too. I figured there had to be something wrong with him. The man is practically perfect. He's gorgeous, intelligent, he's got a great sense of humor, and he's an amazing cook. He's a little OCD and has an unnaturally clean house—hence, the reason I thought he lived with a Martha Stewart clone, but other than that, I haven't found a damn thing wrong with him. It's frustrating as hell. I was kind of banking on the bum thing, and the fact he lived with his mother to keep me safe."

"Safe from what? Safe from falling head over heels in love with him?"

"Oh fuckity, fuck, fuck, fuck."

"My thoughts exactly. Love isn't safe, sugar. They don't make protective gear like shoulder pads and helmets for the heart. This I know. I guess you have to decide if you've got the courage to stick it out. Or are you going turn tail and run?"

She didn't mention that she'd been eyeing the door ever since she'd left Fisher in the bedroom. "I've never run from anything in my life."

Andrew laughed. "Come on, sugar. You can't lie to me. I know you better than I know myself half the time. You've been running from love ever since Jamie

Babcock broke your heart. But you know something? Running from someone who loves you isn't that easy. They tend to chase you, and from what I can see, Fisher's been chasing you from the first day he laid eyes on you. It sounds to me like you just threw the game."

Fisher looked at his knitting and realized that Jessica had turned him into a serial yarn strangler. He was doing his knitting homework and keeping one eye on the clock, wondering if Jessica was still in the house, or if she'd run away. The tension in his knitting was going to shit.

He'd listened for her, but hadn't heard anything. He told himself that it didn't mean she'd left. The plaster walls tended to keep the house noise to a minimum.

When she escaped the bedroom, she'd closed the door, and left him too weak to chase after her. Damn this blasted concussion.

What the hell was he going to do if she left? Shit, she even had the keys to his car—not that he could drive, she'd been right about that. It would kill him, but he'd have to call Trapper or Hunter for help. It would suck, but not as bad as losing Jessica.

He tossed the sampler scarf he'd been trying to knit for her into a bag and stuffed it under the bed. He'd have to figure out how to fix it later. Maybe after he figured how to make things right with Jessica.

He'd just screwed up royally. He never realized he could be such a fucking caveman. He'd planned to give her time, not toss her over his shoulder and carry her off to bed, something he did not once, but twice.

Rubbing his temples, he wished away the ache in his

head and his heart. How did he ever get himself into this mess?

Fisher wasn't a man to just lie around and see what happened, no, concussion or not, he was a man of action—stupid action sometimes, but at least he wasn't letting life pass him by.

He tossed his legs off the bed and tugged on an old pair of sweats. He wasn't going to lie here and wait for her to come to him. He was going after what he wanted, and he wanted Jessica.

Taking his time, he got up slowly—at least the room had stopped spinning, a real improvement over the last time he'd tried to get up. He made it to the door without even holding on to the furniture. He pulled the door open and slid back down the hall, praying that Jessica hadn't run.

When he turned the corner and found her typing away on her computer, he shouldered the wall. Thank God he wasn't going to have to call in the A-Team, or in his brothers' case, the B-Team.

She didn't notice him, so he took the opportunity to watch her. She'd been working all day, and from what he could see, she wasn't upset at all. She looked tired, but at the same time, energized—like someone who'd just had a great workout.

Fisher cleared his throat, and she held up a finger before continuing to type. He sat down on the couch beside her, and she angled her computer away from him. At least she wasn't talking to Andrew—the other man, the man who'd hurt her and left her, and the man she had no problem telling she loved him. Damn, just the thought of it had his head pounding.

Jessica looked up as if she could sense his tension. "You're supposed to be sleeping for another twenty minutes."

He moved closer to her, and she closed the screen on her laptop. "You can't expect me to sleep all day."

"No, but the doctor said you're supposed to stay in bed for three days. Just think. You can sleep for as long as you want now. It's been about twenty-four hours since you got your brains scrambled."

"I didn't scramble my brain. There is nothing wrong with my cognition."

"That's debatable, but there's certainly nothing wrong with your vocabulary. You can play a hell of a scrabble game on my iPhone if you're bored. Your color looks better—you had that Wicked Witch of the West green thing going. Are you feeling any better?"

He took her hand in his and toyed with her fingers. "Actually, I am. The swelling is going down, the knot on my head is back down to golf ball size, and the headache is almost manageable."

"Good." She set her computer aside and rose. "Do you think you can eat something more substantial than soup now? I don't know about you, but I'm starving."

He stood too, maybe a little too quickly, but he wasn't about to let her know that—he still had a little male pride, after all.

He blinked once or twice, until the room stopped swimming, and did his best to smile. "Let's go see what Mom packed for us to eat. She must have been cooking since last night, after Karma called her."

She slid her arm around him, and some of his tension disappeared. He was sure she was trying to prevent him from taking a header, but at least she was touching him. It was a start, and right now, he'd take what he could get.

She shot him a concerned look. "Are you sure you want to go to the kitchen? You can stay here, and I can let you know what we have."

"No, I'm good. I'll just sit at the breakfast bar. I'll be fine."

"Okay, just let me know if you need to lie down."

She was acting as if nothing happened, as if they hadn't had unprotected sex, and he'd never said he loved her, as if she hadn't gotten dressed and run right out of the room. She was also avoiding all eye contact. That couldn't be good.

He climbed up on the bar stool, and she brought him a bottle of water and his pain pills. He'd never taken so many pills in his life, and he was already sick to death of it. He watched her move around the kitchen like she belonged there—okay, maybe not belonged there, but she fit. After calling out options, she proved she could microwave with the best of them.

"I got some good news today while you were sleeping."

Fisher looked up from his shepherd's pie. "My brothers have won the Darwin Award?"

"What's that?"

"It's an award given posthumously to those too stupid to live, thereby eliminating them from the shallow end of the gene pool. Accidental self-sterilization also qualifies."

Jessica chuckled. "Aren't you part of that same gene pool?"

"Yeah, but I swim in the deep end."

"More like you've gone off the deep end. My friend got me an interview for ESPN. They're looking for a new female sports reporter. He already sent them a sample of my work and a few on-screen interviews I had on my blog. They want me to fly out to LA the week after next for a meeting."

"Wow, that's great. Where's the job?"

"New York, I think. But there'll probably be a lot of traveling."

"Oh." He held back the word *fuck*, because he didn't curse in front of women, and he knew he should be happy for her. Happy was not what he was feeling. Panic was more like it, with a mixture of disappointment, and a whole lot of self-pity. "What about your book?"

"I'm still working on it. It's an interview, Fisher, not a job offer. Still, I have an appointment with my friend's agent, just in case. I've never thought about live broadcasting. I mean, I did some in school, but my size was always against me. Maybe with ESPN it'll be different."

"How can your size be anything but an advantage? You're beautiful, and perfectly proportioned. God, Jess, the way you talk, you'd think you were huge."

"I am. The average woman is five foot four. I was five nine by the time I was thirteen. I was taller than every kid in my school and most of the teachers. You heard your brother and cousin. They thought I was a man."

"My brother and cousin both need their eyes checked."

"I'm five eleven and three-quarters, if I slouch. If I wore heels, I'd be taller than you."

"I don't have a problem with that. I don't know why anyone else would either."

"Yeah, well, you're definitely in the minority."

"So, who's this friend of yours?" He knew damn well who it was. It was that creep who'd left her, the one she said she loved.

"Andrew? We went through Columbia together. We've been friends for years. He's the one who dared me to come out here and gave me his house to stay in. He's writing for TV now, but he's hoping to get into screenwriting."

Fisher wanted to ask more, but didn't know how without coming off like a jealous asshole, which, when he thought about it, was exactly what he was. "You know, I have some time off coming. Why don't we go to LA together, maybe head down to San Diego, and stay at the Coronado for the weekend? I promised you romance. This will give me the chance to do it right."

Jess just about choked on her dinner. "Gee, Fisher, that sounds nice, but I kind of told Andrew I'd hang with him for the weekend. We haven't seen each other in ages, and well, I wouldn't feel right just taking off with you and leaving him high and dry."

Fisher pushed his plate away. "Sure. I understand." It didn't mean he liked it. Damn, he couldn't believe how much he didn't like it. But he and Jessica had a deal.

"Besides, you're not going to be able to work until at least Thursday, and even then, you need to take it easy. It wouldn't look good for you to take off that next week."

"I got it, Jess. It's fine."

"Good. I'll only be gone for a few days, and by the time I leave, I have a feeling you're going to be sick of me. You'll be happy to see me go."

"Jess, I love you. I don't think I'll ever get sick of you. Well, not in the next fifty years anyway. Come on. Let's go curl up and watch some TV."

Jessie got up and collected their plates and put them in the sink. "Why don't I help you to the den? And then I've got to clean up the mess I made. I heard the guy who lives here is anal about keeping everything clean. Then I need to get back to my writing."

"I'll take care of the dishes in the morning."

She slid an arm around him and helped him get up. "Oh no, you won't. Doctor Gilg said you're to stay in bed for three days. You're not to do anything more strenuous than walk from the bed to the bathroom."

"I know him. He's a quack."

"He's a neurologist. And he warned me about you. Am I going to have to tie you down to get you to stay in bed?"

He nibbled on her earlobe. "I've got some silk ties, but I get to tie you down first. To hell with the TV, let's just go to bed."

She rolled her eyes, but couldn't disguise the shiver that ran through her. That was something at least. She might not look him in the eye, but she still wanted him. Of course, that didn't stop her from dumping him on the couch, handing him the remote and a bottle of water, and running back to her computer as fast as her long legs would take her. "Just yell if you need anything."

He needed her, and he wanted her tied to his bed—at his mercy. He just didn't think she was inclined to hear that. Hell, she hadn't looked him in the eye since he'd told her he'd loved her.

At ten o'clock, Jessica forced him back to bed, claiming to still be working. At four in the morning, he woke alone and found her asleep in his recliner with her computer still running on her lap. He saved her work, moved her computer, and wished he could pick her up and carry her to bed. He was feeling better, but he still wasn't up for that. Jessica was a handful, in more ways than one.

He tossed the afghan over her and watched her sleep

until the sun came up. Feeling the need for caffeine, and wanting to avoid looking like a love-struck adolescent or worse—a creeper—he tore himself away and headed to the kitchen.

He returned with coffee, heard the shower running, and followed the sound. Coffee could wait. Placing the cups on the counter, he tore off his clothes and stepped in beside her.

"Fisher, what the hell are you doing here?"

He wrapped his arms around her and pulled her in for a kiss. "I brought you coffee, and when I saw you in here alone, I thought I'd join you. Is there a problem?"

"No. I just never showered with anyone before."

"I don't make a habit of it myself, but I can make an exception for you." He poured her shampoo into his hand. "Turn around. I'll wash your hair for you."

She didn't look too happy about it, but she did. Within a minute he was massaging her scalp and the tension out of her shoulders. "I missed you last night."

"I worked late."

"You fell asleep at your computer. I came out to check on you at about four. I saved your work and covered you up. Why didn't you come to bed? Are you avoiding me?"

"No. I was trying to finish a scene, and I guess I was more tired than I thought. It happens."

Fisher didn't believe her, and she still wasn't looking at him—not like she used to. She might not have left physically, but emotionally, she had checked out. It was as if she'd erected some kind of invisible barrier between them, and he wasn't sure how to get past it.

Chapter 15

WEDNESDAY MORNING KARMA KNOCKED ON THE FRONT door to Fisher's house instead of using her key—she knew Fisher would take it away if he remembered she had one. Lord knew he was all over Ben and Hunter about barging in on him and Jessie.

Jessie opened the door, took one look at her, and went back to the recliner. "Fisher's in his room. Make sure he stays there."

Karma stepped inside. "Well, hello to you too. I'm fine. How are you?"

"He's driving me nuts. I think you might need to call for a psych eval."

"For you or him? Maybe the both of you, huh?" She carried the cooler full of food her mom had packed into the kitchen. "So, what's my big brother doing now?"

Jessie followed her like Karma knew she would and pulled herself up to sit on the counter. "I went for a run, and I came home to find him doing my laundry."

Karma did her best to hide her smile as she piled food into the refrigerator. So now she's calling Fisher's place home. Cool. "The nerve of him." She'd lay odds that Fisher scrubbed the bathroom too, but she wasn't about to say so. Fisher was still pissed at her because she'd sent Jessie to the mountains alone. Maybe Karma deserved it, but she had no idea Jessie would actually climb a mountain, trying to get a cell phone signal.

Anyway, Karma was on her best behavior and trying to help Fisher out to get back on his good side. Jessie looked like she was at the end of her rope—and from the looks of it Fisher needed all the help he could get.

Jessie jumped off the counter and paced back and forth between the door and the sink. "Fisher's not supposed to do anything more taxing than walking from the bed to the bathroom, and he's doing laundry."

"What can I say, it's a sickness. All the men in my family are neat freaks. I've just learned to embrace it. Sure, sometimes I go over to their houses and mess things up on purpose. You know, jump up and down on a freshly made bed just to get on their nerves, but really, what's there to complain about? At least you're not expected to do it. And I know from Gina and Toni that if you tried, you'd never do it well enough to please them. Take vacuuming, for instance. A normal person just runs the sweeper, giving it a once-over, right? But not Fisher; he vacuums in patterns. He goes up and down through the whole room, then back and forth across it, and then he vacuums on the diagonal."

"You're pulling my leg, right?"

Karma backed out of the fridge and turned to Jessie, who looked a little sick. "Afraid not. Some people go to therapy—my brothers, they clean. It's a lot cheaper, and us girls don't have to. A win-win situation, if you ask me."

"Karma, he was washing my underwear."

"I figure if a guy is close enough to get me out of my panties, he's welcome to wash them. I'm assuming Fisher's gotten you out of yours a time or two. Am I right?"

The blush covering Jessie's face told the story. "I knew you'd be perfect for each other. Fisher owes me big."

Jessie's mouth was hanging open.

Karma held up her hand. "But don't thank me. Just name your firstborn after me. It better be a girl though—just sayin'."

"But—"

"Thanks to all my hard work, the Kincaid women have almost overtaken the men. When you officially join the family, we'll be even with the guys—well, if we count Jasmine, Ben, and Gina's dog."

"Hold on, Karma. I'm not marrying Fisher."

"Sure you are. Fisher's in love with you, that much is obvious, and well, you're doing a really bad job of avoiding him. There's not a woman around who can withstand the Kincaid charm for long."

Jessie started pacing again. "You don't understand. He's not in love with me. He just thinks he is because he had his brains scrambled, and I saved his life. Or maybe it's Stockholm Syndrome—after all, he keeps saying that I'm holding him captive."

"Na, he loved you before he cracked his head open, and you saved him."

Jessie stopped and squinted. "How do you know that?"

"Hunter told me." Karma reached back into the fridge and pulled out a water. "He knows exactly when it happened, or when Fisher had the panic attack, after he finally figured it out. It's a twin thing."

"A twin thing?"

She cracked the top and took a long drink. "Yeah. Hunter even called Fisher to make sure he was all right."

"That phone call?"

"You were there?" She smacked herself on the forehead. "Of course, you were there. So what'd he look like? Damn, I wish you could have gotten a picture. I'd loved to have seen the look on Fisher's face. So, has he told you yet?"

Jessie ran her hands through her hair and tugged it so tight, her eyebrows rose. "Yeah, but he's wrong."

"I don't think so." Karma looked at Jessie and winced. Ouch, that's gotta hurt. Karma would have paid to have seen a shot of Jessie's face during that conversation too—especially seeing how well she was taking this whole love thing.

"If I just ignore it, maybe when his brain heals, he'll come to his senses."

"Wow, denial ain't just a river in Egypt, is it? So what's your excuse?"

"My excuse for what?" Jessie released her hair, thank God. Karma didn't think she'd want to walk down the aisle bald.

"For falling in love with Fisher."

"I'm not in love with Fisher."

"Uh-huh, sure. Maybe you need a conk on the head to knock some sense into you."

"I have enough sense to know that romantic love doesn't exist. It's lust, plain and simple."

Karma shrugged and took another sip of water. This could take awhile. "Okay, you've been in lust before, right?"

Jessie nodded, but eyed her as if she were looking for Karma's angle. Smart girl.

"Did the guys you were in lust with drive you nuts the way Fisher does?"

"No. But then I never spent much time with them."

"And why was that?"

"Because I didn't want to."

"And I suppose if one of them had gotten hurt, you would have been there for him, taken care of a guy you never spent much time with, right? You'd spend the night, waking him up every hour to make sure he didn't slip into a coma and die, worry about him doing laundry behind your back, make sure he took his medicine."

"Um... they'd never have asked. We didn't have—" She stalled with her mouth open and her hand moving as if trying to gather the invisible Scrabble letters necessary to come up with the right word.

Karma took pity on her and helped her out. "You didn't have the connection you have with Fisher. You didn't love them. Hate to tell you, but you're head-over-running-shoes in love with Fisher. Jessie, welcome to the family."

"But—"

Karma picked up the cooler she'd brought food over in. "Wish I could stay and chat, but I've got to get to work." She waved on her way out. Her work here was done. "Karma has left the building."

———

"I thought I heard Karma's voice."

Fisher was right behind Jessie, so close she felt his breath on her cheek. She wasn't sure how long she'd been standing there. Staring at the closed door. In shock. Waiting for Karma to come back laughing, saying she was just kidding. But Karma didn't come back, and Jessie knew damn well Karma hadn't been joking. She may be wrong, but Karma didn't think so—complete certainty about everyone and everything seemed to be a Kincaid family trait. As much as Jessie wanted to deny everything Karma had said, that little voice in Jessie's head kept telling her that Karma had a point—several in fact.

Fisher wrapped his arms around her waist and drew her back against his big, warm body. "Is there a particular reason you're staring at the front door?"

"Karma just dropped off some food and left."

"That still doesn't answer the question."

"No, no reason."

"You want to move this starefest somewhere more interesting? Sometimes I stare into the refrigerator until I figure out what to eat. We can try that. Or we can stare at the TV together. We can even turn it on first."

"Okay."

"Jess, are you feeling all right, darlin'? You're beginning to scare me."

She was beginning to scare herself too. "I'll live."

"You've been working too hard. Come on." He steered her down the hall toward the den. "Let's see what's on ESPN. That will cheer you up. I've got all five of them. I'm sure you'll find something you want to watch."

Jessie sat beside him on the big leather couch, pulled her legs up, and curled into him. Closing her eyes, she inhaled the scent of Fisher—Ivory soap, Right Guard, pine, and something intrinsically him. She knew it so well, she could pick him out in a lineup blindfolded.

She'd never noticed what any of her other lovers smelled like. She never noticed how their voice deepened and pupils dilated, changing colors when they got excited, or even what color their eyes were. Hell, she couldn't even remember how they kissed, or what they looked like when they came. But with Fisher, she knew, she watched, she noticed, and she felt.

"We can watch *SportsCenter Flashback*."

"Okay."

He lifted her and set her on his lap like she didn't weigh a hundred and forty-five pounds. "Jess, what's the matter, darlin'? I've never seen you so agreeable, not that you're not agreeable. Shit. I didn't mean that. Maybe 'placid' is a better word. Yeah, you're definitely not placid, ever, well, except for now."

"Fisher, do me a favor?"

"Anything."

She looked him in the eye, and she knew it was true. God, he really did love her. No one in her life had ever looked at her that way before, well, except maybe Andrew… She shook her head. But Andrew loved her like a sister. And with Fisher, she was willing to bet a six-figure book deal that what he felt was the furthest thing from brotherly. "Kiss me."

A slow smile spread across his face, and that damn dimple winked. "And I thought you were going to ask for something difficult."

Jessie took a breath a second before his lips touched hers—familiar, exciting, warm. She'd probably kissed Fisher more than any other person on the planet—a plus in her book, since he was one hell of a kisser.

He held her like a delicate flower, and in his arms, she felt like one. He didn't rush, didn't take. He teased and played until she sucked on his tongue. And then, it was as if she flipped a switch—or he stepped into Superman's phone booth. Gone was the easygoing beta, and in his place was a hot, demanding, determined alpha.

Fisher's hold tightened, the kiss deepened, and he groaned, sending shivers through her heart, her mind, her body. It should scare her, but all she could think of was that she wanted more.

More of Fisher—the nice guy who cooked and joked, taught her how to fly-fish, held her while she cried, and shared everything with her. More of the animal who'd grabbed her, tossed her over his shoulder, and took her to heights she'd never imagined existed. The same man who, even when he had a hard time standing, stood against his brothers and shielded her, had her car towed, and somehow got it fixed without her ever figuring out how.

She straddled him, and then she was the one to groan as his hands grabbed her butt and pulled her tight against him.

Fisher raised his hips and looked into her eyes. She knew that look. "God Jess, you slay me. You test my control—hell, you shatter it. I've never lost it before, but with you…"

It was the same for her. She'd cried on him—twice. She never cried, and never in front of anyone, not even her parents—well, not since she was six and broke her arm. With Fisher, after the mortification, and the fear that comes along with possible insanity, she'd felt safe, cared for, cherished. She'd felt loved.

Love—a four-letter word that spelled disaster.

Love—that scary, crazy, thrilling feeling she'd had since she'd met Fisher, the same one she'd had all those times she'd looked at Jamie Babcock, and wondered why he was with her and not the other half-dozen girls falling all over him.

The voice in her head screamed to run, but the look

in Fisher's eyes held her captive. So steady, sure, and possessive, that alpha thing worked like a virtual tattoo, branding her.

Fisher's phone rang and broke the spell. He picked it up and cringed. "It's Karma."

Fisher watched Jessie blanch and wondered if Karma had said something to upset her. He wrapped his arm around Jessie to keep her on his lap and answered, "You stopped by and didn't even say hi to me?"

"I had to get to work. I'm not allowed to lounge around in bed all day with servants to deliver my meals and take care of my every need."

"Don't push it, Karma. I'm off bed rest in a few hours."

"Oh good. Look, we have a Humpin' Hannah's softball game tonight, and you were supposed to play."

"I'm feeling almost back to normal, but I'm not up for playing softball. Sorry, kiddo."

"Fisher, I know that. I'm not an idiot. I was just thinking that Jessie could stand in for you. She's probably a better ballplayer than you are anyway."

"You're probably right. Hold on. I'll ask her."

He held his hand over the speaker. "I was supposed to play softball tonight, and Karma wants to know if you'll stand in for me."

"Sure. Are you going to be okay here alone?"

"I'm off bed rest today, so I'll go along and watch."

She gave him an odd look. "I don't know."

"Oh, come on, Jess. I've been lying around all week. I'm going nuts. Sitting on the bleachers is no more strenuous than sitting on the couch, especially if you're out of reach." He waggled his eyebrows and got a laugh out of her.

"Okay, fine. I'll play. You watch."

He took his hand off the phone. "Jessica said she'd play."

"Great. Just give her your shirt to wear. See you in a couple of hours."

Fisher tossed the phone down and picked Jessica up. She wrapped her arms and legs around him. Yup, he was definitely feeling better.

"Fisher, put me down. What the hell do you think you're doing?"

"Just following doctor's orders. I've got a few more hours of bed rest, and I want to put them to good use."

Trapper had watched Jessie walk Fisher to the stands before the game started. Damn, Fisher had it bad. If Trapper ever acted like such a lovesick pinhead, he hoped someone would put him out of his misery and just shoot him.

Maybe that conk on the head did some real damage. Trapper had seen Fisher with plenty of women over the years, and he was the least possessive person Trapper knew. Hell, half the time he'd have his head stuck so far in his books, he wouldn't even notice when the woman left. With Jessie, it was as if he scanned the crowd, ready to take out anyone who so much as looked her way.

Gramps took a seat, sandwiching Fisher between him and his mom in the bleachers.

Trapper almost felt sorry for Fisher. He was right in the line of fire and had no way of escaping. From the look on mom's face, she was on the warpath. She probably called Gramps on running off to the snack shack for hot dogs again.

Karma sat next to Trapper on the bench. "Fisher's acting like a jealous freak."

Trapper sat back and crossed his legs. "Yeah, someone's gotta talk him off the cliff before he jumps. He looks like he's just itchin' for a fight. If he doesn't watch it, he's gonna end up with his ass in jail, and Jessie on the Tomahawk Trail. She doesn't strike me as the kind of woman who would put up with much bullshit."

"He's in love with her, Trap."

Trapper tugged off his baseball cap and ran his hand through his hair. "Any idiot that looks at him can see that. So what's the problem?"

"Jessie doesn't believe in love—at least not romantic. She swears it's disappearing faster than the incandescent lightbulb, because women have achieved total equality."

Trapper raised an eyebrow. As far as he could tell, Jessie hadn't taken her eyes off Fisher either. "How can she not believe in love? She's in it."

"I know that, and you know that, but Jessie thinks it's lust—a temporary thing."

"Damn, so that's why he's wondering which one of us is going to be his replacement. How the hell is Fisher going to talk her out of that nonsense?"

"I don't know that he can. Hell, I've already tried. And if I can't do it, nobody can."

"Don't you think you've caused enough trouble? The only reason Fisher hasn't taken you over his knee is because one, he's hurt. Two, you don't fight fair. And three, you set him up with Jessie. The fact that he thinks you put her in danger still has you pretty high up there on his shit list."

"How the hell was I supposed to know she'd climb a

mountain when she's afraid of heights? Damn, Trapper. I'm not psychic."

He threw his arm around her. "I know you meant well, but you gotta admit, Fisher has a point. You knew Jessie was driving up in that windup toy car of hers. You knew she'd never make that last leg to the cabin."

"So, I didn't think it through. God, I was busy trying not to bust a gut over the way you jerks fell in line. You know, if you want me to stop messing with you, maybe you should all stop messing with me. I'm twenty-three years old, Trapper. I hardly need my brothers to threaten every man who comes within six feet of me. I have a fifth-degree black belt. I think I can take care of myself."

"Yeah, but that doesn't keep us from worrying."

"And that's my problem, why? It's not like I don't worry about you guys, but you don't see me threatening your dates."

Okay, so she had a point. It didn't mean he had to like it. Trapper shook his head. "I sure hope we win the game in this inning. Jessie hasn't stopped staring at Fisher the whole time he's been sitting there. It's like she can sense his anxiety. Good thing she's not like that on the field."

Jessica was up at bat and hit one right between second and third. She was off and safe at first. The girl ran like a gazelle. When the pitcher had his back turned, she stole second, and at the crack of the bat, she was heading toward third.

Trapper rose to his feet with the rest of the crowd. "Go, go, go!"

Jessica ran for home just as the outfielder bulleted the ball to Danny, the catcher. She hit the dirt. The girl had perfect form and no fear. She slid home, tagging the base before taking out Danny, who fell on top of her.

The ump threw up his arms. "Safe." The crowd went wild. Unfortunately, so did Fisher. He shot out of the stands at a dead run, whipped around the gate, and skidded to a stop a second before Trapper arrived, just as Danny's face lit up with definite interest. He slid his leg between Jessie's, putting his weight on his arms, and raked his eyes over her. "Are you coming to Hannah's after the game?"

Shit. There was nothing left to do but make sure Fisher didn't get his ass arrested.

Trapper stood by while Fisher grabbed Danny.

"Get the hell off her." Fisher tossed him off Jessie like a sack of potatoes, and when Fisher went after Danny, Trapper stepped in.

"Calm down, little brother. If you kill every man that asks your girlfriend out, you're gonna land your ass in jail."

"He was on top of her."

"Yeah, and since she doesn't have a ring on her left hand, or a tattoo that says 'Property of Fisher Kincaid,' Danny had no way of knowing she's taken. She's had a half-dozen offers since the game started and laughed them all off, so chill. She's not on the prowl. You have nothing to worry about. Come on." Trapper threw his arm around Fisher's shoulder. "Go dust her off, and congratulate her on winning the game for us."

Fisher turned to find Hunter had already helped Jessica up. Trapper joined Hunter and lifted her onto their shoulders. Jessica waved her hat, having the time of her life, paying no attention to the fact that both his brothers had their hands on her ass.

Trapper slid her down his body and gave her a kiss on

the cheek before releasing her. "Damn, Jessie, you keep playing like that, and you can keep Fisher's jersey and his place in the lineup. Come on back to Hannah's with us. Your beers are on me."

Trapper kept his arm around Jessica's neck, his hand hanging too damn close to her breasts, as if daring Fisher to say something. Shit, this was Trapper.

"Are you asking for a broken arm, Bro?"

Karma ran right in front of Fisher and gave Jessica a hug. "Holy cow, Jessie! You were amazing. I'll ride over to Hannah's with you."

"Sorry, but I can't go. I've got to get Fisher home."

He was just about to say he'd go too. Jess wasn't the only one suffering from cabin fever. Then his mom came up beside him and put her arm around his waist. "Oh no. Joe and I will take Fisher home and get him all settled in. You kids go on and have fun."

Jessie smiled at his mom. "Are you sure you don't mind?"

"Not at all. You need a break after being cooped up with Fisher for days. It's the least I can do."

"Hey." Fisher put up his hands. "I'm standing right here, you know."

Jessie looked at him. "Yeah, we know from the green tinge to your skin. You'd better go home. You don't look so good. It's past time for your acetaminophen."

"I'm a doctor, Jess. I think I know when I'm supposed to take my meds."

"Well, okay." She turned to Mom and Gramps. "I'll check on him when I get home."

Well, at least she was calling his house home, which was something.

His mother released him and stepped forward. Before

he had the chance, she gave Jessica a hug. "Don't worry about Fisher. He'll be fine. Just have a good time."

Karma grabbed Jessica's arm. "I have your bag. Let's go grab a pool table."

"Great." Jessica gave him a wave and walked away, leaving him with Gramps and his mom. Shit. Before she was ten feet away, she and Karma were surrounded by men.

Gramps rocked back on his heels and stared after Jessica. "You better keep that little filly on a tight rein, son."

"That would be a lot easier to do if you and Mom weren't so damn helpful. Whose side are you on, anyway?"

Fisher saw the look in his mother's eye and protected his head. "Uh, uh, uh. I have a concussion. No head smacks for at least a month. Doctor's orders."

When Gramps pulled into Fisher's driveway, Fisher waved his mother back into the car. "Mom, I've been putting myself to bed for twenty-five years. I don't need help doing it now."

"I know, but I told Jessie I'd make sure you were okay. She didn't see you toss that young man off her like I did. You're just getting off bed rest. You're hardly in any shape to try out for the WWE. What were you thinking?"

He was thinking that the guy was making a play for Jessica. That's what he was thinking. He deserved to be thrown off her. "I was afraid she was hurt. That big guy landed right on top of her."

"And I suppose that's why you threatened to break Trapper's arm too, huh, because you thought she was hurt?"

"You always did have great hearing." He ran his hands through his hair. "Mom, Jessica's special, and she has no clue how incredible she is."

"Fisher, did you watch her? Jessica doesn't even notice the attention."

"Oh, she notices it all right. She just thinks they're staring because she's tall and muscular, not because she's drop-dead gorgeous."

"Well, I'll be. Fisher Michael Kincaid, you've gone and fallen in love with that girl."

Shit. Could this day get any worse? There was no lying to his mom. She had better radar than the air force. "Yeah, but unfortunately, I'm the only one on the love boat. Jessica doesn't believe in love, and I have no idea how to prove it to her."

"Well, acting like a jackass certainly isn't going to help." Gramps laughed so hard he had to hold onto the car door to keep from falling over. "Maybe you should borrow that book on dating that Hunter used. Just make sure she doesn't find it like Toni did."

Kate gave Fisher a hug and whispered in his ear. "As much as it pains me to say it, your grandfather's right. And tomorrow, I expect you to call Trapper and apologize. Just remember, Fisher, Jessica's a smart girl. She'll figure it out eventually. Just be patient—give her time."

He'd promised he would, but by two o'clock in the morning, Jessica still wasn't home, and he was pacing.

Chapter 16

JESSIE SLIPPED HER SHOES OFF AS SHE OPENED THE screen door, so she wouldn't wake Fisher. She stuck her key in the lock, wishing she'd remembered to put some WD-40 on the hinges. She loved the old door. She just didn't love the way it squeaked every time it opened. She slipped in, put her purse on the table, and reached for the lamp, just as the overhead light clicked on. Busted.

Fisher stood at the end of the hall with a weird look on his face.

"What are you doing up? You're supposed to be in bed."

"I was waiting for you." He looked at her funny, his gaze moving between her face and her hands.

She tried to figure out why when she remembered she was holding her shoes. She dropped them by the door. "I took them off outside because I didn't want to wake you."

"That's funny. It looks to me like you were sneaking in."

"Why would I do that?"

"Why would you stay out until two in the morning when your boyfriend's home in bed?"

Jessie tossed her gear next to the door. "I was having fun, and you were supposed to be sleeping. You should have been. You're cranky." She'd missed him all night, which is why she stayed. Lord knew she didn't want to get too used to having him around.

She allowed herself to go to him then, wrap her arms around his waist, and lean in for a kiss, when the fifty she'd stuffed in her bra crinkled against her breast. "Oh, I almost forgot." She stuck her hand in her shirt and pulled out the Jackson to wave it in front of Fisher's face. "Look at what I won. I beat Trapper at pool."

"You did?"

He was shocked, and frankly, she'd been shocked too. For the first time, she wondered if a guy would fall for her old standby. Trapper seemed smarter than most.

"How'd you manage that? I've been playing pool with Trapper all my life, and I've never seen anyone beat him."

"I'm smarter than the average bear, remember?" His arms came around her, and she sucked in a breath, savoring his scent and the feel of him against her. She felt like she'd just come home after being away for a long time, which was strange because this wasn't her home. "I just used his male ego against him."

Fisher's hold tightened, and his hands slid under the hem of her T-shirt. "Do I want to know how you managed that?"

"We were playing Eight-Ball, and he was winning. He really is exceptional at pool."

"That's how he put himself through college and law school."

"Figures. I didn't stand a chance. I was losing by a few balls, and Trapper was going for the eight ball, so I bet him he couldn't bank it twice." She shook her head. "Guys fall for it every time. I only told you because he's too smart to fall for it twice. Though you'd be surprised how many men aren't."

Fisher walked her backward toward the bedroom, switching off the lights, undressing her along the way.

"I finally met Toni. She's a trip, and I mean that in a good way."

"Yeah, my sister-in-law is one-of-a-kind. I'm still amazed she puts up with Hunter."

"He must be doing something right because they didn't stay too long. Karma and Trapper had a bet going over how long it would be before one dragged the other out. It really wasn't Trapper's day. Karma took him for a twenty."

"I swear, I think there's a twenty and a fifty that keep getting passed around the family. They'll bet on pretty much anything."

"They're all great. Well, I'm still not too sure about Hunter. He kept giving me strange looks all night."

"Hunter's more of an observer than a talker."

"Not to mention a little scary. He looks like he's part pit bull. I think he scared Danny away." She shrugged. "Maybe he's the jealous type, but for the life of me, I don't know why. Toni never left his side."

"Danny wasn't after Toni, Jess. He was after you. I'm sure Hunter was just keeping an eye on you."

She let out a laugh, but when she looked at Fisher, he wasn't laughing. He was serious. "Don't be ridiculous. Danny's not the least bit interested in me."

"Yeah, right, that's why he asked you out when he was laying on top of you at home plate."

"I knocked him down. And for your information, Danny didn't ask me out. He asked me if I was going to Hannah's with the group. He was just being friendly." Wasn't he? Not that it mattered. She couldn't

imagine going out with anyone but Fisher. And that was
a problem.

―∿∿―

Jessie was cold. She rolled over to snuggle closer to
Fisher, only to realize he wasn't in bed.

Prying her eyes open, she checked the clock. Twenty
past eight. After the last time they'd made love, Fisher had
mentioned he had rounds at seven. She tried to muster a
modicum of guilt for keeping him up half the night, but
since she'd discovered sex with Fisher sans tears, she failed.

Scooting closer to his side of the bed, she grabbed
his pillow and pulled it to her chest, inhaling his scent
and wishing he'd at least woken her and told her good-
bye. Something was missing… Well, maybe it was just
Fisher and the coffee he always brought her.

She stumbled to the kitchen and found a thermos
of coffee sitting on the counter. She wasn't too sure
about the thermos, but when she poured, the coffee was
steaming. Okay, so maybe she did love Fisher—for his
coffee. The man definitely knew how to satisfy her in
the kitchen, the bedroom, the meadow, and last night,
the hallway was nice too.

She sipped her coffee as she pictured Fisher taking
her up against the wall. He'd had that wild thing going
again. Just the memory of the look in his eyes sent a
shiver through her. She rubbed her shoulder where he'd
given her the love bite that set her flying. Another first.
Shit. Just thinking about it got her hot and bothered.

Her phone rang, and she ran for her purse, thinking
that maybe it was Fisher—no such luck. And no, dammit, she wasn't disappointed. "Hi Mom."

"How was your trip?"

"Great." Jessie grabbed her coffee and sat on the über-clean counter. Fisher must have cleaned the kitchen before he left for work, the freak. She rearranged the cookbooks so they were in a random order. There, that was better.

"I was worried about you the entire time you were gone."

"Yeah, well, I ended up being up at the cabin with a man after all. He was lucky he had a woman with him, since I had to rescue him."

"What?"

Jessie told her mother the story—okay, not the whole story. She left out the dating deal, the really great sex, and the massages. She just told her the part about her car and her fly-fishing, white-water swimming adventure.

"I'm glad I called you, especially if you're not at Andrew's house. I forgot your address on the kitchen table, and I need it to overnight your package."

"You're sending me deli food?"

"Yes, and it's a good thing I bought enough for two, isn't it?"

"I'm not sure how long I'm staying at Fisher's, but I guess you might as well send it here, since he still looked a little green last night."

"That's too bad."

"It's his own fault. He was supposed to stay in bed, but insisted on going to a softball game. I guess I should be thanking my lucky stars he didn't play. And in the morning, when I got home from my run, I caught him doing laundry. Do you believe that? He was washing my clothes. Fisher's such a neat freak. After one visit to his house, I was convinced he lived with his mother."

Her mother laughed. "You can't be serious."

"You would have thought so too. You should see this place. His sister, Karma, tells me he vacuums in patterns, up and down, back and forth, and then diagonal—and that's every time he vacuums. I think he even cleaned the bathroom while I was out."

"Well, no one's perfect."

"Yeah, that's just it. He pretty much is. I haven't found a darn thing wrong with him, and believe me, I've tried."

"What's he do for a living?"

"He's an orthopedist specializing in sports medicine."

"Oh?"

"Yeah, that was real a disappointment. It was much easier when I thought he was a bum. Honestly."

"You'd rather date a bum than a doctor?"

"Of course. It makes it much easier to dump them when things don't work out."

"Jessie, if you didn't date bums or men with gross imperfections, maybe you wouldn't *want* to dump them."

Jessie walked back into the bedroom to grab a pair of Fisher's wool socks. Her feet were like ice cubes. She sat on the bed, set her coffee on the coaster Fisher left there, and rolled her eyes. "Mother, please don't start on this again. I told you how I feel about love and commitment."

"I know, dear. I'm just hoping a wonderful man who's not a bum changes your mind."

"Have you ever known anyone to change my mind?" She pulled up the second sock and wiggled her toes.

"No, but one can hope. And I have to say, Fisher sounds like the perfect man for the job."

"Sorry to disappoint you, Mom, but I'm only staying until I know he's better. God, I thought I'd killed him.

He was out cold, lying on a boulder in the middle of the river, bleeding from the head. I don't think I've ever been so scared."

"Oh honey, I know just how you felt. When we thought your father was having a heart attack, it just about gave me one. I can't imagine my life without him."

Jessie had no problem imagining life without Fisher—the thing was, she didn't like what she saw.

She rattled off Fisher's address and got off the phone as quickly as possible. She needed to stop thinking about him, about life with and without him, about love, or lust, and the way her stomach fluttered whenever he speared her with those green eyes or smiled with the winking dimple. And definitely not the way she felt when he made love to her.

Jessie sipped her coffee and ate a piece of toast over the sink, seeing no reason to dirty a plate.

The house felt empty without him. It wasn't as if she'd seen a lot of him over the last few days. She'd gone out of her way to avoid spending time with him, and she'd done her darnedest to keep him in bed alone, but just hearing him moving around and knowing he was there had been comforting. Even the way he snored was soothing. Yeah, she was definitely questioning her sanity now.

She took the last bite of her toast, and went over the plans she had for the next scene in her manuscript. Dialogue ran through her mind and she hightailed it to her computer, afraid she'd forget it if she didn't get it down right away.

When the doorbell rang hours later, Jessie got out of the chair and her back cracked. Damn, it was a quarter past one and she was still in her pajamas. Okay so they weren't really pajamas; she wore one of Fisher's Rush Medical School T-shirts and a pair of his gym shorts with the drawstrings pulled so tight, the fabric pleated, making them look more like a skirt than shorts. God, she hadn't even stopped to brush her teeth.

"Oh well." She opened the door and there was Fisher's grandfather, with four bags of what smelled like heaven.

"I brought my best girl lunch." He pushed past her and set everything on the breakfast bar before giving her a once-over and smiling. "I hope you're not one of those health food junkies like my Katie, because I brought you the best cheeseburger, french fries, steak fingers, and milk shake in the world."

Jessie couldn't help but smile. She held her hands to her heart and took a big sniff. "I think I'm in love."

Gramps put his arm around her and led her to a stool. "Well, of course you are. No one can resist my grandson for long."

"I wasn't talking about Fisher. I was talking about you. You brought me junk food. Feed me, and I'm yours."

"Jessie, my girl, if I were fifty years younger, I'd take you up on that—at least for a little while." He patted her knee and let out a laugh as he handed her a chocolate shake. "It would break Fisher's heart though, and to tell you the truth, I'm not sure I could handle a filly like you. You're going places, my girl. And I always wanted my woman close at hand. Now don't get me wrong. Fisher doesn't like the idea of another man looking at you, but he doesn't expect you to sit at home waiting for him."

"Mr.—" Shit, she knew his last name wasn't Kincaid, but she couldn't remember.

"Walsh, but you can call me Gramps. Fisher's a good

man, Jessie, and a hard worker. Did you know my grandson graduated second in his class in medical school and was valedictorian in high school and college? The boy always had his head in a book."

"I had no idea." Not that she was surprised. Fisher was annoyingly perfect even then. Sigh… why did intelligence have to be so damn sexy?

Gramps pulled out the burgers and passed her one. "I picked these up from the Westside Drive-In—the best food in town if you ask me. I even got you a surprise for dessert." He took a bag off the bar and put it in the freezer. "Of course, I bought myself one too. I'm a consummate gentleman. I can't stand to see a lady eat dessert alone."

"Gramps, would you grab the ketchup for our fries while you're over there, please?"

"Girl, you're in Boise now. We don't put ketchup on our fries. We use fry sauce." He opened a drawer, took out a kitchen towel, and tied it around his neck like a bib.

When she raised an eyebrow, he patted it into place. "Protection. Katie caught me sneaking a hot dog from the snack shack last night. I got a little mustard on my shirt, and now she's gonna be feeding me even more rabbit food than she usually does. I'm going to suffer for weeks, but I've learned my lesson. She's not gonna catch me again."

"Unless I rat you out."

"Girly, I'm eighty-two years old. If I want to have a cheeseburger and fries with a beautiful woman every now and again, I figure I deserve it. Hell, if it kills me, at least I'll die happy with a smile on my face and a mustard stain on my shirt."

Gramps took out the rest of the food, situating

something he called steak fingers between them, and enough fries to feed a family of four.

The fry sauce looked like a blend of ketchup and either mayo or ranch dressing and maybe relish? She wasn't sure. All she knew was it tasted like heaven on earth.

Boise might not have a great Jewish deli, but they sure knew how to do burgers, fries, and milk shakes. Oh, and those steak fingers were incredible. Gramps was, as he said, the consummate gentleman. He didn't even complain when she ate the lion's share of the steak fingers and french fries.

Jessie hadn't realized how hungry she'd been. Everything Kate and Fisher cooked was so healthy. Her body had been starved for grease, salt, and simple carbs. She took the last bite of her cheeseburger, licked her fingers, and laughed when she caught Gramps wiping his mouth on his bib.

Jessie sat back, full and happy. "Gramps, I can't thank you enough. Not only did you feed me, you pointed out Fisher's one flaw."

"I did no such thing."

"Yes, you did. He's a certifiable health food junkie."

"Not like his momma, he's not. Who do you think I usually buy this feast for?"

"Fisher?"

"Yes, siree bob. Once a month we go out together— when he was a kid, we'd go out once a week, but since I had my heart attack a few years ago, he's made me promise to cut back. This treat will be our little secret." He patted her hand. "Fisher's as close to perfect as a man can be. He's devoted to his family, his work—he loves both with his whole heart—and he's the most gifted and giving person I know. The only thing he was lacking was his other half. Now that he's found you, you both have the world at your feet. You're lucky to find someone to love right when your stars are starting to rise."

"Gramps, I'm afraid you have the wrong idea about Fisher and me."

"Nonsense! These eyes might be old, but they don't miss much. I know you're in love with my grandson, little lady. And if you haven't figured it out yet, it won't be too long because you, my dear, are exceptional, just like Fisher. You're a smart girl. You'll see that life is nothing if you don't have someone to share it with. And for you, that someone is Fisher."

Gramps slid off his stool with the grace of a man half his age. He kissed her cheek and patted her back. "You know, Jessie, it's about time you took a breath. You're going to turn blue soon."

He gave her a smack on the back, and she dragged in a lungful of air. "There you go. Good luck on that interview next week with ESPN. Mitch Seibert would be an idiot if he didn't hire you on the spot." He grabbed his cane and headed toward the door. "I'll just leave the dessert for you and Fisher to have later. I've got to get home. If I'm gone too long, Katie gets suspicious."

"Gramps?"

"Yes?"

"You might want to take off the bib before you go. If Kate sees that, the jig will be up."

He took the towel from around his neck, tossed it to her, and winked before he danced out the door.

———~~~———

Fisher pulled his Roadster into the garage and let out a sigh of relief. Damn, he'd been doing a lot of that lately—every time he realized Jessica hadn't left—yet. But she would leave, that was pretty much a definite. Whether she'd come back was the only question in his mind.

He tossed his knitting he'd taken to class in his backpack, shouldered it and his medical bag, and went around the back of the house to make sure the automatic sprinkler system was set.

Jessica sat on the deck, working on her laptop with a smile on her face, the evening sun shining in her hair. When he closed the gate, she looked up from her computer, spotted him, and smiled. His T-shirt had slipped off her shoulder, showing off her long neck.

"You're home." She put her laptop on the table and met him on the step, looking down at her sock-covered feet. "Sorry. I swiped a pair of your socks. My feet were freezing this morning."

Fisher dropped his pack and his medical bag on the bottom step and held his arms open.

Jessica lunged for him, wrapping her arms around his neck for a kiss.

He'd hoped for a kiss, but hadn't expected that. Fisher was lucky he hadn't ended up on his ass in the grass. He took a step back to regain his balance, gripped her backside with both hands, and kissed her like he'd wanted to since he slid out of bed that morning. It had taken all his willpower not to wake her and watch the smile that lit her face whenever she saw him. Hell, who was he kidding? It had taken all his willpower not to wake her and make love to her again.

Fisher kept kissing her as he carried her into the

house. He didn't stop until he felt the edge of the bed
hit the back of his knees and sat. God, she had him so
worked up. He needed to slow things down, or he was
going to go off like a bottle rocket.

She scooted up on his lap and pulled her shirt off,
tossing it on the floor. His mouth went to her breasts,
as he rolled them both over, tugging her shorts down
her hips.

"No panties?"

"I got so caught up in writing. I never bothered to get
dressed. And then your grandfather came over—"

If there was a way to slow things down, any mention
of his family while they were making love certainly did
the job. He slid his mouth off her breast and looked into
her eyes. At least she didn't look upset. "Gramps came
over?" He rolled off her and stared at the ceiling, trying
to get his breathing under control. It was a miracle she
wasn't halfway to Montana by now.

She snuggled up to him and threw her bare leg over his
waist. "He brought me lunch from the Westside Drive-In."

"Mom's gonna kill him. You'd think he'd give it a
break after getting caught eating a hot dog last night."

The flecks of gold in her eyes sparkled. "He wore a
bib today."

"A bib?"

"Yeah, he tied one of your kitchen towels around his
neck, so he wouldn't drip on his clothes. Unless Kate
smells the grease on him, I think he's safe."

"If her nose is as good as her hearing, he's so busted.
She's got a bullshit detector that hasn't failed yet with
anyone, but maybe my father."

Jess slid over him and sat. "Your father is still alive?"

"As far as I know, but then I haven't heard from him in years, so anything's possible." He gave her waist a squeeze. "The support checks stopped coming on Karma's eighteenth birthday. I don't think any of us has heard from him since."

Jessica came down on top of him, her nose brushing his, her eyes wide. "I'm sorry. I had no idea."

"There's nothing to be sorry for. It's a nonissue. We're lucky he's gone. Mom's one of the strongest women I've ever known, but I don't think she's ever really gotten over him." He wondered if he'd ever get over Jessica. He didn't want reason to find out.

"Luckily, we've always had Gramps. Of course, if he doesn't stop sneaking around eating junk food, he won't be with us much longer. Then again, if Mom catches him, she might just kill him."

Jessica brushed his unruly hair out of his eyes. "Kate loves her father. That much is obvious. I'm sure Gramps is safe."

"Gramps isn't really our grandfather, Jess, though you'd never know it. His daughter-in-law, Ben's mom, and my mom were best friends since they were kids. When Dad ran off, and we lost the house, Gramps and Gran took us in, gave Mom a job, and us a home. When Ben's parents were killed, he moved in, and we've been one big, dysfunctionally happy family ever since."

"When did your grandmother die?"

"When I was twelve. Gramps and Gran were amazing together, a real tag team those two. I wish you could have seen them. If you had, you'd never question the existence of love, that's for sure."

Jessica rested her head on his shoulder. He pulled

her hair band off and slid his hand into her hair, pushing it off her neck, kissing the skin he bared. "What's this?" She had a bruise on her shoulder. He ran his finger over it.

"Oh, that." She smiled that sexy smile that never failed to tent his pants. "That's from last night, up against the wall in the hallway. You don't remember?"

"God, Jess." He kissed the spot he'd bruised. He remembered nipping her shoulder, but damn, he didn't think he'd bit hard enough to bruise her. He'd lost all control—again. "I'm sorry. I never meant to hurt you."

"You didn't, well, not really. I love it when you go all wild on me."

"Yeah, just call me wild."

"I've been thinking about it all day, waiting for you to come home and do it again. That doesn't make me kinky does it?"

Fisher couldn't hold back a laugh. "Considering I'm the one who bit you, do you really think I'm the best judge of that?"

"It's not like I can ask anyone else."

"You did mention tying each other up, if I'm remembering correctly."

She smacked his shoulder. "I'm serious here. You're the only one who has ever wanted me like that."

Doubtful, but he wasn't about to clue her in.

"And you're the only one I want that way."

He could only thank God for that.

"Fisher, I want you so bad, sometimes it scares me."

"Darlin', if it makes you feel better I don't think we're kinky, but I'm always open to suggestions."

She looked like she was about to say something else,

but he cut her off with a kiss. He was determined to get her so hot and bothered, she'd be waiting to jump him as soon as he came home tomorrow.

Jessie expected hot, wild, sweaty, monkey sex. She'd been writing hot sex scenes all day. Hell, for all she knew she might just have to market this book as romantica. Seth and Jenny, her hero and heroine, weren't any better at keeping their hands off each other than she and Fisher were. And she liked it that way. But when Fisher kissed her so tenderly, she felt as if he reached right inside her and touched places she never even knew existed.

He shed his clothes and her inhibitions. He sent her flying using nothing but his mouth and words. When he finally entered her, like a wrecking ball through a pane of glass, he shattered whatever reserve she'd had.

"I love you, Jess." His gaze held hers—strong, steady, hot.

They moved as one, no one leading, no one following. They floated on a river of sensation. Fisher brought her higher, never releasing her from the prison of his gaze, filling her with feeling, so elemental, so strong, so intense, she never wanted the connection to end.

He made love to her slowly, gently, and thoroughly. So deeply it took her breath away.

She wanted to feel like this forever. "Oh God." Fear slammed into her. She tore her gaze away and rolled, dragging him beneath her.

"Just love me, Jess."

She kissed him to shut him up. She couldn't love him, but she could blow his mind. And she did.

Chapter 17

Jessie picked up the package the FedEx guy dropped off the next morning. Deli food. Her heart sang, and her stomach growled. She dug for her phone and texted Fisher:

> Free 4 lunch? I have a surprise, but u have 2 come & get it ;)
> Sry, no time today :(Dinner?
> Sigh. OK :(
> Love u. B home by 7

What the hell was she supposed to say to that? She tossed her phone back into her purse and decided it was a whole lot easier to write dialogue for her characters than it was for herself.

She fixed herself a bagel and lox with schmear, put the food in the refrigerator, and distracted herself with Jenny and Seth's problems instead of her own. Though really, the problems were similar. Of course, her fictional heroine believed in love, just not the fact she was lovable, something the hero seemed to have trouble grasping.

Poor Jenny. Jessie sat at her computer and lost herself in her characters' lives.

Fisher had the day from hell. After he spent three hours in surgery putting the broken bones of a tennis player's hand and wrist back together, he stitched it up, casted it, and sent her to recovery. He dictated his notes and post-op orders, before going to speak with her parents—a conversation he dreaded.

When the Stevenses saw him coming down the hall, Fisher pasted on an encouraging smile. "Alexa came through the surgery beautifully. She's in recovery. You'll be able to go in to see her in a few minutes."

Fisher raised an eyebrow when his patient's father slash tennis coach crossed his arms and spread his feet, as if he was trying not to throttle him.

"And her hand and wrist?"

"There was a lot of damage. The surgery went well, but a lot depends upon how it heals and how Alexa does in physical therapy. Right now, I can only promise you that she'll have a good range of motion and full use of her hand."

"What about her scholarship?" Mrs. Stevens asked. "Her career? Tennis is her life."

Fisher wondered if these people even knew their daughter. Every time he saw her, she talked about tennis, but she also talked about her love of forensics, and the way her practice negatively impacted her studies.

Fisher wasn't sure if Alexa would ever be able to play competitive tennis again. If she couldn't, she'd be okay. She'd been a patient of his long enough for him to know there were a lot of things she could do other than hit a tennis ball. Her parents, on the other hand, seemed to have more invested in making her a pro than they had in doing what was best for their daughter.

"Let's concentrate on Alexa's recovery and her therapy. I'll see her in the morning when I do rounds, and she'll be released by noon. I'd like to see her in my office next week. Just call for an appointment. If you have any questions, don't hesitate to call the service. I'll get right back to you."

Mr. Stevens looked at his wife and then back to Fisher. "When will we know when she can start training?"

"We'll do another set of X-rays at the office and see how she's healing. We won't know any more until then. For now, we need to keep her comfortable. I'll give you prescriptions for pain meds. Keep her in bed and quiet, until I see her. I'd like her to move her fingers, but not use them. The therapist will see her before she leaves and tell you everything you need to know."

He went back to recovery alone because her parents wanted to have dinner. Fisher texted Jessica:

Running late, B home as soon as I can.

He looked up when he heard Alexa move. "Hey, you're in recovery. How are you feeling?"

He waved to the recovery nurse to come over to check Alexa's vitals.

"Thirsty."

"Okay, ice chips coming right up. I'll be right back. You stay put."

She laughed, and he turned, almost running into the nurse bringing Alexa ice chips.

Fisher spent the next half hour feeding ice chips to a sixteen-year-old and answering her questions about medical school, residency, and talking about Jessica and the way she used her athleticism in her work. Alexa reminded him a lot of Jessica. They had the same focus, determination, drive, and intensity. "There's a lot you can do with sports, even if you're not a star athlete you know."

Alexa looked down at her casted arm. "Is it that bad?"

"Alexa, I'm going to give it to you straight. I really don't know. Surgery went well, but there was a lot of damage. Let's see how it heals and what happens with physical therapy. We'll know more in a few weeks." He brushed a tear off her cheek and squeezed her other hand. "I can promise you, you'll have full use of your hand and good range of motion. You should be able to do anything you want."

"Yeah, just not play Centre Court at Wimbledon. My parents are going to be so pissed at me."

"Why? You fell during practice. It was a freak accident. It wasn't anyone's fault."

She nodded, but he doubted she believed him.

"Dr. Kincaid, you don't need to stay here with me. I'm good at being alone. I'm used to it. I really don't mind."

"Na, I have no place important to be. I'll just hang out with you until your folks get back. They ran out to get a bite to eat."

It was nine o'clock before he had Alexa settled in her room, and her parents finally returned. "I'll see you in the morning, kiddo." He gave Alexa's foot a squeeze as he headed for the door. "Mr. and Mrs. Stevens, have a nice night."

Fisher drove home and hoped Jessica got his text. She hadn't answered it, but then he hadn't expected her to. He didn't bother pulling the car into the garage. He just parked on the street and loped to the house. "Sorry, I'm late."

Jessica looked up from her computer. "I hope you didn't eat because I waited for you."

"Good, I'm starving. I had an emergency surgery, and then I stayed with my patient until her parents could pull themselves away from their dinner." He tossed his bags down and leaned over her chair. "I'm sorry, Jess. I just couldn't leave a scared sixteen-year-old lying in recovery all alone."

Jessica set her computer aside and pulled him down for a kiss. "Is she going to be okay?"

"Yeah, she'll be fine. Her tennis career might be over, but I have no doubt she'll be okay either way. She's a great kid. Her parents, on the other hand... Shit Jess, I just don't get some people."

"Do you want to go back to the hospital? I can pack you a sandwich."

"No, she's on pain meds, so she's probably already asleep. I made sure she was settled in her room, and her parents were back before I left. She'll be fine until morning. I'll see her on my rounds. So, what's the surprise, or did I miss it?"

"I made dinner."

"I thought you didn't cook." And from what little he'd seen, she couldn't boil water.

She rose and gave him a kiss. "God, Fisher, give me some credit, will you? I used the word 'made' loosely. You can wipe the look of horror off your face. You'll like it, I promise." She took his hand and dragged him to the kitchen. "Mom sent a care package for us. She went all the way to Edison, New Jersey, to my favorite restaurant in the world: Harold's New York Deli. Look at what she sent."

Jess opened the refrigerator and took out a foot-long package. "Harold's triple decker sandwich—corned beef, pastrami, and brisket." She passed it to him.

"This is one sandwich? It's got to weigh ten pounds. I've delivered babies smaller than this."

"A knish." She took out a foil-wrapped sphere the size of a dinner plate and set it on the counter.

"I'm starting to detect a trend here."

"And a bowl of matzo ball soup." In a gallon bucket.

He took the bucket from her. "You could feed my whole family with the food we have out, and we're all pigs."

"And that's just for starters." She grabbed a bag and a bottle of mustard. "I almost called and invited your grandfather to join us—he'd love this, but I thought he might get in trouble. The sandwich alone has enough cholesterol to cause a heart attack. I hadn't thought of inviting the rest of your family. Sharing only goes so far."

"Thank God. I'm really not into sharing you or the food with anyone." He unwrapped the sandwich that would feed a dozen easily. It was literally a foot tall. "Darlin', you can make me dinner anytime."

"So you're not mad?"

"Why would I be mad?"

"Because you always eat so healthy, and well, this is great, but you have to admit, it would topple over your personal food pyramid. Now with mine, as long as it's balanced right, it sits just fine."

"I'm a believer in the eighty-twenty plan. Eighty percent of the time you eat healthy, and the other twenty is up for grabs. And right now, I can't wait to get my hands on that sandwich. I just don't know how to eat it."

"One bite at a time works for me." She opened the bucket of soup and took a long sniff. "I've been dreaming about Harold's since I stopped there for breakfast on my way to Boise. Mom sent extra rye bread, mustard, two servings of every pickle from the pickle bar—"

"They have a bar for pickles?"

"What, you've never seen a pickle bar? What do you think? They come in only two varieties, Kosher and sweet?"

"Yeah, pretty much."

Jessie rolled her eyes. "You're in for a shock." She scooted around him and grabbed a couple of bowls out of the cabinet. "We're going to have to dissect the matzo ball—since you're the surgeon, I'll leave that to you. It's the size of a bowling ball."

Fisher looked around his kitchen. There were bakery boxes tied with string they hadn't even opened yet, and he'd seen other packages wrapped in butcher paper in the refrigerator. "I can't believe this. There's enough food here to last a week."

"Yeah, isn't it great? Come on, let's gorge."

And gorge they did. Jessica made a sandwich, piled high with the three different kinds of meat, and then proceeded to pull it apart with her fingers, dropping bits into her mouth.

Fisher had never gotten a hard-on watching someone eat before, but then with Jessica, he seemed to spend his life half hard. He was so preoccupied with watching her that he barely tasted his sandwich. Thank God there were plenty of leftovers.

The soup was great. He wasn't sure what was in the spongy thing called a matzo ball, but it tasted amazing. And the knish—man, it was like a potato pie, with almost a phyllo dough crust that Jessica covered with mustard so grainy it cracked when he bit into it. Flavors exploded, and he was lost in what Jessica so aptly called multiple mouth orgasms.

A half hour with Jessica erased a day full of emergencies and people like Alexa's parents—and she hadn't even complained about him being late.

She swore she didn't believe in love, but damned if she didn't spread enough around to drown him in it. He sat back and watched her bite into a cookie the size of a saucer and groan.

"You have to try this. It's a black and white—my favorite cookie in the world."

He'd seen a smaller version sold at Costco. He'd have to remember to pick some up for her. He didn't want her thinking he was a health food nut. "I can't eat another bite."

"Oh, come on, Fisher. You haven't lived until you have a real New York black and white. All we're missing is the chocolate egg cream."

He took a swig of his beer. "Are you homesick?" He'd been so happy to have her there. He never wondered how she felt about leaving the city.

Jessica shrugged. "A little, I guess. I miss my apartment, having my own stuff around, the deli down the street. I miss watching all the games and talking to the players. I miss my job. I was really good at it."

"I know you were. I've read your stuff. It's amazing what you can find on the Internet."

She shot him an incredulous look.

"You're not the only one in this house with a computer, Jess. Why do you think I have Wi-Fi?"

"I can't believe you read my work."

"Why are you surprised? I love you. You're a writer. Of course I'd want to read your work. Heck, I'm dying to read your book, but every time I get near you with your computer, you close it up."

Jessica paled. "You can't read my book. Ever."

"Why not?"

"It's not ready for anyone to read."

"Uh-huh." If Jess were Pinocchio, she'd have a nose the size of a sequoia. "Sure."

Fisher rose and cleared the table, not wanting to show his disappointment—shit, disappointment didn't even cover it—it was more a mixture of fear, hurt, and uncertainty, along with a good bit of anger and bruised ego. He didn't imagine it was a very attractive package. "I don't know about you, but I'm beat. I didn't get much sleep last night."

She followed. "I'll help you clean up, and then I've got some work left to do."

Fisher waved her away. "No, you made dinner. Dishes are on me. Do whatever you need to do, Jess. I'm fine here on my own."

It was a good thing too, since he went to bed on his own. She had her head buried in her computer and didn't even notice he'd locked up the house and disappeared into the bedroom.

When he reached for her at two in the morning, she still wasn't in bed. He laid there building up a full head of steam, until he got up and stomped down the hall. He found her asleep in the chair with her computer on her lap. Damn, the sight of her asleep over her keyboard took all the wind out of him. "What am I going to do with you?" Maybe the better question was "what am I going to do without you?" He couldn't say that aloud though. He saved her work, closed her computer, and picked her up.

"Fisher?"

"Come on, sleepyhead. I'm taking you to bed." Maybe now, he'd get some sleep.

—∿∿—

Jessie woke up alone in bed and didn't remember how she'd gotten there. She heard the front door shut as she pulled her hair off her face and checked the clock, not sure if Fisher was coming or going. Wow, she'd slept past nine—probably coming.

The man in question, dressed in worn jeans and a button-down striped shirt, stepped into the doorway holding two venti Starbucks cups. "I hope one of those is for me."

"Well, I don't know." He leaned against the door-jamb and gave her a look that would singe her panties if she were wearing any.

Damn, she was naked, and she wasn't sure how she'd gotten that way, but she was pretty sure Fisher had something to do with it.

"What are you willing to trade me for it?"

She sat, the sheets pooled at her waist, and heat spread from her belly to between her legs. She was sure if he kept looking at her like that, she'd spontaneously combust. "What do you want?"

"You and me in bed for the rest of the weekend."

"But then who's gonna get the coffee?"

He set their coffees down on the bedside table and

took the top off hers. The scent of vanilla and coffee wafted over and mixed with the scent that was intrinsically Fisher. Talk about an eye-opening combination. "Have I ever let you down before?" He kissed her shoulder before nuzzling her neck.

Had he? "No." He was perfect, and that alone was enough to scare the crap out of her.

He nipped her earlobe, and sparks of need shot through her.

Jessie's heart pounded as she slid the first button of his shirt through the hole.

"So, is it a deal?"

"Fisher, right now, I'm more interested in getting you naked and inside me than in coffee."

"What do you want, Jessica?"

"I want you to love me."

"I do love you. I'll love you forever."

"I didn't mean it that way. I meant it in the physical sense." Or at least she thought she had.

"Unfortunately, you don't get to pick who I love." He pressed his forehead to hers and looked like he was in pain. "And neither do I."

She kissed him to shut him up and ripped his clothes off. She wanted to avoid the "I love you" subject, and sex with Fisher was a great distraction. Too bad there wasn't a shot that kept you from falling in love like the Depo-Provera shot to keep from getting pregnant, and she didn't think the withdrawal method was very reliable either. Abstinence, of course, was foolproof. But Fisher was addicting, and like an addiction, withdrawal would be painful.

Fisher kept her in bed most of the day, but by late

afternoon, he dragged her into the shower. "I have a surprise for you. Unfortunately, it requires us to dress."

"What are we doing?" She soaped his chest, running her hands over his abs and other interesting things.

He pulled her hands away from her favorite plaything, held them behind her back, and nipped her lips. "If I told you, it wouldn't be much of a surprise, would it?"

He made quick work of their shower, much to her dismay, and chased her out of the bedroom as soon as she threw on clothes. When he came out a few minutes later, wearing a tailored suit and tie, he looked like he just stepped off a Hugo Boss billboard. "You look amazing."

He smiled and that damn dimple winked, and her knees went weak. Sheesh, this guy was lethal.

"Where are we going again?"

"I'm not telling."

"Then how am I supposed to know what to wear?"

He took her by the hand and pulled her toward the front door. "I don't suppose you have a little black dress?"

"Nothing so boring. I do have a little red dress though."

"Sounds perfect. Come on."

She pulled out her keys. "Do you want to drive?"

"That was the plan." He tugged her toward the street.

But my car is in the driveway. "Yeah, but mine's right here." He pointed to a silver BMW Roadster parked on the street that she'd never seen before.

"Oh." He opened the door and handed her in. "I didn't think you'd want to take the truck. We'd get some funny looks, especially since I have yet to clean off the upholstery."

He was just full of surprises.

Fisher roamed Andrew's house while Jessica changed. Pictures decorated the walls. "Does Andrew spend a lot of time here?" he called back to her.

"Whenever he can. He likes getting away from LA."

She came up behind him, wrapping her arms around his waist, as he stared at the mantel showing the history of Andrew and Jessica—the two of them with their arms around each other in caps and gowns. He pointed to a photo of Andrew and Jessica dressed to the nines. She rested her chin on his shoulder. "That was at the Emmys last year. His show didn't win."

"Too bad." She smelled really good, not that she didn't always, but she must have put on perfume, because it wasn't her normal scent. Blueberries and vanilla—she smelled edible. "Where was this?" He picked up a picture of Jessica on the pitcher's mound, winding up.

She giggled. "I didn't know he had that." A smile threatened to cut her face in half. "That's me in New Jersey. I was asked to throw the first pitch of the season. I smoked it. It was just a minor league game, but Andrew came out for it. It was a good time."

"And this?" Jessica in a bikini with Andrew's arm around her. "Oahu, I was covering the Vans Triple Crown of Surfing. We turned it into a vacation last year. That's the last time I saw him."

Fisher put the picture back. "I thought you said you were friends."

"We are."

He turned around with a "get real" look on his face—until he saw her—it quickly turned into a "holy shit" look. She couldn't have been in the bedroom for more than five minutes, and she came out looking like a supermodel. The dress was hot, red, barely there, and looked like a silk tube had been shrink-wrapped on her incredible body, which wasn't a bad thing. Fisher just wasn't so sure he wanted any other man to look at her while she was wearing it. He let out a wolf whistle. "Wow. You're beautiful." His gaze went from her simple updo that made him want to pull out all the pins and run his hands through her hair, to the dress—what there was of it, down her long, long, long legs to her bare feet. "Where are your shoes?"

She held out a pair of red stilettos and put a hand to her stomach.

"Do you need help putting them on?"

"No, but they're four-inch heels."

"I see that."

"I could wear my black flats."

"Are those uncomfortable or something?"

She shook her head.

"Are you going to fall on your face if you wear them?"

She laughed. "No, but I'll be about an inch taller than you."

"Is that a problem for you?"

"No."

"Then put them on, and let's go."

———

Hours later, as Fisher swayed with Jessica on the dance floor to soft, sexy jazz, he figured he scored a touchdown in the game of romance. He'd surprised her all right. Taking her to Chandler's Steak House, the best, most romantic restaurant in Boise, was a brilliant play, if he did say so himself.

"Fisher?" Jess was barefooted and wrapped around him, her head on his shoulder, her body pressed against him.

"Hmm?"

"Take me home."

"I thought you'd never ask." The whole way home, all he could think of was how he'd manage getting her out of that damn dress without ripping it.

Jessie picked up her phone and smiled when she saw Andrew's name. "Andrew, how's it going?"

"Hey, I got a call from my neighbor worried that you've disappeared. Is everything okay? You didn't kill Fisher or anything, did you?"

"No, I didn't kill him, and yes, everything is fine. Why?"

"You haven't been home in two weeks. I guess your little dating deal is still going on, huh?"

"Yeah, it is. I keep trying to go home, but whenever I do, something comes up."

Andrew laughed uproariously.

"Andrew James Monahan, you have a dirty mind."

"Dirty, but accurate. Jessie, face it, you wouldn't be staying there if you didn't like that thing that keeps coming up."

Jessie rolled her eyes and wished they were Skyping, so Andrew would see it, but then, it would have been offset by the redness in her cheeks. "I was all set to leave on Monday after I went for a run with Fisher, but by the time I got showered and changed, Karma called with a fashion emergency, so Fisher's sister-in-law Toni, Karma, and I had to shop."

"Spare me the details, please. It's bad enough I write about this stuff, I don't want to listen to it too."

"I got an outfit for my interview, so it was productive. By the time we got back, Fisher, Hunter, and Trapper were cooking dinner."

"Sure, okay."

"Then Tuesday, Kate came over with mums and needed help planting them."

"Did you tell whoever Kate is that whenever you buy a plant, it's dead within a month?"

"Yes, I warned her, but the Kincaids aren't much for listening—at least not to me—they're more the steam-rolling kind."

"Wow, and you allowed yourself to be swayed?"

"No, but—"

"You did. Jessie, either these people are mind-benders, or you're losing your touch."

"Yeah, that's kind of what I'm afraid of. Then Wednesday, Grampa Joe came over for our weekly greasefest. I swear, if Kate finds out what he does when we're together, she's going to kill us both. But Gramps said he'd die happy."

"You call him Gramps?"

"Well, Mr. Walsh seems a little formal when you're fighting over steak fingers and sucking down chocolate shakes."

"*The* Joe Walsh? Jessie, do you have any idea who Joe Walsh is?"

"Yeah, he's Fisher's grandfather, kinda sorta. Anyway, Kate has him on a strict diet, so he comes to me to cheat."

"Joe Walsh is like the seventh richest man in the country. He's on the Forbes list."

"He's a sly old man, but you can't help but love him. And Wednesday night, I played on the Humpin'

Hannah's softball team again. And then, we all went to the bar—"

"How's the book coming?"

"Great. It's practically writing itself. I'm in the calm before the storm stage."

"Sounds like it. So how's Fisher feel about you coming out for an interview?"

"Fine, I guess. We haven't talked much about it."

"Or me, obviously."

"No, I talk about you. I had to go home to get dressed up, and he saw all the pictures—I never even noticed them before."

"Yeah, sometimes for a journalist, you're pretty myopic. Unless there's sports involved, you're just not very observant."

"That's not true."

"What color are my eyes?"

"What does it matter?"

"I rest my case. So, you got dressed up? What'd you do?"

"He's teaching me about romance, remember? He took me to Chandler's."

Andrew whistled. "It takes months to get reservations there. But then, I guess when your grandfather is Joe Walsh, you can get a table anywhere."

"It's not like that, Andrew. You'd never know Gramps is rich. He's just like I always wished my grandparents were. He's a trip, actually."

"I see."

"What's that supposed to mean?"

"Absolutely nothing, sugar. I'm happy for you. I really am."

"Happy about what?"

When Andrew didn't answer, she checked her phone to make sure she wasn't cut off. "What is it?"

"Not for me to say, but I'd suggest having a real heart-to-heart with Fisher."

"Oh no. He keeps telling me he loves me, and he's making me crazy."

"So, I guess he's fully recovered from the concussion?"

"Oh yeah, he's fine."

"And he's still in love with you?"

God, now it was her turn to not answer. It was time to leave. Things were getting entirely too cozy. Nights were spent curled up in Fisher's arms, and well, she couldn't really complain about that.

"I'm leaving tonight. No matter what. I have to pack."

"Okay, sugar. Call me if you need me. If I don't hear from you, I'll see you tomorrow."

"Yeah, see you."

She ended the call. No matter what happened, she had to leave tonight. She needed to talk to Fisher. He'd been watching her all day, avoiding any mention of her trip to LA and her interview.

She stuffed her phone in her purse by the door and looked around the living room. She'd written most of her book right there in Fisher's recliner. Her notes lay on the table beside it—a table she didn't remember being there the first time she'd fallen asleep there writing. Fisher must have moved a table over for her. She was really gonna miss that chair—it was writing nirvana.

She straightened up her notes and put them in her messenger bag. While she was away, she'd finish her book, and try to figure out what to do about Fisher without him distracting her.

After dinner Jessie felt like the elephant in the room was sitting on her chest. She and Fisher had curled up on the couch and were watching ESPN, not that she could concentrate on the game. God, her eye was twitching, her head ached, and she wondered if she wasn't coming down with something.

Fisher pulled her onto his lap, and she swallowed hard. "Jess, don't go tomorrow."

"What are you talking about?" Her stomach tied itself into knots. "I have to." She wrapped her arms around herself. "I have meetings, an interview, and Andrew's expecting me."

"You don't have to do anything." Fisher tightened his hold, trapping her against him. His mouth close to her ear, she could feel the words he said—low, smooth, determined, demanding. "Stay with me. Finish your book. Give yourself some time. Give us some time."

Jess opened her mouth and then closed it, swallowing back her anger, and doing her best to think past the voice in her head screaming for her to run and run fast. The weight on her chest increased tenfold, and she couldn't draw in a deep breath. She had to get up. She had to move, or she'd scream. "Let me go."

"I don't want to."

"It's not your choice, it's mine." She broke the bond of his arms, climbed off his lap, and went to the bedroom, tossing everything she'd brought into her bag.

"You're leaving now?" Of course, Fisher would follow her.

"I'm flying out in the morning, and I need to go home and pack. I'm not going to my interview in jeans and a Mets T-shirt."

"We need to talk, Jess." He tried catching her arm as she left the bathroom, but she pulled out of his grasp.

"There's nothing to talk about." She couldn't think when he was touching her, not about leaving anyway. "You don't need me here, and I have a lot to do. I've already stayed way too long."

"Jess, I don't want you to leave like this."

"Like what?"

"In the middle of a fight."

"Fisher, this isn't a fight." She stuffed her feet into her sneakers, avoiding his gaze, praying she didn't throw up the dinner he'd fixed. "I can't do this. Don't you understand? This job could be the break of a lifetime. It could be even better than my work at the *Times*. And Andrew set it up. This isn't just about you and me. It's about Andrew too. It would make Andrew and me look bad if I suddenly canceled. I won't do that to either of us."

"So this is about Andrew?" He blocked the door to the hall. "I thought we had a deal, a partnership, or doesn't that mean anything?"

"Fisher, I don't know what you're getting at. It was research, and you've known about this interview since I have." She didn't look at him. She couldn't. She concentrated on stuffing everything she could think of in her bag and then zipped it up. If she left something, so be it. When she could no longer avoid it, she looked at him, standing like a sentry in the doorway, filling the space, stealing the oxygen from the room. "What's your problem?"

"You're my problem. You're flying off to LA and staying with another man who is clearly in love with you. You're interviewing for a job that will put you on the other side of the country, and as far as I can see, you haven't given any consideration to what this will do to us or to me. That's my problem."

She couldn't believe he went there. "Andrew's not in love with me. We're friends." Wow, Fisher had that sexy-angry look down. She remembered it, and unfortunately, it had the same effect on her as it had at the foot of the mountain she'd climbed the first time she'd seen him pissed.

"Bullshit. I saw the way he looked at you when you were Skyping. Hell, he has a veritable shrine to you at his house."

Jessie went nose to nose with him, and not in a good way. "You spied on me while I was having a private conversation with Andrew?"

"You told him you loved him—"

"I do." She held her bag in front of her to keep from slugging him. "I love him like a brother. Andrew is my best friend. My only friend."

"Some friend. You said he left you."

"What the hell did you expect him to do? He got a job and moved to LA." She threw up her hands, letting her bag flop against her side. "Why am I explaining this to you? This is none of your business."

"The hell it's not. You're mine. That makes it my business."

Jessie didn't want to be anyone's anything, but knowing that Fisher got all bent out of shape and possessive over the likes of her, embarrassingly enough, made her want to squeal like a five-year-old spotting her first Barbie Dream House. She tamped it down and channeled her old softball coach. "You don't own me." She pushed him back. "You don't tell me where I can and can't go." She shoved him again. "And you sure as hell don't pick my friends." This time, she shoved with both hands, pushing him against the wall of the hall. "You are not my keeper." Jessie turned on her heel and hurried toward the living room.

"I love you, Jess. I want to be your partner, not your keeper." Fisher followed, hot on her heels.

She grabbed her computer and stuffed it into her messenger bag, blinking back tears, unable to breathe as the pain slammed into her. She had to make a clean break. She had to keep him from following her. If he did, she'd never be able to pull this off. Fuckity, fuck, fuck fuck.

She hoisted the bag over her shoulder and squared off at the front door. "What do you want from me?"

Fisher took her arms and pulled her up against him. "I want to know what the hell am I to you?"

"Temporary."

Chapter 18

TEMPORARY? FISHER SANK INTO A CHAIR AS THE SLAM-ming of the door reverberated through his skull. He never knew one word had enough strength to knock the air out of him and cause him physical pain, but that one did.

Gramps always said, "Boy, never ask a question you don't want to know the answer to. You'll surely get it." Shit. Of all times for the old man to be right—but Fisher had wanted the answer, just not the one he got. Fuck.

Getting drunk was out of the question. He had early rounds in the morning. Plus, he was depressed enough as it was, and adding alcohol would just make matters worse—if that were possible.

When the phone rang, he ran for it, praying it was Jess. When he saw Hunter's name on the caller ID, he let it go to voice mail and did the only think he knew that would keep him busy and from going completely insane. He cleaned. Everything.

―⁓―

Jessie dragged her carry-on off the plane, toward the baggage area. She passed the security point, wonder-ing what Fisher was doing. He'd had early rounds, but didn't see patients until one. She'd thought about calling Karma and asking her to check on him. But after what she'd said to him, the way she'd hurt him, she didn't think Karma would even speak to her, no less do anything to ease her mind or her guilt.

She almost walked into Andrew before she saw him. His smile fell as soon as his eyes met her red-rimmed ones.

"Oh sugar, it went that bad, huh?"

Jessie couldn't even speak. She just nodded and walked into Andrew's open arms and leaked all over his shoulder.

"What happened?"

"I was so scared he'd follow me, that I wouldn't be able to leave him. I eviscerated him and everything we had together. I was mean and cruel, and I hurt him. I don't know if I can live with it, Andrew. I can't sleep—every time I close my eyes, I see the pain in his face."

She'd thought what Jamie had done had hurt, but it was nothing compared to what she'd done to Fisher and herself.

Still, if it hurt this much, she couldn't imagine what it would feel like a year from now, if she had stayed.

——⁓——

At ESPN Jessie was shuffled from office to office. She had three back-to-back interviews with executives, did screen tests of a play-by-play, conducted an on-camera interview, met other commentators, and did a mock sports talk segment. By the time the day was over, she figured they had an hour of footage and enough information about her to know her blood type and the date of her last menstrual cycle.

Mitch Seibert walked her out of the office and down to the lobby. He stopped just beyond security. "Well, Jessie, it was nice meeting you. We'll give you a call next week once a decision is made."

"Great. Thanks so much for the opportunity to interview. I enjoyed it. You have a great team."

"Good. I hope everything works out. Oh, and be sure to tell your grandfather hello for me, will you?"

"Excuse me? Mitch, my grandfather's dead."

The man blanched and took a step back. "Oh God, I had no idea. I just spoke to him the week before last. What happened? I know he had a heart attack a few years ago…"

"Hold on, Mitch. You wouldn't happen to be talking about Joe Walsh would you?"

"Yeah, he called me and told me I'd be an idiot not to hire you on the spot. Joe gave me my start back when I was at Boise State. He's the smartest man I've ever met. He's been my mentor since I played Bronco football."

Jessie blew out a breath. "Grampa Joe is fine, but he's not my grandfather. He just kind of adopted me."

Mitch wiped his brow with a handkerchief, looked like he was about to cry with relief, and then laughed. "That old coot. Leave it to him to spot the best talent I've seen in a long time. But damn, Jessie, you scared the hell out of me." He took a deep breath and blew it out. "I don't get out to see him often enough. You give him my love and tell him I'll have that bottle of his favorite whiskey under my coat next time I come to the house."

She laughed. "He's got you trained too, huh?"

"Kate would skin us if she knew half the things the old man did."

"Guilty. We've been hitting the Westside Drive-In pretty hard lately."

Mitch put his arm around her. "Next time you come out, bring me an order of steak fingers, will you?"

"I'll get right on that. It was a pleasure to meet you,

Mitch, I'm sorry about the confusion. I really didn't mean to scare you like that. I had no idea Gramps had *his* fingers in this deal."

"I had the interview scheduled before he called about you. I told him about my past work with Andrew, who, I might add, is your biggest fan next to Joe. It was a co-incidence, but I gotta say, the old man still has an eye for talent. You did great, Jessie. You'll definitely be hearing from us soon, so don't go making any long-term plans until you do. Okay? We'll be in touch with your agent."

She reached out and gave Mitch a hug. "That's great to hear. Thanks."

❧

By the time Trapper got to Humpin' Hannah's Wednesday night, Fisher was six thousand calories ahead and two sheets to the wind.

Karma tilted her head toward Fisher at the other end of the bar and mouthed, "Do something."

Hunter came up behind Trapper and stole the beer Karma had just poured. Typical. Trapper did what he always did, patiently putting up with his younger siblings. Shit. He had problems of his own. He was in no mood to deal with Fisher's heartache, but as usual, he didn't have much of a choice.

"Looks like there's trouble in paradise." Hunter took a long draw off Trapper's stolen Guinness. "I've been calling Fisher since Sunday, and he hasn't answered yet. He's never gone underground that long."

Trapper shook his head. It was going to be a long night. "Let's flip to see who takes him home."

Hunter took a quarter out of his pocket. "You call it."

"Heads."

Hunter smiled as he spied the coin—of course, he didn't show it to Trapper. "Looks like you're it."

"Damn, and I just cleaned my car."

"Maybe Karma will be nice and send him home with a bucket."

Trapper grabbed his beer and looked over to Hunter. "You ready?"

Hunter took another swig. "Not much choice. Let's go."

Damn, when Trapper got a look at Fisher, he saw himself five years ago. Not a good reminder. "Hey, Fisher. What's going on?"

Trapper took a seat beside Fisher, and Hunter flanked him. "You've been AWOL lately."

"It was temporary." He shook his head, which rested on his hand, and upset the balance.

"What's temporary?" If Trapper hadn't grabbed his shoulder, Fisher's head would have hit the bar.

"Jessica said I am," Fisher slurred. "She's got herself a new research partner, and she said she loves him, Trapper. That's it. I'm giving up women. All of 'em."

Hunter leaned over. "Man, that's harsh."

"Damn." Fisher was never much of a drinker. He'd always been too busy working or studying to spend much time partying. The last time Trapper had heard Fisher slur was on his twenty-first birthday. Trapper had to take him home that night too—and ended up buying a new pair of boots after Fisher puked all over the ones Trapper had been wearing. Trapper looked down—at least he wasn't wearing his favorites. That was something anyway. He nodded to Hunter. "If I end up losing another pair of boots, you're buying me replacements."

"Gladly. Just as long as they're not mine."

Fisher continued as if he hadn't heard Hunter. "Jessica's off in La-La Land with that guy Andrew who's in love with her. I bet he's not temporary."

Karma slid over to them and reached for the bottle of Macallan 18 sitting in front of Fisher.

"Hey, that's mine."

Karma was faster. "Not anymore, it's not. Fisher Michael Kincaid, you're officially cut off." She gave Trapper and Hunter the evil eye. "Boys, you need to get him out of here. He's been holding up the bar too long. God, he's been here since opening, and I'm not a babysitter."

Trapper smiled his best smile. "I don't suppose I can use your car, can I? I think the fresh air will do Fisher good."

"Not on your life." She wiped down the bar. "I'll give you a bucket." She handed him a bucket that once contained margarita salt.

"Great, thanks."

She patted Fisher's cheek. "Don't worry, sweetie. Jessie will be back in a few days, and things will be all right. She couldn't even describe that guy, Andrew. There's no chemistry."

"He loves her, and she loves him. I heard them."

Trapper scrubbed his face with his hands. "Shit. It's gonna be a long night." He threw Fisher's arm over his shoulder, helped his little brother off the stool, and grabbed the bucket. Hunter took the other side, and they hustled Fisher out the door and into the Sequoia. Trapper buckled him in, stuck the bucket between his legs, and rolled down the window, before leaning Fisher's head out. "You're going to owe me so big."

Fisher let out a snore. Great.

Hunter rocked back on his heels. "You stay with him tonight, and I'll stop by in the morning."

Trapper threw his cowboy hat in the back seat. He'd really hate for Fisher to mistake that for a bucket. "Follow me to his house. He's already asleep. I might need a hand carrying him in."

"No problem. I'll follow you." Hunter gave him a wave and walked away. Lucky bastard.

Trapper made the drive without incident. He walked around the truck and waited for Hunter. "Come on, let's get him inside. He's out cold."

Hunter pulled the door open, and Trapper thanked God he hadn't released the seat belt yet. It was the only thing keeping Fisher in the car. Between the two of them, they got Fisher onto the porch and had him leaning against the wall, while Hunter unlocked the door. "You couldn't have unlocked the damn door before we got him out of the truck?"

"Hey, I didn't hear you suggest anything."

Fisher looked up. "I don't feel so good." He leaned forward, and there went a perfectly good pair of boots.

Shit. It was going to be a long fucking night.

"Gramps, you have to do something." Karma couldn't believe she was begging. "I promised the guys I wouldn't interfere again, but someone has to. I can't stand to see Fisher like this. It's all my fault."

Gramps got up from behind his desk and walked to the window to look out over his empire—part of it anyway.

Karma hated coming to Gramps's office. Since she

was out of diapers, her mother had always insisted she "dress appropriately." In mom-speak that meant wearing a skirt or dress and the toe-strangling shoes that came along with it. Needless to say, it took a major family emergency to get her up to the twenty-ninth floor of the Walsh Building.

Gramps crossed his arms. "Karma, first of all, this isn't your fault. Jessie and Fisher have to find their own way. If they don't want it badly enough, maybe they're not meant to be together."

"Oh, come on, Gramps. You know they're perfect for each other. They just have their timing screwed up, which is amazing, because I really thought they were on the same circadian rhythm, you know. They were constantly running into each other. But it turns out when it comes to love, Jessie and Fisher are on opposite sides of the bell curve. He's fast, she's slow, and that spells disaster."

Gramps let out a laugh. "Jessie fell just as hard and fast for your brother as he did for her, even an old fool like me could see that. She's just been hurt. That girl's as skittish as a sixteen-point buck on the first day of huntin' season. She'll come around."

Karma threw herself into one of the big leather chairs in front of Gramps's desk, almost forgetting she was wearing a skirt. Damn, she really hated keeping her legs crossed. "I don't know, Gramps. Jessie really hurt Fisher. You didn't see him last night. Trapper and Hunter had to pour him out of the bar."

"That boy's never much of a drinker."

"And Fisher tossed his cookies all over Trapper's boots."

"Why'd you let him drink so damn much?"

Karma stood and stomped over to the old man. "Have you ever known any one of my brothers, or Ben for that matter, to ever listen to me? Why do you think I always have to trick them?"

"I always thought it was because you can, and you enjoy pullin' the wool over their eyes."

"Okay, you've got me there. You'd think they'd know by now not to underestimate me. But it doesn't change the fact that they never listen to a word I say."

"I assume you have a devious plan brewing in that pretty little head of yours." He slicked back what was left of his white hair. "What's it gonna be this time?"

"Nothing. It would be too obvious. They'll be expecting me to do something. But you, on the other hand…"

"Jessie will be back in town on Friday."

Karma rubbed her hands together. "And my sources say she starts training at Starbucks on Monday."

"Well, shit. If I knew she needed a job that badly, I would have hired her myself."

"She's writing a book, and she's just doing the Starbucks thing for the health benefits. Plus, it will give her time to write."

He sat down. "I know plenty of people in publishing. What kind of book is she writing?"

"Promise not to tell anyone?" Karma sat forward.

"Scout's honor."

"Yeah, like you were ever a Boy Scout. But it's too good not to tell you. Jessie's writing a romance."

Gramps let out a guffaw. "Now that's one book I've got to read. The girl doesn't recognize love when she's up past her waders in it, and she's writing a romance? You know, now that I think about it that might make some kind of strange sense after all. Sometimes you have to know something in here." He pointed to his head. "To figure things out in here." He pointed to his heart.

He walked around his desk and pressed the button for his intercom. "Shamus, get me Mitch Seibert on the phone." His eyes sparkled. "Okay, girly, get out of here, so I can formulate a plan."

"I knew I could count on you." She went around his desk and kissed his cheek. "After all, I learned from the master."

"You're cleaning?"

Jessie turned away from the kitchen sink she was scrubbing to find Andrew staring at her. "I got into the habit at Fisher's. He's a neat freak right down to the way he folds his towels." She took the kitchen towel and folded it in thirds. "See, the man is sick. He folds the kitchen towels in thirds lengthwise and then in half, but the bath towels have to be folded in thirds and then thirds again. And you can't just stuff them in the closet. Nooo, you have to put the rounded edge facing out like a display at Neiman Marcus."

"Imagine."

"And he even folds his underwear. I mean, who does that?"

"Not me, that's for sure, and certainly not you. Yup." Andrew poured himself a cup of coffee. "Neat drawers are a definite sign of a sick mind."

"Exactly."

"Yeah, he sounds like a real loser. He cooks, cleans, is a veritable God in bed—"

"Who told you that?"

"You did."

Jessie felt her face flame. She remembered telling Andrew that Fisher was perfect, but she hadn't gone into specifics, had she?

"Sugar, you've complained about every lover you've ever had—not that you've had many, but I heard all about their shortcomings, shall we say, with the very notable exception of Dr. Fisher Kincaid. That and the bruise on your shoulder, the one you've taken to rubbing like a Buddha's belly for luck tells me all I need to know. It also explains why you haven't been sleeping or eating, and why you've been walking around my place like a zombie."

She opened her mouth to protest, but shut it. What could she say? He was right. She was miserable. She'd never been so miserable in her entire life.

He took her hand. "I'm worried about you, sugar. You've even stopped writing. I've never seen that happen. Writing to you is like breathing—it's necessary to live. You haven't written a word in days."

"I'm stuck." She shrugged and pulled her hand away from his. God, just touching Andrew, even platonically, made her feel as if she were cheating on Fisher. "I wrote the big black moment, and I did it so well. I don't know how to ever put the pieces back together again."

"So, rewrite it."

"That's the thing. This is the only way I can see it. Andrew, I love my characters, but I can't help but think if they did get back together, I'd just be setting them up for an even bigger heartbreak in the future."

"Maybe you should get a job writing soaps. That's what they're looking for."

"Jenny and Seth are so different. She's all junk food and crackers in bed, and he's a granola with an unhealthy relationship with his vacuum cleaner."

"Sounds kinky."

She did her best to smile, but from the look on Andrew's face, she'd missed her mark. She was so selfish. She'd been there all week, and Andrew had spent his vacation time plying her with food, alcohol, really bad jokes, and chocolate. A corpse would have been better company than she'd been. And unfortunately, she found out the hard way that the out-of-sight-out-of-mind theory of heartbreak recovery didn't work. Out-of-sight just seemed to magnify the problem. At least, if she were in Boise, she might see Fisher and make sure he was okay.

"Do you want me to read the manuscript and tell you what I think? At least then, we'd be able to brainstorm an ending. That's why most writers have critique partners in the first place. Sometimes you get so involved with the story and the characters, you can't see the forest for the trees."

"Sure, let me just get my Thumbdrive. You can download it on your computer." She went to the door where her bags were packed and ready to go and pulled out her keys with her Thumbdrive on them. "Here you go. We use the same writing program, so you can comment, and we can email it back and forth."

Andrew took it from her, and she followed him into his office. "It'll be like college all over again. Remember how we used to critique each other's stuff?"

"Yeah, I remember." She leaned on his desk wondering what she'd ever done to deserve a great friend like Andrew.

"Thanks for everything. You're the best friend I've ever had. I really don't know what I'd do without you."

He pulled her Thumbdrive from his laptop and handed it back to her. "No thanks necessary. We've always been there for each other, sugar. I just want you to be happy. If Fisher makes you happy, maybe you should see if you two can work things out. He sounds like a great guy, except for the whole OCD problem. Though, from the looks of it, it's catching. Pretty soon, you'll be folding your underwear."

She did laugh at that. Even her laugh sounded rusty to her ears. She checked the time on her phone, the one Fisher hadn't dialed, or texted, or anything. But then what did she expect? After what she'd said, Fisher would never forgive her, no less want her back. She let out a sigh. "We'd better be going if I'm going to make my plane."

Andrew stood and pulled her along with him. "Before you go, promise me something."

"What?"

"Promise me you'll think about talking to Fisher."

When she started to protest, he put his finger on her lips. "If the woman I love was in love with me, I'd move heaven and earth to be with her. Even if that meant getting down on my hands and knees, begging forgiveness. Pride doesn't keep you warm at night. Believe me. Unrequited love is a cold and humbling experience."

"What if she loves you and you just don't know it? If you never asked her—"

"No. She's in love with someone else, and he gives her something I never could. He's a better man for her than I am."

"I hope she appreciates you."

"She does." He tugged on her hands, pulling her off the edge of his desk. "Come on. If I don't get you to the airport on time, I might not get rid of you before you start folding my underwear."

If Fisher didn't have to go to work, he wouldn't, but then he wasn't sure what the hell he'd do. There were only so many beer cozies a guy could knit. He figured more than a six-pack for each brother and cousin seemed a bit obsessive.

He'd made Karma a Dr. Who scarf long enough to make a noose. He'd thought about leaving it like that to freak out his brothers, but they seemed freaked out enough, and to be honest, he was afraid they wouldn't see it as a joke.

He'd cleaned everything before he'd gone off the veritable deep end. Once his workweek was done, he'd hit the bar harder than he'd ever remembered. The ensuing hangover and spin around the toilet bowl of depression seemed to bring out his closet slob—one he never knew existed. But looking around the house, he couldn't summon the energy to care.

Fisher sent Trapper a new pair of Lucchese boots to make up for the pair he'd ruined. Damn, he'd never live that one down. He was still routinely reminded of the pair he'd ruined on his twenty-first birthday, the first and last time he'd been drunk—until his crash and burn with Jessica.

Shit. Just thinking of her had the power to knock the wind out of him, send him reeling, and leave him feeling sick.

She'd be back in town today. It was a good thing he was on call for the next three days—he'd traded with one of his partners just to keep from making a fool of himself and begging Jess to take him back. He figured he'd embarrassed himself enough over the last week to last a lifetime—which would probably be about the same amount of time it would take him to get over her.

He'd taken to sitting in her chair, staring into space, and knitting. He picked up the ruined scarf he'd started for Jessica and pulled the needles out, ripping out the stitches the way she'd ripped out his heart. Maybe he'd salvage the yarn and make his mother a hat or something.

His front door slammed open and Gramps walked in. Damn, that would teach him to bolt the door—not that a lock would ever stop the old man. It might have given Fisher a minute to straighten up. But then, looking around, he figured he'd need the entire hospital's cleaning staff in order to get it done in under an hour.

His eyes met with Gramps, and Fisher realized he was not only sitting with a pile of purple yarn on his lap, but his eyes were embarrassingly close to leaking.

He picked up the yarn he'd strangled more than once and tossed it in a bag, but not before the old man got a load of what he was doing.

"I lost a bet."

"You lost a hell of a lot more than a bet, boy." He looked around and let out a whistle. "So this is what rock bottom looks like."

"Yeah, I guess so."

Gramps stepped over a pile of newspaper, planted his cane in front of him, and leaned over Fisher. "So, what the hell are you gonna do to get the girl back?"

"Nothing. She said I was temporary, Gramps. What the hell do you say to that?"

"Bullshit, poppycock, and hell no, just for starters."

"Bullshit didn't go over well when I tried it earlier."

"So she knocked you down. Are you gonna sit here and wallow in self-pity, or are you going after what you want?"

Wallowing was about all he was capable of—well, that and losing himself in his job. He had to get through two more hours of wallowing though, and it didn't look as if Gramps was going anywhere in a hurry.

When Fisher didn't answer, Gramps hit him with his cane and pushed a pile of crap off the couch. "Do you think I got your grandmother on the first try, boy? I chased that woman for a year and a half, before I was even able to steal a kiss. Hell, I asked her to marry me a good half-dozen times before she said yes. What do you think would have happened had I acted like you?"

Fisher hoped that was a rhetorical question. He couldn't fathom what Gramps's life would have been like without Gran. Just like he couldn't fathom what his life would be like without Jess.

"Jessie James is one hell of a woman. Maybe you're not man enough to handle her."

Fisher'd had enough. He stood and got in his grandfather's face. "I had no problem handling Jessica. I handled her just fine. I just couldn't keep her from running away."

"Then what the hell are you doing sitting here? You need to get off your ass and chase her. I happen to know her plane lands in less than an hour."

Fisher took a step back and scrubbed his hands over his face. "I'm on call for the next three days."

Gramps shook his head, suddenly looking every day of his eighty-two years. "I never thought I'd see the day when I'd be disappointed in you, Fisher. I thought I'd raised you better than to hide behind your stethoscope. Maybe you don't deserve Jessie after all."

Shit. Fisher didn't think he could fall any farther. Seeing the look on Gramps's face gave him the extra push he'd needed to go all the way.

Fisher's pager rang. He pulled it off his belt and checked the message. "I have an emergency. I'll call you when I get off, okay?"

Gramps didn't answer, he didn't follow, and Fisher didn't have time to deal with him or anything else right now. "I gotta go, Gramps. Lock up on the way out."

Chapter 19

JESSIE SAT AT STARBUCKS AND STUDIED THE TRAINING manual. The new black polo and black pants she wore matched her mood. She'd been home since Friday and hadn't seen Fisher yet. At least not in the flesh—he was her constant companion in every other way though. She couldn't help but think of him day and night, no matter how much she tried not to. Fisher showed up in her dreams, her thoughts, hell, even in her conversations.

Laura, or Lady Gaga, as Jessie chose to think of her, made herself at home at the table and set down two lemonade iced teas. "So, how's Fisher?"

"I don't know. I haven't seen him since I got back from LA."

Laura pulled off her cap. "I didn't mean 'how is he?'" She waggled her eyebrows. "I meant, how is he… in the sack? It's been the topic of the month behind the bar."

Jessie schooled her face and blinked back the tears gathering in her eyes. She hoped to God she was PMSing, because her eyes were leaking almost constantly lately.

The manager, Steph, chose that moment to step up to the table. "You don't have to answer that, Jessie. Not that we're not interested, mind you, but even we have a bit of decorum, though it seems to be lost on Laura." Steph gave Laura a pointed look. "Trudi is going to take you through the opening procedures tomorrow, since you'll be taking over for her when she goes on vacation next month."

"Okay."

Luckily, Laura only had a ten-minute break. She put her cap and apron back on and went to work the drive-thru. Jessie listened with half an ear to the headset. "Welcome to Starbucks. My name is Laura. What can I get you?"

"We called in an order for the hospital."

"Oh, right. Do you have Fisher's cup with you?"

"I sure do."

"Drive on up."

Jessie stood to stretch and get a look at the girl bringing Fisher his coffee. Laura caught her. She switched the headset to private. "Blonde hair, blue eyes, big boobs — your usual nightmare."

Jessie shrugged. "She's getting coffee for everyone."

"Yeah, but she's the only one who keeps Fisher's cups in her car."

Jessie took off her hat. "I'm going on my half." She walked outside and sat on the patio, sipping her coffee and checking her messages. Andrew had called three times. He was turning into a regular mother hen.

"So, have you seen him?"

"No, but I saw the blonde sent to fetch his coffee."

"Ooh, is that jealousy I hear?"

"Lay off, Andrew."

"So... I see you're still in the same lovely mood you were in when you left."

"What do you expect?"

"I expected you to be sick of yourself by now. Have you done any writing?"

"No, I'm still stuck. But I heard from our agent. She loves the partial of the book, and she's just waiting for me to finish it. She still hasn't heard from ESPN though."

"That doesn't mean anything, Jessie. These things take time."

"I know. It's just... Andrew, I don't know if I can stay here."

"What do you mean?"

"Fisher is everywhere. I go for a run, and even though I haven't seen him, it's like he's running beside me. I go home, and he's there. I come to work at Starbucks, and everyone wants to know how he is in bed. I'm thinking of quitting and just going home, Andrew. I can crash with my parents until I find out what's happening with ESPN." She looked around to make sure no one was listening. "I just don't want to go through training here at 'Bucks and then not be able to handle seeing Fisher every morning. I don't want to leave them high and dry either."

"Jessie, take a breath. Don't do anything right now. Give it a week or two."

"I don't think I can. My eyes have been leaking almost nonstop. God, I can't control it. What if I see him and fall apart?"

"Well, it hasn't scared him off yet, has it?"

"That's just it. It has. When I left, I did a hell of a job. He knew when I was coming home, and he hasn't even tried to contact me. It's over."

"I thought that was what you wanted, sugar."

"Yeah, that's what I thought too."

<hr/>

Karma let herself into Fisher's house and then stepped out to make sure she was in the right one. Fisher's home rivaled her place when it came to a mess.

When she walked into the kitchen, she figured he'd just stolen the biggest pig award from her. She swatted flies that had begun to colonize on the food left on the dishes in the sink. "God, Fisher. When you fall, you do it with gusto, don'tcha?"

She never thought she'd see the day that she'd clean up after one of her big brothers, but it was clear Fisher needed help—it was time for a cleaning intervention.

She pulled her phone out and called in reinforcements. "Hunter? We have a situation. You need to get your butt down to Fisher's. It looks like a herd of moose took up residence in here—and they weren't housebroken."

"If this is a joke Karma, it's not funny."

"It's not a joke, and I'm not laughing. Gramps called and told me Fisher's lost it. I came down to check it out for myself. You're not gonna believe it."

"Where's Fisher?"

"At the hospital. Gramps said he's on call for three days. This can't wait though. Things are already getting ripe, if you know what I'm sayin'."

She heard Hunter groan.

"I'll do my best to straighten things up, but it's going to take a cleaning crew. So I thought I'd leave the details to you and Trapper."

"Karma. This is Fisher we're talking about. How bad can it be?"

"You're just gonna have to see it for yourself. But take my word for it, you need to call Trapper for this one, Bro. Oh, and bring your own gloves. I'm using

Fisher's while I go around collecting his dirty underwear. You might want to bring a camera, so you can
blackmail him with the evidence of his insanity later."

"You're gonna share?"

She left the gross kitchen for the boys—she figured
it was bad enough she had to clean her own. In this
case, she'd gladly share the wealth—she didn't want
to be stingy.

Karma walked around the house picking up clothes.
Fisher had obviously slept on the couch, or at least that's
where he'd dropped his drawers. "Eww." It grossed her
out even with gloves on. There was just something unnatural about picking up your brother's skivvies. She
figured she'd do a few loads of wash before she had to
leave for work. After all, being a caring sister only went
so far.

She opened the washer and found it full of red clothes.
She rolled her eyes. In her world, there were colors, and
there were whites. In Fisher's, he had whites, lights,
reds, and darks. "Well, Fisher, welcome to Karma's
world." He was just gonna have to deal.

Karma tossed the reds in the drier and his whites in
the washer, turned it on hot, and ignoring the measuring
cup, threw in some detergent. God, was he anal or what?
Who measured laundry detergent?

Karma let the wash run, while she stripped his bed.
She knew he'd appreciate having fresh sheets to fall into
when he got off call. She was tempted to short-sheet the
bed, but congratulated herself on withstanding temptation. After all, she was trying to get off his shit list, not
climb a few rungs.

After only a few mishaps, she'd folded his laundry

and stacked it on his dresser. She was just glad she wasn't going to be there when Fisher and the guys got in. Suzie Homemaker she wasn't.

———— ·∿· ————

Fisher spent the better part of eight hours in surgery, playing operation with the victim of a donorcycle crash. He had no problem with motorcycles—hell, he had one of his own, but he did have a problem with people too stupid to wear helmets and protective gear. In an accident between a tractor trailer and a motorcycle, the bike always lost.

He showered, dressed, and left the hospital determined to go home and get some sleep. Unfortunately, his car seemed to have a mind of its own. Before he even realized it, he was parked down the street from Jessie's house. He sat there thinking about his grandfather's accusation that he was hiding behind his stethoscope. He'd been dead-on, as usual. When he'd almost lost his patient on the table, he decided to stop wasting time. He was going to get Jessica back. He didn't want to live without her.

When she stepped out the front door and ran for the sidewalk, it was as if the sun came out and shone down on her. He smiled for the first time since she'd left, and it matched the smile on her face. But instead of turning toward him, she ran straight. Fuck, she ran straight into the open arms of Andrew. He picked Jessica up, spun her around, and set her down. Andrew threw his arm around her shoulder, her arm settled naturally around Andrew's waist, and together they walked into the house. She was happy, and Fisher was wondering if he'd live. He was crushed worse than that biker had been. Jessica James was his Mack Truck.

Fisher's hand squeezed the steering wheel so tight that he was surprised he hadn't dented it. The pain took his breath. It was as if he'd been stabbed through the heart.

He wasn't sure how long he sat there, but eventually one of the neighbors gave him a dirty look. He threw the Beemer in gear and headed home. Alone.

—⁓—

"Andrew!" Jessie ran out the door and threw her arms around him. "What the heck are you doing here?" The idiot had called her from the street. "Why didn't you tell me you were coming?"

"I didn't want you to try to talk me out of it. It's just one less fight we're going to have."

"We never fight. Why are we going to fight?"

"Because you're not gonna like what I have to say."

Jessie took a deep breath and shrugged her shoulders, before wrapping her arm around Andrew's waist. "Well, if we're gonna have a knockdown, drag-out fight, we better get the tequila out." They walked through the door, and Jessie headed straight to the kitchen. She reached for the tequila and two shot glasses, while Andrew grabbed the limes, oranges, and lemons and cut them into regimented wedges. "I went to the grocery store and bought the fruit all by myself. Fisher would have been so proud to see me in the produce aisle. He thought I didn't know where it was."

"Salt or sugar?"

She'd never seen Andrew so damn serious. He had actually lined up the wedges. "You tell me."

"Sugar."

She blew out a relieved breath, licked the web of

flesh between her thumb and pointer finger, and sugared it. "I'm ready."

Andrew handed her a shot. "You're a hell of a writer, damned hot too. I was reading a chapter at Wendy's, and the sex was so hot I couldn't leave until the tent in my pants deflated. I was late for a meeting."

She licked her hand, tossed back the shot, and grabbed a piece of orange. "Heaven."

Andrew followed her, preferring the lime over the orange—there was no accounting for taste.

"Next?" Damn, one shot, and she was already feeling the buzz. She tried to remember the last time she'd eaten.

"Sugar." Andrew poured, which was a good thing, because she'd been all thumbs lately. "Adrian, our agent, really loved the partial you sent her."

"I already knew that."

"Yeah, but I'm trying to get you tipsy, so go ahead and drink anyway."

"Okay." She licked the sugar off her hand and poured the shot down her throat, chasing it with a sweet orange. "I love getting my five servings of fruits and veggies this way."

"Sugar."

"Andrew, I haven't been eating much lately. I'm definitely getting tipsy."

"Good. A couple more shots, and we'll switch to salt."

The two of them licked and slurped their way through the tequila and an entire orange.

"Salt."

"Damn, I wuth afraid of that." She salted her hand and waited for the ax to drop.

Andrew poured the shots. "I don't think you're writing fiction, Jessie."

"What?"

"Take the shot, and I'll explain."

Jessie had to concentrate on her aim. Damn, she was getting skunked. The salt wasn't nearly as satisfying as the sugar had been. She drank then sucked on a lemon. Her lips were numb. "Okay, shoot."

"I don't think you were writing fiction."

"You jusht said that." Andrew looked fuzzy. "Of course, I was writing fiction."

"No, sugar."

"Great. We're back to oranges."

Andrew shook his head and came around beside her. The next thing she knew, he was walking her down the hall. "Sugar, you didn't write Jenny and Seth's story. You wrote Jessie and Fisher's story." He kissed her cheek in front of her bedroom door. "You need to get some sleep. I have a stop to make. I'll be back in a flash though."

"Hmm? I'm not tired, I'm drunk."

"Yes, you are." He helped her to bed and pulled the covers up to her chin. "I'll see you later."

"Promise?" It was as if the curtain fell. The film was cut. Her world went black.

―⁓―

Fisher peeled away from Jessie's—make that Andrew's—house and sped home feeling like the world's only living heart donor. He was mentally and physically exhausted and wasn't looking forward to another night of trying and failing to sleep on the couch. He needed to just grow a pair of balls and change the sheets on his bed. He'd been avoiding it, because the sheets had still held Jessica's scent, and in his sick mind, he seemed to equate smelling her to having her. After the loving reunion he'd just witnessed, he didn't think even his subconscious mind would buy it now.

Fisher walked into his house and did a double take. Maybe he had really lost his mind. When he'd left the house a few days ago, he wondered if he'd return to find it condemned by the health department, and now it looked as if a cleaning tornado had come through the place.

Maybe the entire last week had just been one long, nasty dream, and any moment now, he'd awaken next to Jessica and make love to her.

He scratched his head, kicked his shoes off, and saw his knitting with Karma's Dr. Who scarf sticking out. Shit. That reality meant he was definitely living this nightmare.

Fisher pulled his shirttails out of his pants and unbuttoned it on the way down the hall toward the bedroom. He closed the blackout shades, tossed off the rest of his clothes, and turned down the somehow freshly made bed. At this point, he couldn't care less who'd cleaned his house and changed his sheets; he was just happy he wouldn't have to prove he had the balls to do it himself. He lay down, grabbed Jessie's pillow, held it to his chest, and did his best to pretend it was her.

Sleep came slowly, but it came, until the banging at the door awoke him. Damn, Fisher opened his gritty eyes and remembered where he was—in his bed, alone, and someone was banging on the door like a madman. In the darkened room, Fisher grabbed a pair of shorts from his bureau, tugged them on as he ran, and threw open the door. Fisher stared at the man he'd seen kissing Jessica, and for the first time, really regretted taking the Hippocratic oath. The "do no harm" part stuck in his craw. Without that line, Fisher could break the guy's legs and then fix them.

"Nice shorts." Andrew looked as if he were holding back a laugh.

Fisher glanced down to find his once white tennis shorts were now bright pink. He groaned and scrubbed his hand over his face. Karma.

"Don't tell me you actually let Jessie do your laundry?"

"Do you really want to go there?" The sound of Jessica's name coming from this guy made Fisher want to take the binder Andrew held and shove it right up his ass. "I'm working on maybe six hours of sleep in the last three days. You've taken your life in your hands showing up here. You're either brave, stupid, or you have a death wish."

"Right now, I'm leaning toward stupid."

Fisher left the door wide open, not really caring what Andrew did, and headed to the kitchen. He needed coffee if he had any hope of dealing with his replacement without committing murder.

Andrew was right about being stupid. He followed Fisher into the kitchen and set the binder on the bar. Fisher put on a pot of coffee, leaned against the counter, and crossed his arms to keep from reaching over the bar and throttling the man. "Do you want to tell me what the hell you're doing here? 'Cause I gotta warn you, if you're here to gloat, you won't be leaving without the help of paramedics."

"I'm not a patient."

"Yet."

Andrew shook his head, and then looked into Fisher's eyes. "Let's cut to the chase, Fisher. You don't like me, and believe me, after what you've done to Jessie,

I really don't like you. But this isn't about me or you, it's about Jessie. She's my best friend, and I love her too damn much to sit by and watch her suffer when I can do something about it. I want her to be happy and after reading this," he said and shoved the binder toward Fisher. "Even a blind man can see you make her happy."

"What is it?" Fisher took the brown manuscript binder and opened it. *Call Me Wild*, by Jessie James.

"This is her book? It's finished?"

"No, it seems she's missing her research partner." Andrew rubbed his forehead. "Look. I just drank the better part of a bottle of tequila. If you want me to continue this discussion, it would help if you poured me some of that coffee you just made."

"Sure. Have a seat." Fisher filled two mugs and passed one over to Andrew, who took a sip. Fisher took pity on the guy, dug a water out of the refrigerator, and slid it across the bar. "You might want to drink that too."

"Thanks." Andrew stared at the water bottle, picking the paper label off, while Fisher watched. Andrew appeared to be fighting an internal war and losing.

Andrew raised his gaze to meet Fisher's. "Read the manuscript. Jessie drank as much as I did, but she hasn't eaten or slept in days, so it hit her pretty hard. She's at home sleeping it off. She won't be up for a few hours at least." Andrew took a deep breath and a sip of coffee. "Shit. Maybe I should have stuck with tequila." He rubbed his chest. "I can't believe I'm doing this," he mumbled almost to himself and then squared his shoulders. "I'm warning you. If you hurt her, Fisher, they won't find the pieces of your body."

"I love Jessica. I'd never hurt her, but she said I

was temporary." Man, just saying that word made his chest ache.

Andrew nodded and then met Fisher's gaze. "Yeah, I know." He patted the top of the manuscript. "Read this, and you'll see there's nothing temporary about you. Jessie's my best friend. We've never been anything more than best friends. Don't make her choose between us—it will hurt her, and it might just kill me."

Fisher nodded. "This conversation never took place."

"Okay, good." Andrew stood and swayed on his feet. "Someone has to be there when Jessie wakes up. Is it going to be you or me?"

"Me." Fisher picked up the manuscript. "Thanks... Jessica's really lucky to have a friend like you."

Andrew stood straighter, his eyes piercing Fisher's. "You take good care of her, and don't make me regret this."

"I won't."

"Okay." Andrew's shoulders slumped. He set his coffee down and headed for the door.

"Where are you going?"

Andrew turned. "Hell if I know. LA, I guess."

"You can stay here. There's a guest room upstairs. Besides, you can't leave without saying good-bye to Jessica."

"Fine, but you better get over there. I don't want her waking up alone."

Fisher threw on a shirt and shoes and grabbed the manuscript. He was out of the house in no time flat. He let himself into Jessie's house and went to check on her. Man, was she a sight for sore eyes. He sat beside her and brushed the hair off her face. Her eyes blinked open and shut.

"Fisher, you're here," she mumbled and curled around him.

"Hey, darlin', I heard you had too much to drink."

"I had fruit."

"That's good. I'll be right outside if you need anything. Okay?"

"Uh-huh."

It was beginning to get dark, so Fisher left the bathroom light on and the door open, in case she needed to make a run for it.

He picked up the manuscript and read. The girl could definitely write. The story was engaging, the characters were well-rounded, the emotions were high, the sex was smokin' and eerily familiar, and the fear Jenny felt every time Seth told her he loved her was palpable. She'd been terrified. If Jessica's backstory even remotely resembled Jenny's, well, shit…

When Jenny told Seth he was temporary, he couldn't have explained how he'd felt as accurately as Jessica had. It was as if she'd crawled into his mind and took up residence. She knew him. She loved him, just like Jenny loved Seth. When he'd read what Jenny's next week was like without Seth, his heart broke all over again.

And to think Fisher had thought it was hard to be on the receiving end of that conversation. It didn't compare to the horror that Jenny had felt—the guilt, the fear, the loss that she knew she'd brought on herself.

He left the manuscript on the table. It was after midnight, and Jessica was still sleeping. From what Jenny had been through, he surmised Jessica hadn't been able to sleep any better without him than he'd been able to sleep without her. He went to her, slid under the covers, and pulled her into his arms.

Chapter 20

JESSIE SHOT UP IN BED, AND HER HAND WENT TO HER HEAD to keep it from exploding. What the hell had happened? She'd dreamt that she'd spent the night in Fisher's arms. It had seemed so real, she could swear she still smelled him. But he wasn't there, and her bed looked like a bomb exploded in it—signs of a restless night. Still, except for being extremely hung over, for the first time in a week, Jessie felt rested. She figured tequila was good for something.

Gingerly, she slid out of bed and went to the bathroom to brush her teeth, caught a glimpse of herself in the mirror, and cringed. The dark circles under her eyes made the rest of her face look even paler than she suspected the nausea did. She opened the door, and the scent of coffee drew her to the kitchen.

"Andrew, from now on, we are not doing sugar."

"You should probably lay off the tequila instead."

Jessie looked up and swore she saw Fisher sitting in her kitchen. The sun shone through the window at his back. "Fisher?" She put one hand on the wall to steady herself, the other on her pounding head, and closed her eyes. Breathe. God, now her eyes were playing tricks on her. Maybe she was still dreaming. After all, the man before her was dressed completely in cotton candy pink. Her Fisher never wore pink, well, not that she'd ever seen. When she opened her eyes again, he was still there, pink shorts and all. "Nice shorts."

He stepped toward her. "It's a long story. I was just about to bring you coffee."

She reached out and touched his face, the stubble rough against her fingers. "You're really here." Her eyes sprang a major leak, and her hand trembled. She thought he nodded, but it was hard to tell through the flood in her eyes.

"A little birdie told me you had a bad case of writer's block and still needed your research partner."

A rush of blood roared through her ears. Fuckity, fuck, fuck, fuck. She covered her mouth and ran, slamming the bathroom door behind her, before making a two-pointer into the porcelain hoop.

She washed out her mouth and splashed her face. God, could she be any less attractive?

"Jessica, are you all right?"

She couldn't hide in the bathroom forever. She opened the door, peeked out, then shut the door again and leaned against it. He was still there looking worried.

"You should sip water. It will help."

Nothing was going to help. Fisher was here in her house—okay, Andrew's house—on the other side of a bathroom door, sounding as if he cared. Everything she had rehearsed to say to him flew out the proverbial window as soon as she laid eyes on him. She'd imagined so many make up scenarios, but none of them had involved puking.

"Jess, darlin', open the door."

She took a deep breath and turned the handle. She'd have to get through this. She'd apologize and hope for the best. If he never wanted to see her again, that would be fair. She looked into those green eyes and took a deep breath. "I don't think I could feel much worse after what I said to you when I left. I was cruel and mean, and well, I was scared 'cause I felt… Anyway, I didn't mean it—any of it. I'm sorry."

When Fisher didn't say anything, she glanced up from wringing her hands. Fuck. She was becoming her mother.

He looked at her in the same way a doctor looks at patient when he has bad news. All concerned and seriously stone-faced. She did not want to hear Fisher's bad news. She already knew what it was. He wasn't taking her back. He didn't love her anymore.

She wiped her eyes with the back of her hands and went to the bedroom, opening her closet, and pulling out her bag. "I can't stay here. Everywhere I go reminds me of you. I can't go to the Albertsons. I can't run. I can't go to Humpin' Hannah's. I can't even go into Starbucks. I told Steph I made a mistake taking the job. God, some blonde came through the drive-thru with your cup, and my eyes leaked. I just want to go home."

"I think you're right. You'll feel better once we get you home."

So much for him wanting her back. She wanted to curl up on the bed and just disappear.

"Sit down, and tell me what's yours."

"Just the clothes." Jessie sat on the edge of the bed, wrapped her arms around herself and rocked, trying not to cry.

"Okay." He gave her shoulder a squeeze. "I'll take care of it. Do you want some tea and toast first?"

"I don't have anything but fruit, and after last night, I don't think I'll be able to eat another orange or lemon for a while."

"That's understandable."

Fisher was even the perfect ex—just watching him fold her clothes hurt. Within a few minutes, everything was packed.

"I'll go put these in the car, and we can go." Fisher shouldered the bags. "You need to get some food into you."

Jessie followed him down the hall and watched him carry her things out the front door. God, how was she supposed to drive away from him?

Her head pounded, and she went to the kitchen, needing to sit and get a grip before she dissolved into a puddle of tears. She grabbed the coffee Fisher had poured her and took a tentative sip, sat at the table, and flipped open Andrew's binder to see what he was working on. Anything to stop thinking of Fisher packing her car for the long drive home. The title jumped out at her. *Call Me Wild*, by Jessie James. The lukewarm coffee she held slopped over her hand.

"Hey, be careful with that." Fisher took the coffee from her and wiped up the spill. "That's my only copy. You're really a fabulous writer, darlin', but there were a few inaccuracies."

"You read it?"

"Every word." He sat beside her and threw his arm around the back of her chair. "The story was riveting, but Seth wasn't really a closet knitter."

"No?"

"Maybe he was after Jenny dumped him, but he'd only taken a knitting class because he lost a bet with his brothers. You see, he'd been in kind of a funk, and they bet him he couldn't pick up a woman on Ladies' Night at Hannah's. It wasn't as if he couldn't. He just wasn't interested, and he was never the kind of guy who was only out to get laid. He lost the bet and found himself signed up for three beginning knitting classes."

"That makes sense, knowing Seth's brothers. Those guys will bet on anything."

"Exactly."

"And Seth had it bad for Jenny, well before his little sister tricked him into going to the cabin."

"Why?"

"I don't know. Jenny was beautiful. That first day when they ran into each other at Starbucks, he looked into her eyes and saw a woman who was so strong, so self-assured, but had no idea how amazing she was. She pushed him and challenged him and had him tied up in knots. He was so busy trying to catch her that he'd fallen in love without even realizing it. When he figured it out, it scared the hell out of him. You see, he'd never met a woman he could picture spending his life with."

Fisher tore his eyes away, took a deep breath, and straightened his back, as if gathering his courage. "Jessica, I'd never met a woman I could picture spending my life with until I met you."

"Yeah?" She turned to him and crossed her arms, her fingers digging into her biceps. "Then why did you pack my bags so I could go back to my parents' on Long Island?"

"I packed your bags so you can go home. With me."

"Your home? But Fisher, I don't want this to be a temporary research thing. I want this to be a permanent gig."

He stood and picked up her coffee cup. "Okay."

She stood too, and tossed the napkin on the table. "Okay what? What is okay?"

"Okay, I'll marry you. Call it research for your next book." He tapped the top of the manuscript. "Darlin', this one isn't going to print."

"What did you say?" She dropped her arms and stood nose to nose with him.

"I said," he spoke through clenched teeth, "this book isn't going to print."

"No." She pushed on his hard chest. "Before that."

"The part about you coming home with me?"

"No." She pushed him again. "After that."

"Dammit, Jessica. Marry me." He grabbed her hand and held it to his chest. "I can't go through this again. I lost it when you left. My house went to shit. I'm surprised it wasn't condemned by the health department. It got so bad Karma did my laundry. Now, everything that I owned that was white is pink. I puked on Trapper's boots. Do you have any idea how much it cost to replace them? I knit three six-packs of beer cozies and a scarf long enough to hang myself with. And I'll be damned if you'll ever have another research partner. You got that? I don't think I can take it."

God, she loved it when he went all alpha on her. "I guess that explains the outfit, so okay."

"Okay what?" Fisher looked like he was about to strangle her.

"Okay, I'll marry you." She wrapped her arms around him. "I love you, Fisher. Let's go home."

Fisher carried Jessica into his house and let out a breath as relief rushed through him. Andrew must still be upstairs. He carried Jessica back toward the bedroom and closed the door behind him. He kissed her and set her down on the bed and straightened. "I'll get you something to eat. You just rest."

She got on her knees and scooted toward him, tugging on his T-shirt. "I'm not hungry—for food."

Fisher just about groaned. "Darlin', we have a houseguest, and I wouldn't put it past the whole family to show up. They have a sick sixth sense about these things."

She kissed him hard and long, and when she slid her hands into his pink shorts, he'd forgotten what he was saying.

"Fisher? Do you love me?"

"God, yes."

She kissed a path from one nipple to the other, and licked her way to his fly, and he swallowed hard. His shorts hit the floor.

"I want you so bad it scares me. I need you. Inside me. Now."

Fisher was lost in a frenzy of rediscovery—her taste, her scent, the texture of her skin fascinated him. He licked and teased and played, until she begged for mercy. He floated on sighs of pleasure and passion, on nips of temptation, and the heady freedom to love Jess freely with nothing withheld.

Jess stared into his eyes, unflinching. When he entered her, it was if the last piece of his heart fell into place. They moved as one, and together they rode the crest and flew and shattered, holding tight to each other.

"I'm crushing you." Fisher rolled off her and spooned his body around hers. Her long hair draped over his arm, his hand against her stomach.

Jessica's snuggled closer, and he followed her into the first good sleep he'd had in days.

"I have a bad feeling about this, and I called Mom." Karma stood on Fisher's front lawn, crossed her arms, and looked at Hunter and Toni. "I'm not gonna take the fall for this one, Hunter. I've joined MA—Meddlers Anonymous. I think you should leave Fisher alone." She shot Toni an I-can't-believe-you-let-him-talk-you-into-this look.

Toni just shrugged and looked away as Hunter gave Karma his patented pesky-older-brother pout. "You always were a snitch. The neighbor called me because she was worried. She said there was a strange man here last night. We have to at least check it out."

"What do you think? That Fisher's batting for the other team?"

"He did swear off women that night at Hannah's."

"Get real. Maybe he just has a friend over from college or med school. You know, he does have a life."

He headed toward the porch and threw that same look over his shoulder. She was tempted to kick him. She would have, if she didn't know mom was on her way.

Trapper walked up beside her and rocked back on his heels. "Don't even think about it, Karma."

"I can think about all I want." She put her hands on her hips, rolled her eyes, and stuck out her tongue just for good measure. "I just can't do it. Hunter's acting like an ass again, and he won't listen to reason."

"Hi, Toni." Trapper kissed her on the cheek.

"I tried distracting him." Toni fingered her studded collar. "But he was acting like a nervous nanny all night."

Hunter shrugged. "I'm getting some pretty strong mixed signals. I don't understand it. I've tried calling him, but he must have his phone off. It goes straight to voice mail."

"Or maybe—" Karma pushed his chest. "He just doesn't want to talk to you."

"I'm worried, Karma, Something big is happening, and I'm not in the loop."

Brothers, you can't train 'em, you can't shoot 'em, but damn, she did love 'em. "Now, you know how Fisher's felt ever since you and Toni got married. Something big happened, and he wasn't in the loop either. It's enough to throw off any twin's game."

"Yeah, well, his game moved to a whole other conference if you ask me." He pointed to the mango-green Karmann Ghia convertible with California plates. "Do you know any straight man who would be caught dead in that?"

Maybe not in Boise. "Sure, I do. Anyone in LA. Not everyone needs a four-wheeler to feel like a real man."

"Forgive me if I don't take your word for it." Hunter put his hands on his hips, his feet spread, doing his macho-man-of-the-mountain impression. "I still haven't recovered from Fisher's last stint in the psycho-city jail. I ruined a perfectly good pair of gloves cleaning up the disaster that losing Jessie created. And Steph at Starbucks said that Jessie's quit and is moving back home, so I can guaran-ass-tee, it's not her. Besides, she drives a red Mini Cooper."

Trapper smiled. "I ended up getting two pairs of really nice boots out of the deal. Not bad for a few hours of work."

Gramps's White Lincoln pulled up to the curb, and Mom rushed out, followed closely by Gramps. "Who called this family meeting?"

Karma and Trapper pointed to Hunter. Karma stepped up and gave her mom a kiss on the cheek. "I've been trying to talk him out of it."

Mom gave her a sideways glance. "No, you just don't want to get blamed for it."

"Hi, Mom." Trapper tipped his cowboy hat back and leaned in for a kiss. "Who else is coming?"

"Ben and Gina are on their way."

Karma sidled over to Gramps. "What's this I hear about Jessie moving home?" she whispered behind her hand.

Grampa winked. "Don't you worry, girly. I've got it all under control."

Ben and Gina walked hand-in-hand across the lawn, Gina's five-inch spikes sinking into the grass.

Hunter looked around. "Everyone ready?"

Mom stopped at the door as Hunter grabbed his key. "At least knock first."

"Yeah, we wouldn't want to give the burglar a fright," Hunter snapped, and both Mom and Toni smacked him on the head.

Hunter knocked twice and unlocked the door. The whole family swarmed in.

Jessie called Fisher, trying to get him back, but it wasn't her voice she was hearing. "Fisher Michael Kincaid."

She opened her eyes. God, it was happening again. It wasn't a dream.

The door to the bedroom slammed open, and she jumped.

"We're staging an intervention."

Crap. That was Hunter—damn him, and his twin thing.

"Don't tell me that body next to Fisher's is Jessie's. I know for a fact she went back home to Long Island."

Jessie could swear she heard the sound of pictures being snapped. And her clothes were strewn all over the floor.

"Karma, put that camera down."

Kate was there? In the bedroom? Could this get any more embarrassing?

"If it's a guy under that sheet, I sure hope he can play baseball as well as Jessie."

Oh God no, not Trapper too.

Grampa Joe laughed. "Well, if it is a man under that sheet with Fisher, he wears a bra."

Fuckity, fuck, fuck, fuck. Her face flamed so hot, she was surprised the sheet wasn't smoldering. Jessie made sure everything was covered and poked Fisher. "I know you're awake. Do something. They're your family."

"No," he whispered, "they're our family." Her head was on his shoulder, and even with the blackout shades, Fisher had the sheet pulled up over their heads. He inched it down, uncovering both their faces. Keeping his arm around her, he sat up, forcing her to join him. God, the whole family was there, and one tiny woman she'd never even met before.

"Hunter, if you say another word about my fiancée"—Fisher's arm tightened around her—"I'll kick your ass, and Jessica will help me. Believe me, you don't want to get on her bad side."

Gramps picked up her bra with the rubber tip of his cane and tossed it onto the bed. "Sounds like we've got some celebratin' to do instead of intervenin'. You two take your time, and come out whenever you're ready.

We're in no rush." He winked at her. "I knew you'd figure it out. I'm gonna have me some exceptional great-grandbabies soon. I can feel it."

Kate took a tissue out of her sleeve and patted her eyes. "Okay, everyone out. Let's give them time to get dressed."

"Thanks, Mom," Fisher said as she herded the crew out.

Jessie fell back onto the pillows. "That's it. We're changing the locks and putting one on the bedroom door. This is ridiculous."

"I told you they had a sick sixth sense, didn't I? Welcome to the family."

Karma ducked her head as her mother slapped her and tore the camera out of her hands.

"I can't believe you took pictures."

"Well, at least we have a memento from the day Fisher got engaged. Jessie looks cute with her hair a mess and her face all red."

Gina stepped over and looked. "Sometimes I'm really glad we live in Brooklyn. I wouldn't want you storming into our bedroom."

Hunter snorted. "Ben always locks it. I checked."

Gramps sat on the recliner. "Some damn thing's poking me in the ass." He reached behind him and pulled out circular knitting needles attached to what looked like a tube of camouflage. "I never figured Jessie for a knitter."

Trapper smiled and pushed the brim of his cowboy hat back. "She's not. That's Fisher's."

Gramps looked over at Hunter. "Well, shit son, no wonder why you were so worried about Fisher. When did he take up actin' like a woman?"

At least Hunter had the decency to look ashamed. "When he lost a bet, Trapper bought him knitting lessons." Of course, Hunter would blame it all on Trapper. Mom hit the both of them, so he got his.

"What the hell is he knitting, anyway?" Gramps examined the project.

Fisher stepped into the living room, tugging a very embarrassed Jessie behind him. "Camo beer cozies."

Gramps got up, went right to Jessie, and threw his arms around her. "I'm so proud of you, girl. Welcome to the family."

"Thanks, Gramps."

He took her left hand in his. "Well, damn Fisher. Where the hell is her ring?"

"I don't have one yet. It's not like I planned this."

"Shit, you've known you wanted to marry her for weeks now. You don't ask a woman to put up with the likes of you without giving her a nice, big diamond. Haven't I taught you boys anything?"

"Hey." Hunter took his wife's hand in his. "I had a ring when I proposed."

Toni laughed. "Yeah, but he didn't get down on one knee, and it didn't look like an engagement ring, so I just assumed it was a sorry-I-acted-like-an-ass present."

Gina laughed. "I got mine in front of the justice of the peace and my ex-boyfriend on our first wedding day. I wondered if it was a fake. I mean, who buys a real diamond for a sham of a marriage?"

Everyone turned and smiled. "Ben," they chorused.

Jessie's phone rang, and she ran into the bedroom to take it. Karma didn't think Jessie could look any happier, but when she came back to join them, she did. She whispered something in Fisher's ear, and he picked her up and kissed her. "Jessica got the job with ESPN, and she's based here in Boise covering the Northwest."

Karma looked over to Gramps, who winked at her. She mouthed the words "thank you." God, Karma loved her family.

She heard footsteps and turned to see a stranger walking down the stairs. "You must be Andrew." How Jessie didn't notice what Andrew looked like was amazing. No wonder Fisher was having puppies at the thought of Jessie staying with him. "I'm Karma Kincaid, Jessie's future sister-in-law. Welcome to the family."

Andrew smiled. "Congratulations, sugar." Andrew gave Fisher a look, pulled Jessie into his arms, and gave her a smacking kiss on the cheek. "I'm happy for you."

"Andrew, I got the ESPN job too. I'll be based here in Boise."

"That's fabulous. I knew you'd get it."

"Well, I don't think I could have survived, and Fisher and I wouldn't have been able to fix things without you."

"Na, I didn't have much to do with it." He shook Fisher's hand. "Congratulations."

Fisher turned the shake into a guy hug. "Andrew, thanks for everything."

Andrew nodded and backed toward the door. Karma knew an escape plan when she saw one. She stepped over, leaned against the door, shot Andrew a smile, and raised an eyebrow. Foiled again. "Everyone… this is Andrew Monahan, Jessie's best friend since they went to Columbia together. Andrew, this is…" She started the introductions, and even remembered to introduce Gina to Jessie. When she looked at her watch, she cringed—she had to leave, or she'd be late for work. She really didn't want to miss this. "Okay, I'm having an impromptu engagement party for Jessie and Fisher tonight at Hannah's. After all, I'm the one who fixed them up together." She pointed at Andrew. "And you are the only one from Jessie's side, so you'd better show up."

"I wouldn't miss it." He was friendly enough, but his eyes kept cutting back to Gina. He finally went over to her. "Excuse me, but do I know you?"

Ben put his arm around his wife.

Andrew smiled at Ben and then looked back at Gina. "No, really, it's not a pickup line. You look so familiar. Where'd you grow up?"

"New York."

"I know what it is. It's the eyes. Hey, Jessie, doesn't Gina look just like my friend Angel Anderson?"

"Angel? You mean the pitcher from the Jersey Jackals?"

"Yeah, that's him. He's my mom's best friend's son. I swear, you have the same eyes. They look copper when the sun hits them. I've never seen that before. I spent a few summers hanging out with Angel and getting paid for it. He was too old for a nanny and too young to get around by himself. We used to go sailing—he's a great kid, and now he's playing minor league baseball. Needless to say, his parents aren't happy. They sent the kid to Princeton, and instead of getting a real job, he joined a minor league team. Personally, I'm proud of him. There will be plenty of time to put his education to work for him."

Gina's eyes went wide. "Do you have a picture of him?"

They had the attention of the whole room now. Jessie looked from Gina to Fisher before answering. "Andrew, isn't he in that one of me throwing out the first pitch?"

"Yeah... I think so."

It was apparent that Gina's interest was making Andrew nervous.

Fisher shook his head. "Andrew, Gina's little brother was given up for adoption when he was newborn, and she's been looking for him. It was a private adoption, so it hasn't been easy."

Gina nodded. "I realize it's a long shot, but right about now, any news is welcome. How old is he?"

"Um... I don't know. Twenty-two or twenty-three. I never asked, but I always assumed Angel was adopted. He's dark and Hispanic, and his parents are fair-haired Caucasian. Maybe you're related or something. You just never know."

Karma smiled at Andrew. "You certainly don't."

Karma looked over to Trapper, who stood off on his own, so solitary—the family Rock of Gibraltar. She wondered who he leaned on when his world went to hell. But then, she'd never seen it happen. Hmm... He'd been a bit of a downer for the last two weeks, since he came back from one of his frequent seventy-two-hour excursions. Interesting...

Fisher kissed Jessica, and the two of them practically glowed. "My work here is done." Karma turned around. "I'm off to Humpin' Hannah's. See you at eight for the party." She waved and walked out the door. "Karma has left the building."

Acknowledgments

Writing is a solitary endeavor, but a writer's life isn't. I'm lucky to have the love and support of my incredible family. My husband, Stephen, who after twenty-two years of marriage, is still the man of my dreams. My children, Tony, Anna, and Isabelle, who in spite of being teenagers, are my favorite people to hang out with. They make me laugh, amaze me with their intelligence and generosity, and make me proud every day.

My parents, Richard Williams and Ann Feiler, and my stepfather George Feiler, who always encouraged me, and continue to do so.

My wonderful critique partners Deborah Villegas and Laura Becraft. They shortened my sentences, corrected my grammar, and put commas where they needed to be. They listened to me whine when my muse took a vacation, gave me great ideas when I was stuck, and answered that all-important question: Does this suck? They help me plot, love my characters almost as much as I do, and push-challenge me to be a better writer. They are wonderful friends, talented writers, and the sisters of my heart.

I owe a debt of gratitude to their families, who so graciously let me borrow them during my deadline crunch. So, to Robert, Joe, Elisabeth, and Ben Becraft, and Ruben, Alexander, Donovan, and Cristian Villegas, you have my thanks and eternal gratitude.

I'd also like to thank my other critique partners who are always there when I need a fresh eye—Grace Burrowes, Hope Ramsay, and April Line.

I wrote most of this book in the Carlisle Crossing Starbucks, and I have to thank all my baristas for keeping me in laughter and coffee while my computer and I camped out in their store. They were always there for me when I was searching for the right word or falling asleep at my computer. I don't think I could have written this book without them. I also need to thank a few of the customers who have become wonderful friends: Dana and Steven Gossert, and Alan Monahan, for giving me an excuse not to write.

As always, I have to thank my wonderful agent Kevan Lyon for all she does, my team at Sourcebooks, my editor Deb Werksman, and my publicist Beth Pehlke.

About the Author

Robin Kaye was born in Brooklyn, New York, and grew up in the shadow of the Brooklyn Bridge next door to her Sicilian grandparents. Living with an extended family that's a cross between *Gilligan's Island* and *The Sopranos*, minus the desert isle and illegal activities, explains both her comedic timing and the cast of quirky characters in her books.

She's lived in half a dozen states, from Idaho to Florida, but the romance of Brooklyn has never left her heart. She currently resides in Maryland with her husband, three children, two dogs, and a three-legged cat with attitude.

Robin would love to hear from you. Visit her website at www.robinkayewrites.com. Or email her at robin@robinkayewrites.com.